ULTIMATE
SPIDER-MAN
LEARNING CURVE

LEARNING CURVE

WRITER
BRIAN MICHAEL BENDIS

PENCILS
MARK BAGLEY

INKS
ART THIBERT

COLORS
TRANSPARENCY DIGITAL

LETTERS
COMICRAFT

ASSISTANT EDITOR
BRIAN SMITH

COLLECTIONS EDITOR
JEFF YOUNGQUIST

EDITOR
RALPH MACCHIO

ASSISTANT EDITOR
JENNIFER GRÜNWALD

INSPIRATION
BILL JEMAS

BOOK DESIGNER
JEOF VITA

EDITOR IN CHIEF
JOE QUESADA

PUBLISHER
DAN BUCKLEY

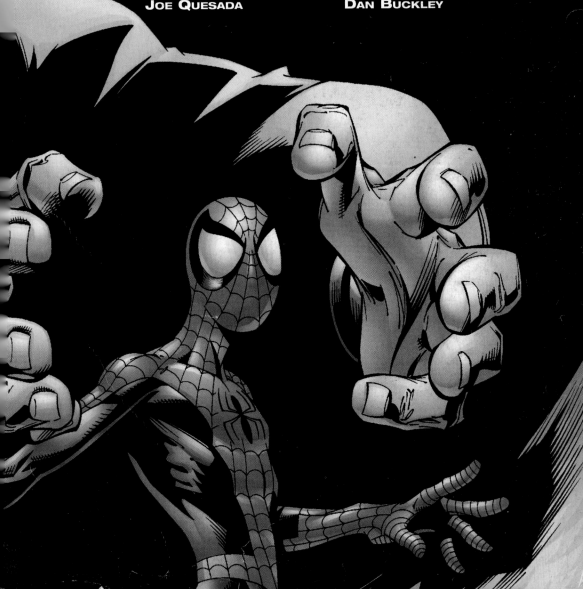

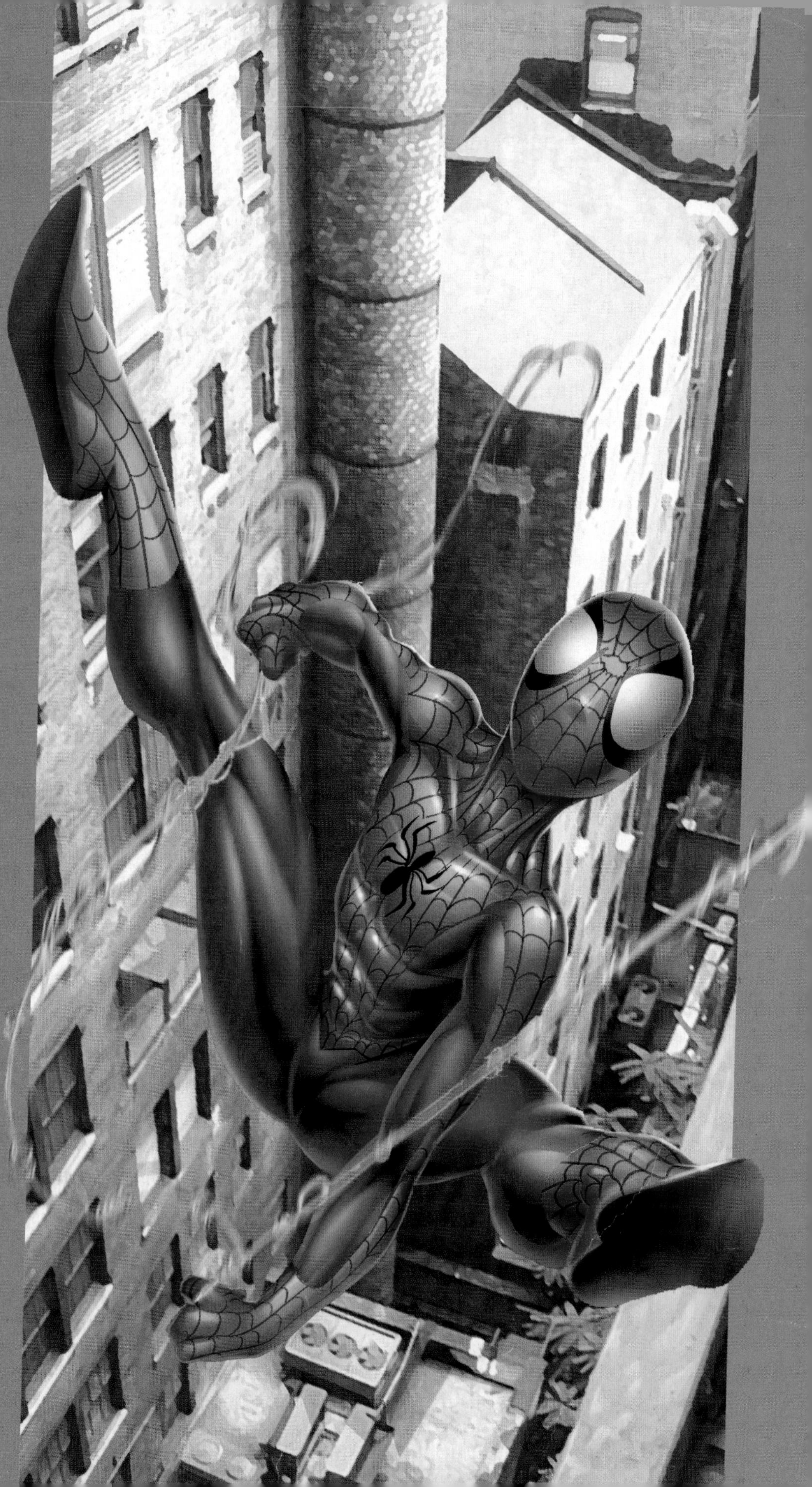

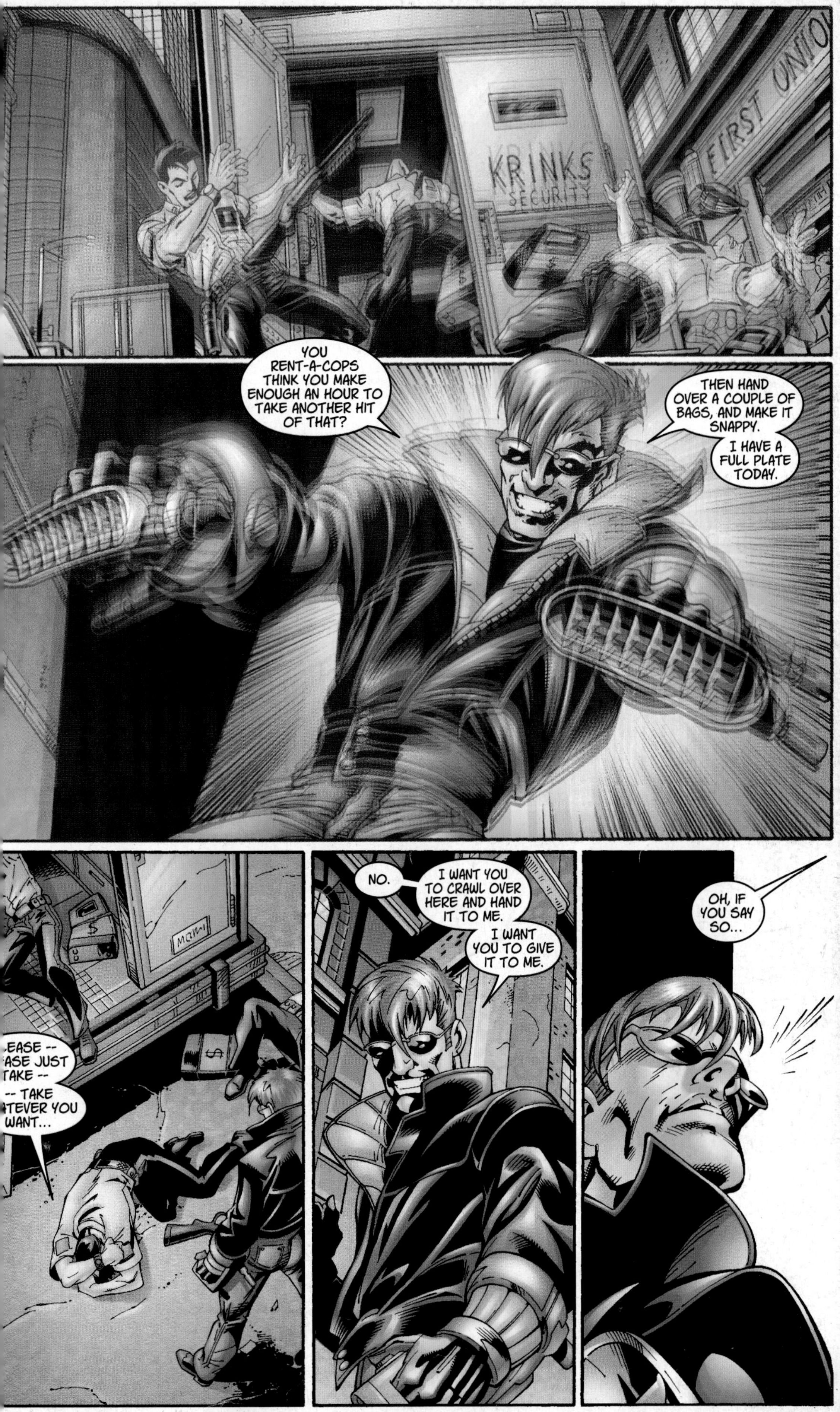
KRINKS SECURITY
FIRST UNION
YOU RENT-A-COPS THINK YOU MAKE ENOUGH AN HOUR TO TAKE ANOTHER HIT OF THAT?
THEN HAND OVER A COUPLE OF BAGS, AND MAKE IT SNAPPY.
I HAVE A FULL PLATE TODAY.
EASE -- ASE JUST TAKE --
-- TAKE TEVER YOU WANT...
NO.
I WANT YOU TO CRAWL OVER HERE AND HAND IT TO ME.
I WANT YOU TO GIVE IT TO ME.
OH, IF YOU SAY SO...

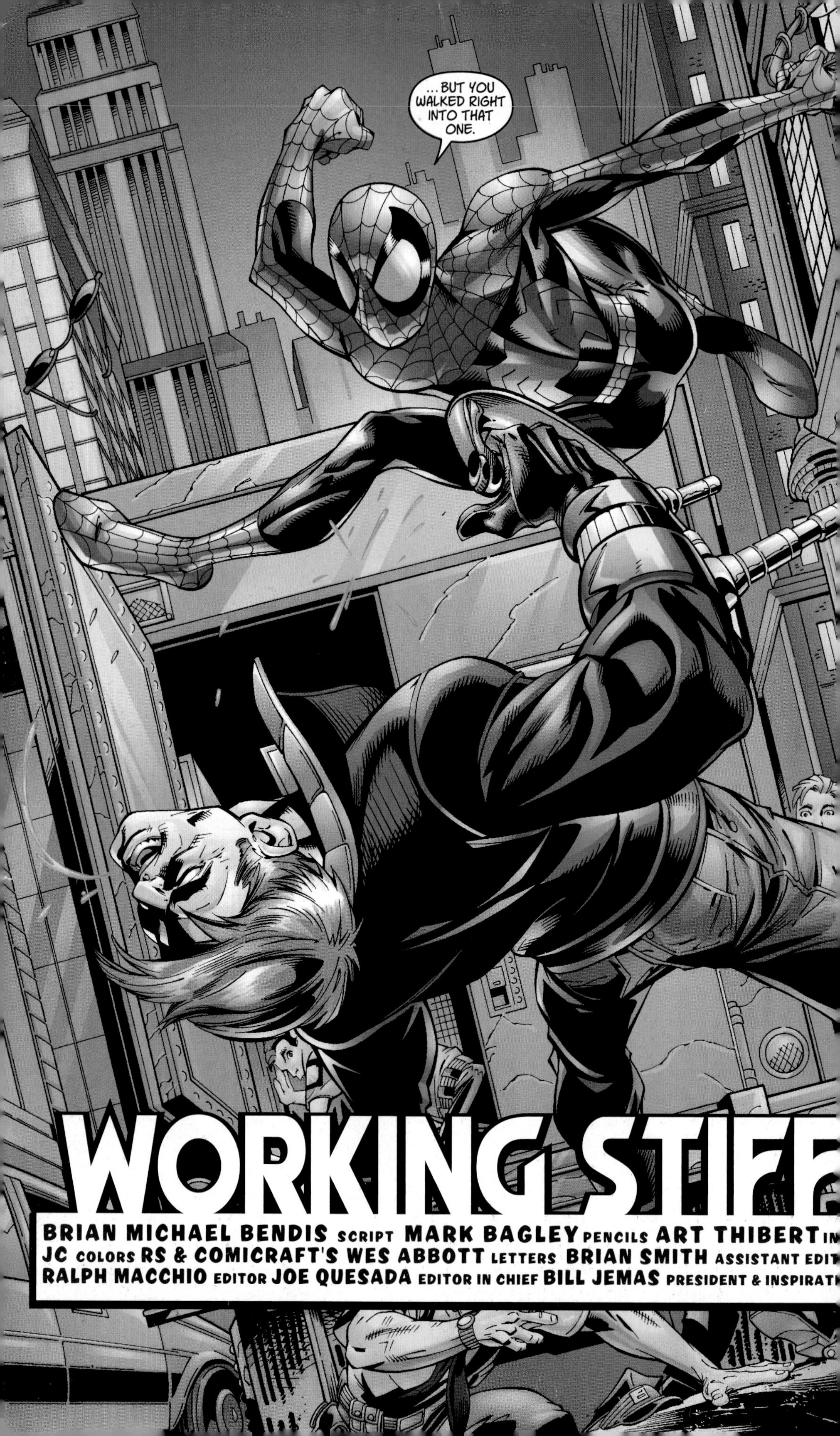

...BUT YOU WALKED RIGHT INTO THAT ONE.
WORKING STIFF
BRIAN MICHAEL BENDIS SCRIPT MARK BAGLEY PENCILS ART THIBERT IN
JC COLORS RS & COMICRAFT'S WES ABBOTT LETTERS BRIAN SMITH ASSISTANT EDIT
RALPH MACCHIO EDITOR JOE QUESADA EDITOR IN CHIEF BILL JEMAS PRESIDENT & INSPIRATI

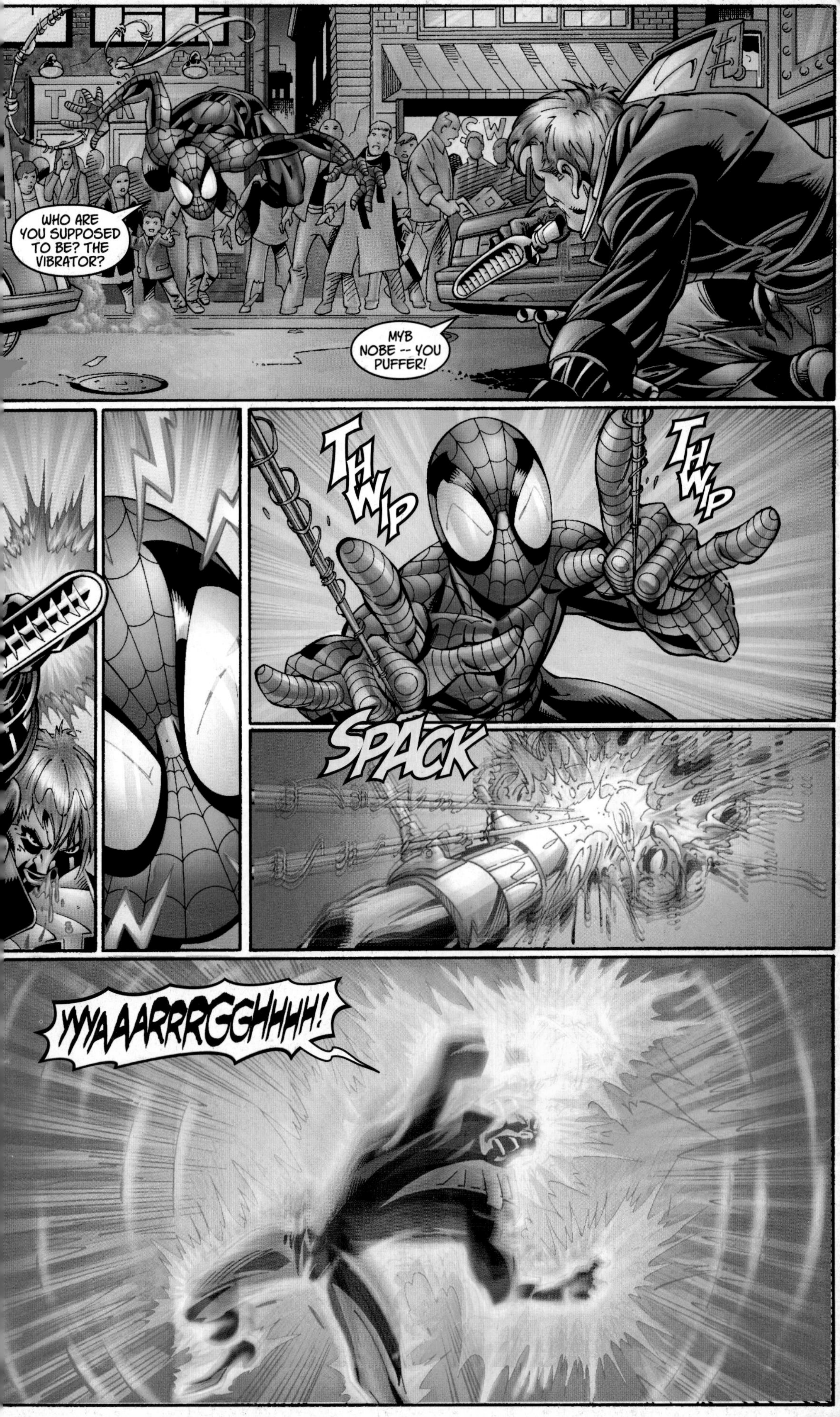
WHO ARE YOU SUPPOSED TO BE? THE VIBRATOR?
MYB NOBE -- YOU PUFFER!
THWIP
THWIP
SPACK
YYAAARRRGGHHHH!

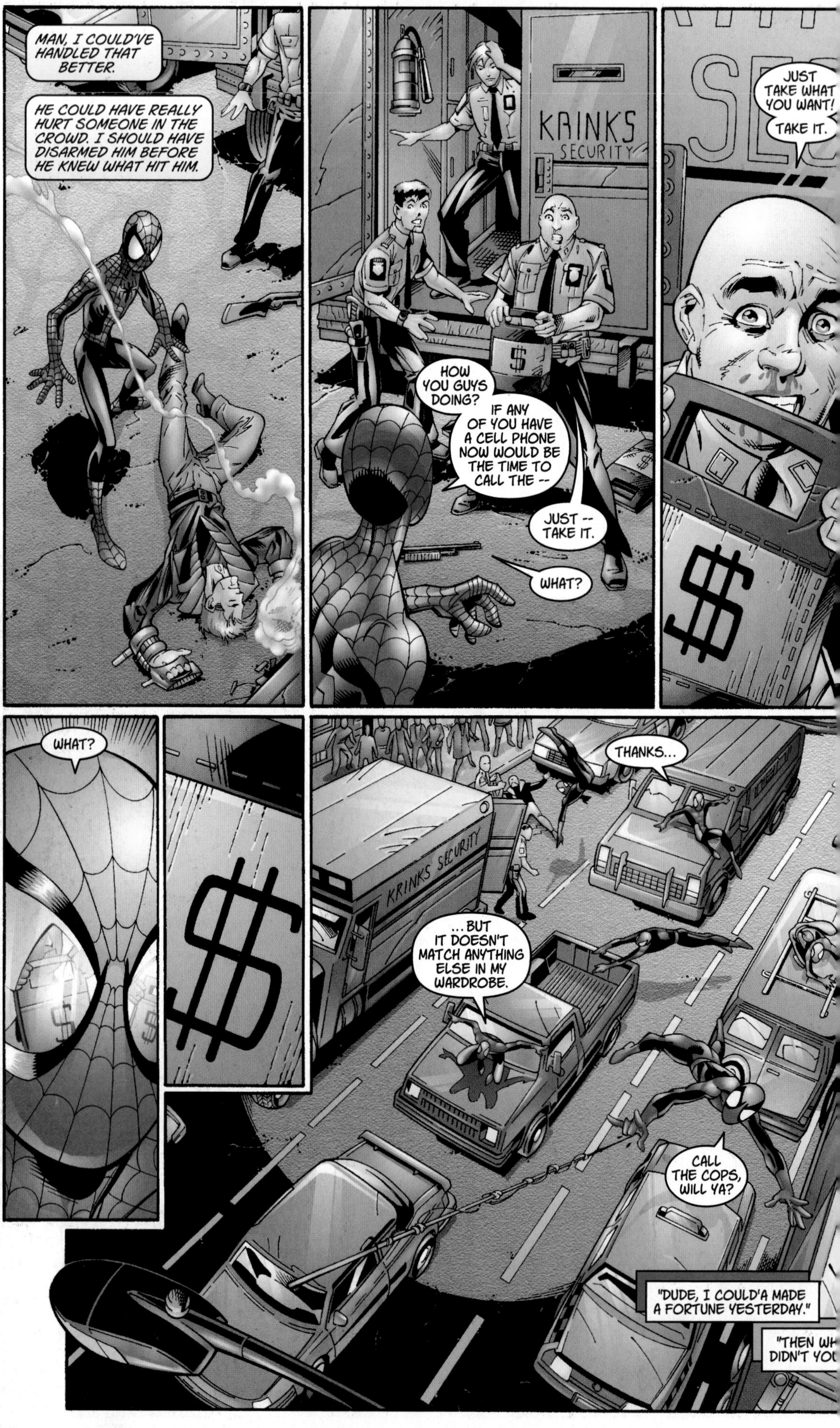
MAN, I COULD'VE HANDLED THAT BETTER.
HE COULD HAVE REALLY HURT SOMEONE IN THE CROWD. I SHOULD HAVE DISARMED HIM BEFORE HE KNEW WHAT HIT HIM.
KRINKS SECURITY
HOW YOU GUYS DOING?
IF ANY OF YOU HAVE A CELL PHONE NOW WOULD BE THE TIME TO CALL THE --
JUST -- TAKE IT.
WHAT?
JUST TAKE WHAT YOU WANT!
TAKE IT.
WHAT?
THANKS...
KRINKS SECURITY
...BUT IT DOESN'T MATCH ANYTHING ELSE IN MY WARDROBE.
CALL THE COPS, WILL YA?
"DUDE, I COULD'A MADE A FORTUNE YESTERDAY."

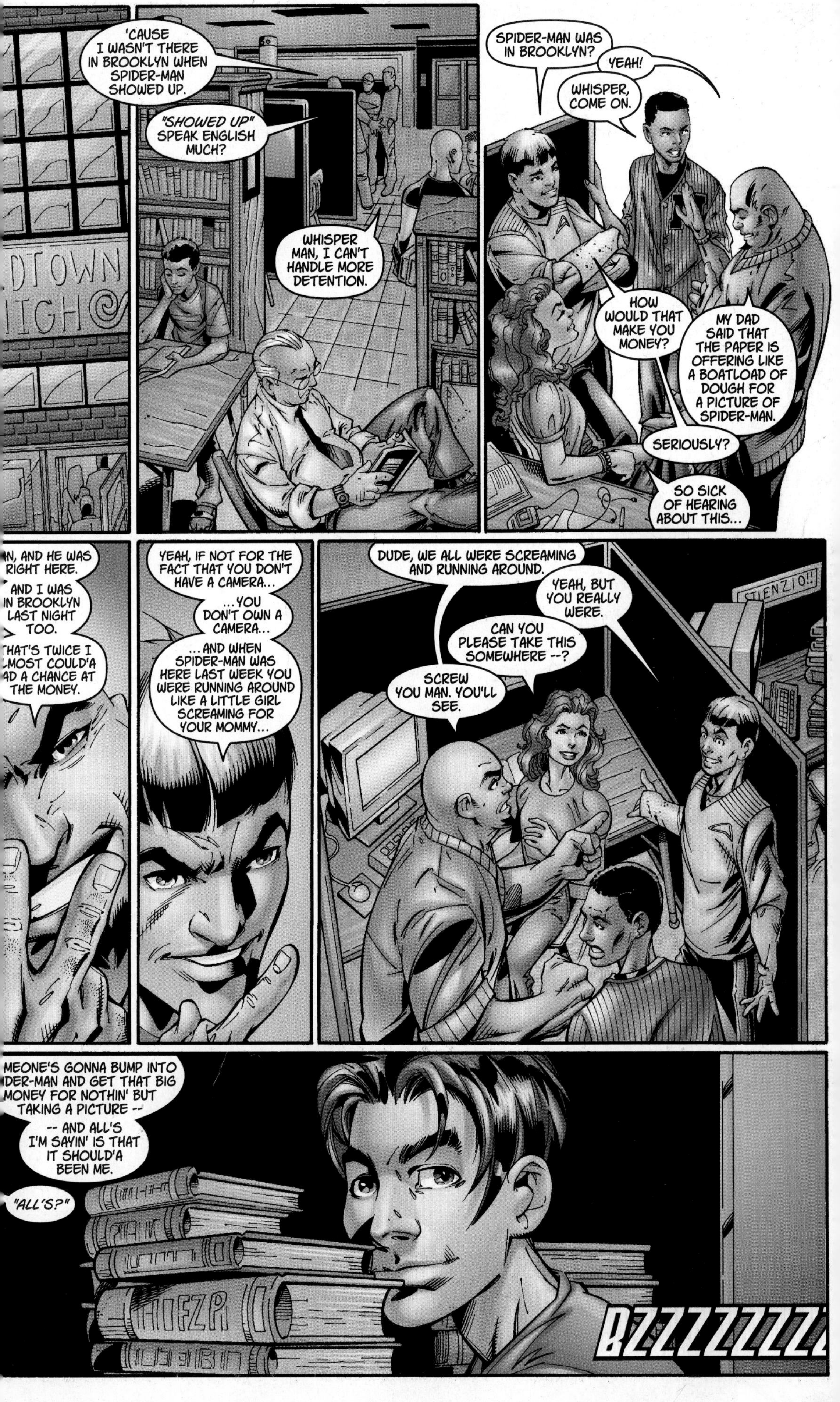
'CAUSE I WASN'T THERE IN BROOKLYN WHEN SPIDER-MAN SHOWED UP.
"SHOWED UP" SPEAK ENGLISH MUCH?
WHISPER MAN, I CAN'T HANDLE MORE DETENTION.
SPIDER-MAN WAS IN BROOKLYN?
YEAH!
WHISPER, COME ON.
HOW WOULD THAT MAKE YOU MONEY?
MY DAD SAID THAT THE PAPER IS OFFERING LIKE A BOATLOAD OF DOUGH FOR A PICTURE OF SPIDER-MAN.
SERIOUSLY?
SO SICK OF HEARING ABOUT THIS...
N, AND HE WAS RIGHT HERE.
AND I WAS IN BROOKLYN LAST NIGHT TOO.
THAT'S TWICE I LMOST COULD'A AD A CHANCE AT THE MONEY.
YEAH, IF NOT FOR THE FACT THAT YOU DON'T HAVE A CAMERA...
...YOU DON'T OWN A CAMERA...
...AND WHEN SPIDER-MAN WAS HERE LAST WEEK YOU WERE RUNNING AROUND LIKE A LITTLE GIRL SCREAMING FOR YOUR MOMMY...
DUDE, WE ALL WERE SCREAMING AND RUNNING AROUND.
YEAH, BUT YOU REALLY WERE.
CAN YOU PLEASE TAKE THIS SOMEWHERE --?
SCREW YOU MAN. YOU'LL SEE.
MEONE'S GONNA BUMP INTO DER-MAN AND GET THAT BIG MONEY FOR NOTHIN' BUT TAKING A PICTURE --
-- AND ALL'S I'M SAYIN' IS THAT IT SHOULD'A BEEN ME.
"ALL'S?"
BZZZZZZZ

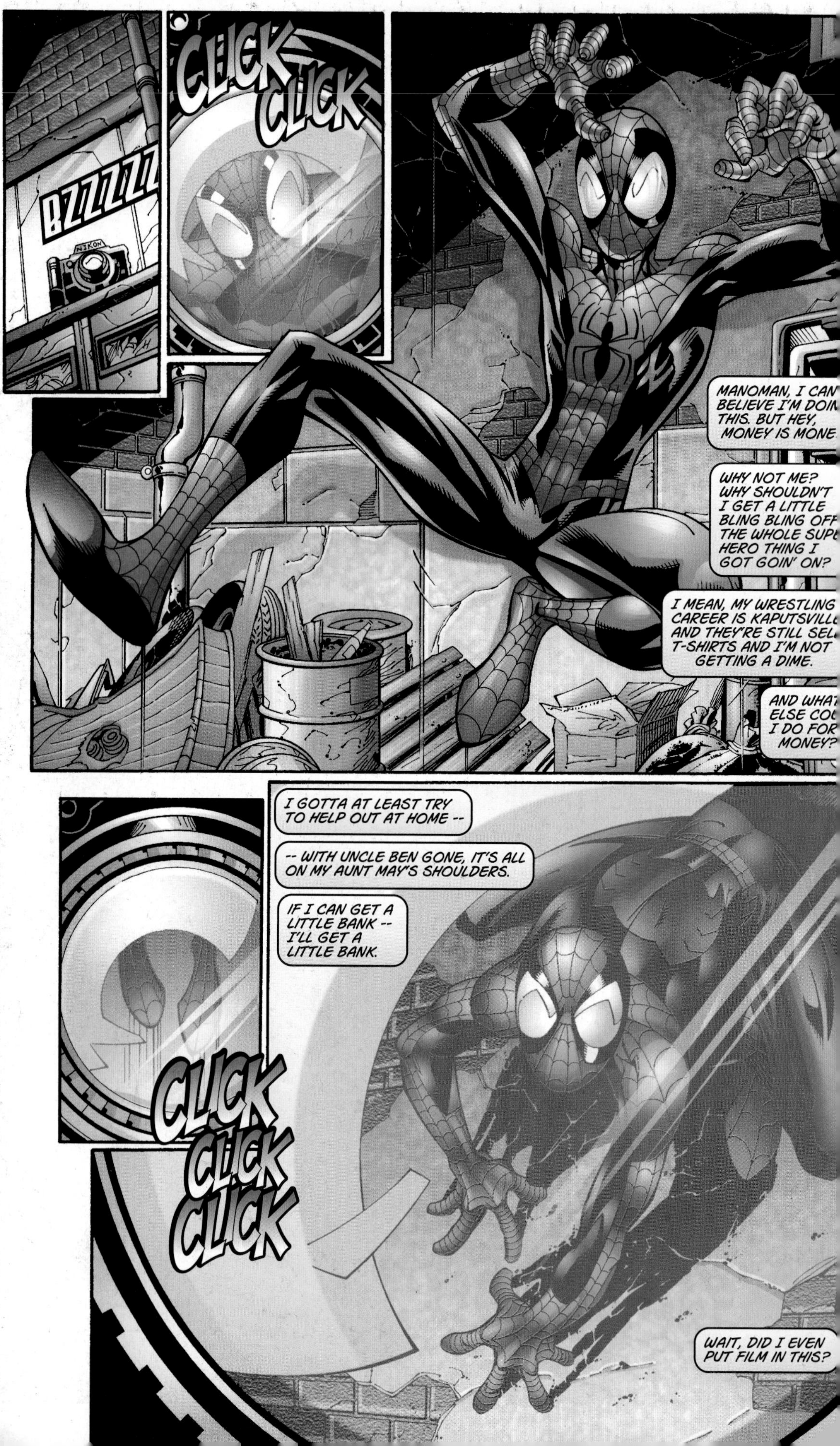
BZZZZZ
CLICK CLICK
MANOMAN, I CAN BELIEVE I'M DOIN THIS. BUT HEY, MONEY IS MONE
WHY NOT ME? WHY SHOULDN'T I GET A LITTLE BLING BLING OFF THE WHOLE SUPE HERO THING I GOT GOIN' ON?
I MEAN, MY WRESTLING CAREER IS KAPUTSVILL AND THEY'RE STILL SEL T-SHIRTS AND I'M NOT GETTING A DIME.
AND WHA ELSE CO I DO FOR MONEY?
I GOTTA AT LEAST TRY TO HELP OUT AT HOME --
-- WITH UNCLE BEN GONE, IT'S ALL ON MY AUNT MAY'S SHOULDERS.
IF I CAN GET A LITTLE BANK -- I'LL GET A LITTLE BANK.
CLICK CLICK CLICK
WAIT, DID I EVEN PUT FILM IN THIS?

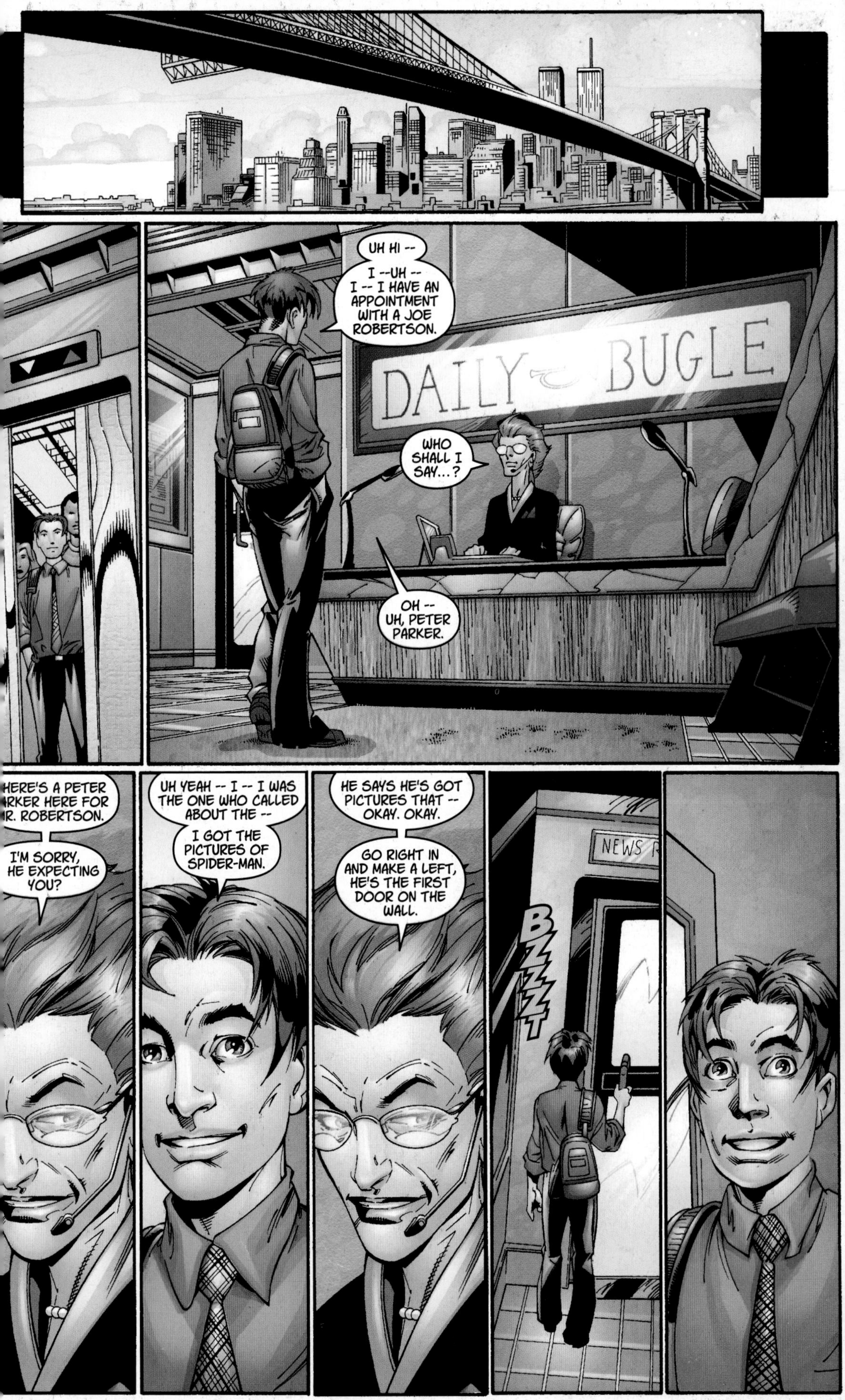
UH HI --
I --UH -- I -- I HAVE AN APPOINTMENT WITH A JOE ROBERTSON.
DAILY BUGLE
WHO SHALL I SAY...?
OH -- UH, PETER PARKER.
HERE'S A PETER ARKER HERE FOR R. ROBERTSON.
I'M SORRY, HE EXPECTING YOU?
UH YEAH -- I -- I WAS THE ONE WHO CALLED ABOUT THE --
I GOT THE PICTURES OF SPIDER-MAN.
HE SAYS HE'S GOT PICTURES THAT -- OKAY. OKAY.
GO RIGHT IN AND MAKE A LEFT, HE'S THE FIRST DOOR ON THE WALL.
NEWS
BZZZT

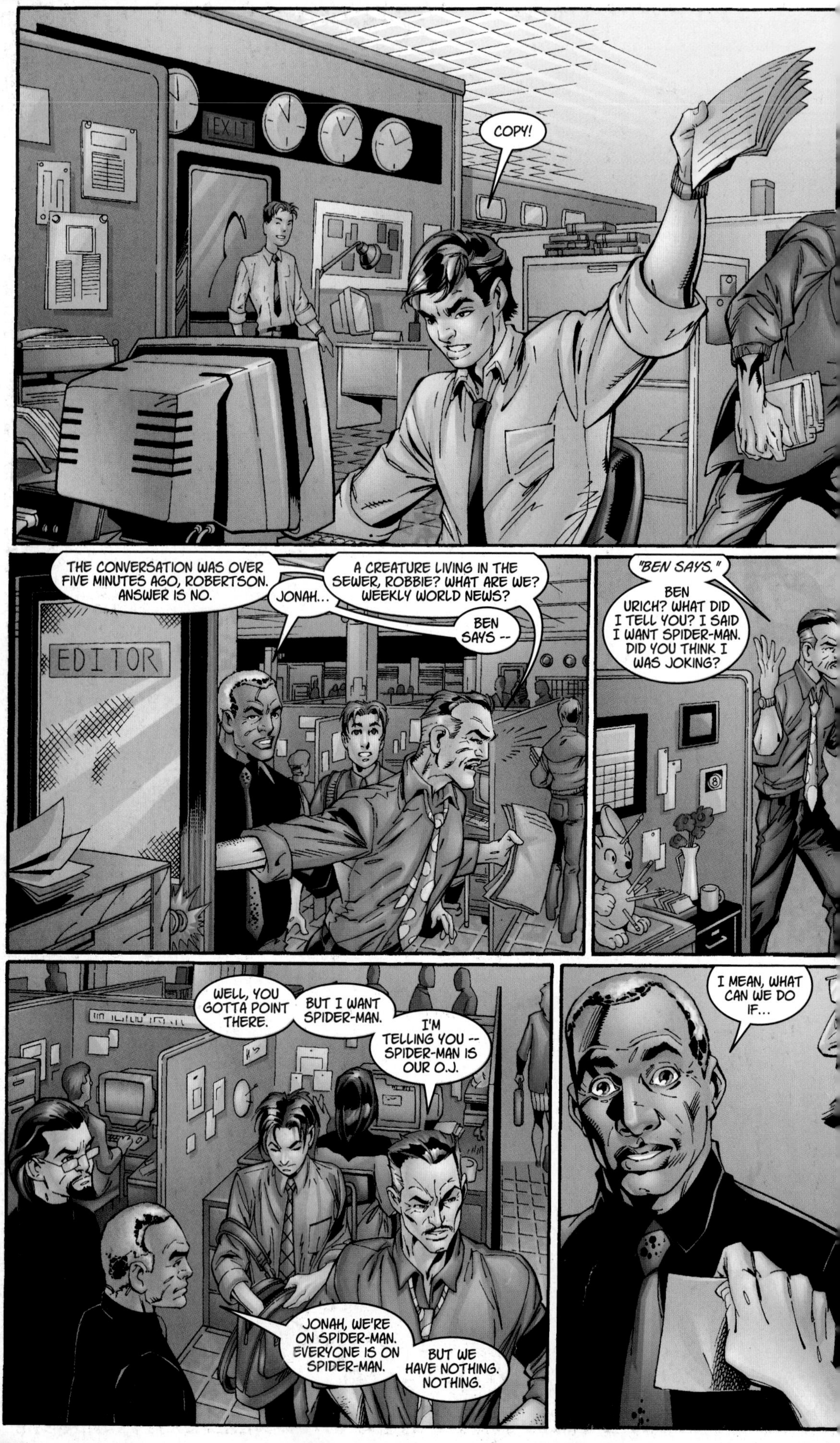

EXIT
COPY!
EDITOR
THE CONVERSATION WAS OVER FIVE MINUTES AGO, ROBERTSON. ANSWER IS NO.
A CREATURE LIVING IN THE SEWER, ROBBIE? WHAT ARE WE? WEEKLY WORLD NEWS?
JONAH...
BEN SAYS --
"BEN SAYS."
BEN URICH? WHAT DID I TELL YOU? I SAID I WANT SPIDER-MAN. DID YOU THINK I WAS JOKING?
WELL, YOU GOTTA POINT THERE.
BUT I WANT SPIDER-MAN.
I'M TELLING YOU -- SPIDER-MAN IS OUR O.J.
JONAH, WE'RE ON SPIDER-MAN. EVERYONE IS ON SPIDER-MAN.
BUT WE HAVE NOTHING. NOTHING.
I MEAN, WHAT CAN WE DO IF...

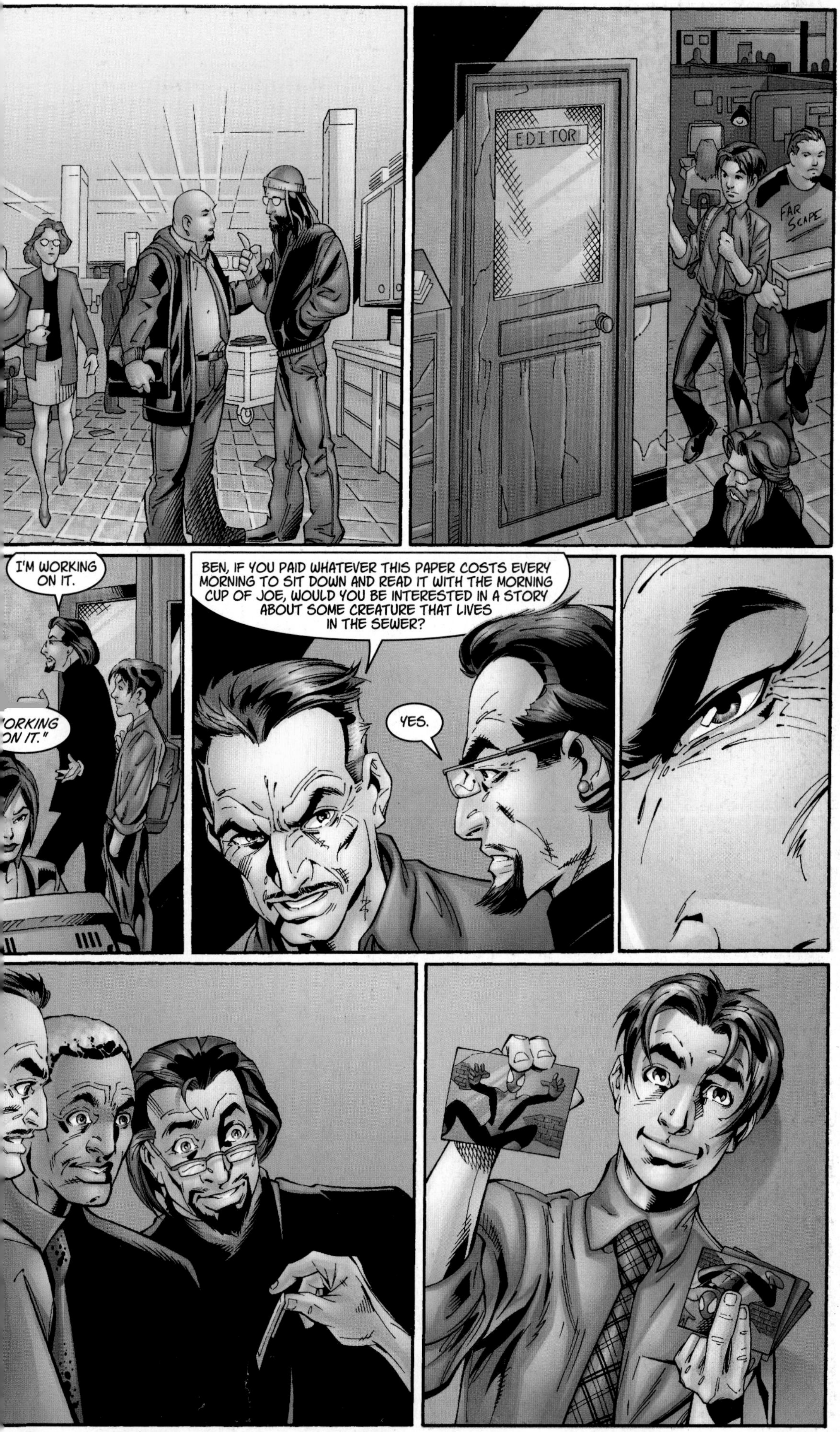
EDITOR
FAR SCAPE
I'M WORKING ON IT.
"WORKING ON IT."
BEN, IF YOU PAID WHATEVER THIS PAPER COSTS EVERY MORNING TO SIT DOWN AND READ IT WITH THE MORNING CUP OF JOE, WOULD YOU BE INTERESTED IN A STORY ABOUT SOME CREATURE THAT LIVES IN THE SEWER?
YES.

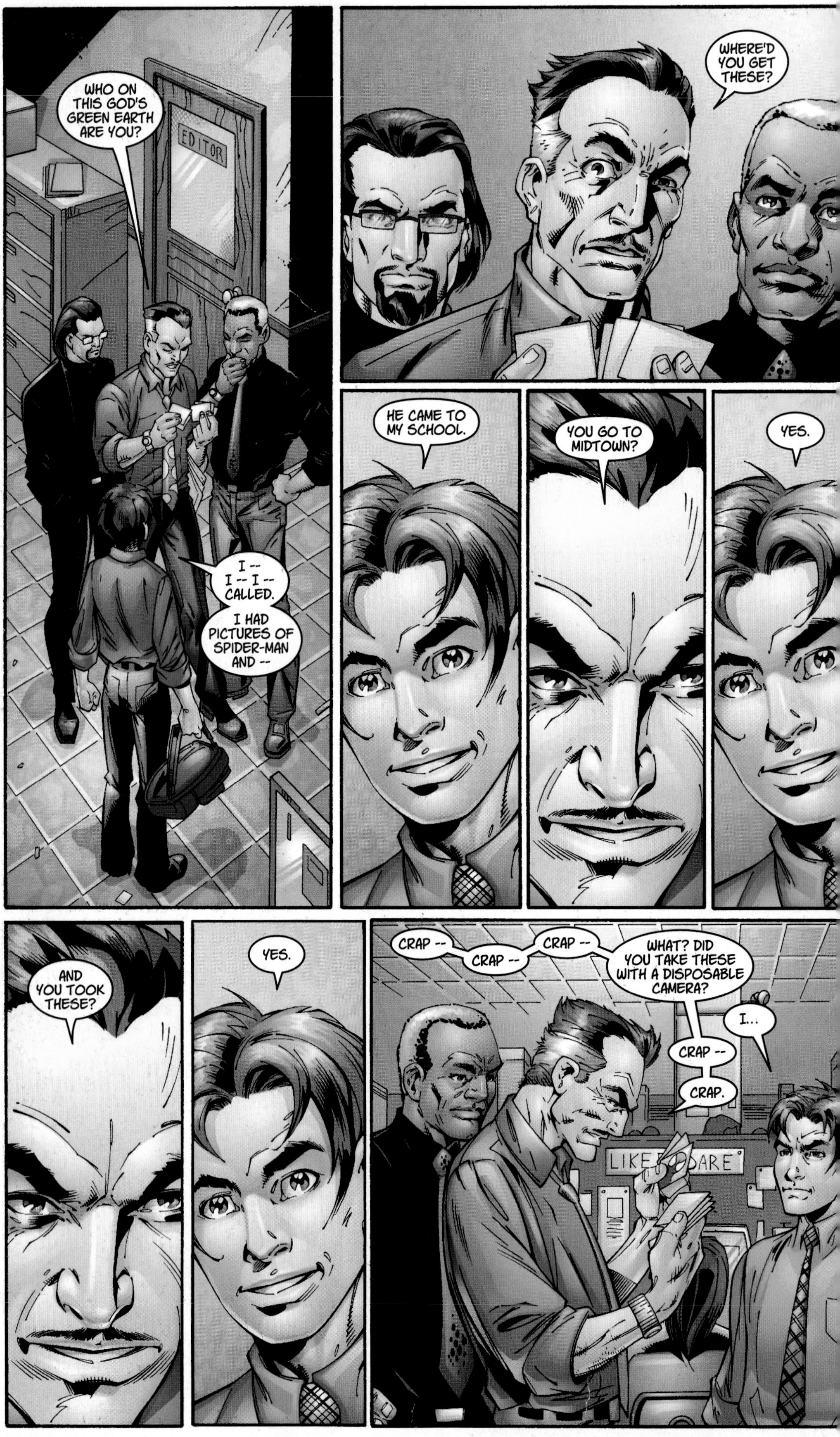
WHO ON THIS GOD'S GREEN EARTH ARE YOU?
EDITOR
I -- I -- I -- CALLED.
I HAD PICTURES OF SPIDER-MAN AND --
WHERE'D YOU GET THESE?
HE CAME TO MY SCHOOL.
YOU GO TO MIDTOWN?
YES.
AND YOU TOOK THESE?
YES.
CRAP --
CRAP --
CRAP --
WHAT? DID YOU TAKE THESE WITH A DISPOSABLE CAMERA?
I...
CRAP --
CRAP.

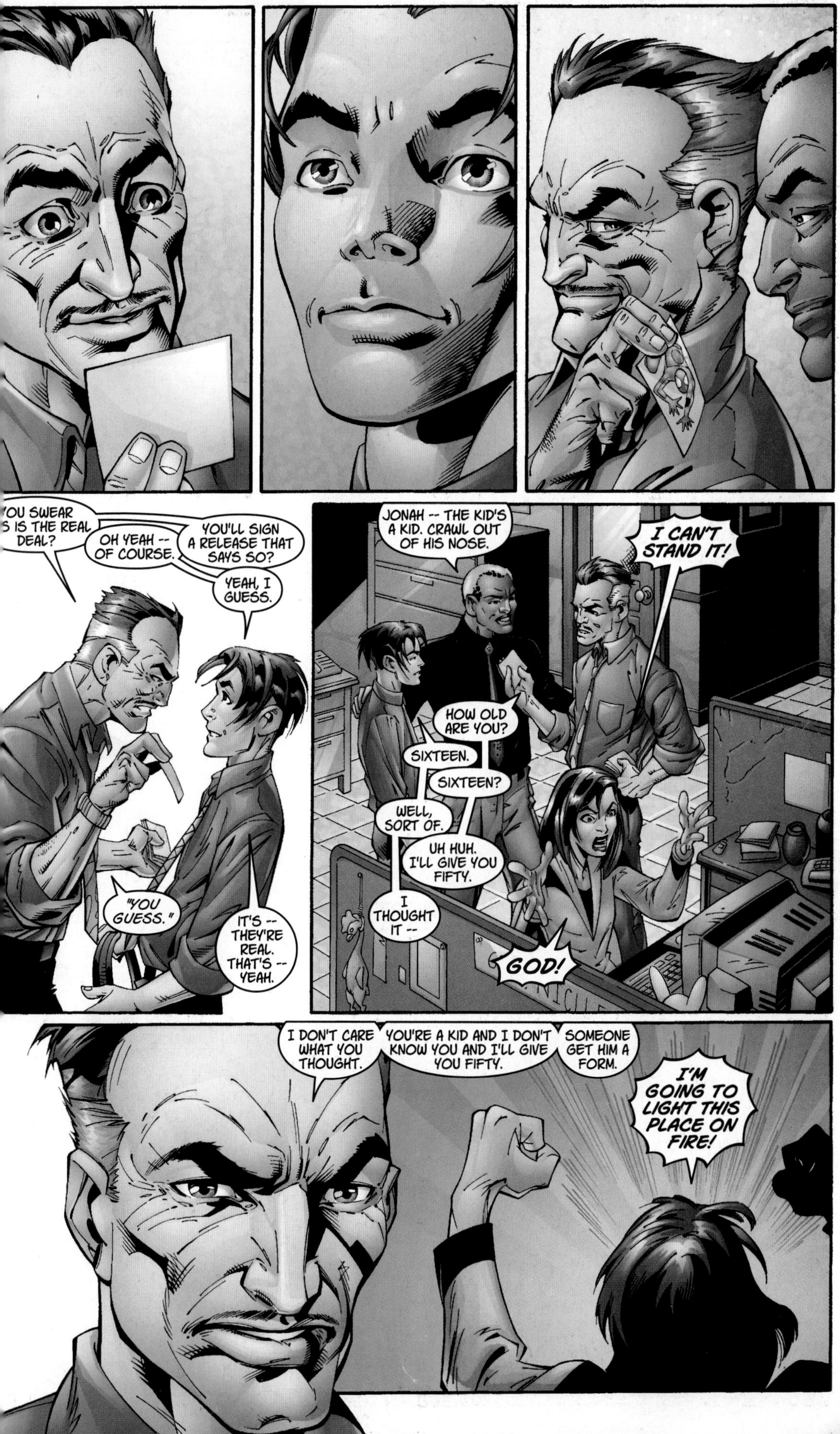
YOU SWEAR
S IS THE REAL DEAL?
OH YEAH -- OF COURSE.
YOU'LL SIGN A RELEASE THAT SAYS SO?
YEAH, I GUESS.
"YOU GUESS."
IT'S -- THEY'RE REAL. THAT'S -- YEAH.
JONAH -- THE KID'S A KID. CRAWL OUT OF HIS NOSE.
I CAN'T STAND IT!
HOW OLD ARE YOU?
SIXTEEN.
SIXTEEN?
WELL, SORT OF.
UH HUH. I'LL GIVE YOU FIFTY.
I THOUGHT IT --
GOD!
I DON'T CARE WHAT YOU THOUGHT.
YOU'RE A KID AND I DON'T KNOW YOU AND I'LL GIVE YOU FIFTY.
SOMEONE GET HIM A FORM.
I'M GOING TO LIGHT THIS PLACE ON FIRE!

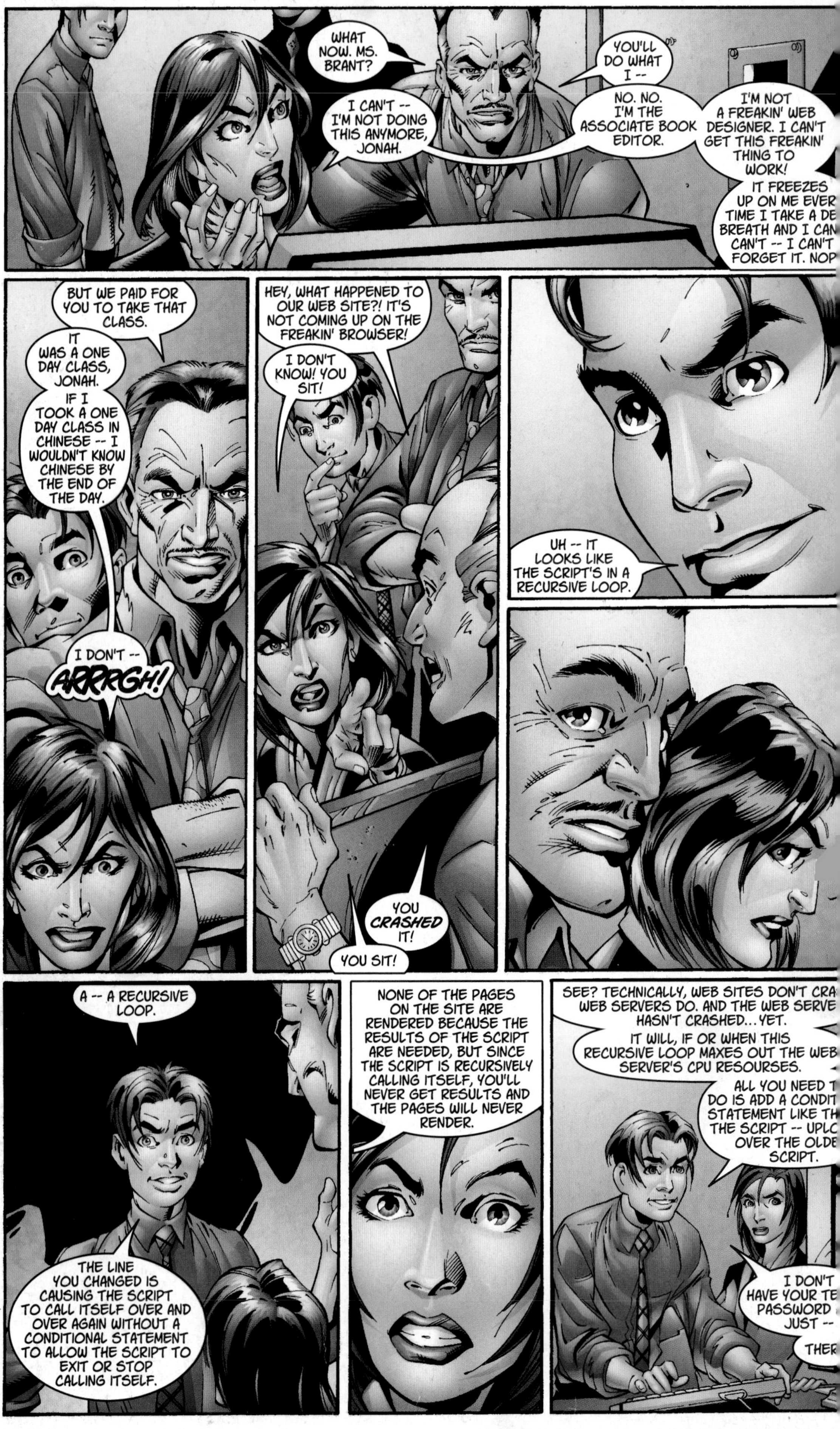

WHAT NOW. MS. BRANT?
I CAN'T -- I'M NOT DOING THIS ANYMORE, JONAH.
YOU'LL DO WHAT I --
NO. NO. I'M THE ASSOCIATE BOOK EDITOR.
I'M NOT A FREAKIN' WEB DESIGNER. I CAN'T GET THIS FREAKIN' THING TO WORK!
IT FREEZES UP ON ME EVER TIME I TAKE A DE BREATH AND I CAN CAN'T -- I CAN'T FORGET IT. NOP
BUT WE PAID FOR YOU TO TAKE THAT CLASS.
IT WAS A ONE DAY CLASS, JONAH.
IF I TOOK A ONE DAY CLASS IN CHINESE -- I WOULDN'T KNOW CHINESE BY THE END OF THE DAY.
I DON'T --
ARRRGH!
HEY, WHAT HAPPENED TO OUR WEB SITE?! IT'S NOT COMING UP ON THE FREAKIN' BROWSER!
I DON'T KNOW! YOU SIT!
YOU CRASHED IT!
YOU SIT!
UH -- IT LOOKS LIKE THE SCRIPT'S IN A RECURSIVE LOOP.
A -- A RECURSIVE LOOP.
THE LINE YOU CHANGED IS CAUSING THE SCRIPT TO CALL ITSELF OVER AND OVER AGAIN WITHOUT A CONDITIONAL STATEMENT TO ALLOW THE SCRIPT TO EXIT OR STOP CALLING ITSELF.
NONE OF THE PAGES ON THE SITE ARE RENDERED BECAUSE THE RESULTS OF THE SCRIPT ARE NEEDED, BUT SINCE THE SCRIPT IS RECURSIVELY CALLING ITSELF, YOU'LL NEVER GET RESULTS AND THE PAGES WILL NEVER RENDER.
SEE? TECHNICALLY, WEB SITES DON'T CRA WEB SERVERS DO. AND THE WEB SERVE HASN'T CRASHED... YET.
IT WILL, IF OR WHEN THIS RECURSIVE LOOP MAXES OUT THE WEB SERVER'S CPU RESOURSES.
ALL YOU NEED T DO IS ADD A CONDIT STATEMENT LIKE TH THE SCRIPT -- UPLC OVER THE OLDE SCRIPT.
I DON'T HAVE YOUR TE PASSWORD JUST --
THER

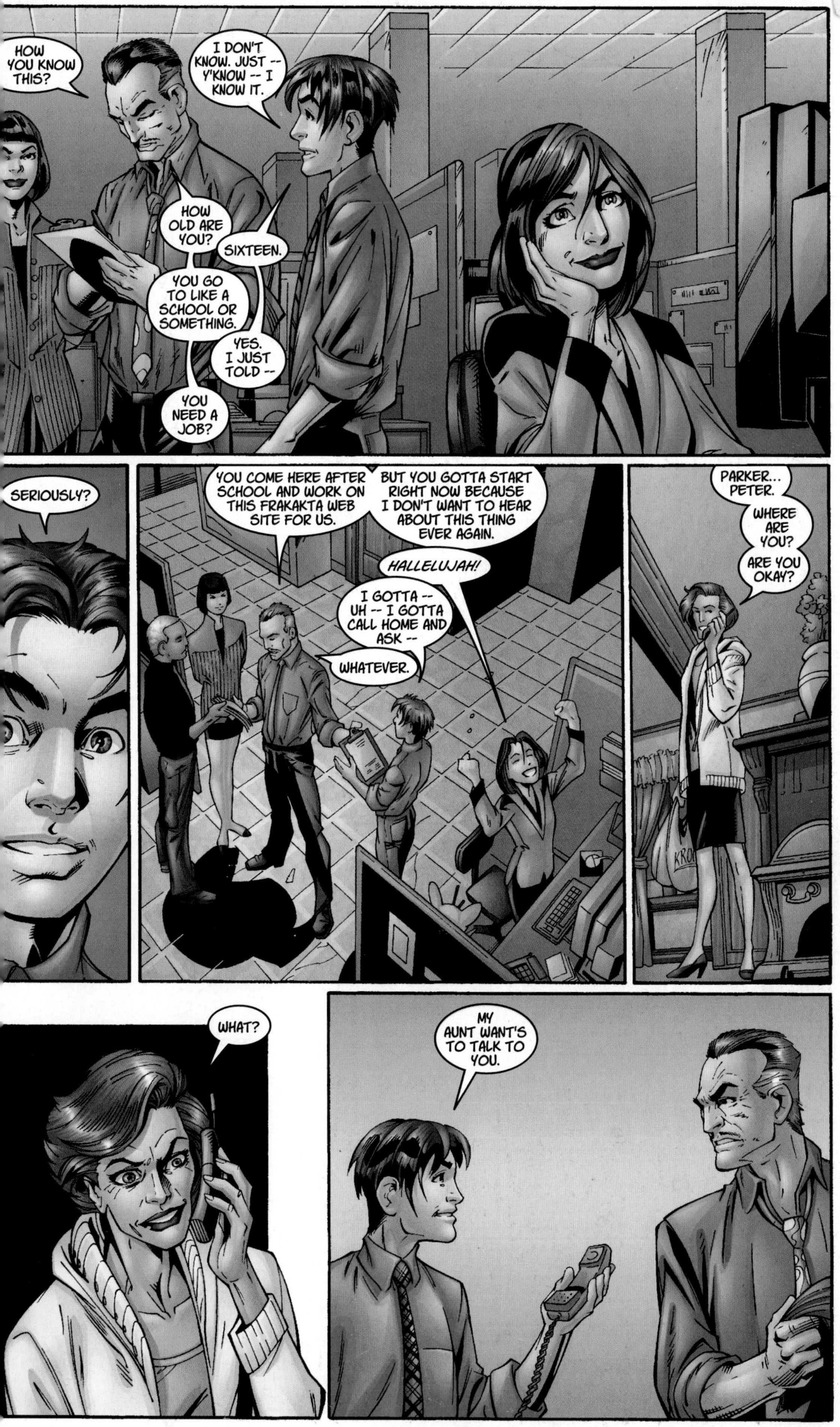
HOW YOU KNOW THIS?
I DON'T KNOW. JUST -- Y'KNOW -- I KNOW IT.
HOW OLD ARE YOU?
SIXTEEN.
YOU GO TO LIKE A SCHOOL OR SOMETHING.
YES. I JUST TOLD --
YOU NEED A JOB?
SERIOUSLY?
YOU COME HERE AFTER SCHOOL AND WORK ON THIS FRAKAKTA WEB SITE FOR US.
BUT YOU GOTTA START RIGHT NOW BECAUSE I DON'T WANT TO HEAR ABOUT THIS THING EVER AGAIN.
HALLELUJAH!
I GOTTA -- UH -- I GOTTA CALL HOME AND ASK --
WHATEVER.
PARKER... PETER.
WHERE ARE YOU?
ARE YOU OKAY?
WHAT?
MY AUNT WANT'S TO TALK TO YOU.

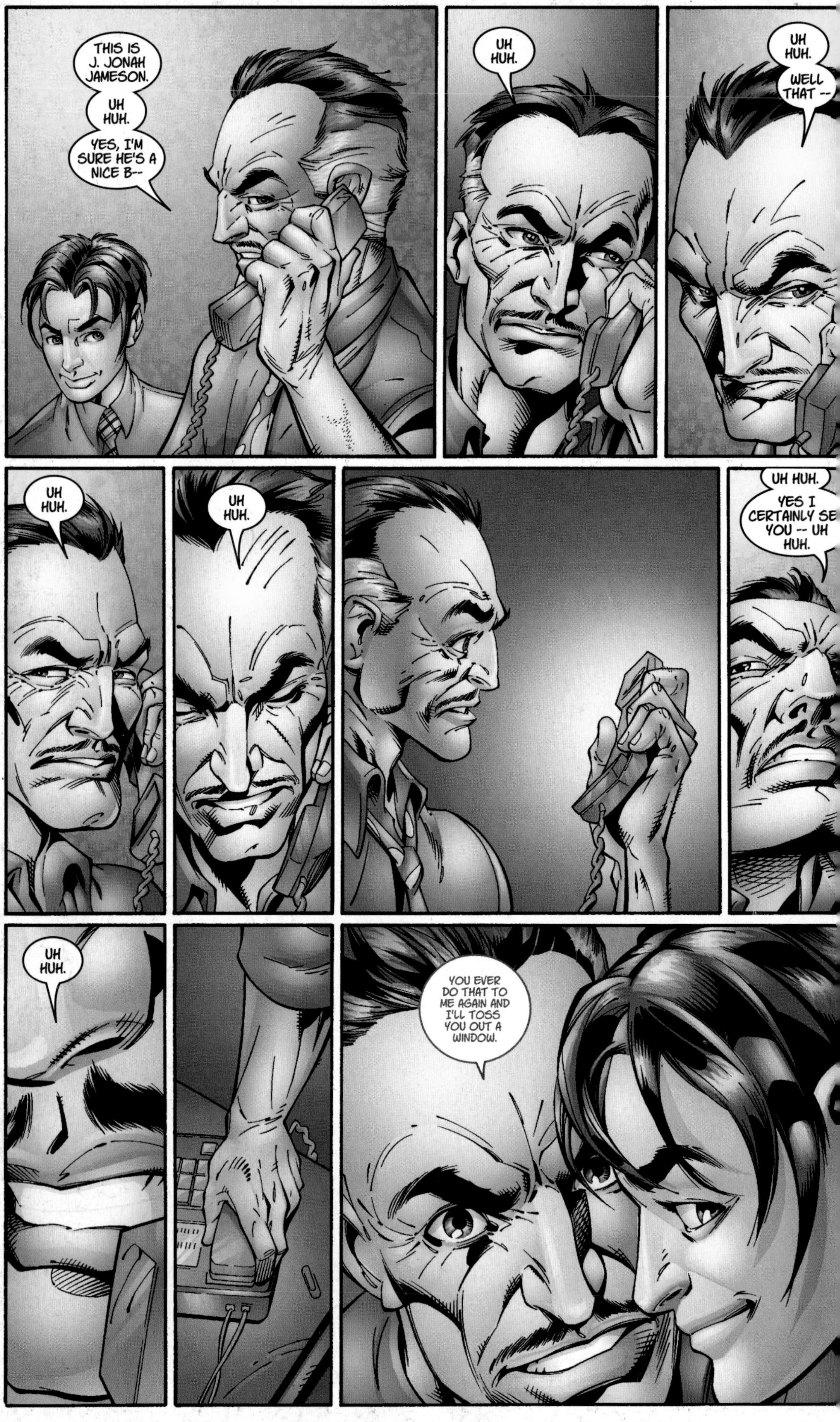
THIS IS J. JONAH JAMESON.
UH HUH.
YES, I'M SURE HE'S A NICE B--
UH HUH.
UH HUH.
WELL THAT --
UH HUH.
UH HUH.
UH HUH.
YES I CERTAINLY SE YOU -- UH HUH.
UH HUH.
YOU EVER DO THAT TO ME AGAIN AND I'LL TOSS YOU OUT A WINDOW.

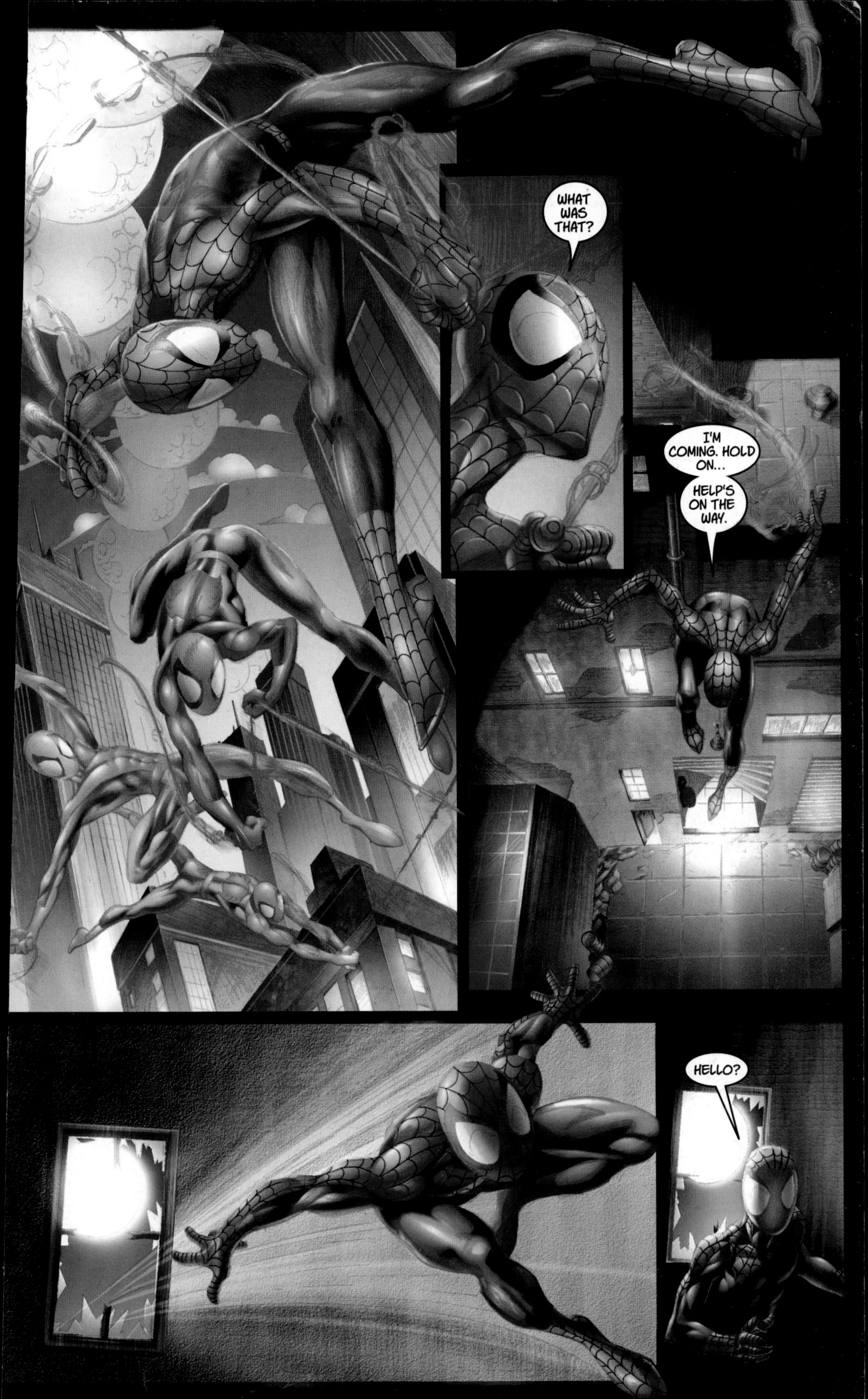
WHAT WAS THAT?
I'M COMING. HOLD ON...
HELP'S ON THE WAY.
HELLO?

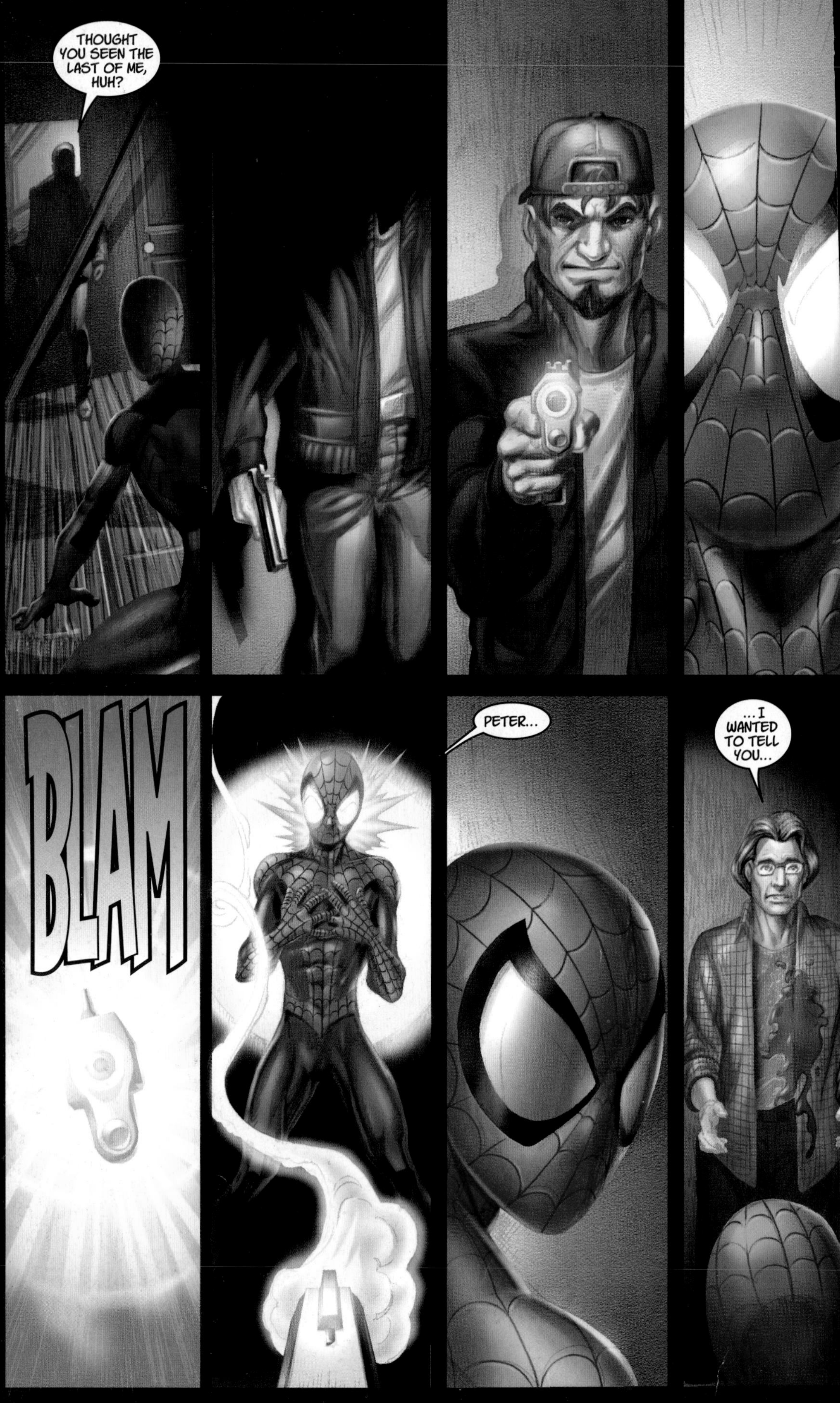
THOUGHT YOU SEEN THE LAST OF ME, HUH?
BLAM
PETER...
...I WANTED TO TELL YOU...

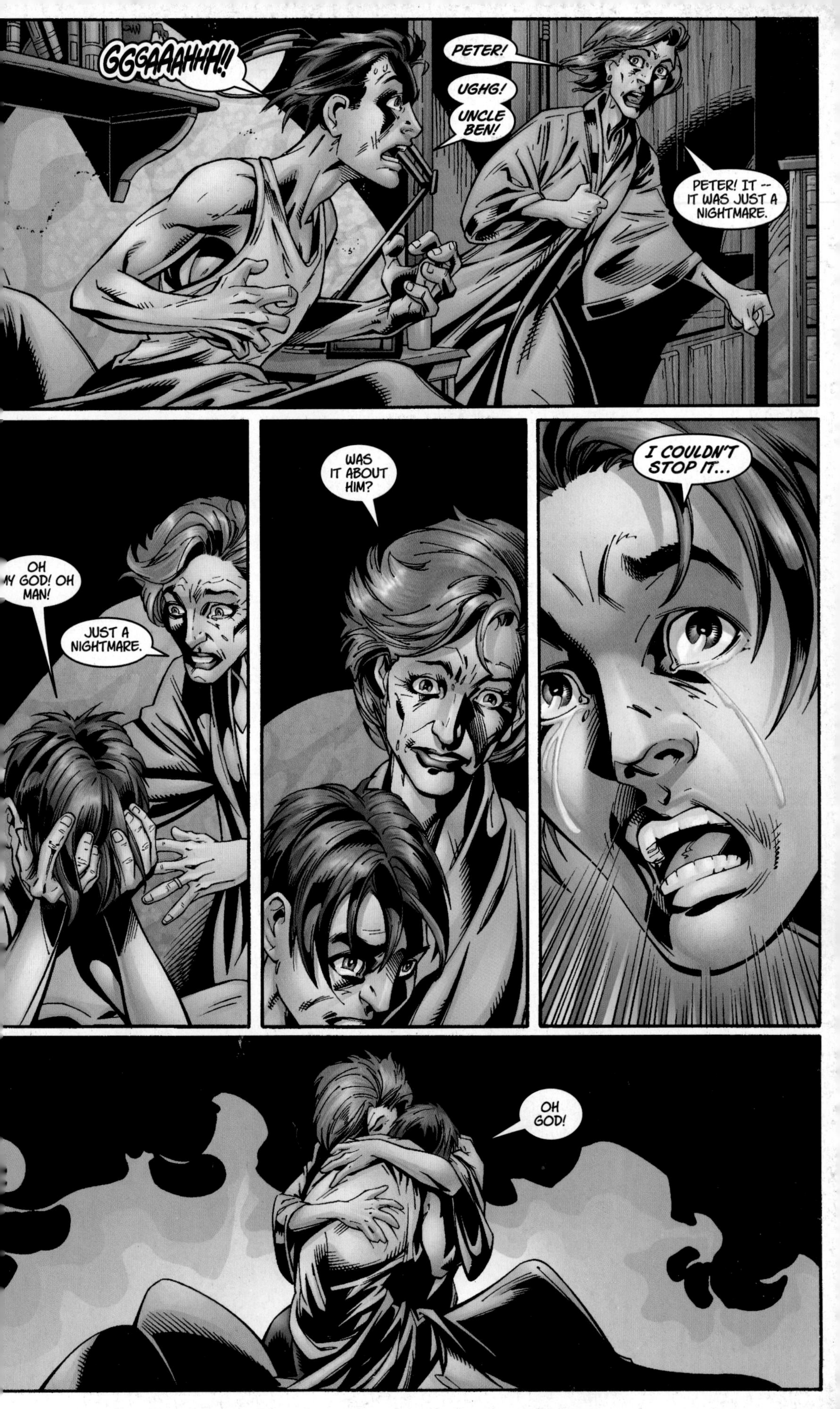
GGGAAAHHH!!
PETER!
UGHG!
UNCLE BEN!
PETER! IT -- IT WAS JUST A NIGHTMARE.
OH MY GOD! OH MAN!
JUST A NIGHTMARE.
WAS IT ABOUT HIM?
I COULDN'T STOP IT...
OH GOD!

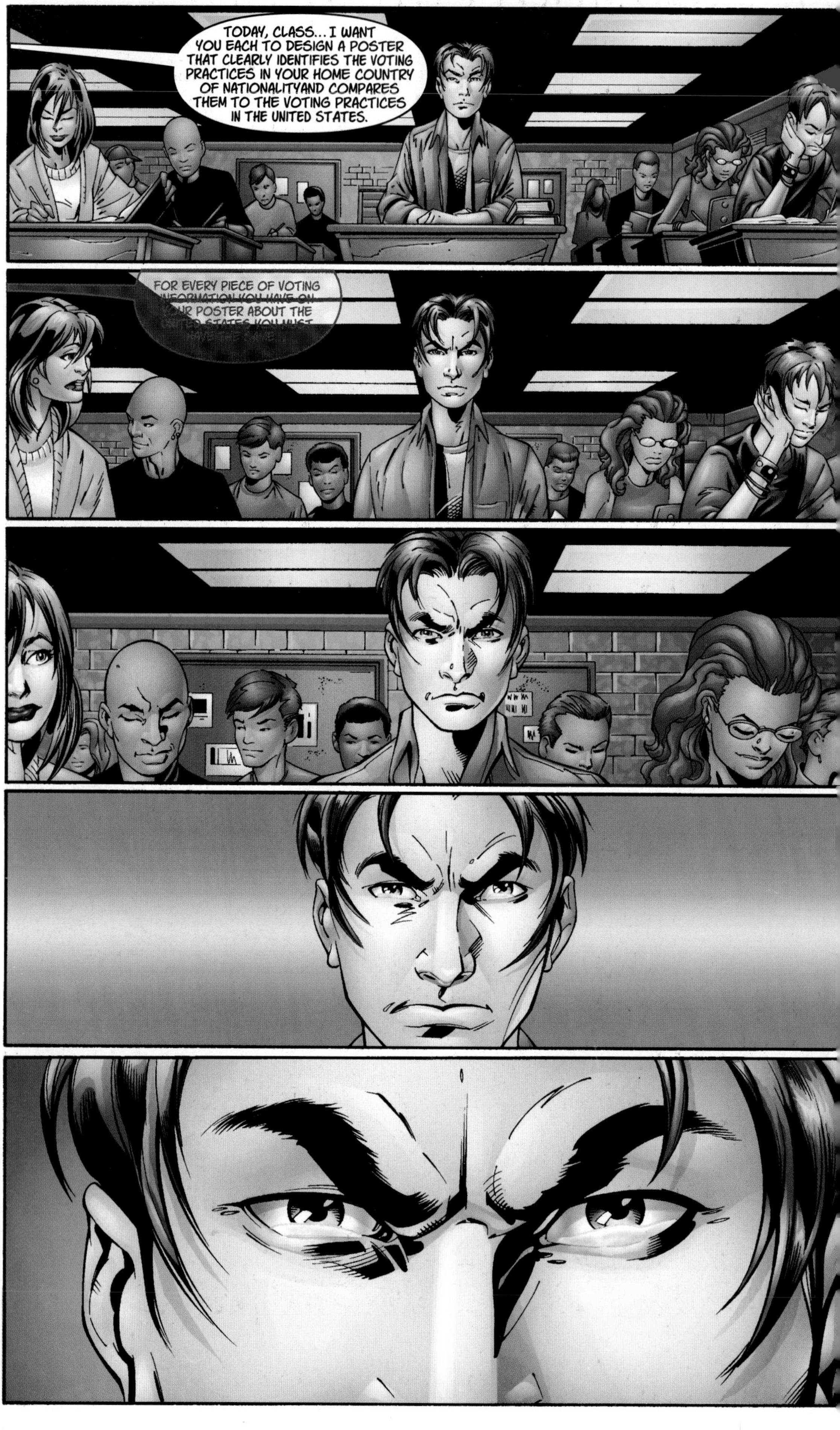
TODAY, CLASS... I WANT YOU EACH TO DESIGN A POSTER THAT CLEARLY IDENTIFIES THE VOTING PRACTICES IN YOUR HOME COUNTRY OF NATIONALITYAND COMPARES THEM TO THE VOTING PRACTICES IN THE UNITED STATES.
FOR EVERY PIECE OF VOTING
POSTER ABOUT THE

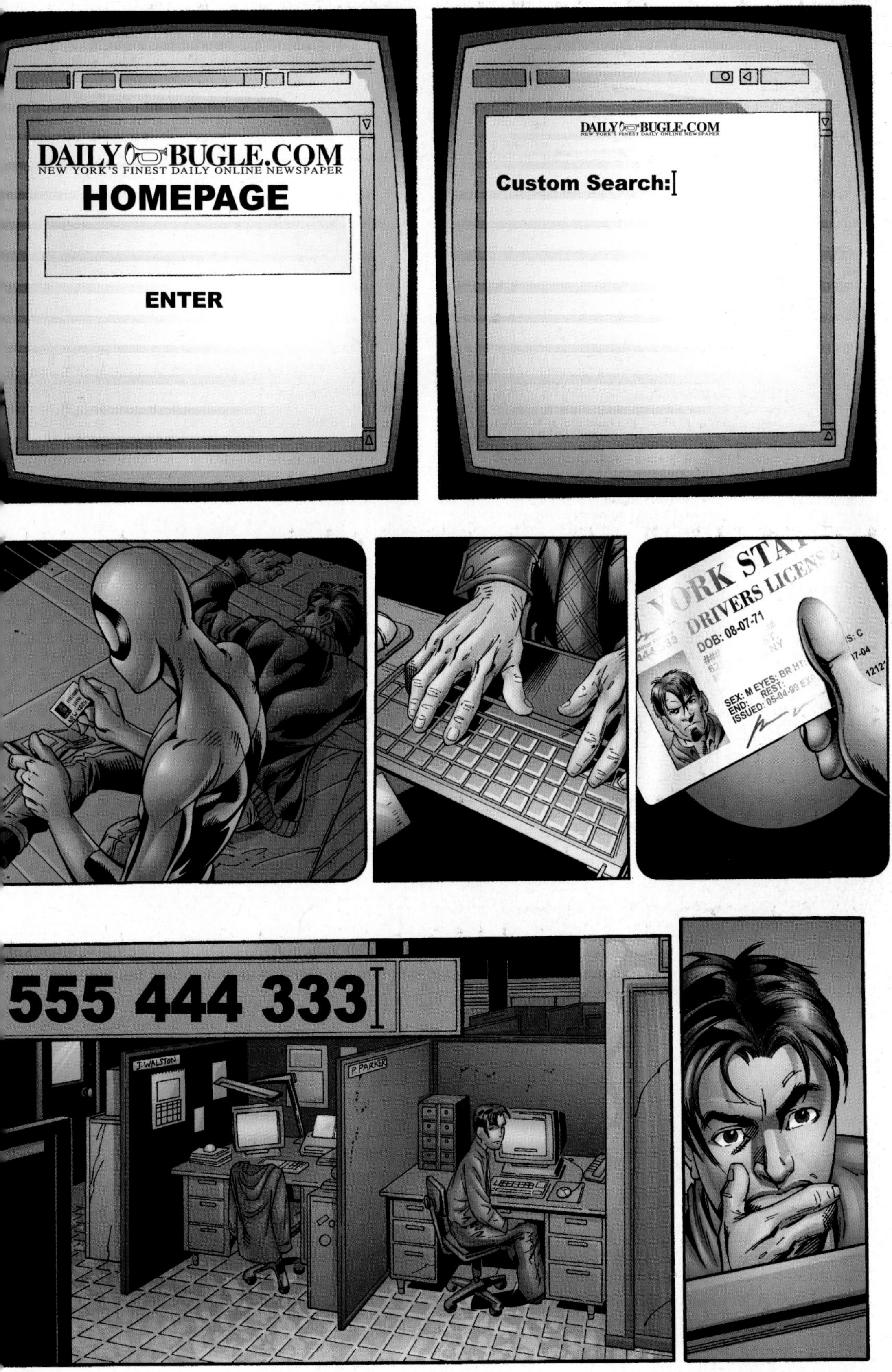
DAILY BUGLE.COM
NEW YORK'S FINEST DAILY ONLINE NEWSPAPER
HOMEPAGE
ENTER
DAILY BUGLE.COM
NEW YORK'S FINEST DAILY ONLINE NEWSPAPER
Custom Search:
DRIVERS
DOB: 08-07-71
SEX: M EYES: BR
END:
REST:
ISSUED: 05-04-99
555 444 333
J. WALSTON
P. PARKER

ITEM'S FOUND: 2

Police bust bosses at "The Cage." A hot spot for alleged organized crime.

More?

ITEM: 2

ORGANIZED CRIME IN NEW YORK CITY
an overview by Ben Urich

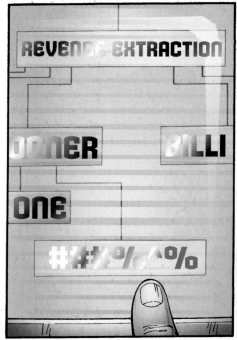

REVENGE EXTRACTION

ODNER   BILLI

ONE

#%#%^%

WILSON FISK
THE KINGPIN

ENFORCEM

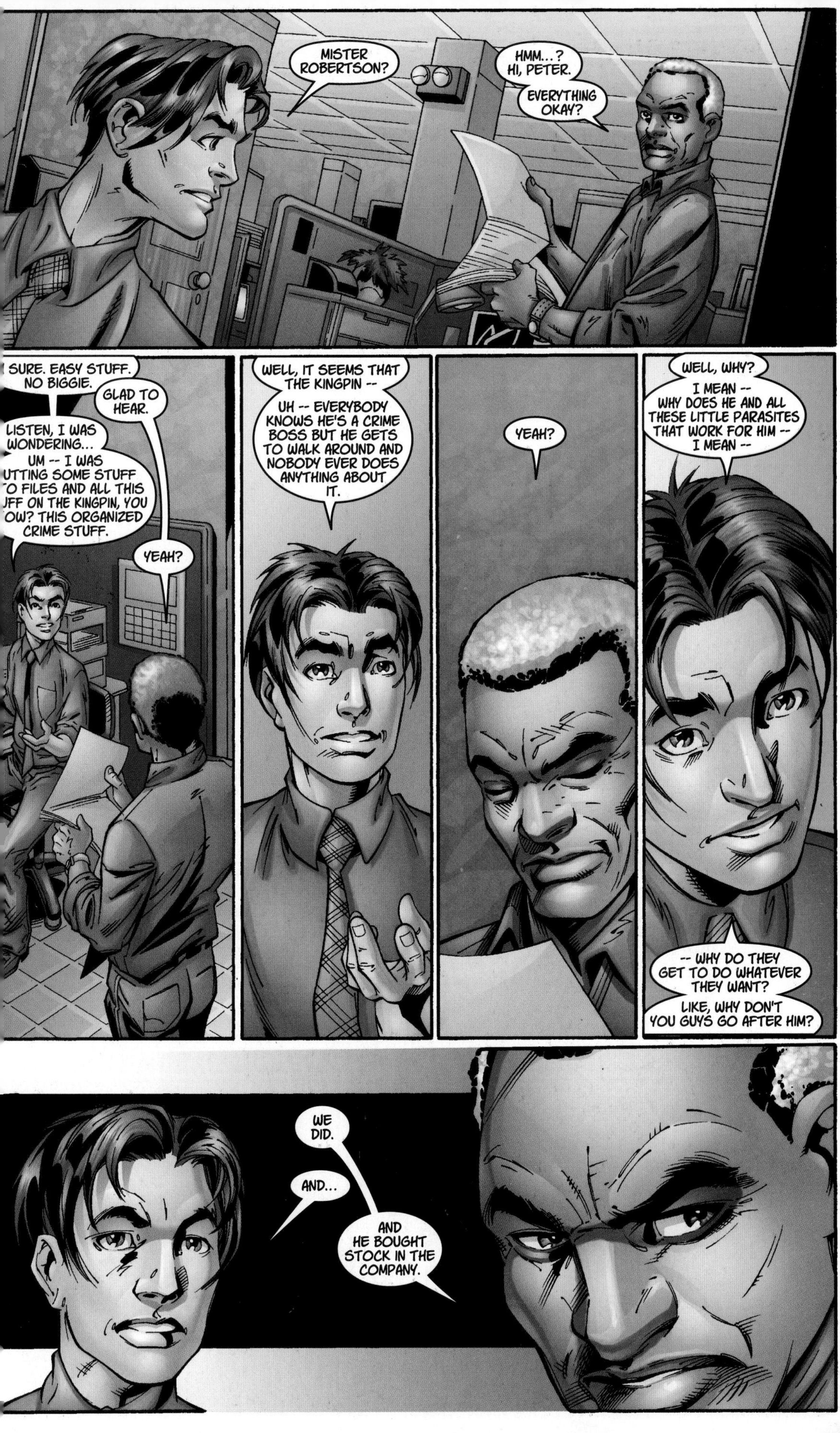
MISTER ROBERTSON?
HMM...? HI, PETER.
EVERYTHING OKAY?
SURE. EASY STUFF. NO BIGGIE.
GLAD TO HEAR.
LISTEN, I WAS WONDERING...
UM -- I WAS UTTING SOME STUFF TO FILES AND ALL THIS UFF ON THE KINGPIN, YOU OW? THIS ORGANIZED CRIME STUFF.
YEAH?
WELL, IT SEEMS THAT THE KINGPIN --
UH -- EVERYBODY KNOWS HE'S A CRIME BOSS BUT HE GETS TO WALK AROUND AND NOBODY EVER DOES ANYTHING ABOUT IT.
YEAH?
WELL, WHY?
I MEAN -- WHY DOES HE AND ALL THESE LITTLE PARASITES THAT WORK FOR HIM -- I MEAN --
-- WHY DO THEY GET TO DO WHATEVER THEY WANT?
LIKE, WHY DON'T YOU GUYS GO AFTER HIM?
WE DID.
AND...
AND HE BOUGHT STOCK IN THE COMPANY.

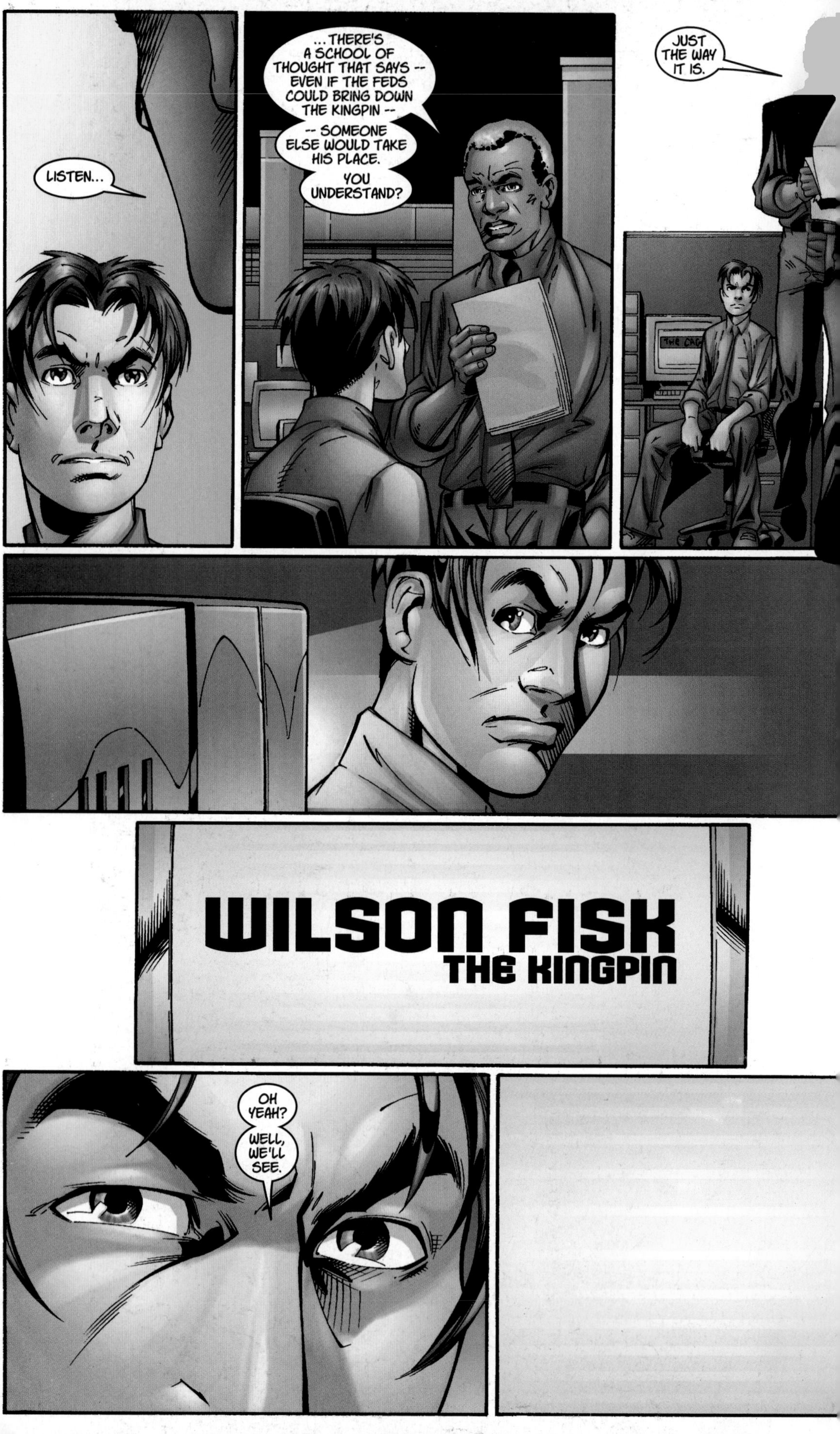
LISTEN...
... THERE'S A SCHOOL OF THOUGHT THAT SAYS -- EVEN IF THE FEDS COULD BRING DOWN THE KINGPIN --
-- SOMEONE ELSE WOULD TAKE HIS PLACE.
YOU UNDERSTAND?
JUST THE WAY IT IS.
WILSON FISK
THE KINGPIN
OH YEAH?
WELL, WE'LL SEE.

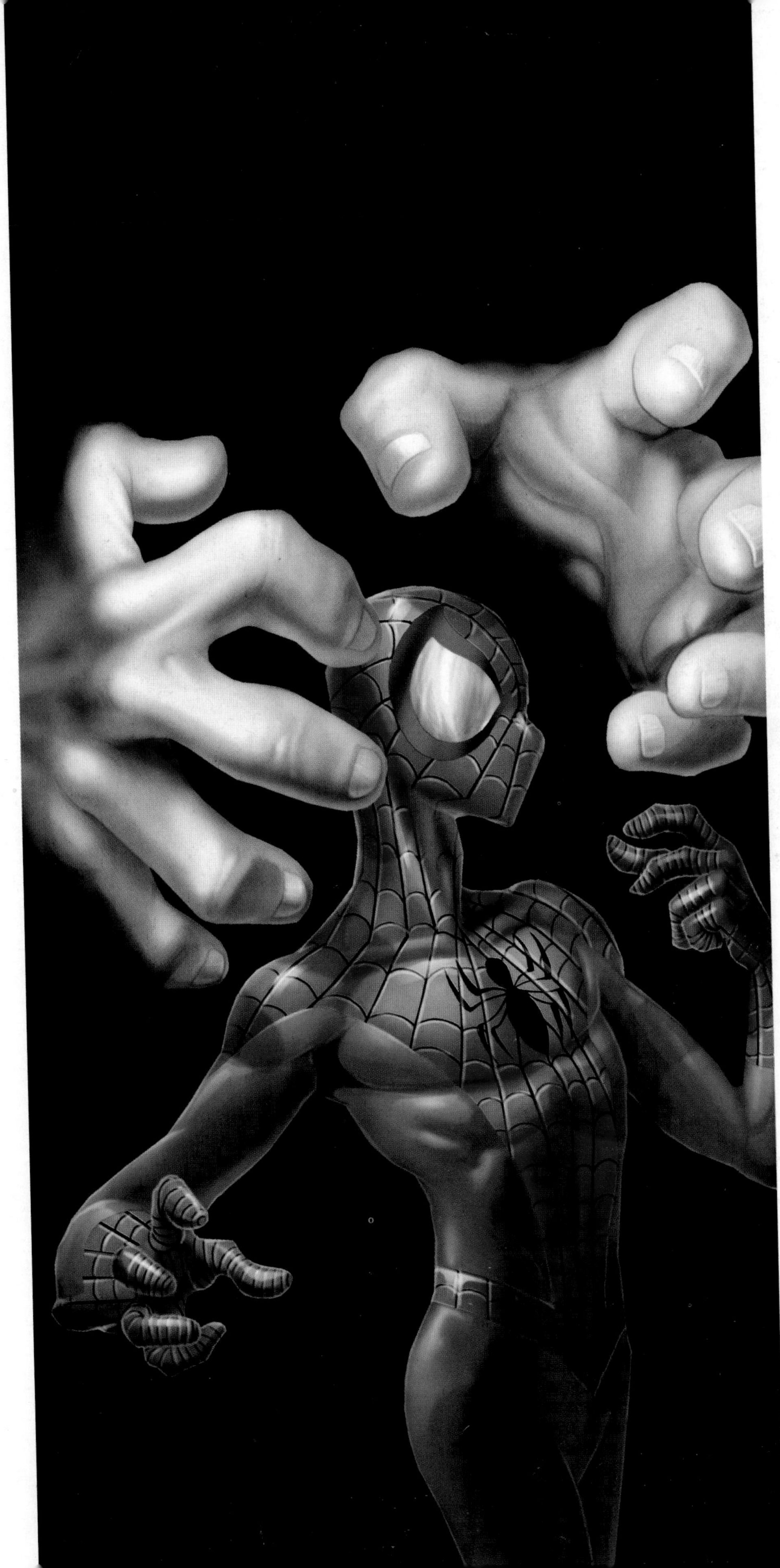

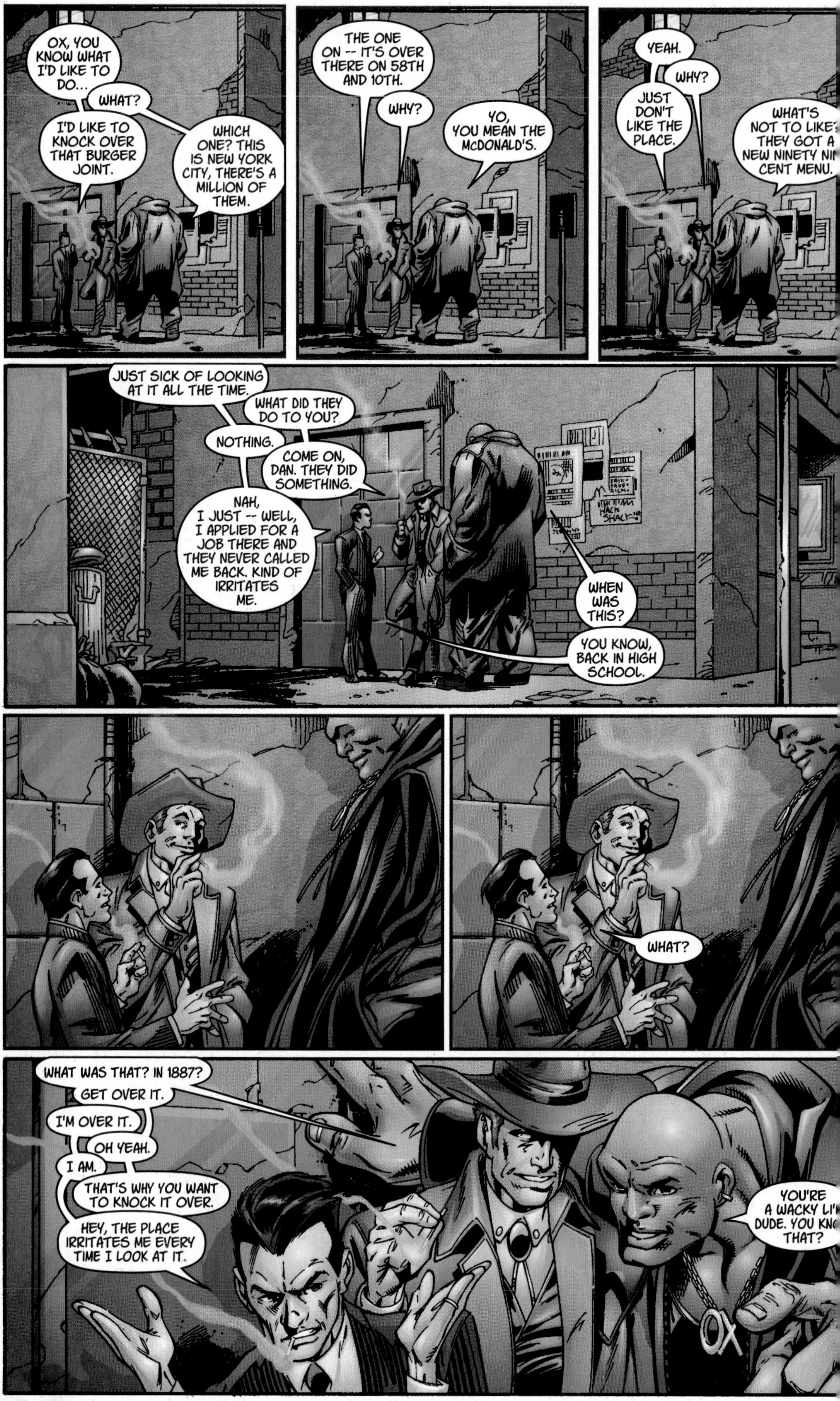
OX, YOU KNOW WHAT I'D LIKE TO DO...
WHAT?
I'D LIKE TO KNOCK OVER THAT BURGER JOINT.
WHICH ONE? THIS IS NEW YORK CITY, THERE'S A MILLION OF THEM.
THE ONE ON -- IT'S OVER THERE ON 58TH AND 10TH.
WHY?
YO, YOU MEAN THE McDONALD'S.
YEAH.
WHY?
JUST DON'T LIKE THE PLACE.
WHAT'S NOT TO LIKE? THEY GOT A NEW NINETY NI CENT MENU.
JUST SICK OF LOOKING AT IT ALL THE TIME.
WHAT DID THEY DO TO YOU?
NOTHING.
COME ON, DAN. THEY DID SOMETHING.
NAH, I JUST -- WELL, I APPLIED FOR A JOB THERE AND THEY NEVER CALLED ME BACK. KIND OF IRRITATES ME.
WHEN WAS THIS?
YOU KNOW, BACK IN HIGH SCHOOL.
WHAT?
WHAT WAS THAT? IN 1887?
GET OVER IT.
I'M OVER IT.
OH YEAH.
I AM.
THAT'S WHY YOU WANT TO KNOCK IT OVER.
HEY, THE PLACE IRRITATES ME EVERY TIME I LOOK AT IT.
YOU'RE A WACKY LI' DUDE. YOU KN THAT?

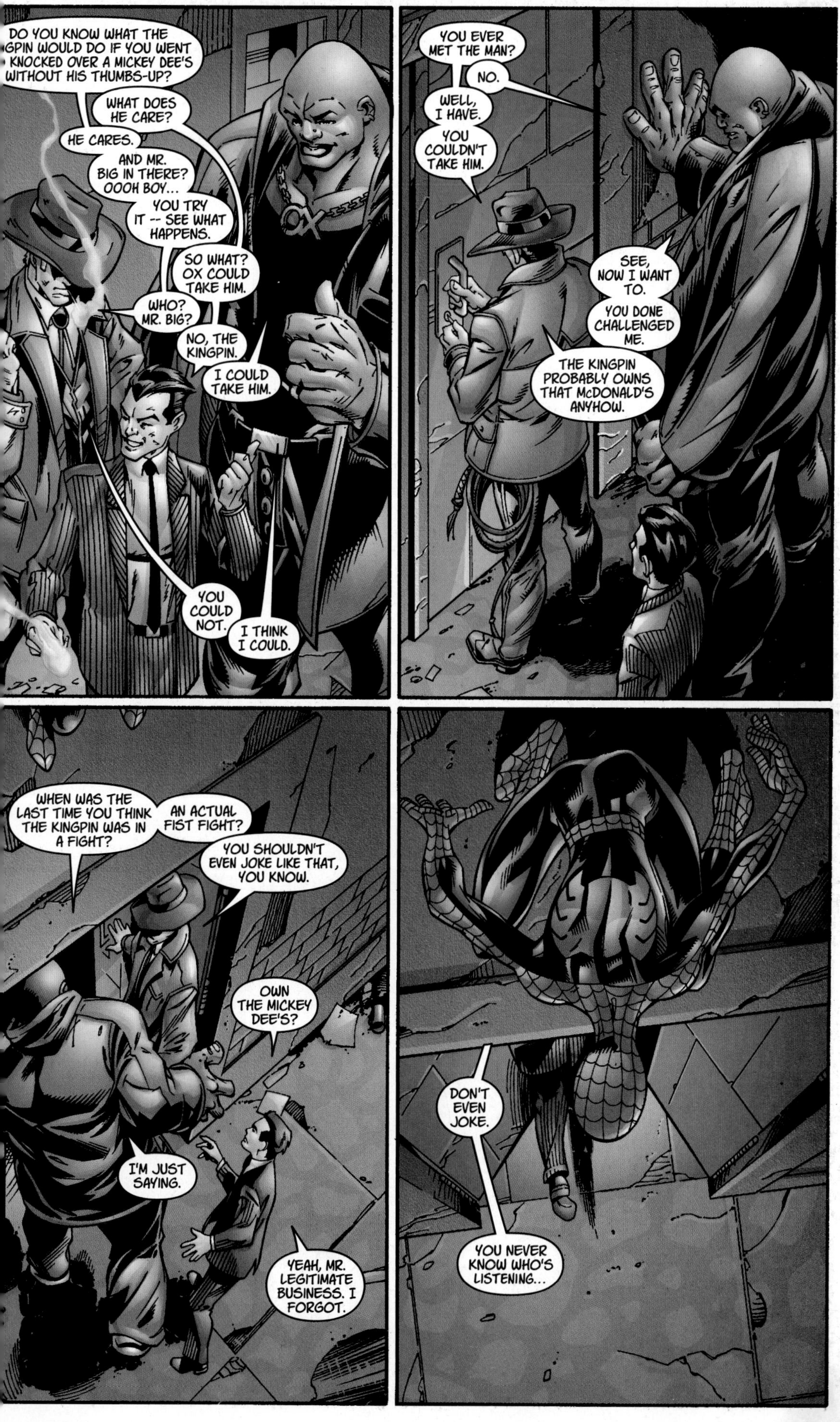
DO YOU KNOW WHAT THE KINGPIN WOULD DO IF YOU WENT KNOCKED OVER A MICKEY DEE'S WITHOUT HIS THUMBS-UP?
WHAT DOES HE CARE?
HE CARES.
AND MR. BIG IN THERE? OOOH BOY...
YOU TRY IT -- SEE WHAT HAPPENS.
SO WHAT? OX COULD TAKE HIM.
WHO? MR. BIG?
NO, THE KINGPIN.
I COULD TAKE HIM.
YOU COULD NOT.
I THINK I COULD.
YOU EVER MET THE MAN?
NO.
WELL, I HAVE.
YOU COULDN'T TAKE HIM.
SEE, NOW I WANT TO.
YOU DONE CHALLENGED ME.
THE KINGPIN PROBABLY OWNS THAT McDONALD'S ANYHOW.
WHEN WAS THE LAST TIME YOU THINK THE KINGPIN WAS IN A FIGHT?
AN ACTUAL FIST FIGHT?
YOU SHOULDN'T EVEN JOKE LIKE THAT, YOU KNOW.
OWN THE MICKEY DEE'S?
I'M JUST SAYING.
YEAH, MR. LEGITIMATE BUSINESS. I FORGOT.
DON'T EVEN JOKE.
YOU NEVER KNOW WHO'S LISTENING...

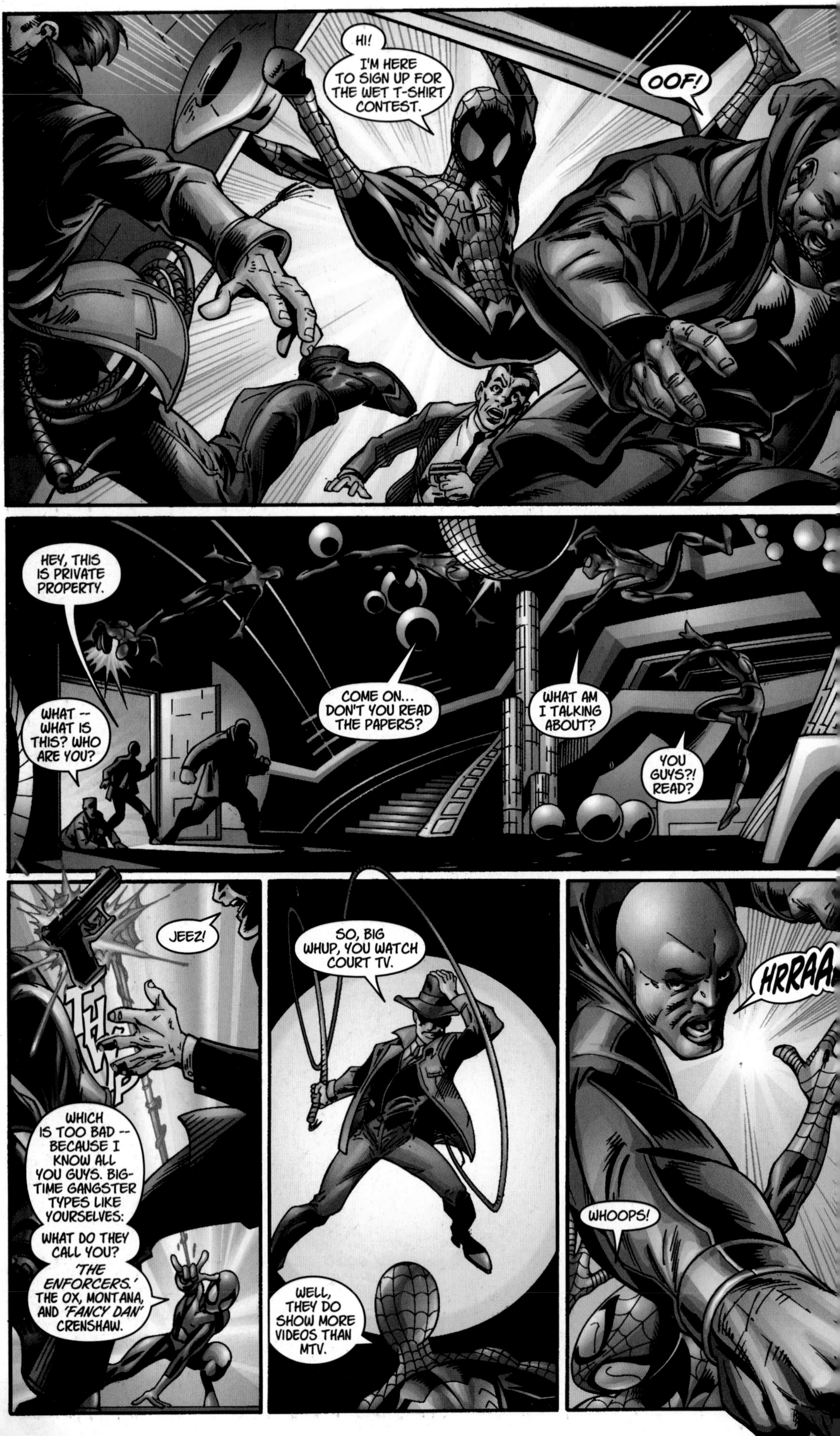
HI!
I'M HERE TO SIGN UP FOR THE WET T-SHIRT CONTEST.
OOF!
HEY, THIS IS PRIVATE PROPERTY.
WHAT -- WHAT IS THIS? WHO ARE YOU?
COME ON... DON'T YOU READ THE PAPERS?
WHAT AM I TALKING ABOUT?
YOU GUYS?! READ?
JEEZ!
WHICH IS TOO BAD -- BECAUSE I KNOW ALL YOU GUYS. BIG-TIME GANGSTER TYPES LIKE YOURSELVES:
WHAT DO THEY CALL YOU?
'THE ENFORCERS.' THE OX, MONTANA, AND 'FANCY DAN' CRENSHAW.
SO, BIG WHUP, YOU WATCH COURT TV.
WELL, THEY DO SHOW MORE VIDEOS THAN MTV.
HRRAA
WHOOPS!

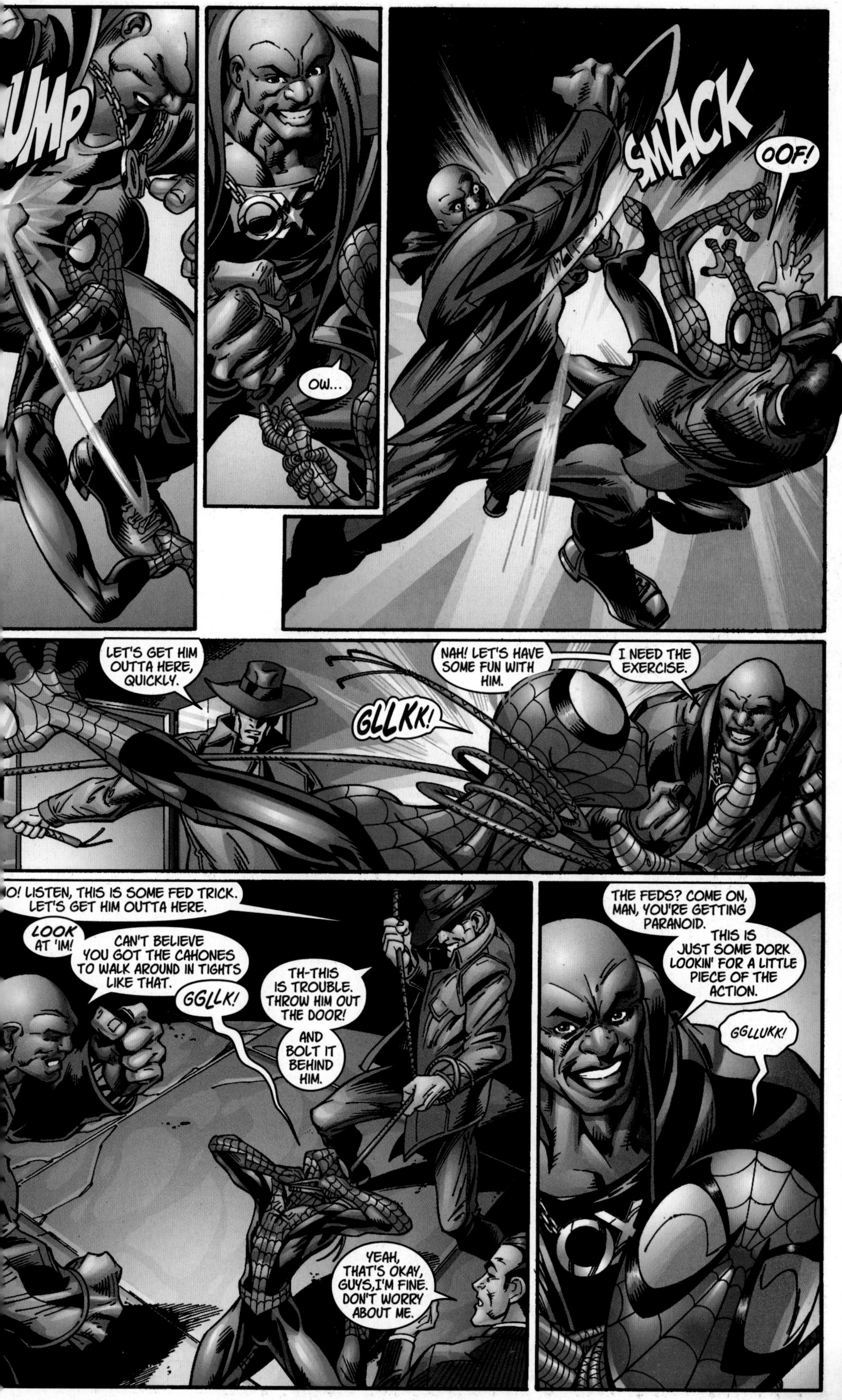
UMP
OW...
SMACK
OOF!
LET'S GET HIM OUTTA HERE, QUICKLY.
GLLKK!
NAH! LET'S HAVE SOME FUN WITH HIM.
I NEED THE EXERCISE.
O! LISTEN, THIS IS SOME FED TRICK. LET'S GET HIM OUTTA HERE.
LOOK AT 'IM!
CAN'T BELIEVE YOU GOT THE CAHONES TO WALK AROUND IN TIGHTS LIKE THAT.
GGLLK!
TH-THIS IS TROUBLE. THROW HIM OUT THE DOOR!
AND BOLT IT BEHIND HIM.
YEAH, THAT'S OKAY, GUYS, I'M FINE. DON'T WORRY ABOUT ME.
THE FEDS? COME ON, MAN, YOU'RE GETTING PARANOID.
THIS IS JUST SOME DORK LOOKIN' FOR A LITTLE PIECE OF THE ACTION.
GGLLUKK!

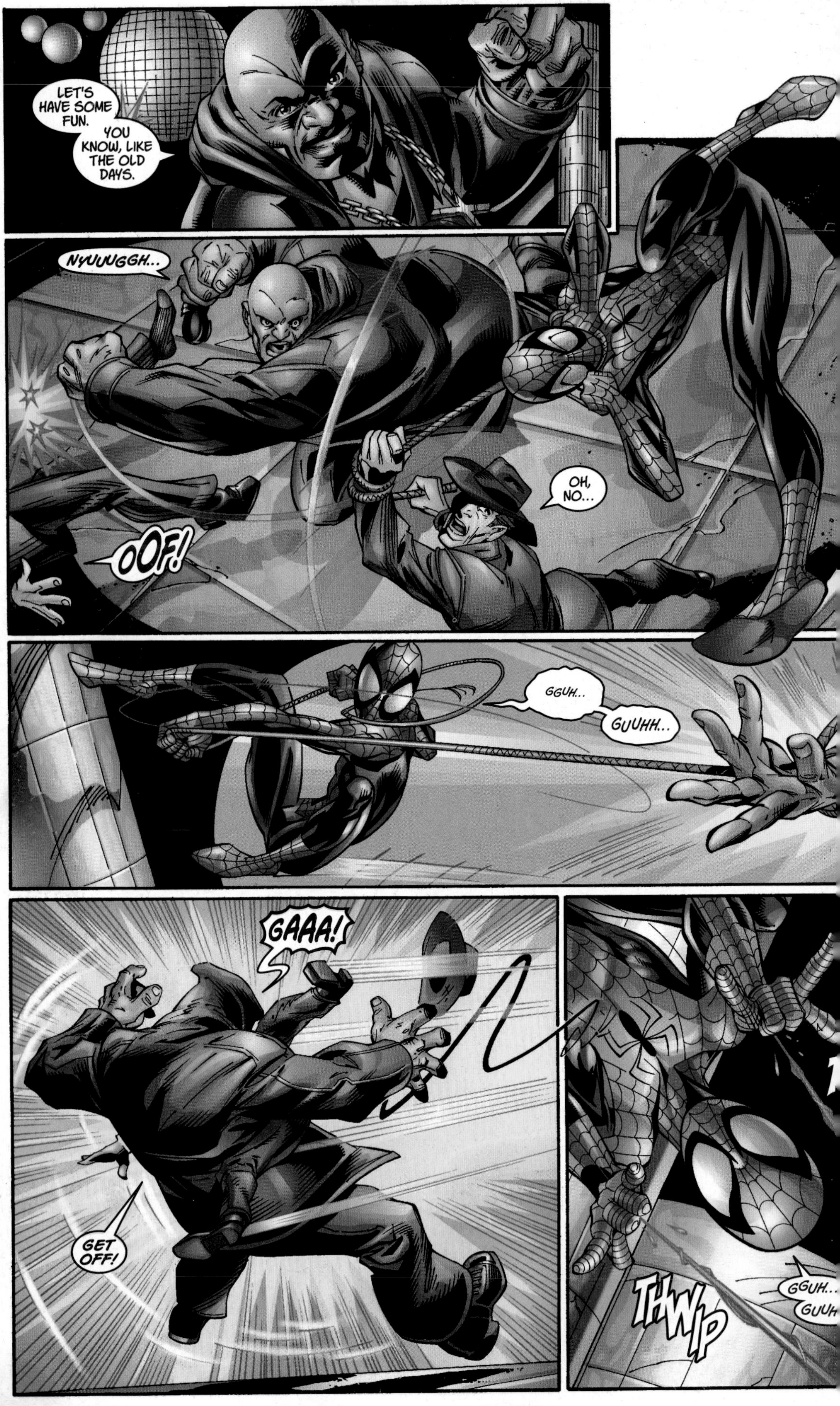
LET'S HAVE SOME FUN.
YOU KNOW, LIKE THE OLD DAYS.
NYUUUGGH...
OH, NO...
OOF!
GGUH...
GUUHH...
GAAA!
GET OFF!
THWIP
GGUH...
GUUH

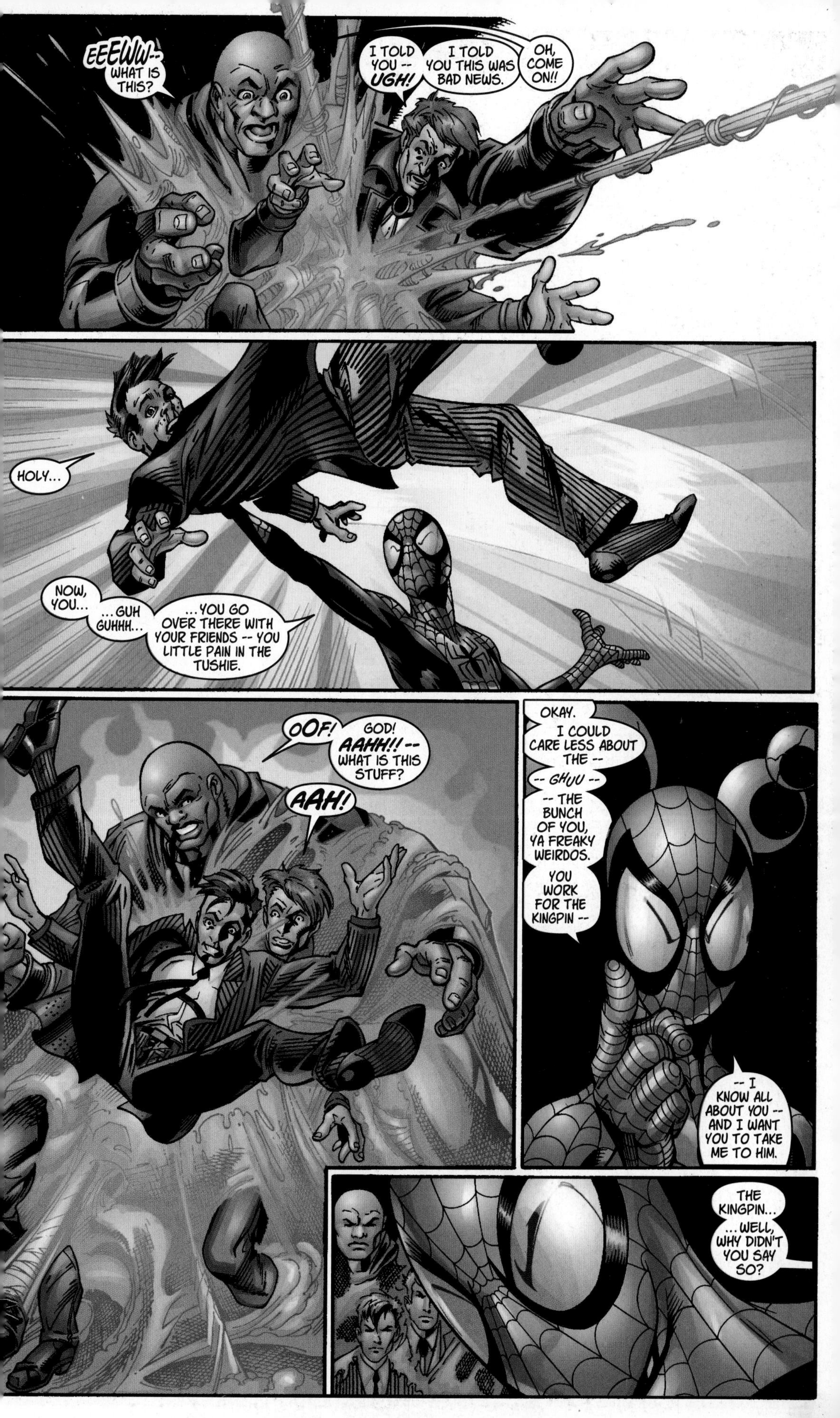
EEEWW-- WHAT IS THIS?
I TOLD YOU -- UGH!
I TOLD YOU THIS WAS BAD NEWS.
OH, COME ON!!
HOLY...
NOW, YOU...
...GUH GUHHH...
...YOU GO OVER THERE WITH YOUR FRIENDS -- YOU LITTLE PAIN IN THE TUSHIE.
OOF!
GOD! AAHH!! -- WHAT IS THIS STUFF?
AAH!
OKAY.
I COULD CARE LESS ABOUT THE --
-- GHUU --
-- THE BUNCH OF YOU, YA FREAKY WEIRDOS.
YOU WORK FOR THE KINGPIN --
-- I KNOW ALL ABOUT YOU -- AND I WANT YOU TO TAKE ME TO HIM.
THE KINGPIN...
...WELL, WHY DIDN'T YOU SAY SO?

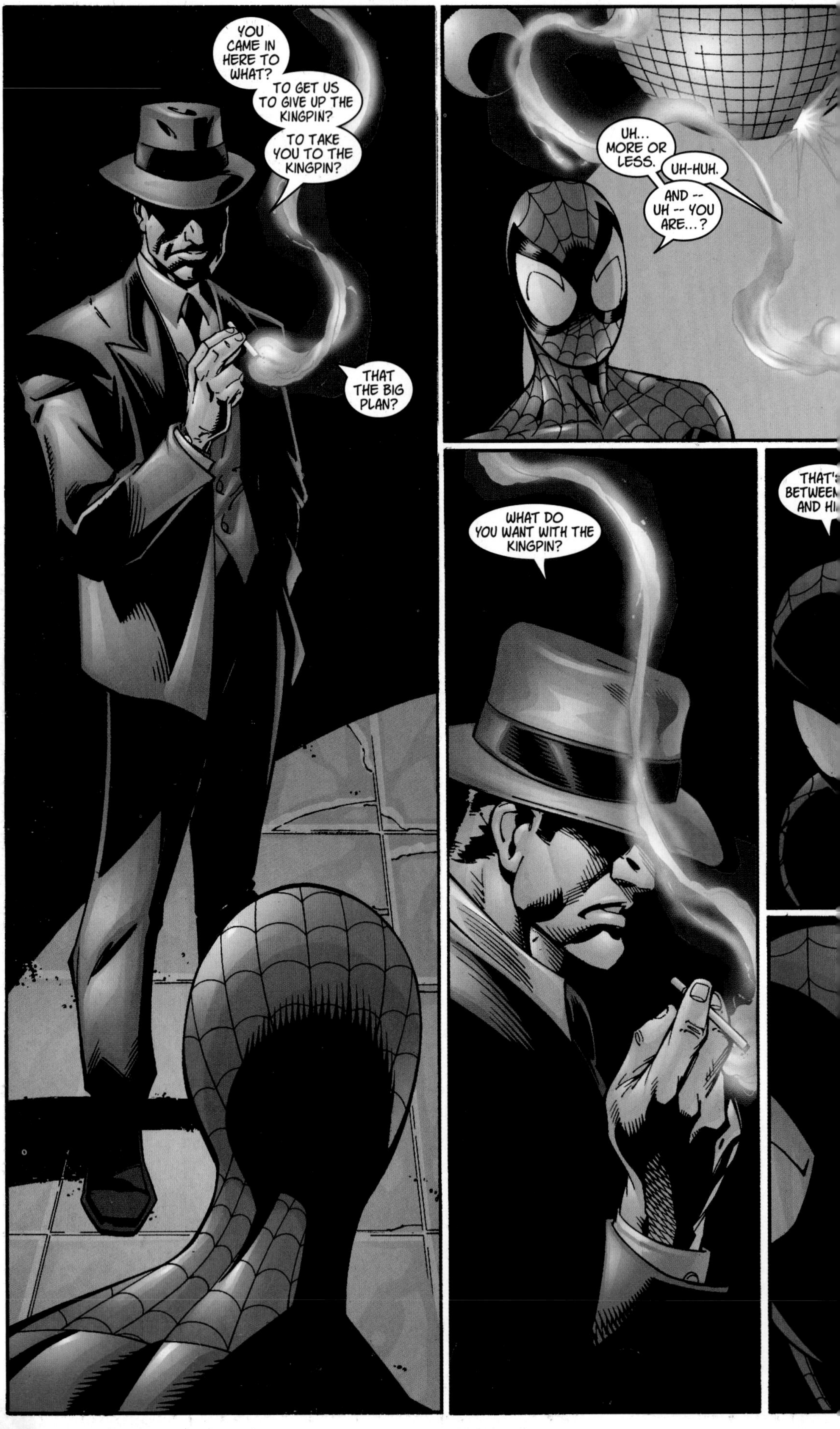
YOU CAME IN HERE TO WHAT?
TO GET US TO GIVE UP THE KINGPIN?
TO TAKE YOU TO THE KINGPIN?
THAT THE BIG PLAN?
UH... MORE OR LESS.
UH-HUH.
AND -- UH -- YOU ARE...?
WHAT DO YOU WANT WITH THE KINGPIN?

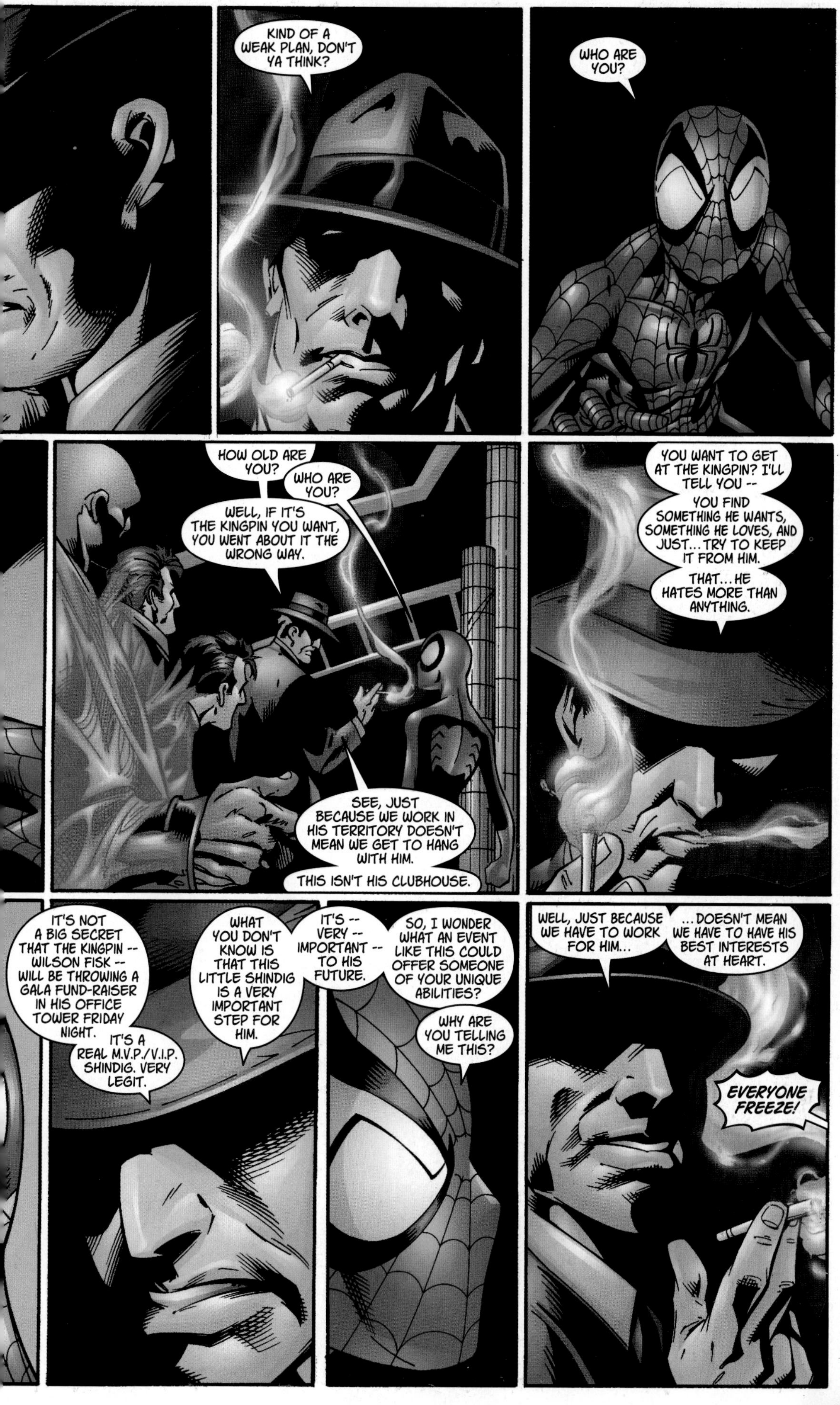
KIND OF A WEAK PLAN, DON'T YA THINK?
WHO ARE YOU?
HOW OLD ARE YOU?
WHO ARE YOU?
WELL, IF IT'S THE KINGPIN YOU WANT, YOU WENT ABOUT IT THE WRONG WAY.
SEE, JUST BECAUSE WE WORK IN HIS TERRITORY DOESN'T MEAN WE GET TO HANG WITH HIM.
THIS ISN'T HIS CLUBHOUSE.
YOU WANT TO GET AT THE KINGPIN? I'LL TELL YOU --
YOU FIND SOMETHING HE WANTS, SOMETHING HE LOVES, AND JUST... TRY TO KEEP IT FROM HIM.
THAT... HE HATES MORE THAN ANYTHING.
IT'S NOT A BIG SECRET THAT THE KINGPIN -- WILSON FISK -- WILL BE THROWING A GALA FUND-RAISER IN HIS OFFICE TOWER FRIDAY NIGHT.
IT'S A REAL M.V.P./V.I.P. SHINDIG. VERY LEGIT.
WHAT YOU DON'T KNOW IS THAT THIS LITTLE SHINDIG IS A VERY IMPORTANT STEP FOR HIM.
IT'S -- VERY -- IMPORTANT -- TO HIS FUTURE.
SO, I WONDER WHAT AN EVENT LIKE THIS COULD OFFER SOMEONE OF YOUR UNIQUE ABILITIES?
WHY ARE YOU TELLING ME THIS?
WELL, JUST BECAUSE WE HAVE TO WORK FOR HIM...
...DOESN'T MEAN WE HAVE TO HAVE HIS BEST INTERESTS AT HEART.
EVERYONE FREEZE!

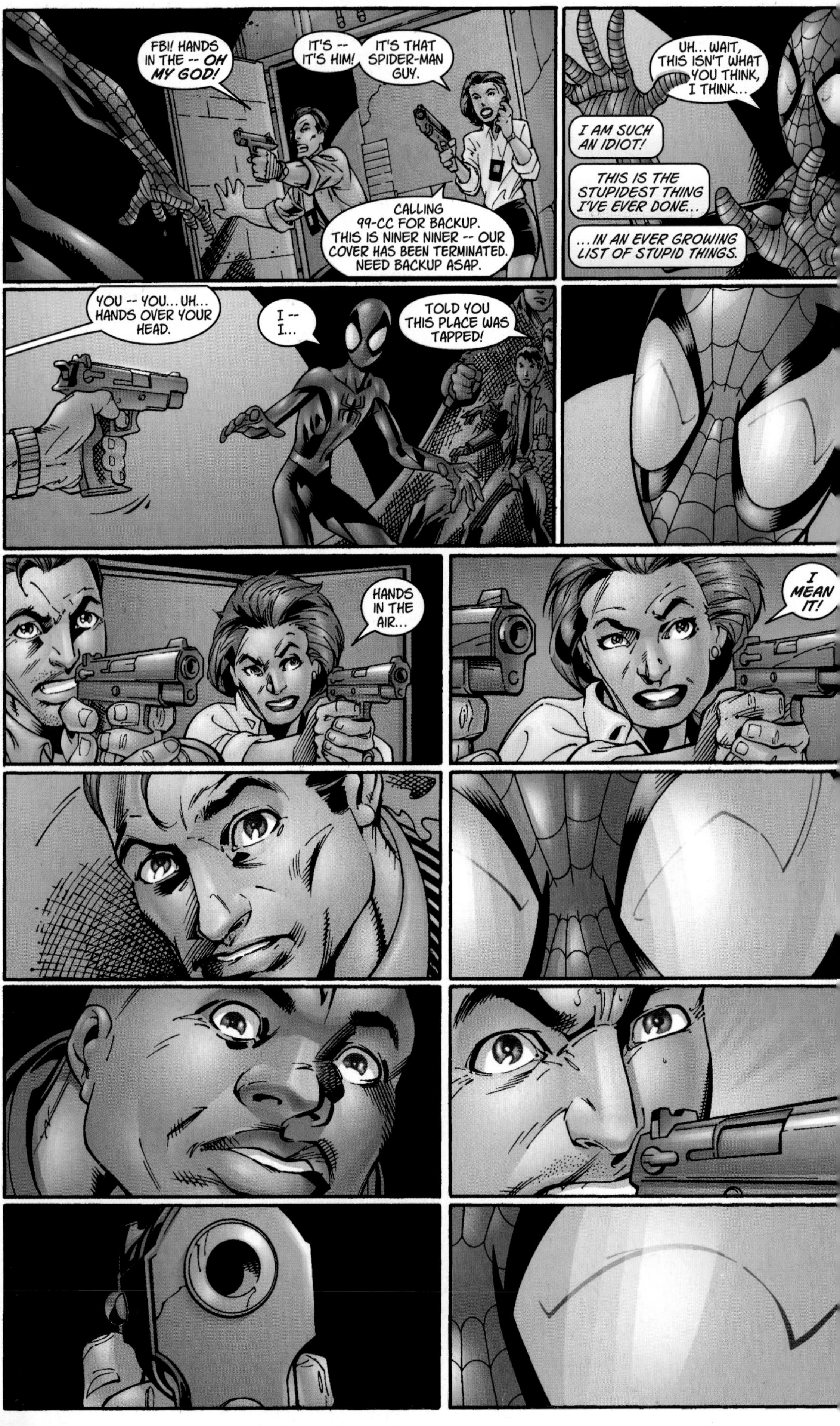

FBI! HANDS IN THE -- OH MY GOD!
IT'S -- IT'S HIM!
IT'S THAT SPIDER-MAN GUY.
CALLING 99-CC FOR BACKUP. THIS IS NINER NINER -- OUR COVER HAS BEEN TERMINATED. NEED BACKUP ASAP.
UH... WAIT, THIS ISN'T WHAT YOU THINK, I THINK...
I AM SUCH AN IDIOT!
THIS IS THE STUPIDEST THING I'VE EVER DONE...
...IN AN EVER GROWING LIST OF STUPID THINGS.
YOU -- YOU... UH... HANDS OVER YOUR HEAD.
I -- I...
TOLD YOU THIS PLACE WAS TAPPED!
HANDS IN THE AIR...
I MEAN IT!

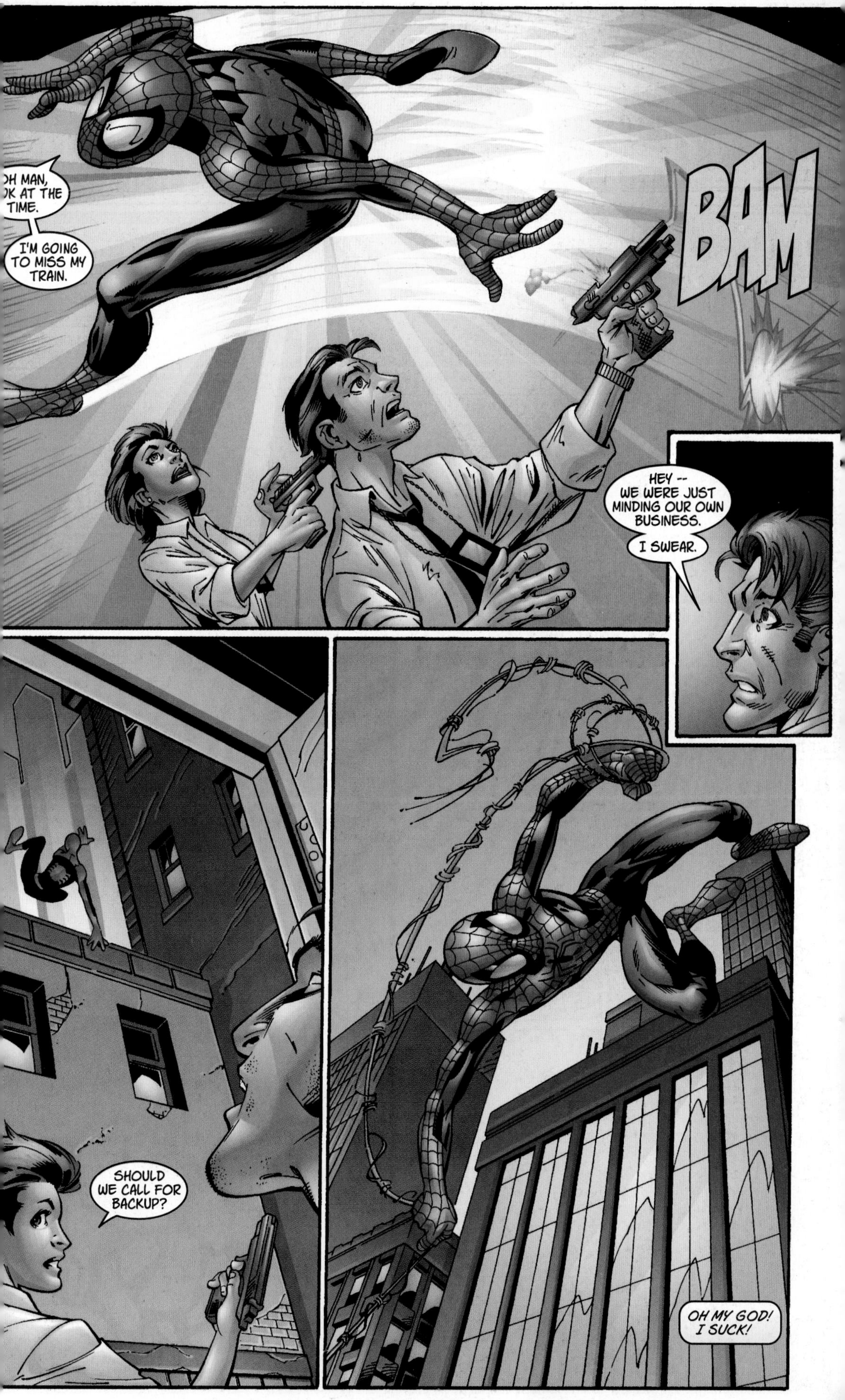

OH MAN, LOOK AT THE TIME.
I'M GOING TO MISS MY TRAIN.
BAM
HEY -- WE WERE JUST MINDING OUR OWN BUSINESS.
I SWEAR.
SHOULD WE CALL FOR BACKUP?
OH MY GOD! I SUCK!

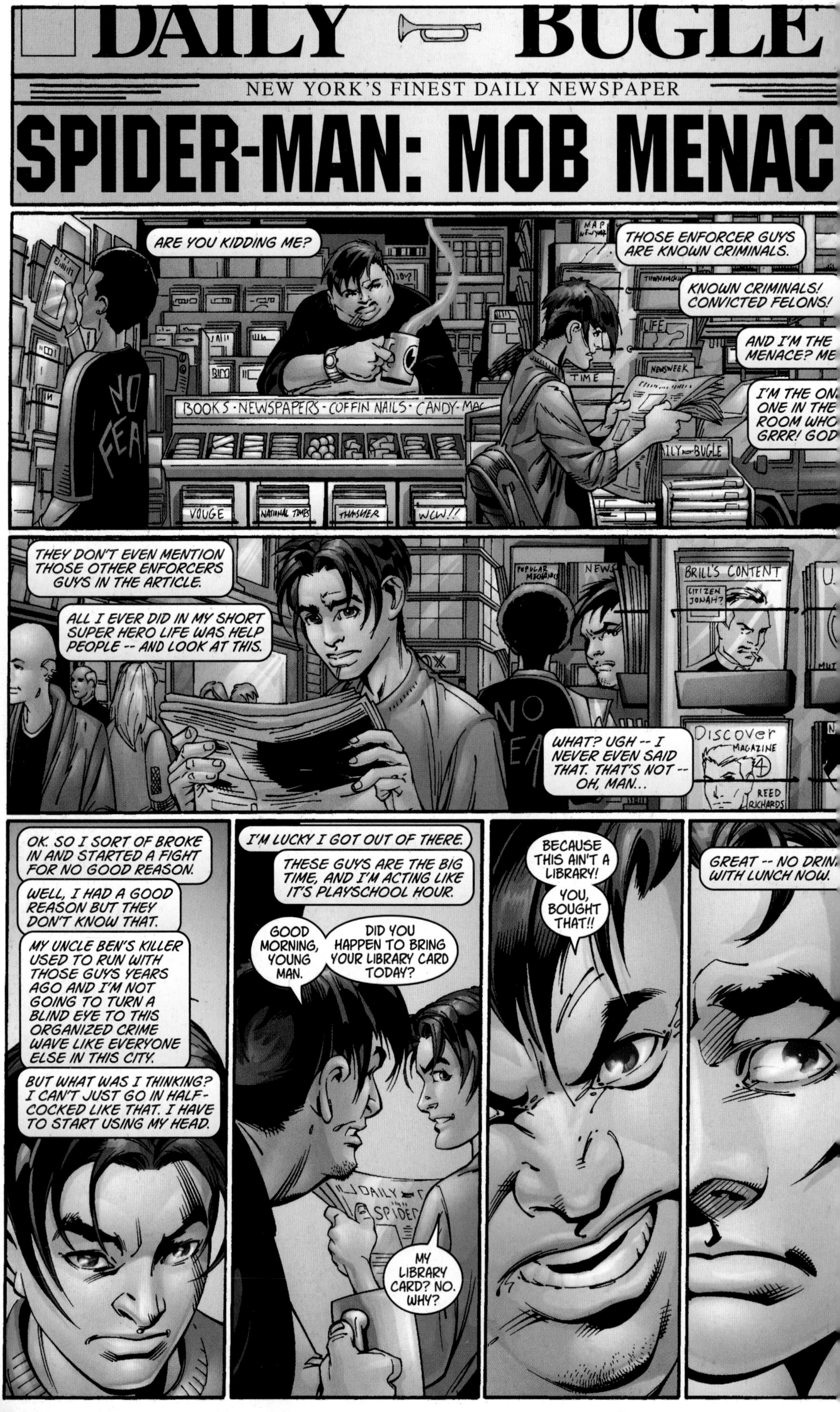
DAILY BUGLE
NEW YORK'S FINEST DAILY NEWSPAPER
SPIDER-MAN: MOB MENAC
ARE YOU KIDDING ME?
THOSE ENFORCER GUYS ARE KNOWN CRIMINALS.
KNOWN CRIMINALS! CONVICTED FELONS!
AND I'M THE MENACE? ME
I'M THE ON ONE IN THE ROOM WHO GRRR! GOD
BOOKS · NEWSPAPERS · COFFIN NAILS · CANDY · MAC
VOUGE
NATIONAL TIMES
THASHER
WCW!!
NO FEA
THEY DON'T EVEN MENTION THOSE OTHER ENFORCERS GUYS IN THE ARTICLE.
ALL I EVER DID IN MY SHORT SUPER HERO LIFE WAS HELP PEOPLE -- AND LOOK AT THIS.
BRILL'S CONTENT
CITIZEN JONAH?
WHAT? UGH -- I NEVER EVEN SAID THAT. THAT'S NOT -- OH, MAN...
Discover MAGAZINE
REED RICHARDS
OK. SO I SORT OF BROKE IN AND STARTED A FIGHT FOR NO GOOD REASON.
WELL, I HAD A GOOD REASON BUT THEY DON'T KNOW THAT.
MY UNCLE BEN'S KILLER USED TO RUN WITH THOSE GUYS YEARS AGO AND I'M NOT GOING TO TURN A BLIND EYE TO THIS ORGANIZED CRIME WAVE LIKE EVERYONE ELSE IN THIS CITY.
BUT WHAT WAS I THINKING? I CAN'T JUST GO IN HALF-COCKED LIKE THAT. I HAVE TO START USING MY HEAD.
I'M LUCKY I GOT OUT OF THERE.
THESE GUYS ARE THE BIG TIME, AND I'M ACTING LIKE IT'S PLAYSCHOOL HOUR.
GOOD MORNING, YOUNG MAN.
DID YOU HAPPEN TO BRING YOUR LIBRARY CARD TODAY?
MY LIBRARY CARD? NO. WHY?
BECAUSE THIS AIN'T A LIBRARY!
YOU, BOUGHT THAT!!
GREAT -- NO DRIN WITH LUNCH NOW.

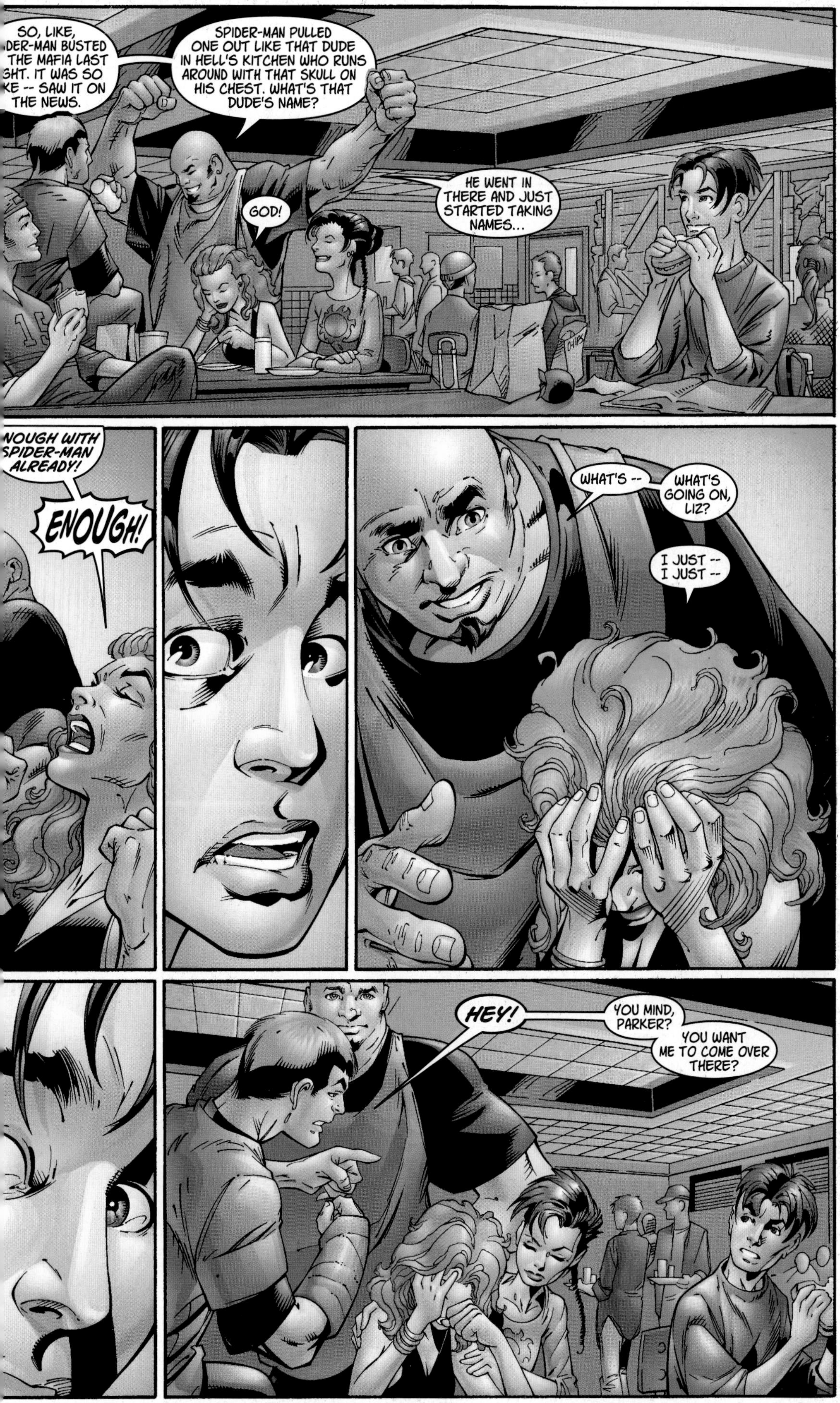
SO, LIKE, DER-MAN BUSTED THE MAFIA LAST GHT. IT WAS SO KE -- SAW IT ON THE NEWS.
SPIDER-MAN PULLED ONE OUT LIKE THAT DUDE IN HELL'S KITCHEN WHO RUNS AROUND WITH THAT SKULL ON HIS CHEST. WHAT'S THAT DUDE'S NAME?
GOD!
HE WENT IN THERE AND JUST STARTED TAKING NAMES...
NOUGH WITH SPIDER-MAN ALREADY!
ENOUGH!
WHAT'S --
WHAT'S GOING ON, LIZ?
I JUST -- I JUST --
HEY!
YOU MIND, PARKER?
YOU WANT ME TO COME OVER THERE?

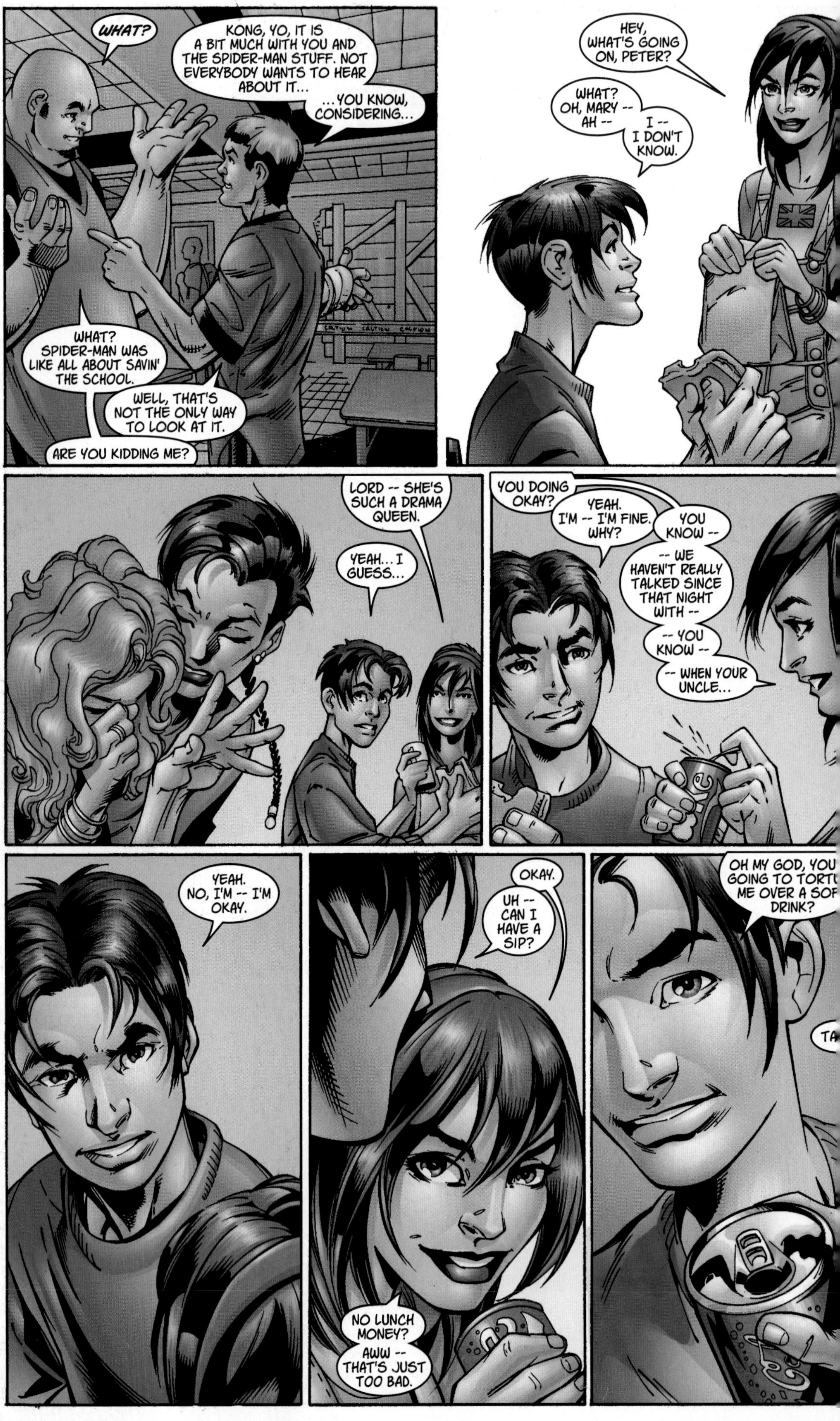
WHAT?
KONG, YO, IT IS A BIT MUCH WITH YOU AND THE SPIDER-MAN STUFF. NOT EVERYBODY WANTS TO HEAR ABOUT IT...
...YOU KNOW, CONSIDERING...
WHAT? SPIDER-MAN WAS LIKE ALL ABOUT SAVIN' THE SCHOOL.
WELL, THAT'S NOT THE ONLY WAY TO LOOK AT IT.
ARE YOU KIDDING ME?
HEY, WHAT'S GOING ON, PETER?
WHAT? OH, MARY -- AH --
I -- I DON'T KNOW.
LORD -- SHE'S SUCH A DRAMA QUEEN.
YEAH... I GUESS...
YOU DOING OKAY?
YEAH. I'M -- I'M FINE. WHY?
YOU KNOW --
-- WE HAVEN'T REALLY TALKED SINCE THAT NIGHT WITH --
-- YOU KNOW --
-- WHEN YOUR UNCLE...
YEAH. NO, I'M -- I'M OKAY.
OKAY.
UH -- CAN I HAVE A SIP?
NO LUNCH MONEY?
AWW -- THAT'S JUST TOO BAD.

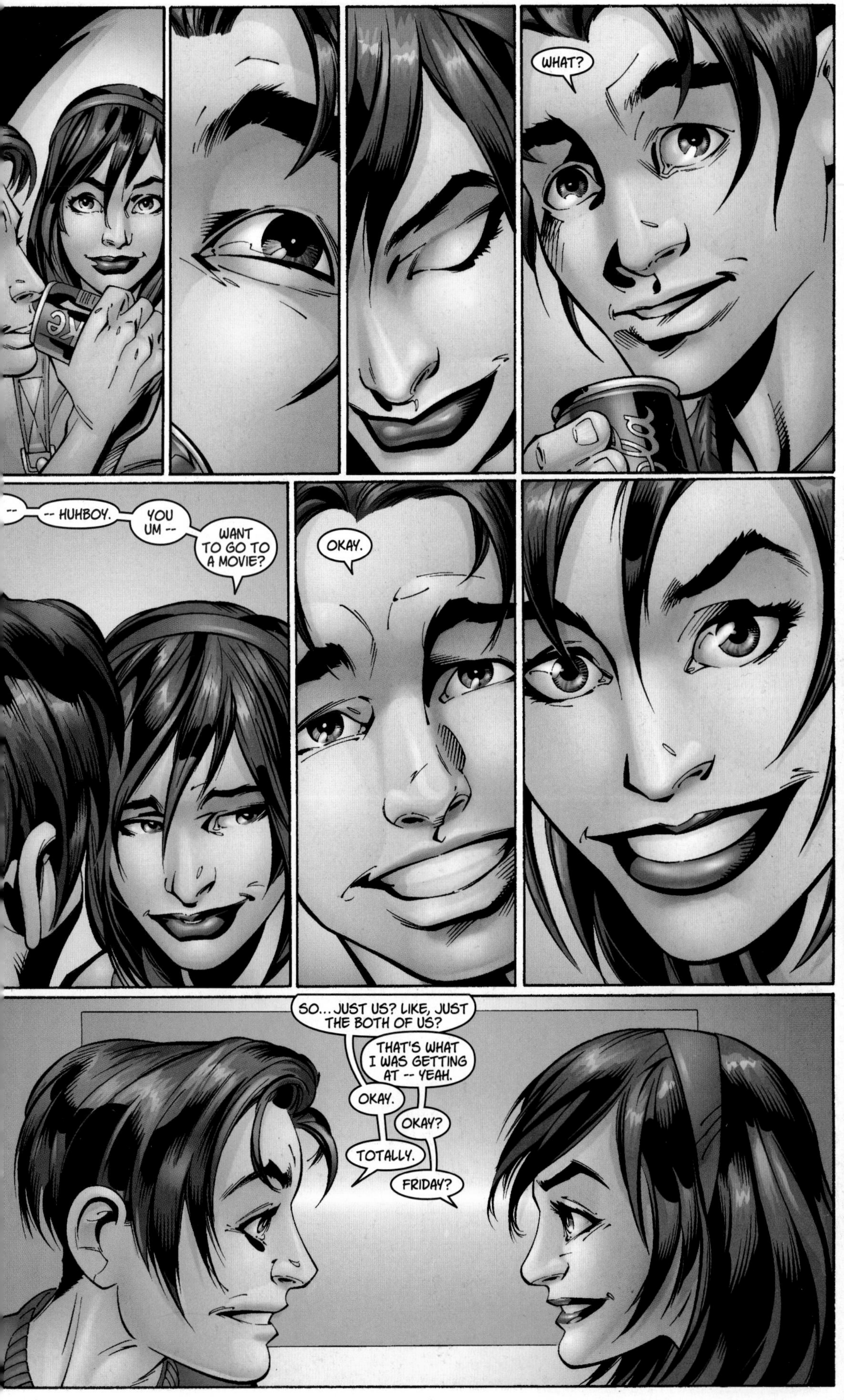
WHAT?
-- -- HUHBOY.
YOU UM --
WANT TO GO TO A MOVIE?
OKAY.
SO... JUST US? LIKE, JUST THE BOTH OF US?
THAT'S WHAT I WAS GETTING AT -- YEAH.
OKAY.
OKAY?
TOTALLY.
FRIDAY?

IT'S NOT A BIG SECRET THAT THE KINGPIN -- WILSON FISK -- WILL BE THROWING A GALA FUND-RAISER IN HIS OFFICE TOWER FRIDAY NIGHT.

SO, I WONDER WHAT AN EVENT LIKE THIS COULD OFFER SOMEONE OF YOUR UNIQUE ABILITIES?

LET'S SAY SATURDAY.

WHAT'S GOING ON FRIDAY?

UH -- WORK.

I -- YEAH -- HAVE TO WORK AT THE PAPER.

OH YEAH -- DUH.

SO, YOU CAN DO SATURDAY?

I CAN DO SATURDAY.

COOL. IT'LL BE FUN.

IF I PICK THE MOVIE.

I KNEW THAT WAS COMING.

JUST AS LONG AS WE BO KNOW WHO'S CHARGE.

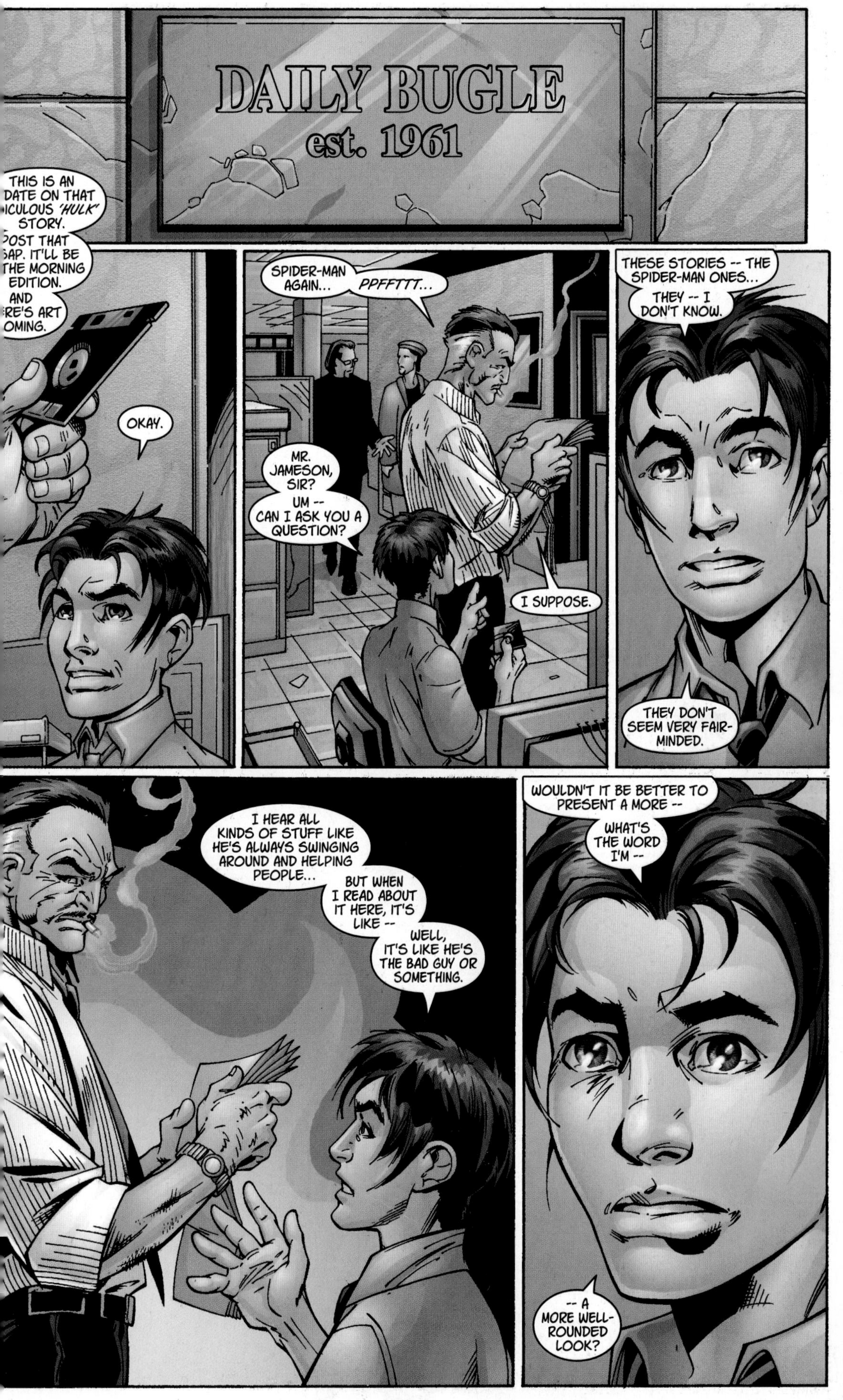
DAILY BUGLE
est. 1961
THIS IS AN
DATE ON THAT
ICULOUS 'HULK' STORY.
POST THAT
SAP. IT'LL BE THE MORNING EDITION.
AND
RE'S ART
OMING.
OKAY.
SPIDER-MAN AGAIN...
PPFFTTT...
MR. JAMESON, SIR?
UM -- CAN I ASK YOU A QUESTION?
I SUPPOSE.
THESE STORIES -- THE SPIDER-MAN ONES...
THEY -- I DON'T KNOW.
THEY DON'T SEEM VERY FAIR-MINDED.
I HEAR ALL KINDS OF STUFF LIKE HE'S ALWAYS SWINGING AROUND AND HELPING PEOPLE...
BUT WHEN I READ ABOUT IT HERE, IT'S LIKE --
WELL, IT'S LIKE HE'S THE BAD GUY OR SOMETHING.
WOULDN'T IT BE BETTER TO PRESENT A MORE --
WHAT'S THE WORD I'M --
-- A MORE WELL-ROUNDED LOOK?

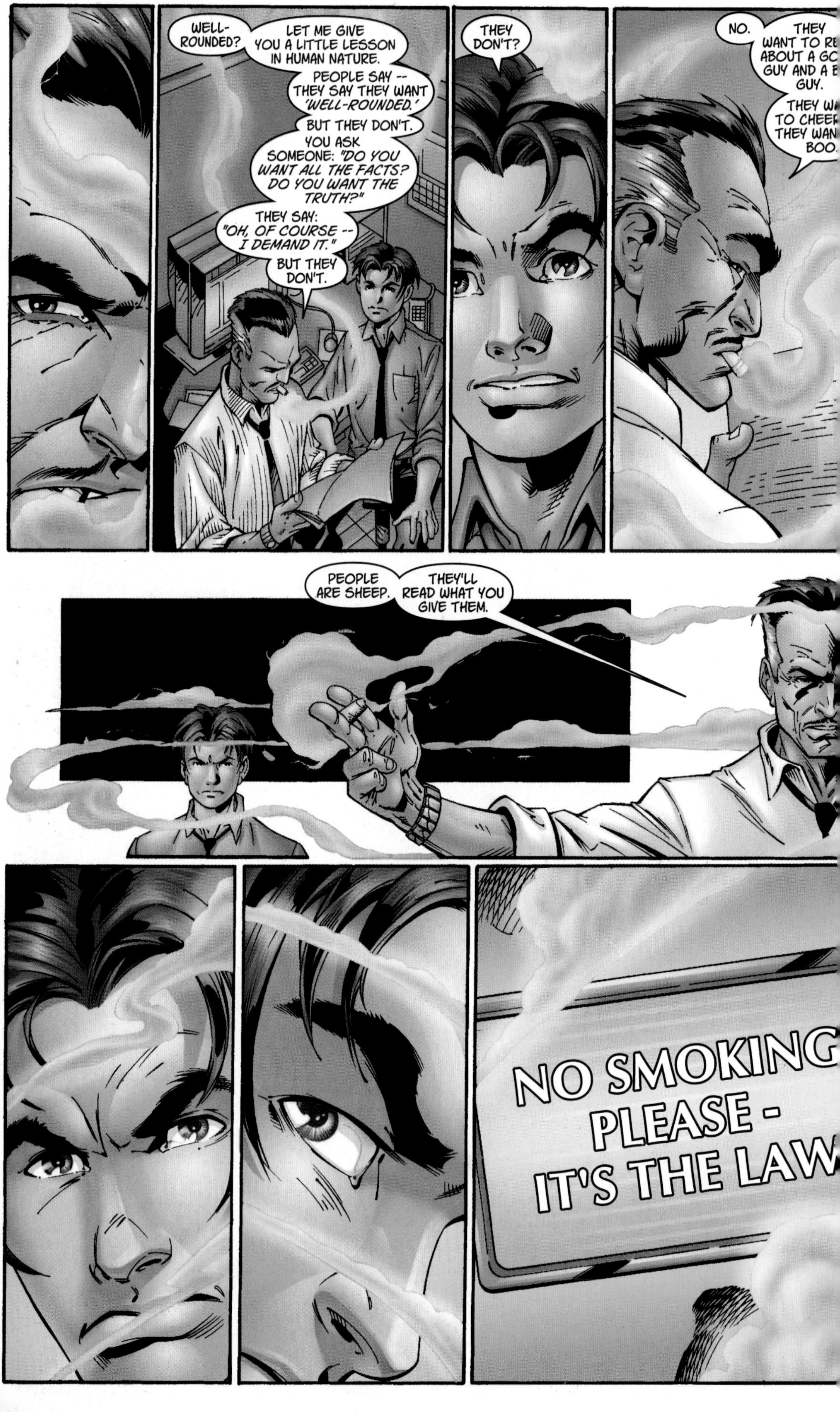
WELL-ROUNDED?
LET ME GIVE YOU A LITTLE LESSON IN HUMAN NATURE.
PEOPLE SAY -- THEY SAY THEY WANT 'WELL-ROUNDED.'
BUT THEY DON'T.
YOU ASK SOMEONE: "DO YOU WANT ALL THE FACTS? DO YOU WANT THE TRUTH?"
THEY SAY: "OH, OF COURSE -- I DEMAND IT."
BUT THEY DON'T.
THEY DON'T?
NO.
THEY WANT TO RE ABOUT A GO GUY AND A B GUY.
THEY WA TO CHEER THEY WAN BOO.
PEOPLE ARE SHEEP.
THEY'LL READ WHAT YOU GIVE THEM.
NO SMOKING PLEASE - IT'S THE LAW

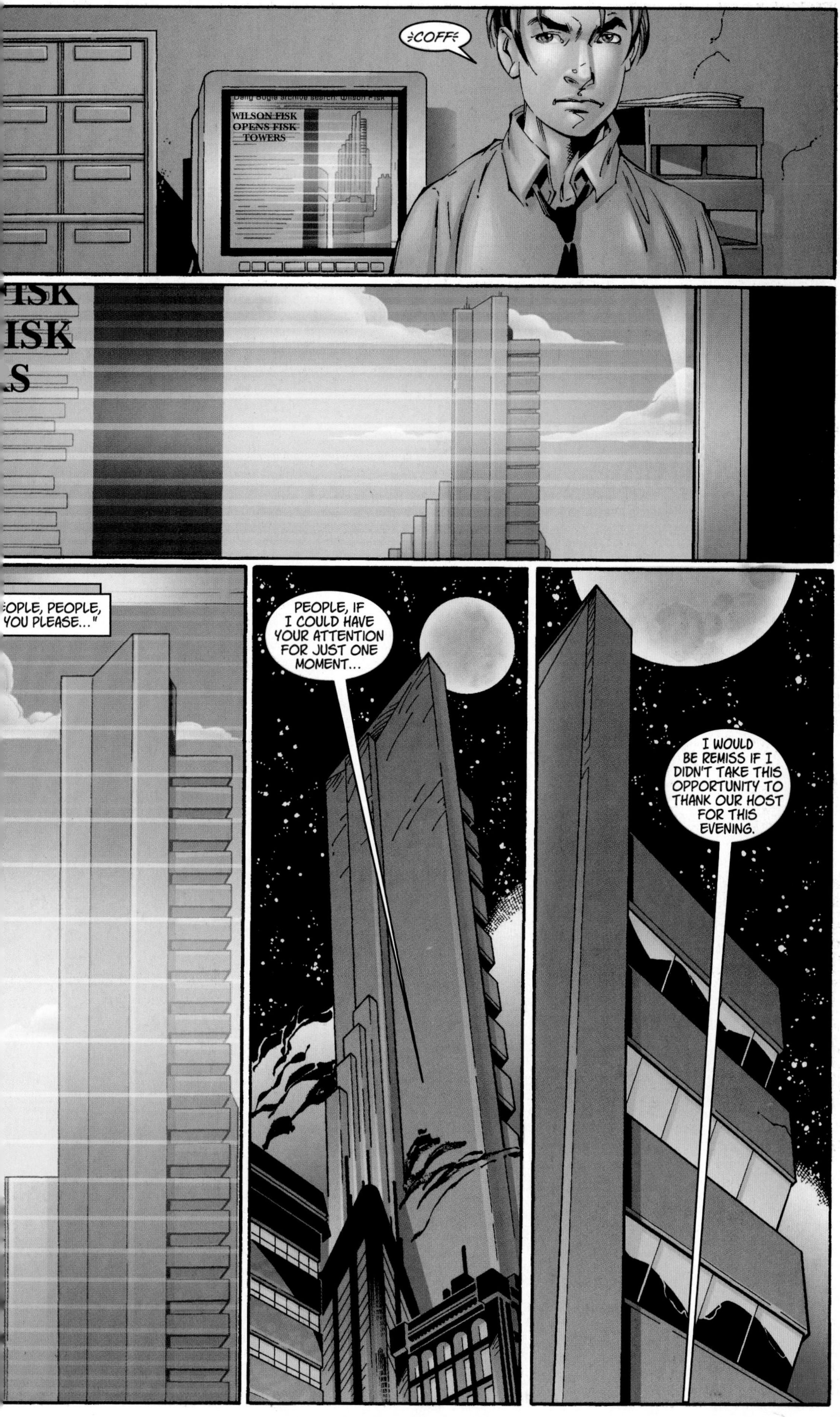
COFF
Daily Bugle archive search: Wilson Fisk
WILSON FISK
OPENS FISK
TOWERS
ISK
ISK
S
OPLE, PEOPLE,
YOU PLEASE..."
PEOPLE, IF I COULD HAVE YOUR ATTENTION FOR JUST ONE MOMENT...
I WOULD BE REMISS IF I DIDN'T TAKE THIS OPPORTUNITY TO THANK OUR HOST FOR THIS EVENING.

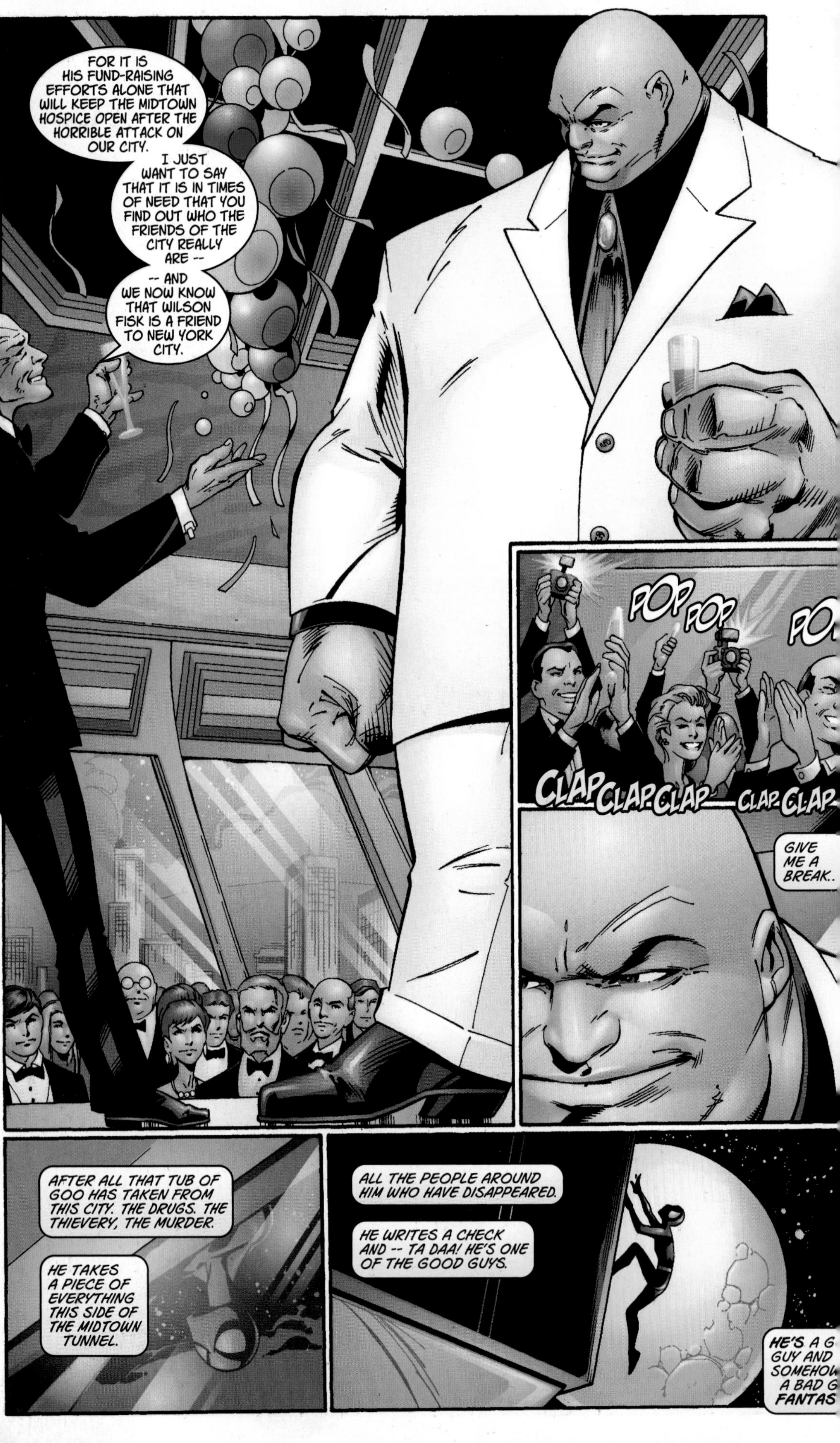
FOR IT IS HIS FUND-RAISING EFFORTS ALONE THAT WILL KEEP THE MIDTOWN HOSPICE OPEN AFTER THE HORRIBLE ATTACK ON OUR CITY.
I JUST WANT TO SAY THAT IT IS IN TIMES OF NEED THAT YOU FIND OUT WHO THE FRIENDS OF THE CITY REALLY ARE --
-- AND WE NOW KNOW THAT WILSON FISK IS A FRIEND TO NEW YORK CITY.
POP POP
CLAP CLAP CLAP CLAP CLAP
GIVE ME A BREAK..
AFTER ALL THAT TUB OF GOO HAS TAKEN FROM THIS CITY. THE DRUGS. THE THIEVERY, THE MURDER.
HE TAKES A PIECE OF EVERYTHING THIS SIDE OF THE MIDTOWN TUNNEL.
ALL THE PEOPLE AROUND HIM WHO HAVE DISAPPEARED.
HE WRITES A CHECK AND -- TA DAA! HE'S ONE OF THE GOOD GUYS.

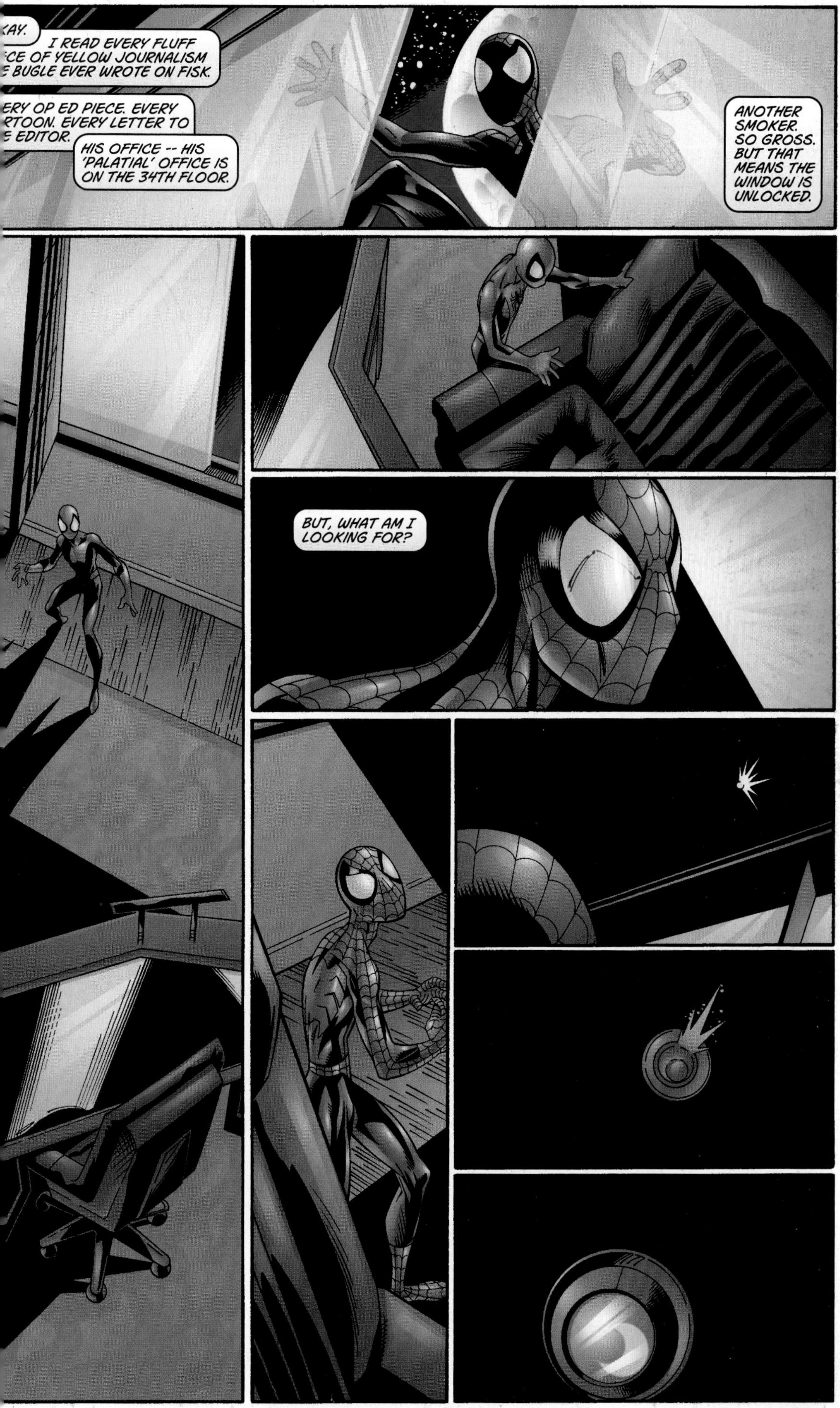

KAY.
I READ EVERY FLUFF
CE OF YELLOW JOURNALISM
E BUGLE EVER WROTE ON FISK.
ERY OP ED PIECE. EVERY
RTOON. EVERY LETTER TO
E EDITOR.
HIS OFFICE -- HIS 'PALATIAL' OFFICE IS ON THE 34TH FLOOR.
ANOTHER SMOKER. SO GROSS. BUT THAT MEANS THE WINDOW IS UNLOCKED.
BUT, WHAT AM I LOOKING FOR?

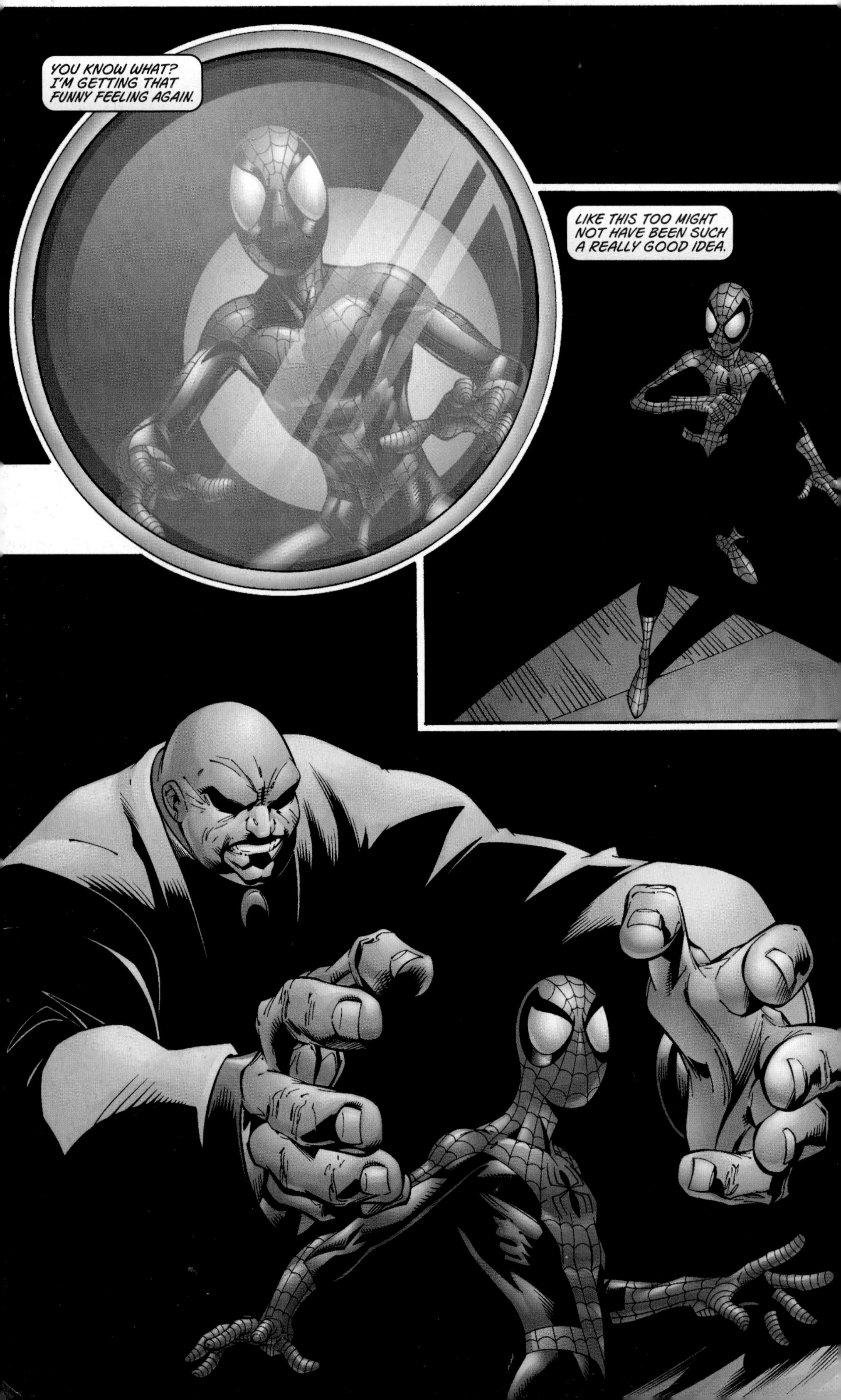
YOU KNOW WHAT? I'M GETTING THAT FUNNY FEELING AGAIN.
LIKE THIS TOO MIGHT NOT HAVE BEEN SUCH A REALLY GOOD IDEA.

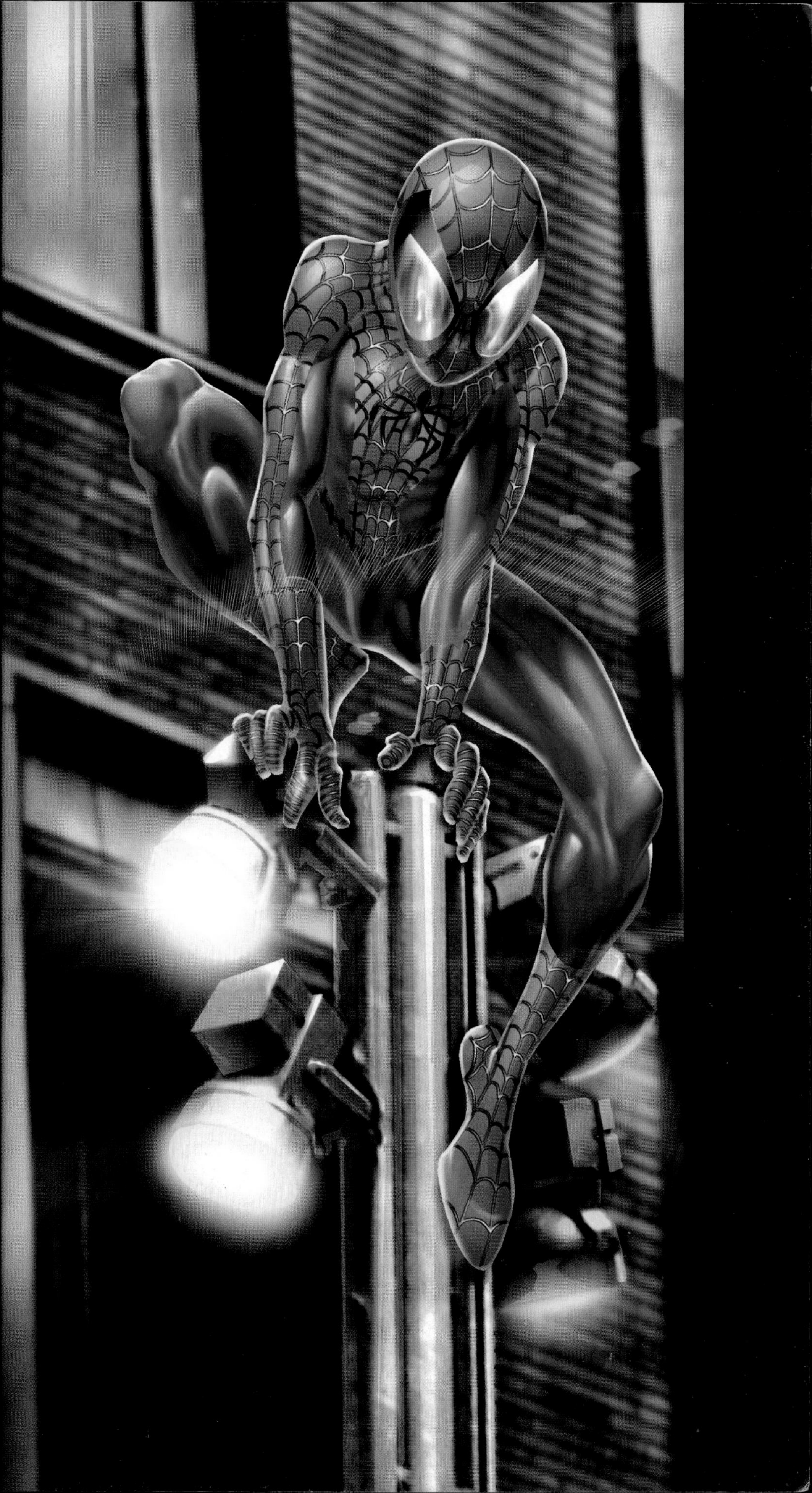

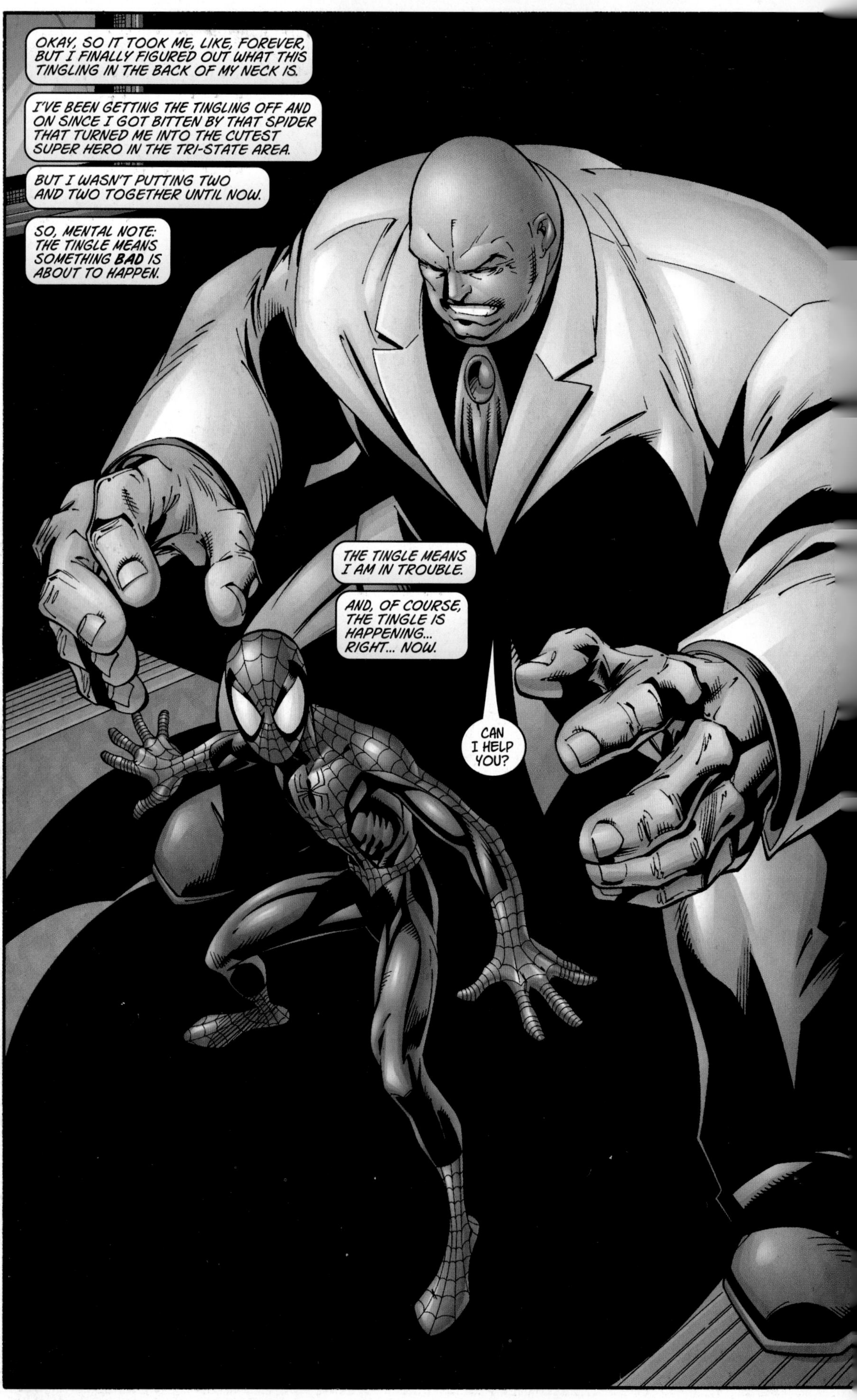
OKAY, SO IT TOOK ME, LIKE, FOREVER, BUT I FINALLY FIGURED OUT WHAT THIS TINGLING IN THE BACK OF MY NECK IS.
I'VE BEEN GETTING THE TINGLING OFF AND ON SINCE I GOT BITTEN BY THAT SPIDER THAT TURNED ME INTO THE CUTEST SUPER HERO IN THE TRI-STATE AREA.
BUT I WASN'T PUTTING TWO AND TWO TOGETHER UNTIL NOW.
SO, MENTAL NOTE: THE TINGLE MEANS SOMETHING **BAD** IS ABOUT TO HAPPEN.
THE TINGLE MEANS I AM IN TROUBLE.
AND, OF COURSE, THE TINGLE IS HAPPENING... RIGHT... NOW.
CAN I HELP YOU?

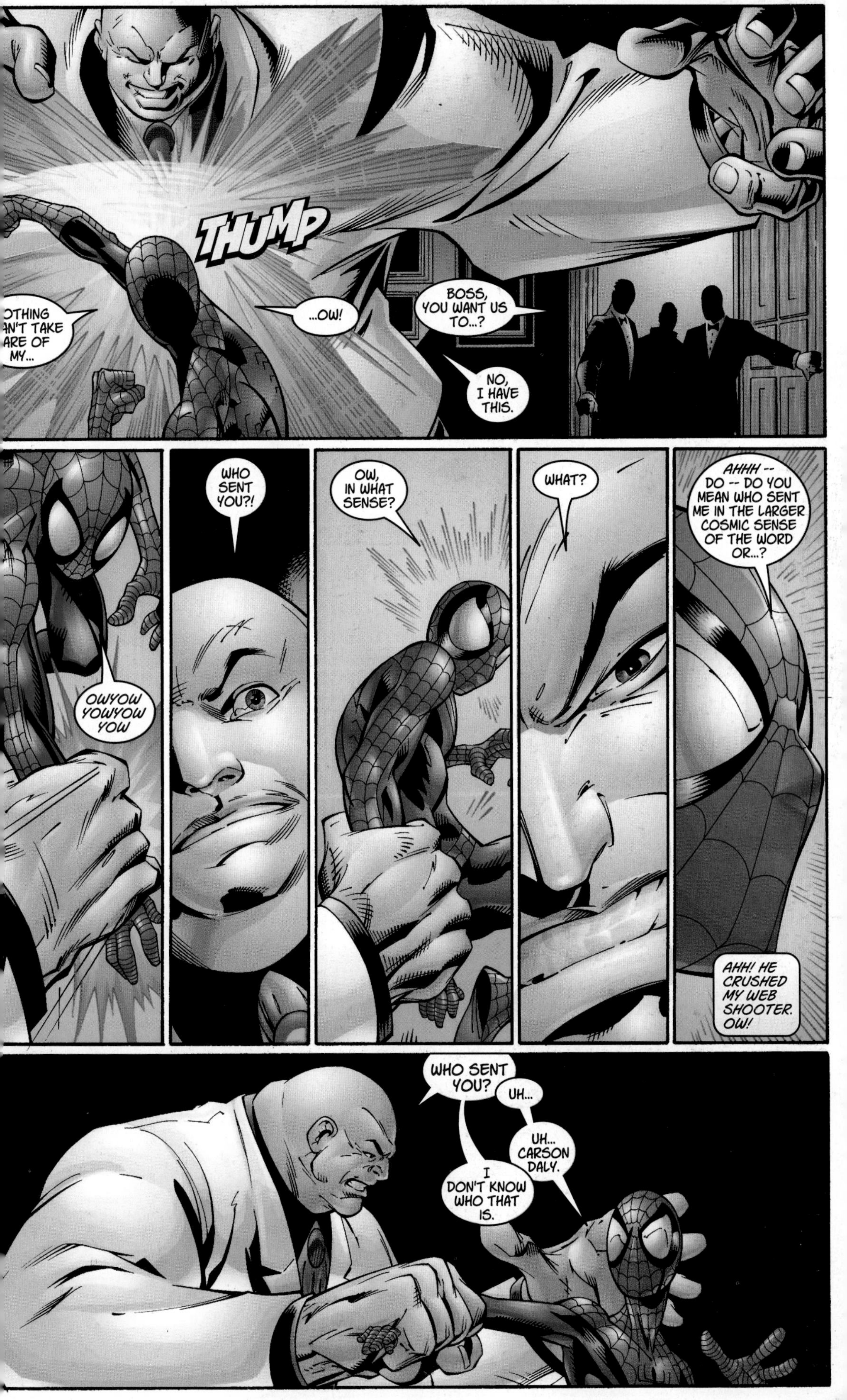

THUMP
OTHING
AN'T TAKE
ARE OF
MY...
...OW!
BOSS, YOU WANT US TO...?
NO, I HAVE THIS.
OWYOW YOWYOW YOW
WHO SENT YOU?!
OW, IN WHAT SENSE?
WHAT?
AHHH -- DO -- DO YOU MEAN WHO SENT ME IN THE LARGER COSMIC SENSE OF THE WORD OR...?
AHH! HE CRUSHED MY WEB SHOOTER. OW!
WHO SENT YOU?
UH...
UH... CARSON DALY.
I DON'T KNOW WHO THAT IS.

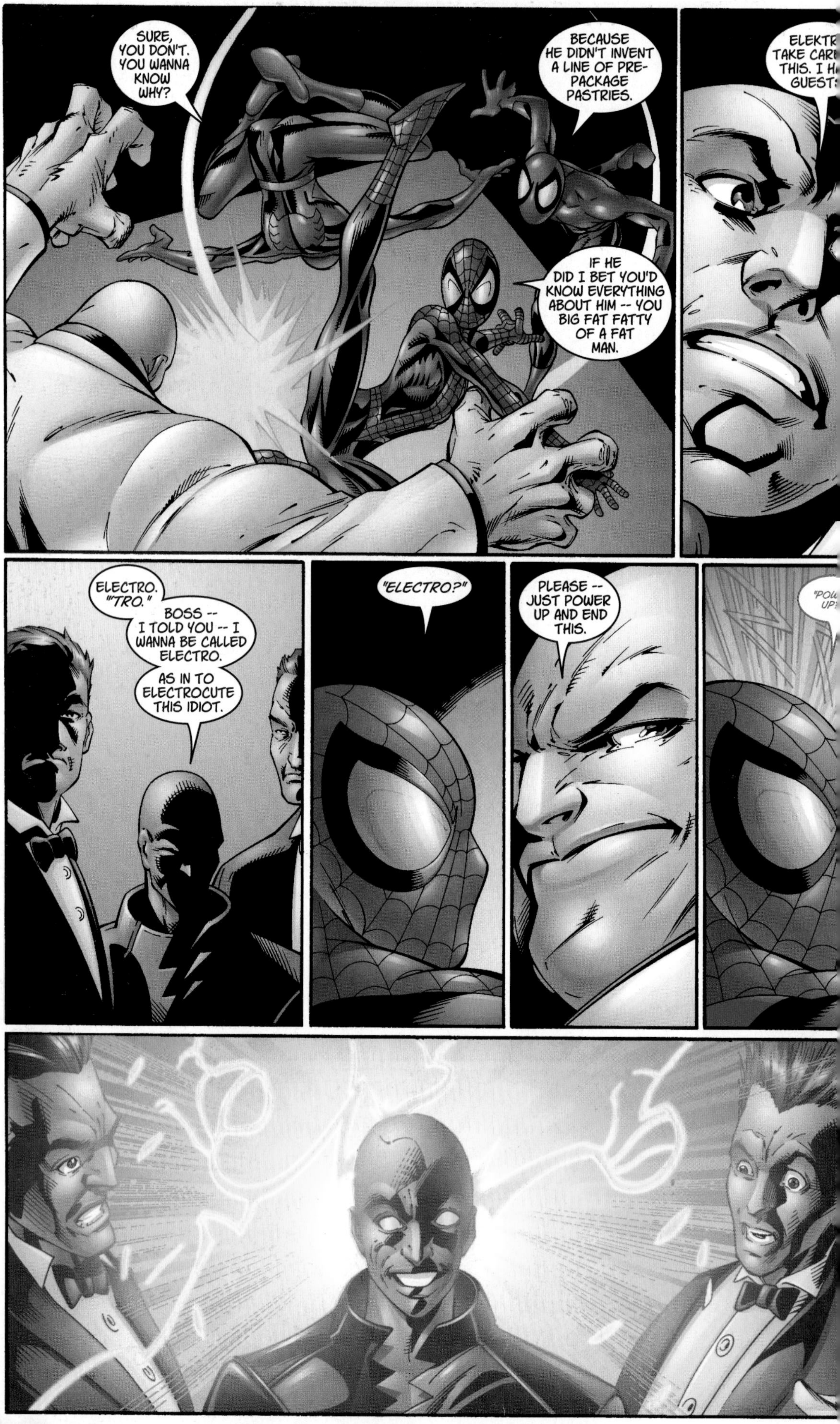

SURE, YOU DON'T. YOU WANNA KNOW WHY?
BECAUSE HE DIDN'T INVENT A LINE OF PRE-PACKAGE PASTRIES.
IF HE DID I BET YOU'D KNOW EVERYTHING ABOUT HIM -- YOU BIG FAT FATTY OF A FAT MAN.
ELEKTR TAKE CAR THIS. I H GUEST
ELECTRO. "TRO."
BOSS -- I TOLD YOU -- I WANNA BE CALLED ELECTRO.
AS IN TO ELECTROCUTE THIS IDIOT.
"ELECTRO?"
PLEASE -- JUST POWER UP AND END THIS.
"POW UP

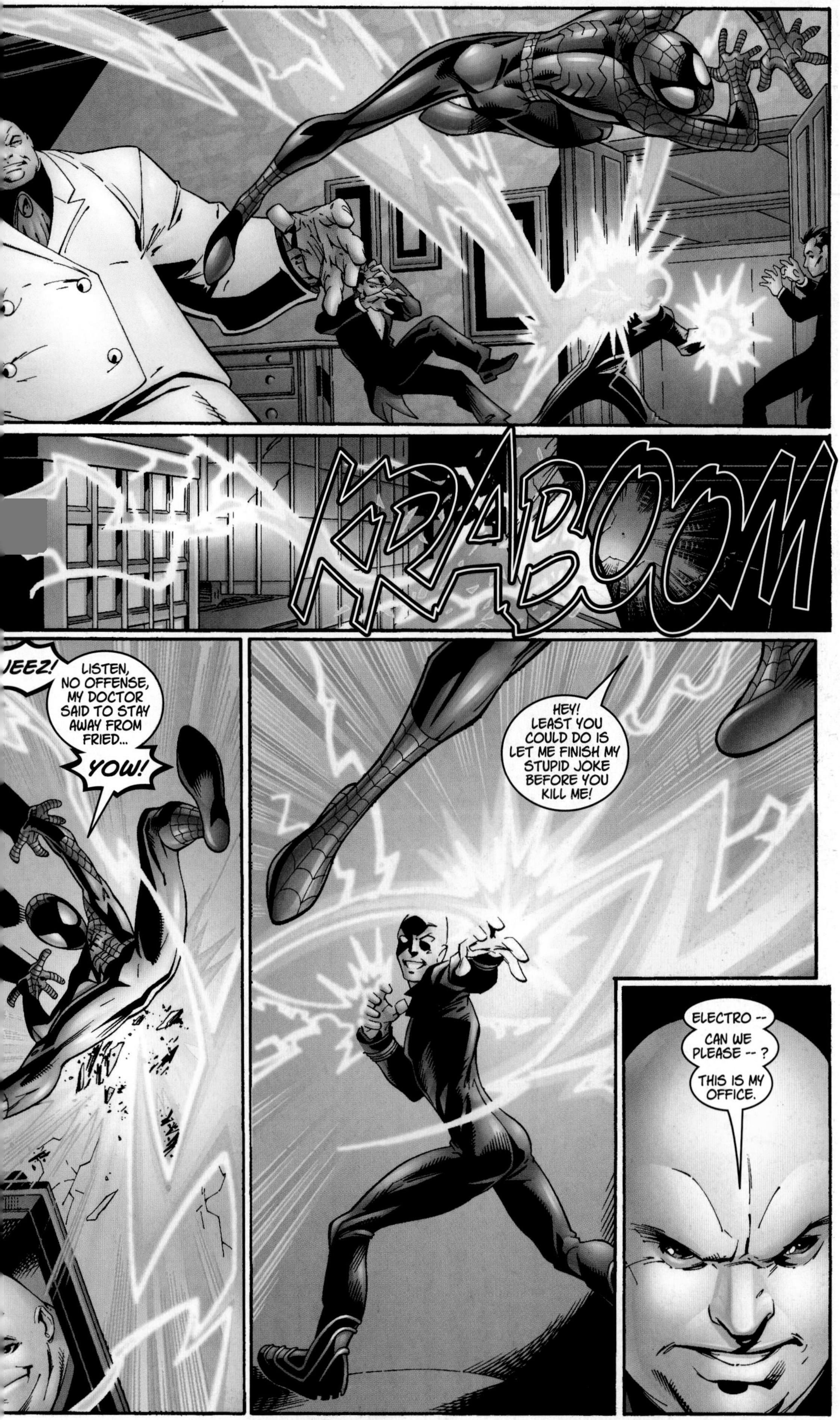
KRAABOOM
JEEZ!
LISTEN, NO OFFENSE, MY DOCTOR SAID TO STAY AWAY FROM FRIED...
YOW!
HEY! LEAST YOU COULD DO IS LET ME FINISH MY STUPID JOKE BEFORE YOU KILL ME!
ELECTRO --
CAN WE PLEASE -- ?
THIS IS MY OFFICE.

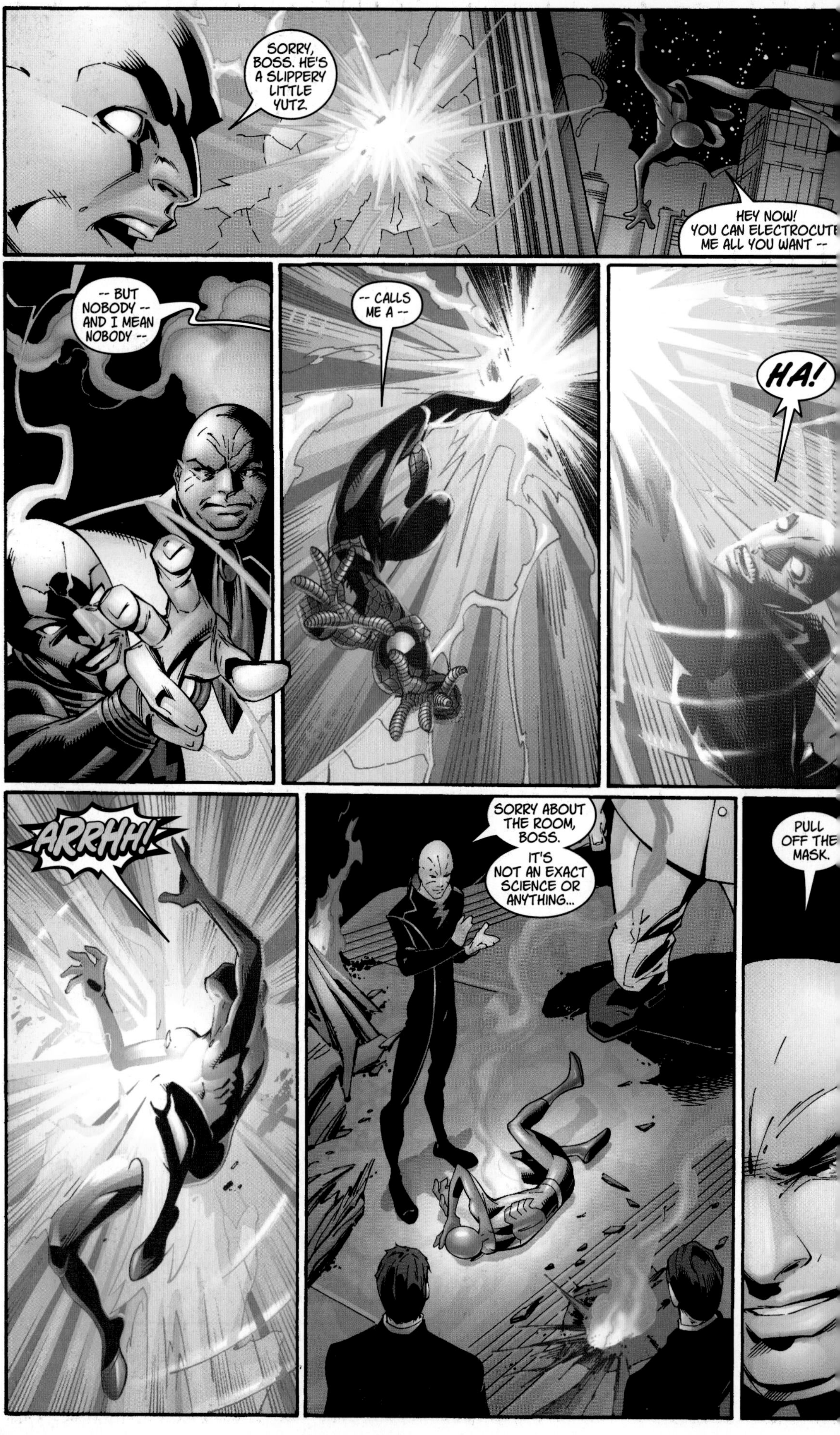
SORRY, BOSS. HE'S A SLIPPERY LITTLE YUTZ.
HEY NOW! YOU CAN ELECTROCUTE ME ALL YOU WANT --
-- BUT NOBODY -- AND I MEAN NOBODY --
-- CALLS ME A --
HA!
ARRHH!
SORRY ABOUT THE ROOM, BOSS.
IT'S NOT AN EXACT SCIENCE OR ANYTHING...
PULL OFF THE MASK.

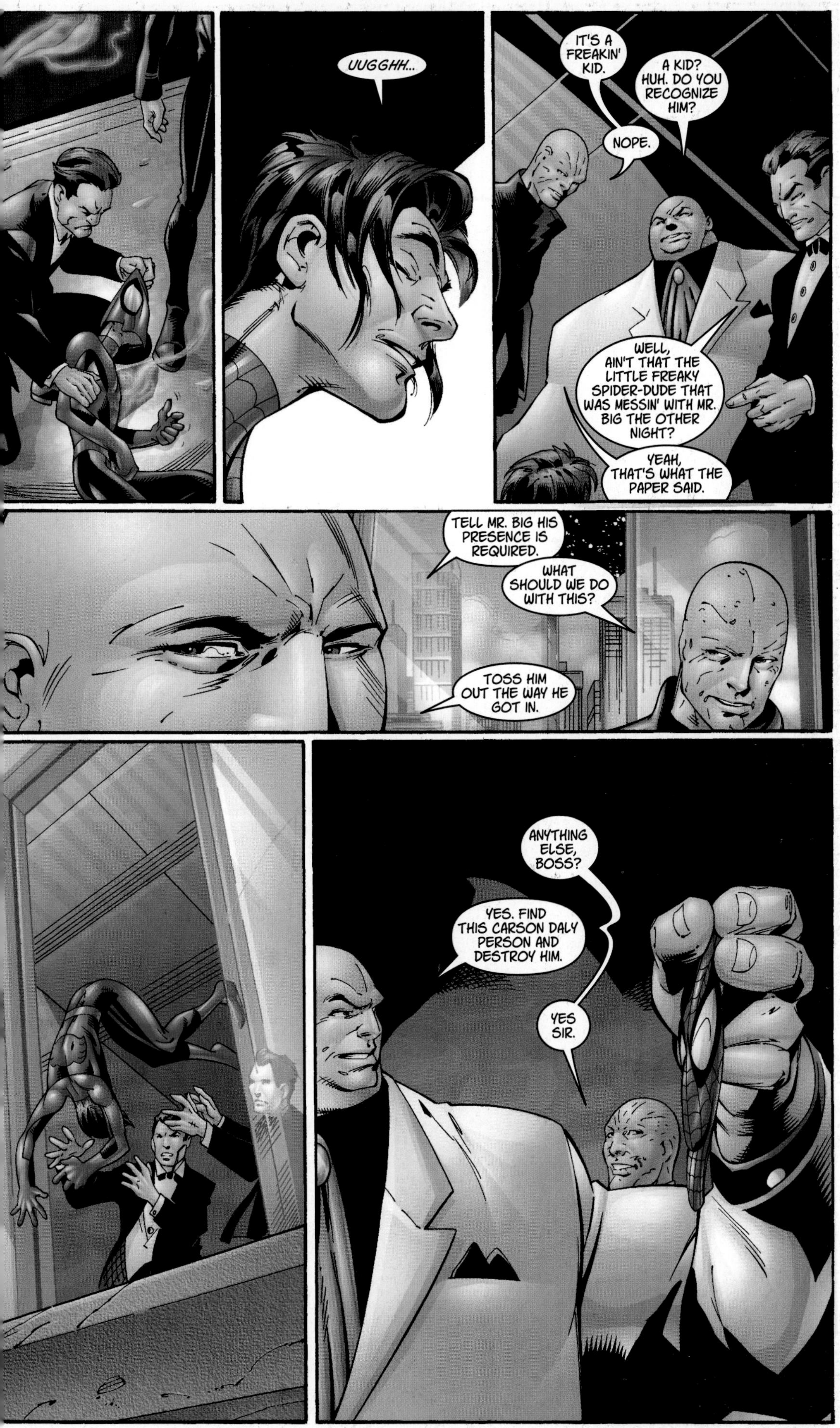
UUGGHH...
IT'S A FREAKIN' KID.
A KID? HUH. DO YOU RECOGNIZE HIM?
NOPE.
WELL, AIN'T THAT THE LITTLE FREAKY SPIDER-DUDE THAT WAS MESSIN' WITH MR. BIG THE OTHER NIGHT?
YEAH, THAT'S WHAT THE PAPER SAID.
TELL MR. BIG HIS PRESENCE IS REQUIRED.
WHAT SHOULD WE DO WITH THIS?
TOSS HIM OUT THE WAY HE GOT IN.
ANYTHING ELSE, BOSS?
YES. FIND THIS CARSON DALY PERSON AND DESTROY HIM.
YES SIR.

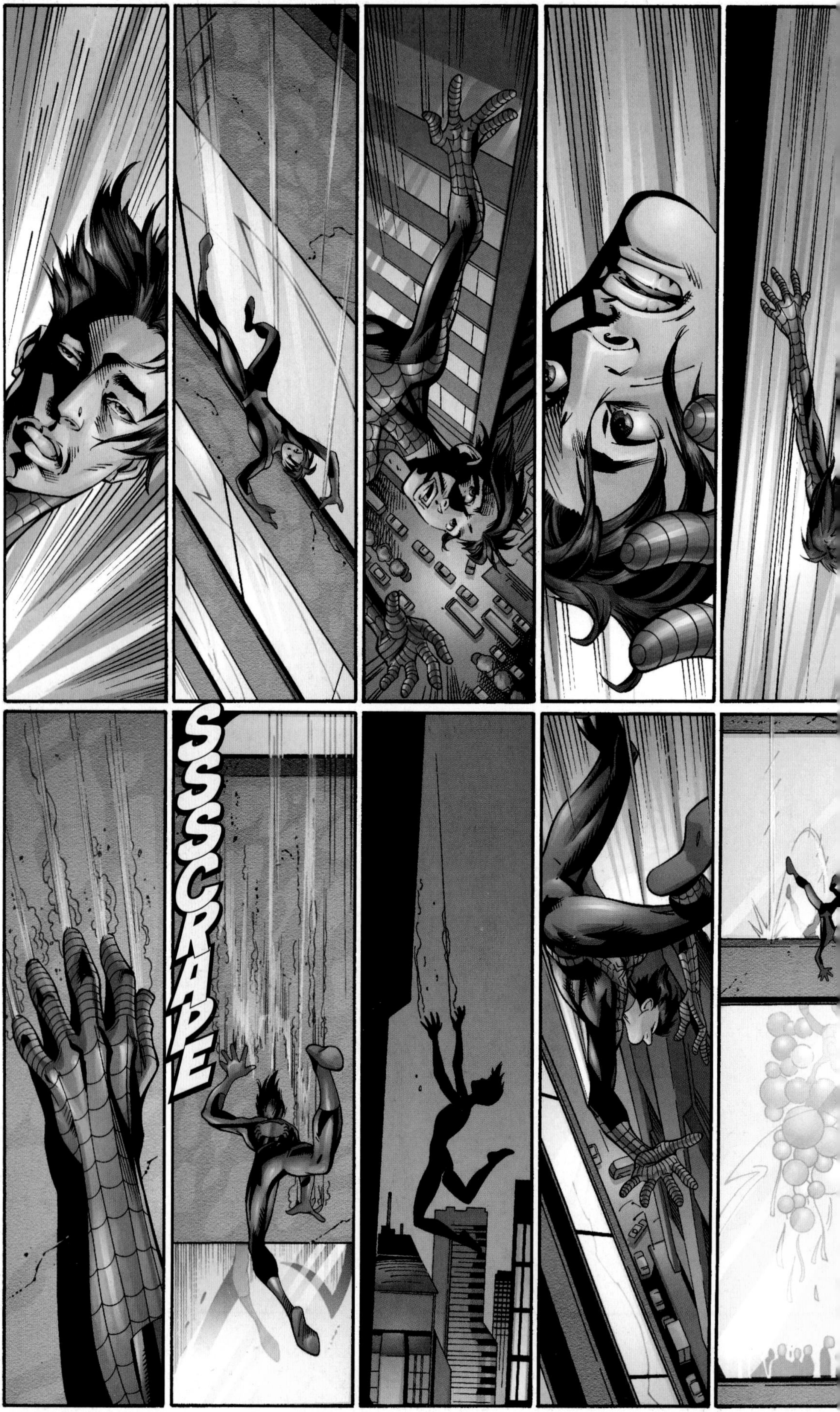
SSSCRAPE

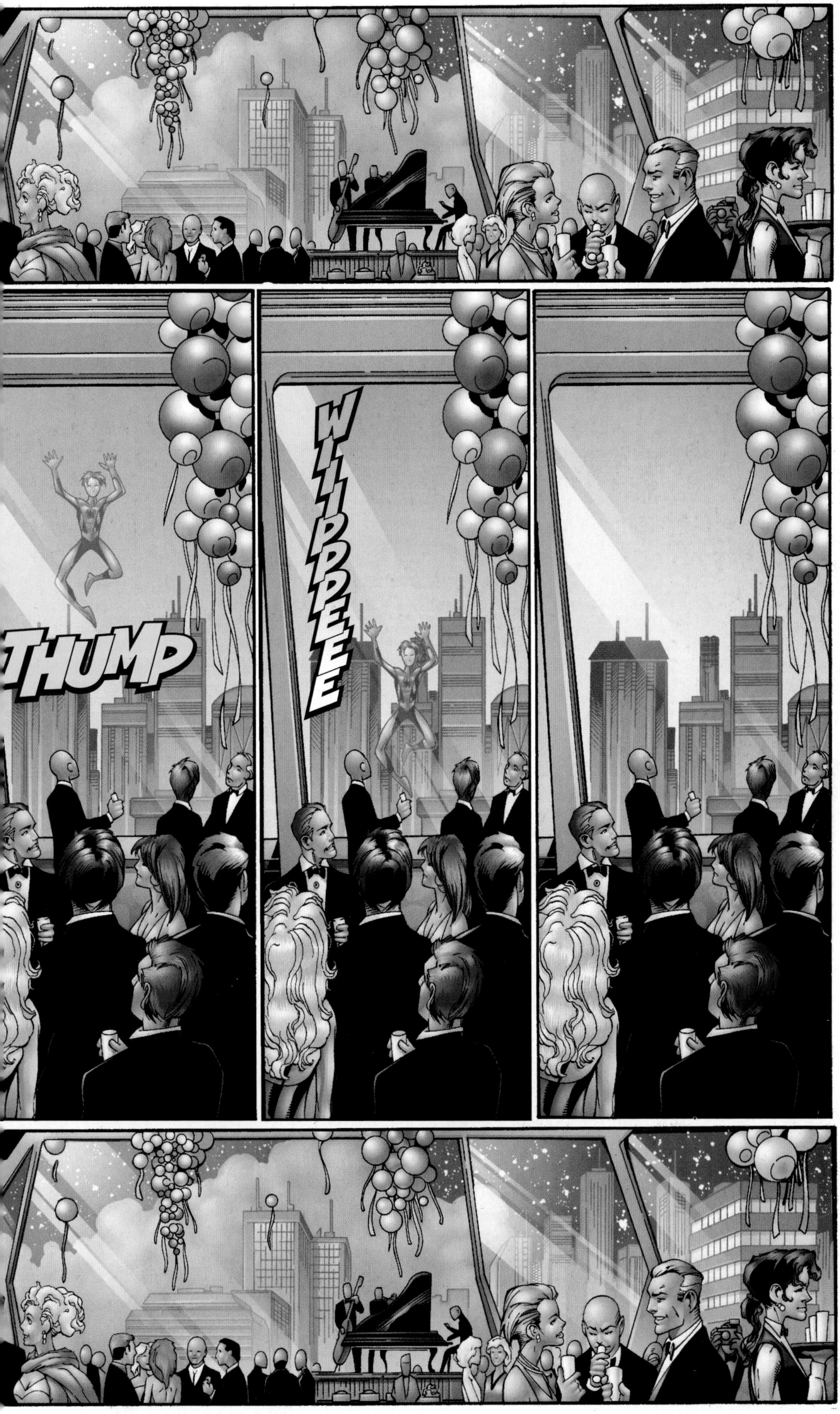
THUMP
WHIPPEEE

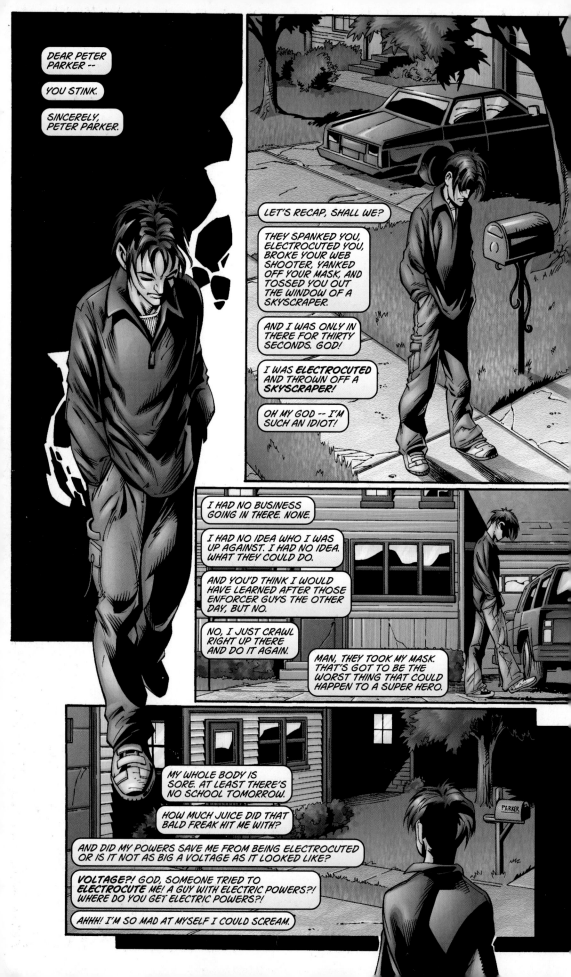

DEAR PETER PARKER --

YOU STINK.

SINCERELY,
PETER PARKER.

LET'S RECAP, SHALL WE?

THEY SPANKED YOU, ELECTROCUTED YOU, BROKE YOUR WEB SHOOTER, YANKED OFF YOUR MASK, AND TOSSED YOU OUT THE WINDOW OF A SKYSCRAPER.

AND I WAS ONLY IN THERE FOR THIRTY SECONDS. GOD!

I WAS ELECTROCUTED AND THROWN OFF A SKYSCRAPER!

OH MY GOD -- I'M SUCH AN IDIOT!

I HAD NO BUSINESS GOING IN THERE. NONE.

I HAD NO IDEA WHO I WAS UP AGAINST. I HAD NO IDEA. WHAT THEY COULD DO.

AND YOU'D THINK I WOULD HAVE LEARNED AFTER THOSE ENFORCER GUYS THE OTHER DAY, BUT NO.

NO, I JUST CRAWL RIGHT UP THERE AND DO IT AGAIN.

MAN, THEY TOOK MY MASK. THAT'S GOT TO BE THE WORST THING THAT COULD HAPPEN TO A SUPER HERO.

MY WHOLE BODY IS SORE. AT LEAST THERE'S NO SCHOOL TOMORROW.

HOW MUCH JUICE DID THAT BALD FREAK HIT ME WITH?

AND DID MY POWERS SAVE ME FROM BEING ELECTROCUTED OR IS IT NOT AS BIG A VOLTAGE AS IT LOOKED LIKE?

VOLTAGE?! GOD, SOMEONE TRIED TO ELECTROCUTE ME! A GUY WITH ELECTRIC POWERS?! WHERE DO YOU GET ELECTRIC POWERS?!

AHHH! I'M SO MAD AT MYSELF I COULD SCREAM.

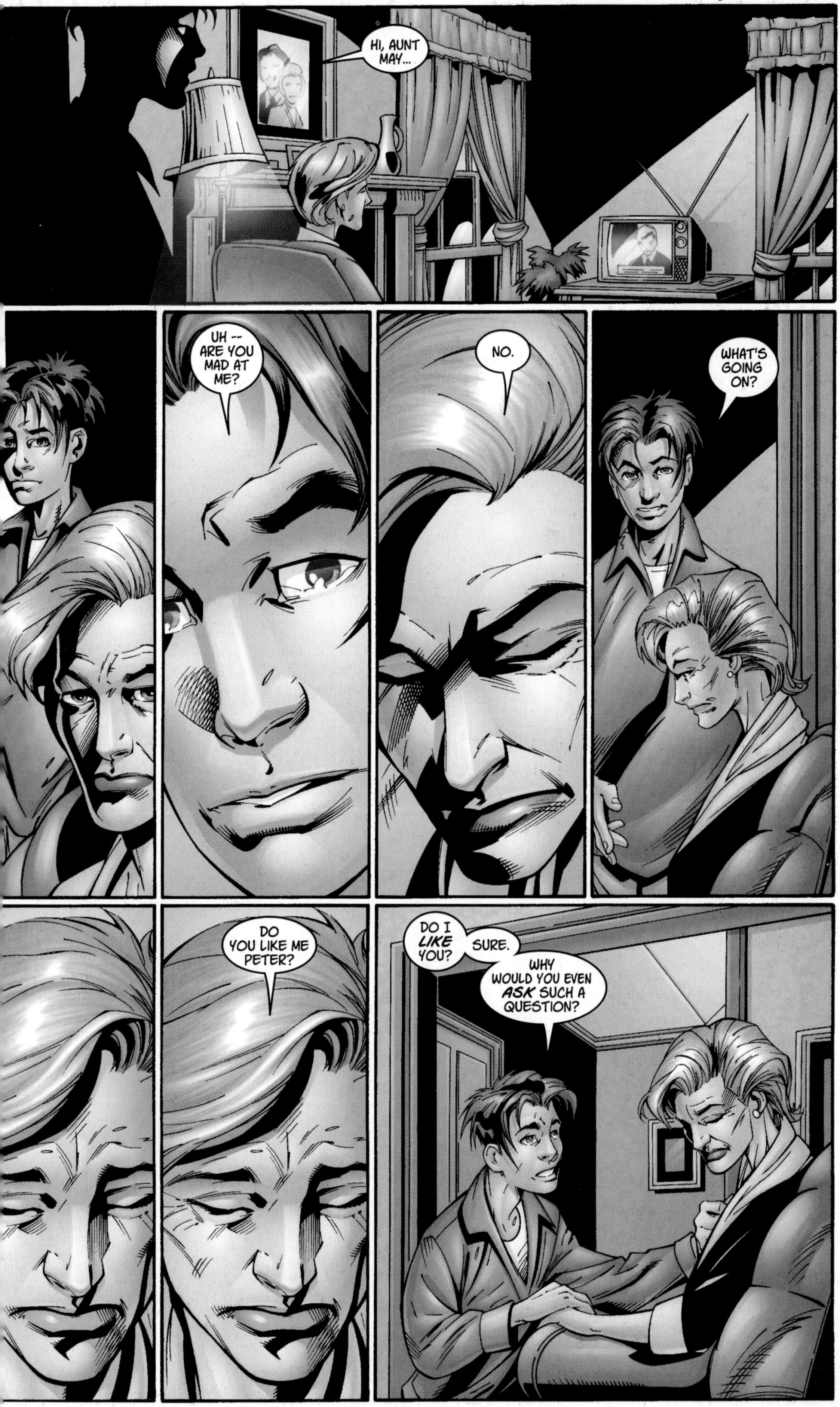
HI, AUNT MAY...
UH -- ARE YOU MAD AT ME?
NO.
WHAT'S GOING ON?
DO YOU LIKE ME PETER?
DO I *LIKE* YOU?
SURE.
WHY WOULD YOU EVEN *ASK* SUCH A QUESTION?

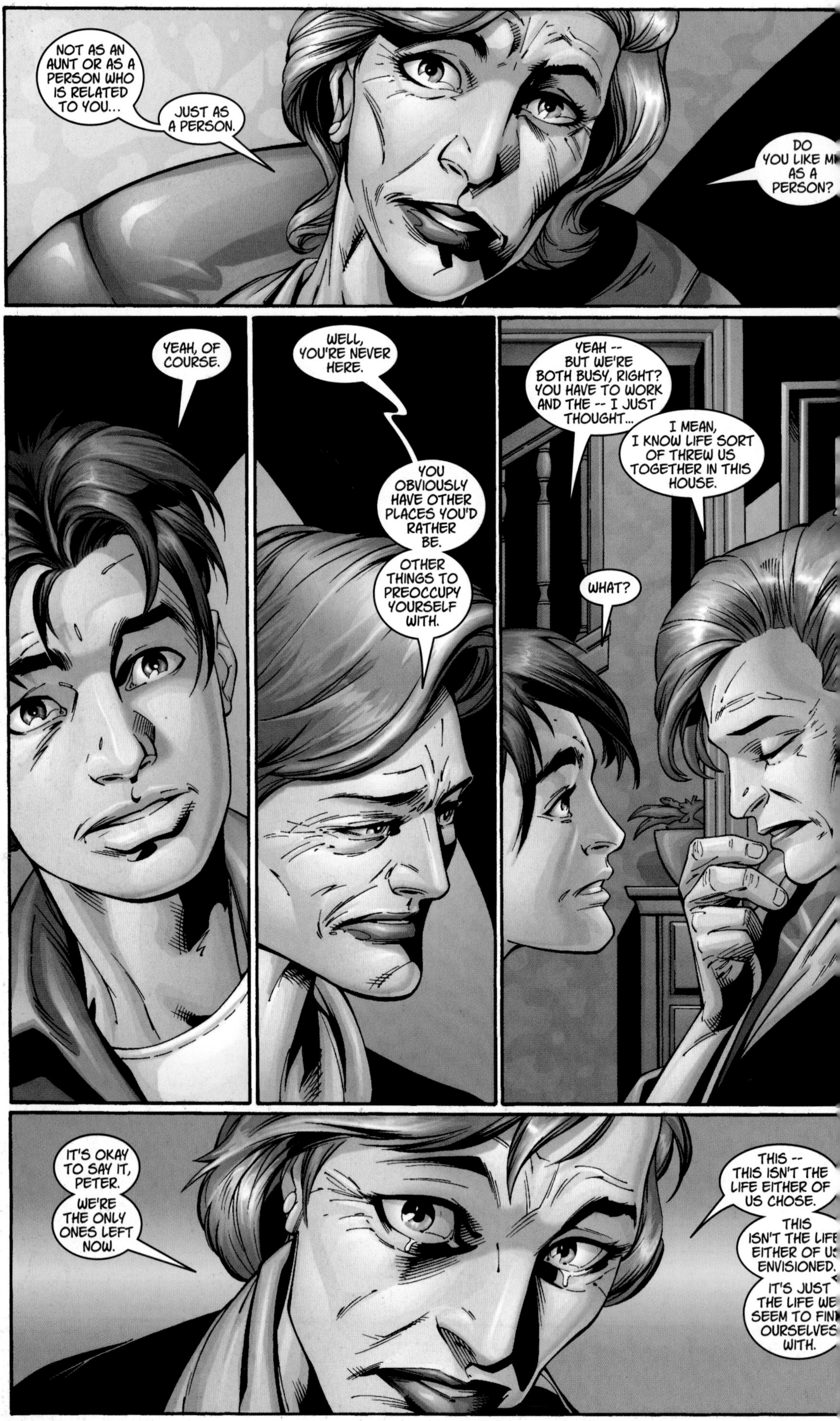
NOT AS AN AUNT OR AS A PERSON WHO IS RELATED TO YOU...
JUST AS A PERSON.
DO YOU LIKE ME AS A PERSON?
YEAH, OF COURSE.
WELL, YOU'RE NEVER HERE.
YOU OBVIOUSLY HAVE OTHER PLACES YOU'D RATHER BE.
OTHER THINGS TO PREOCCUPY YOURSELF WITH.
YEAH -- BUT WE'RE BOTH BUSY, RIGHT? YOU HAVE TO WORK AND THE -- I JUST THOUGHT...
I MEAN, I KNOW LIFE SORT OF THREW US TOGETHER IN THIS HOUSE.
WHAT?
IT'S OKAY TO SAY IT, PETER.
WE'RE THE ONLY ONES LEFT NOW.
THIS -- THIS ISN'T THE LIFE EITHER OF US CHOSE.
THIS ISN'T THE LIFE EITHER OF US ENVISIONED.
IT'S JUST THE LIFE WE SEEM TO FIND OURSELVES WITH.

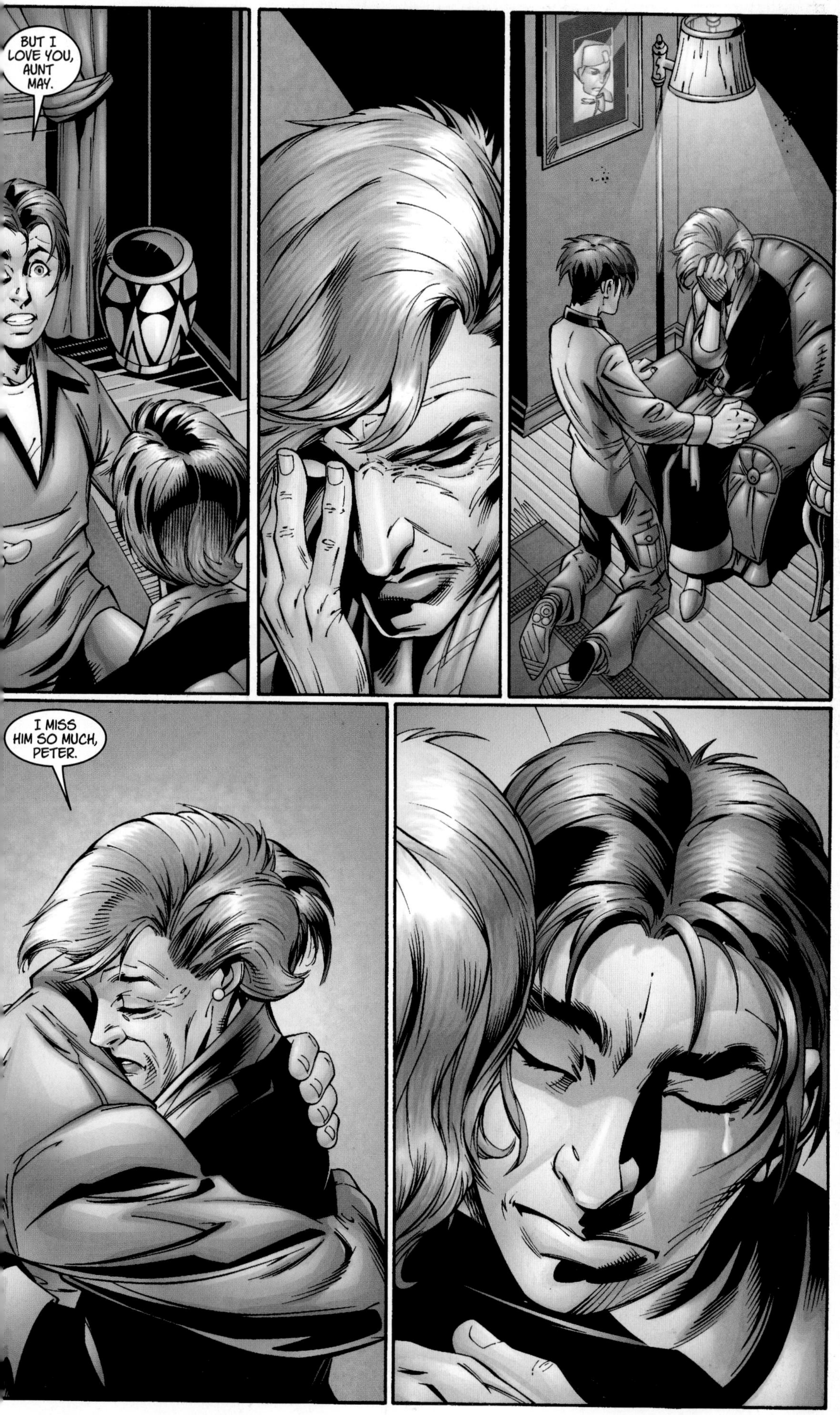
BUT I LOVE YOU, AUNT MAY.
I MISS HIM SO MUCH, PETER.

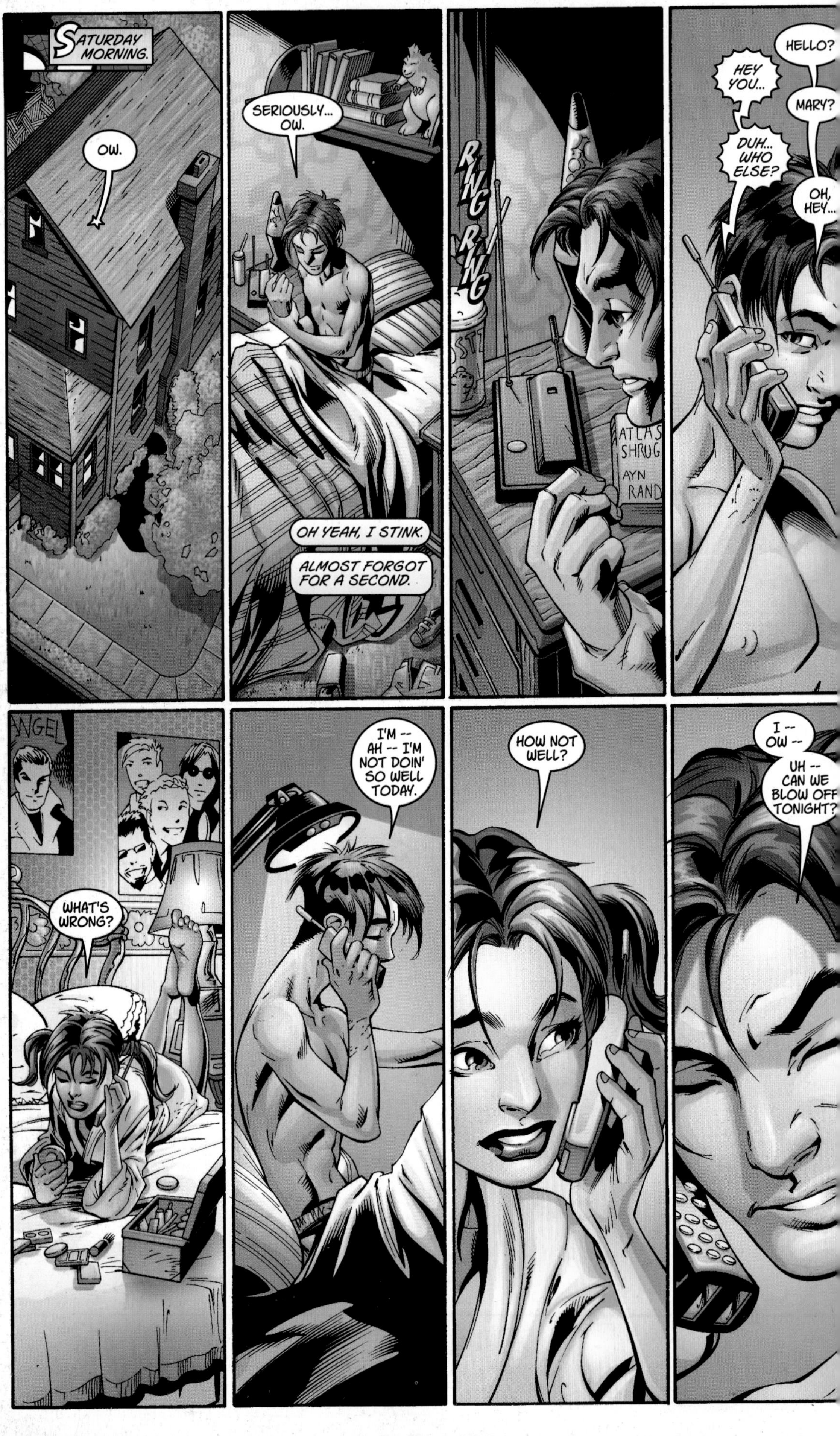
SATURDAY MORNING.
OW.
SERIOUSLY... OW.
OH YEAH, I STINK.
ALMOST FORGOT FOR A SECOND.
RING RING
ATLAS SHRUG AYN RAND
HELLO?
HEY YOU...
MARY?
DUH... WHO ELSE?
OH, HEY...
ANGEL
WHAT'S WRONG?
I'M -- AH -- I'M NOT DOIN' SO WELL TODAY.
HOW NOT WELL?
I -- OW --
UH -- CAN WE BLOW OFF TONIGHT?

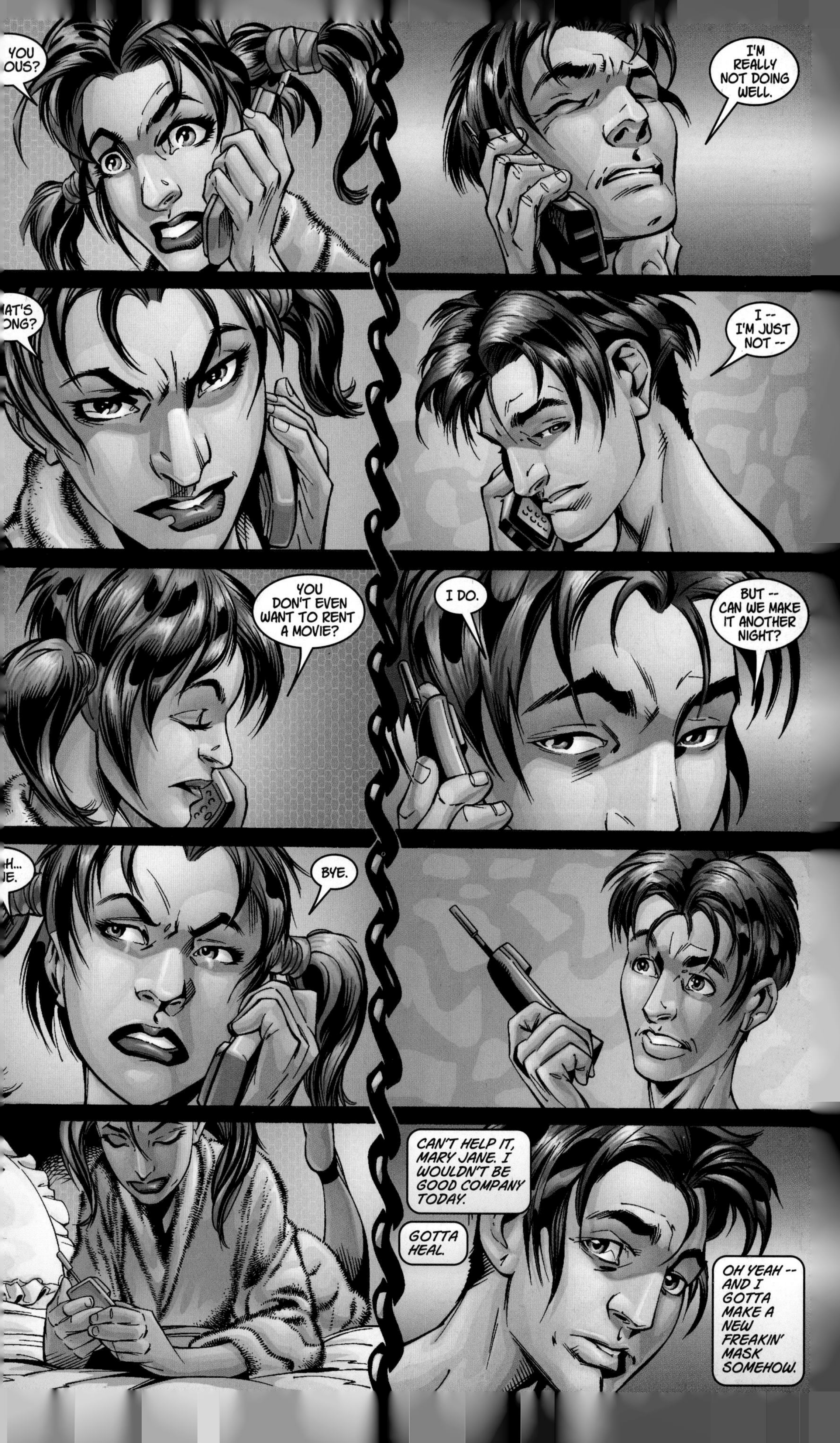
I'M REALLY NOT DOING WELL.
I -- I'M JUST NOT --
YOU DON'T EVEN WANT TO RENT A MOVIE?
I DO.
BUT -- CAN WE MAKE IT ANOTHER NIGHT?
BYE.
CAN'T HELP IT, MARY JANE. I WOULDN'T BE GOOD COMPANY TODAY.
GOTTA HEAL.
OH YEAH -- AND I GOTTA MAKE A NEW FREAKIN' MASK SOMEHOW.

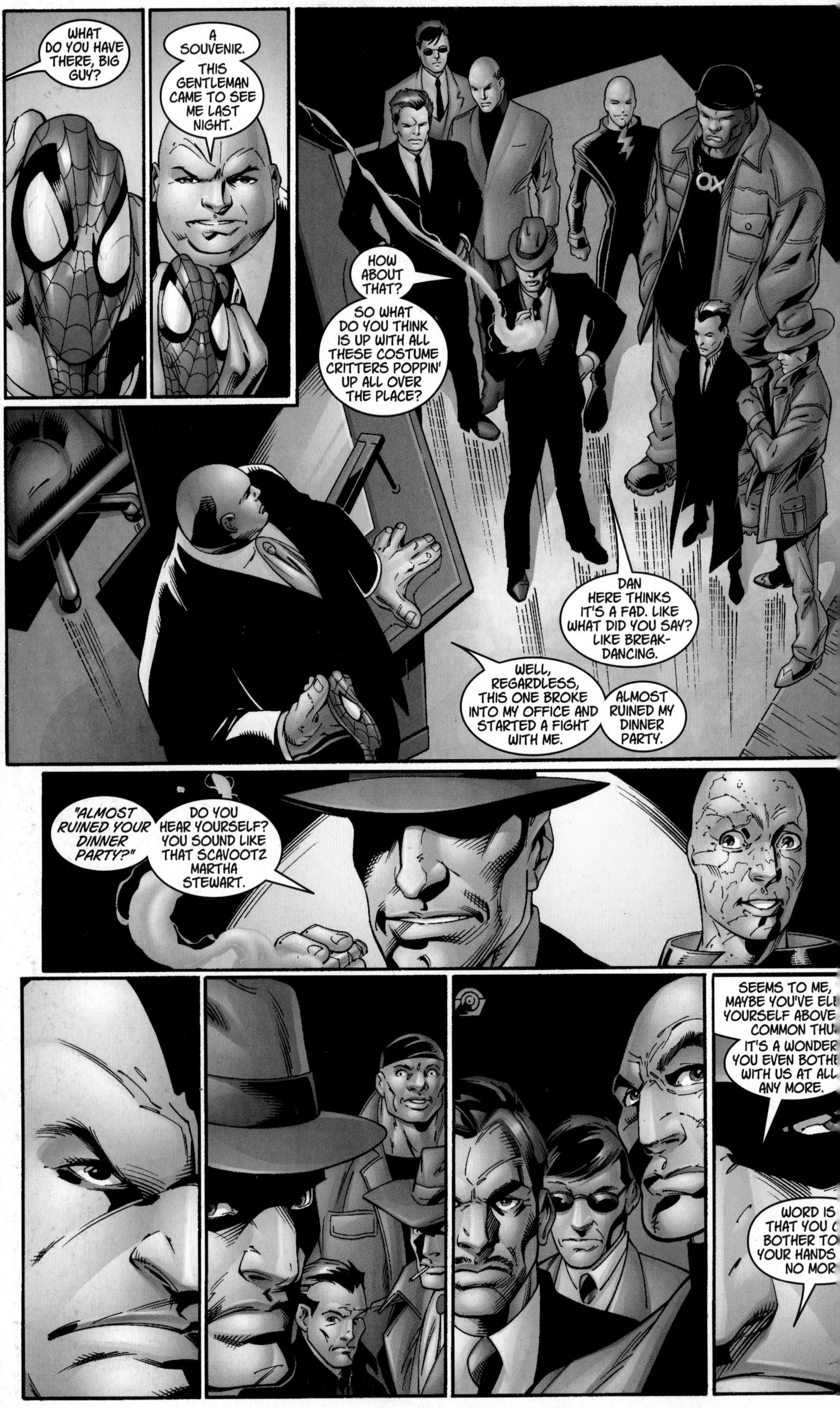
WHAT DO YOU HAVE THERE, BIG GUY?
A SOUVENIR.
THIS GENTLEMAN CAME TO SEE ME LAST NIGHT.
HOW ABOUT THAT?
SO WHAT DO YOU THINK IS UP WITH ALL THESE COSTUME CRITTERS POPPIN' UP ALL OVER THE PLACE?
DAN HERE THINKS IT'S A FAD. LIKE WHAT DID YOU SAY? LIKE BREAK-DANCING.
WELL, REGARDLESS, THIS ONE BROKE INTO MY OFFICE AND STARTED A FIGHT WITH ME.
ALMOST RUINED MY DINNER PARTY.
"ALMOST RUINED YOUR DINNER PARTY?"
DO YOU HEAR YOURSELF? YOU SOUND LIKE THAT SCAVOOTZ MARTHA STEWART.
WORD IS THAT YOU

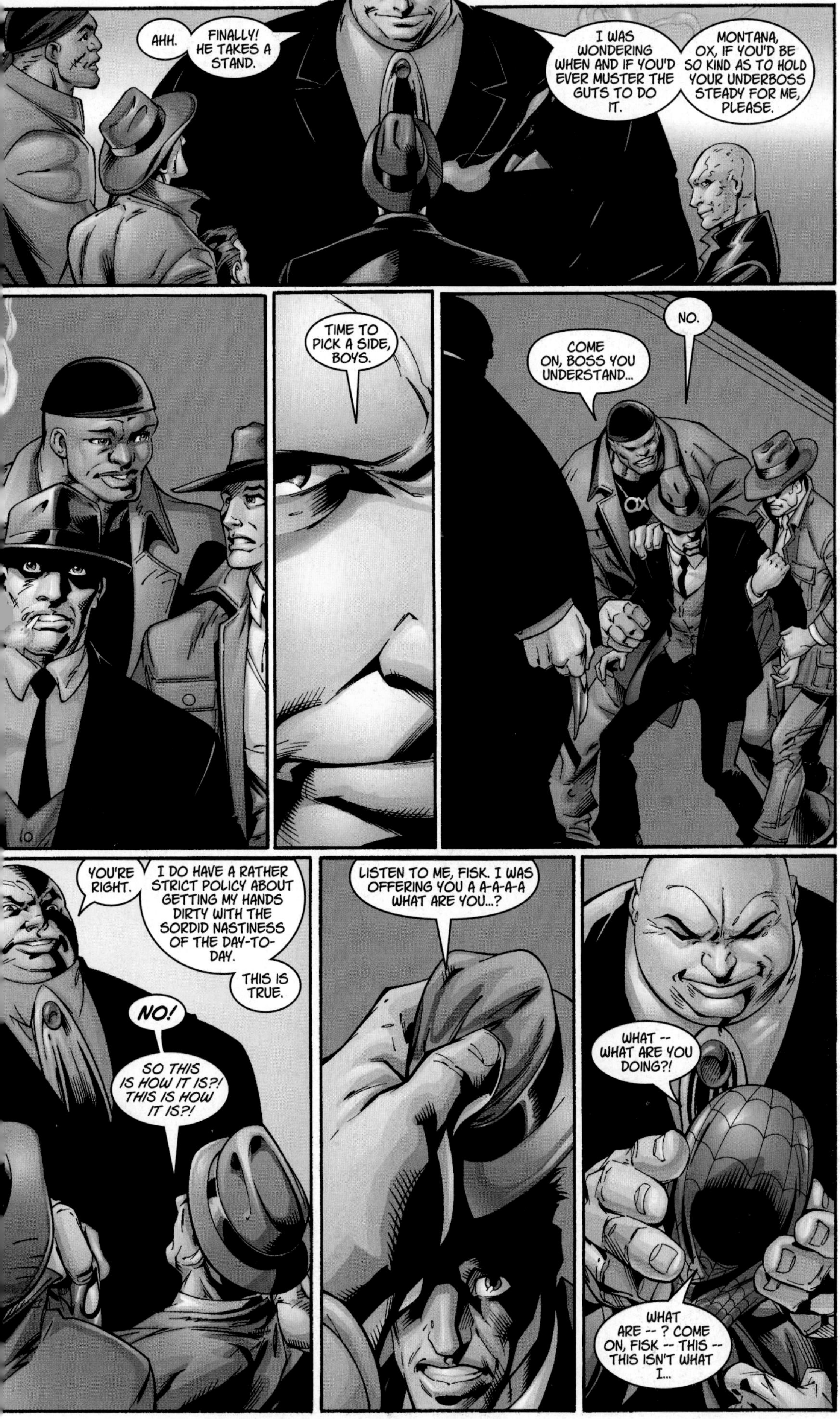
AHH.
FINALLY! HE TAKES A STAND.
I WAS WONDERING WHEN AND IF YOU'D EVER MUSTER THE GUTS TO DO IT.
MONTANA, OX, IF YOU'D BE SO KIND AS TO HOLD YOUR UNDERBOSS STEADY FOR ME, PLEASE.
TIME TO PICK A SIDE, BOYS.
COME ON, BOSS YOU UNDERSTAND...
NO.
YOU'RE RIGHT.
I DO HAVE A RATHER STRICT POLICY ABOUT GETTING MY HANDS DIRTY WITH THE SORDID NASTINESS OF THE DAY-TO-DAY.
THIS IS TRUE.
NO!
SO THIS IS HOW IT IS?! THIS IS HOW IT IS?!
LISTEN TO ME, FISK. I WAS OFFERING YOU A A-A-A-A WHAT ARE YOU...?
WHAT -- WHAT ARE YOU DOING?!
WHAT ARE -- ? COME ON, FISK -- THIS -- THIS ISN'T WHAT I...

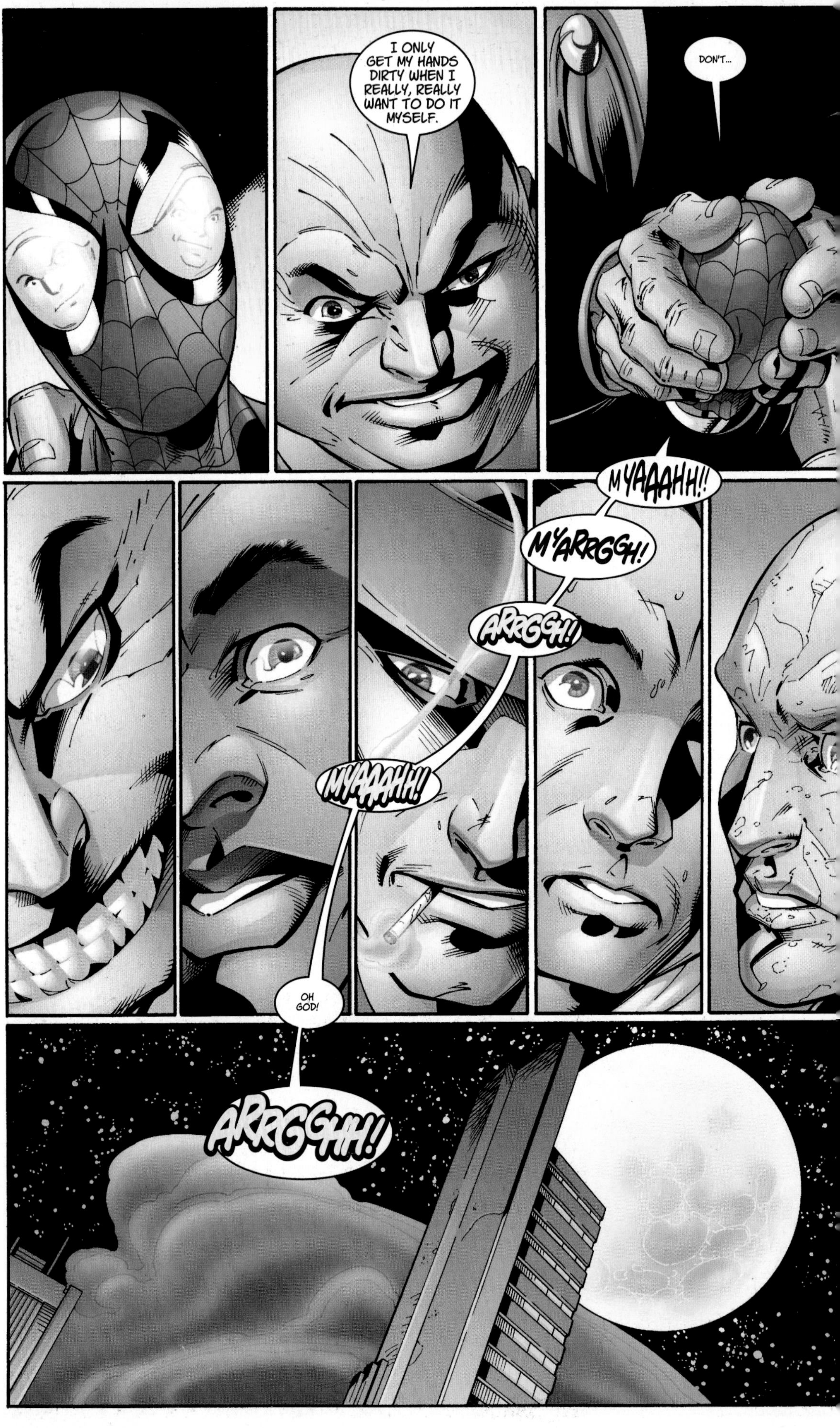
I ONLY GET MY HANDS DIRTY WHEN I REALLY, REALLY WANT TO DO IT MYSELF.
DON'T...
MYAAAHH!!
MYARRGGH!
ARRGGH!
MYAAAHH!
OH GOD!
ARRGGHH!

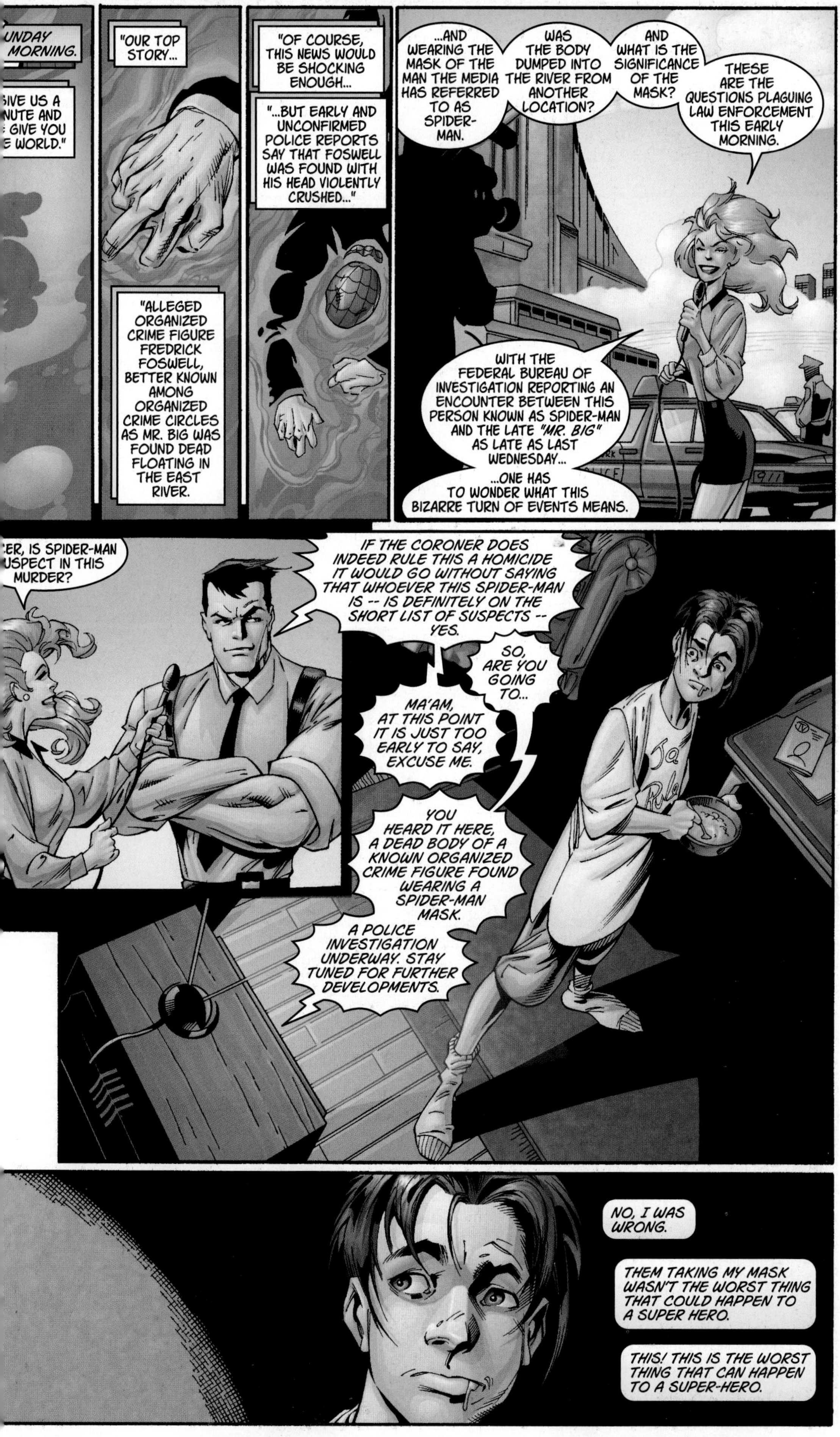
UNDAY MORNING.
GIVE US A NUTE AND E GIVE YOU E WORLD."
"OUR TOP STORY...
"ALLEGED ORGANIZED CRIME FIGURE FREDRICK FOSWELL, BETTER KNOWN AMONG ORGANIZED CRIME CIRCLES AS MR. BIG WAS FOUND DEAD FLOATING IN THE EAST RIVER.
"OF COURSE, THIS NEWS WOULD BE SHOCKING ENOUGH...
"...BUT EARLY AND UNCONFIRMED POLICE REPORTS SAY THAT FOSWELL WAS FOUND WITH HIS HEAD VIOLENTLY CRUSHED..."
...AND WEARING THE MASK OF THE MAN THE MEDIA HAS REFERRED TO AS SPIDER-MAN.
WAS THE BODY DUMPED INTO THE RIVER FROM ANOTHER LOCATION?
AND WHAT IS THE SIGNIFICANCE OF THE MASK?
THESE ARE THE QUESTIONS PLAGUING LAW ENFORCEMENT THIS EARLY MORNING.
WITH THE FEDERAL BUREAU OF INVESTIGATION REPORTING AN ENCOUNTER BETWEEN THIS PERSON KNOWN AS SPIDER-MAN AND THE LATE "MR. BIG" AS LATE AS LAST WEDNESDAY...
...ONE HAS TO WONDER WHAT THIS BIZARRE TURN OF EVENTS MEANS.
CER, IS SPIDER-MAN USPECT IN THIS MURDER?
IF THE CORONER DOES INDEED RULE THIS A HOMICIDE IT WOULD GO WITHOUT SAYING THAT WHOEVER THIS SPIDER-MAN IS -- IS DEFINITELY ON THE SHORT LIST OF SUSPECTS -- YES.
SO, ARE YOU GOING TO...
MA'AM, AT THIS POINT IT IS JUST TOO EARLY TO SAY, EXCUSE ME.
YOU HEARD IT HERE, A DEAD BODY OF A KNOWN ORGANIZED CRIME FIGURE FOUND WEARING A SPIDER-MAN MASK.
A POLICE INVESTIGATION UNDERWAY. STAY TUNED FOR FURTHER DEVELOPMENTS.
NO, I WAS WRONG.
THEM TAKING MY MASK WASN'T THE WORST THING THAT COULD HAPPEN TO A SUPER HERO.
THIS! THIS IS THE WORST THING THAT CAN HAPPEN TO A SUPER-HERO.

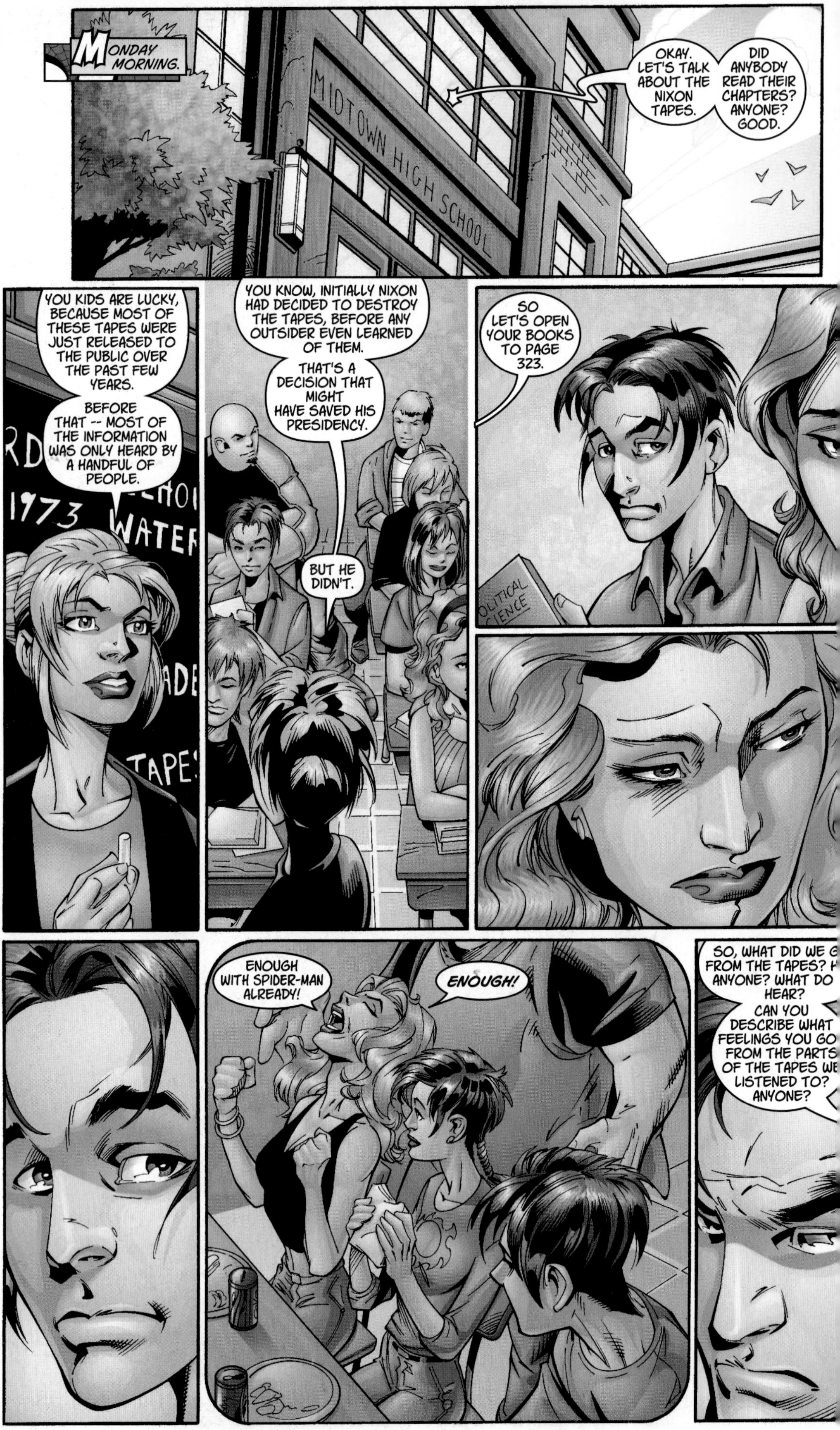
MONDAY MORNING.
MIDTOWN HIGH SCHOOL
OKAY. LET'S TALK ABOUT THE NIXON TAPES.
DID ANYBODY READ THEIR CHAPTERS? ANYONE? GOOD.
YOU KIDS ARE LUCKY, BECAUSE MOST OF THESE TAPES WERE JUST RELEASED TO THE PUBLIC OVER THE PAST FEW YEARS.
BEFORE THAT -- MOST OF THE INFORMATION WAS ONLY HEARD BY A HANDFUL OF PEOPLE.
1973
WATER
TAPES
YOU KNOW, INITIALLY NIXON HAD DECIDED TO DESTROY THE TAPES, BEFORE ANY OUTSIDER EVEN LEARNED OF THEM.
THAT'S A DECISION THAT MIGHT HAVE SAVED HIS PRESIDENCY.
BUT HE DIDN'T.
SO LET'S OPEN YOUR BOOKS TO PAGE 323.
OLITICAL
IENCE
ENOUGH WITH SPIDER-MAN ALREADY!
ENOUGH!
SO, WHAT DID WE G
FROM THE TAPES? H
ANYONE? WHAT DO
HEAR?
CAN YOU DESCRIBE WHAT FEELINGS YOU GO FROM THE PARTS OF THE TAPES WE LISTENED TO? ANYONE?

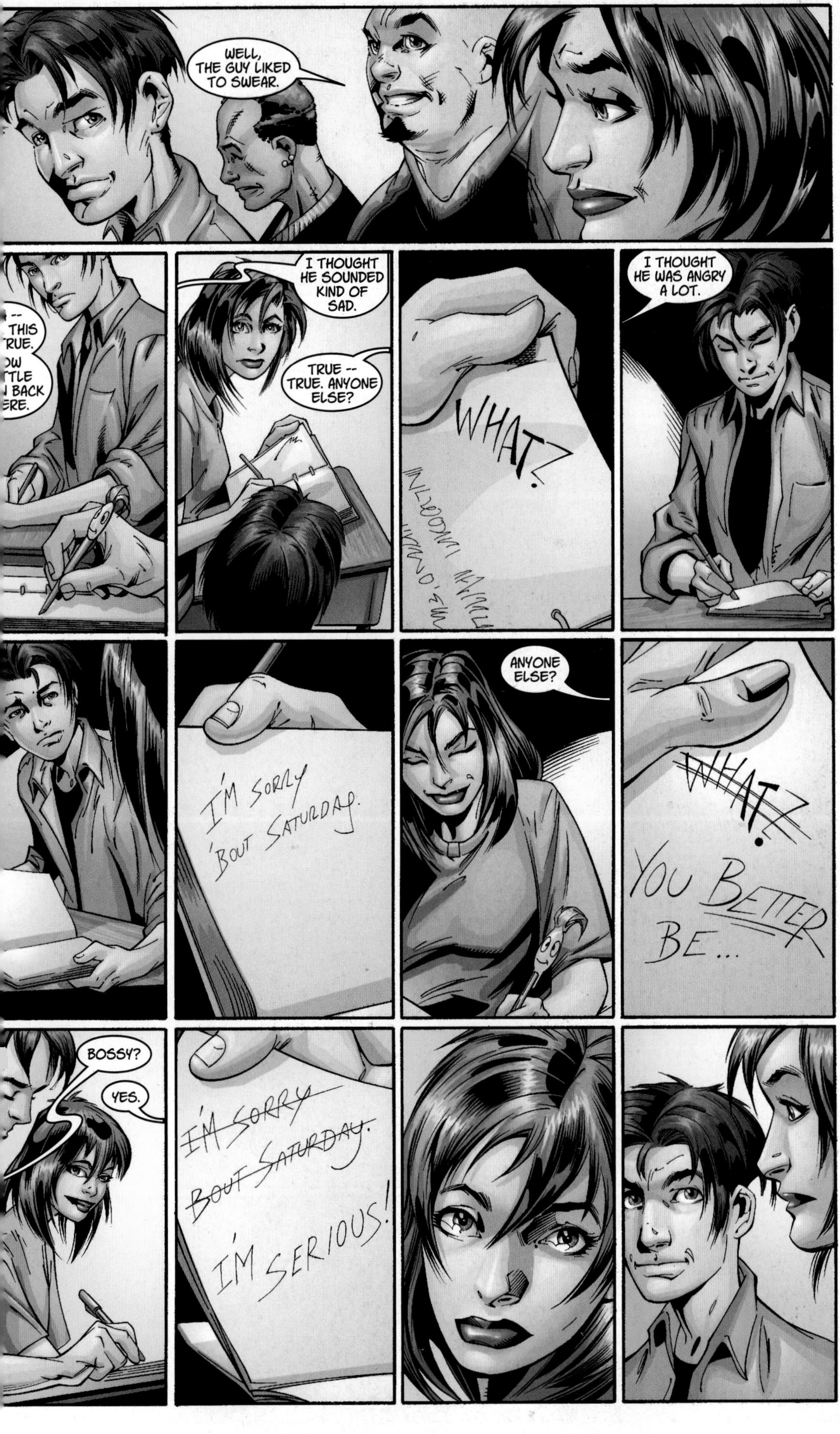
WELL, THE GUY LIKED TO SWEAR.
I THOUGHT HE SOUNDED KIND OF SAD.
TRUE -- TRUE. ANYONE ELSE?
WHAT?
I THOUGHT HE WAS ANGRY A LOT.
I'M SORRY 'BOUT SATURDAY.
ANYONE ELSE?
WHAT?
YOU BETTER BE...
BOSSY?
YES.
I'M SORRY 'BOUT SATURDAY.
I'M SERIOUS!

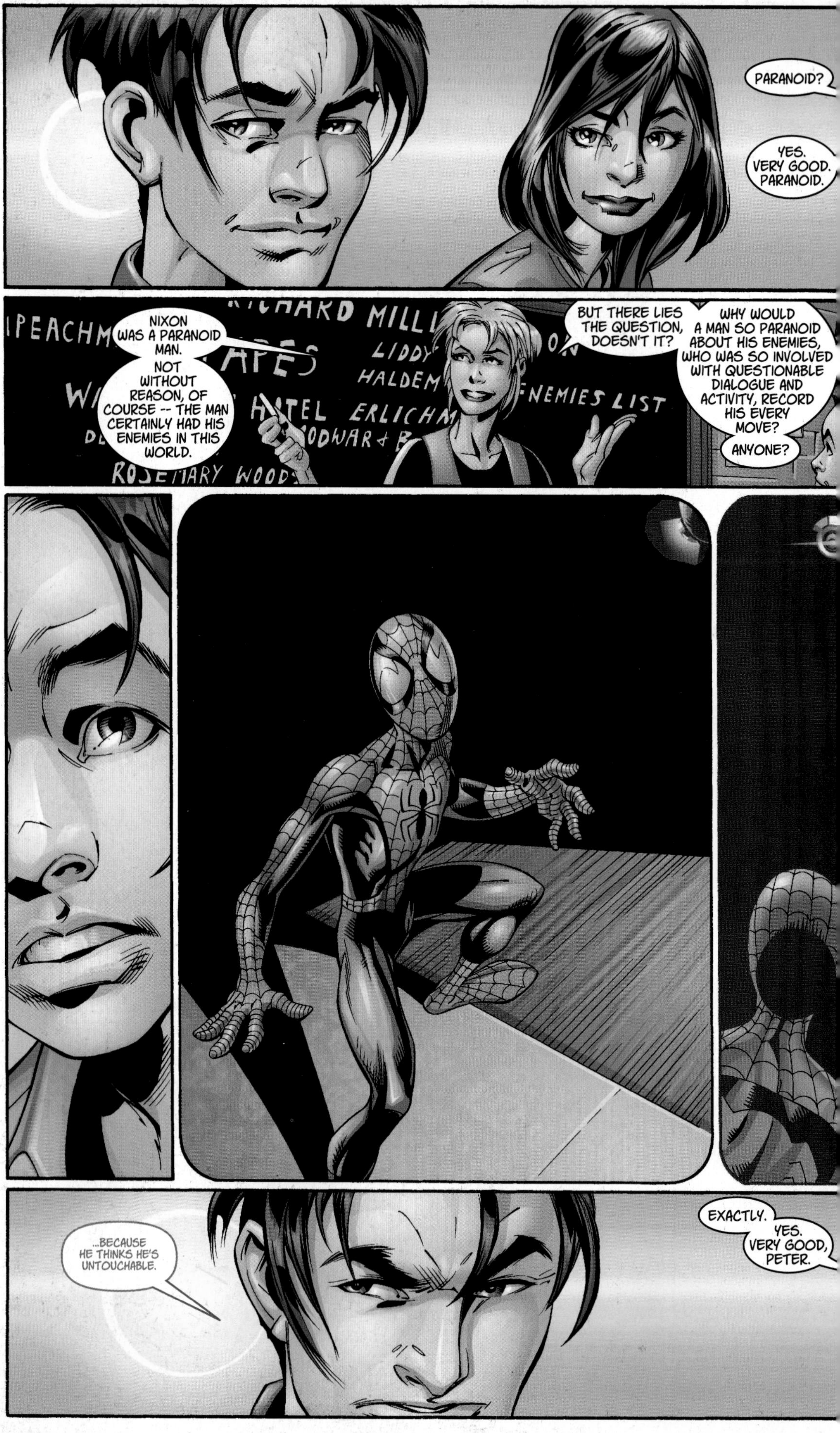
PARANOID?
YES. VERY GOOD. PARANOID.
NIXON WAS A PARANOID MAN.
NOT WITHOUT REASON, OF COURSE -- THE MAN CERTAINLY HAD HIS ENEMIES IN THIS WORLD.
BUT THERE LIES THE QUESTION, DOESN'T IT?
WHY WOULD A MAN SO PARANOID ABOUT HIS ENEMIES, WHO WAS SO INVOLVED WITH QUESTIONABLE DIALOGUE AND ACTIVITY, RECORD HIS EVERY MOVE?
ANYONE?
...BECAUSE HE THINKS HE'S UNTOUCHABLE.
EXACTLY.
YES. VERY GOOD, PETER.

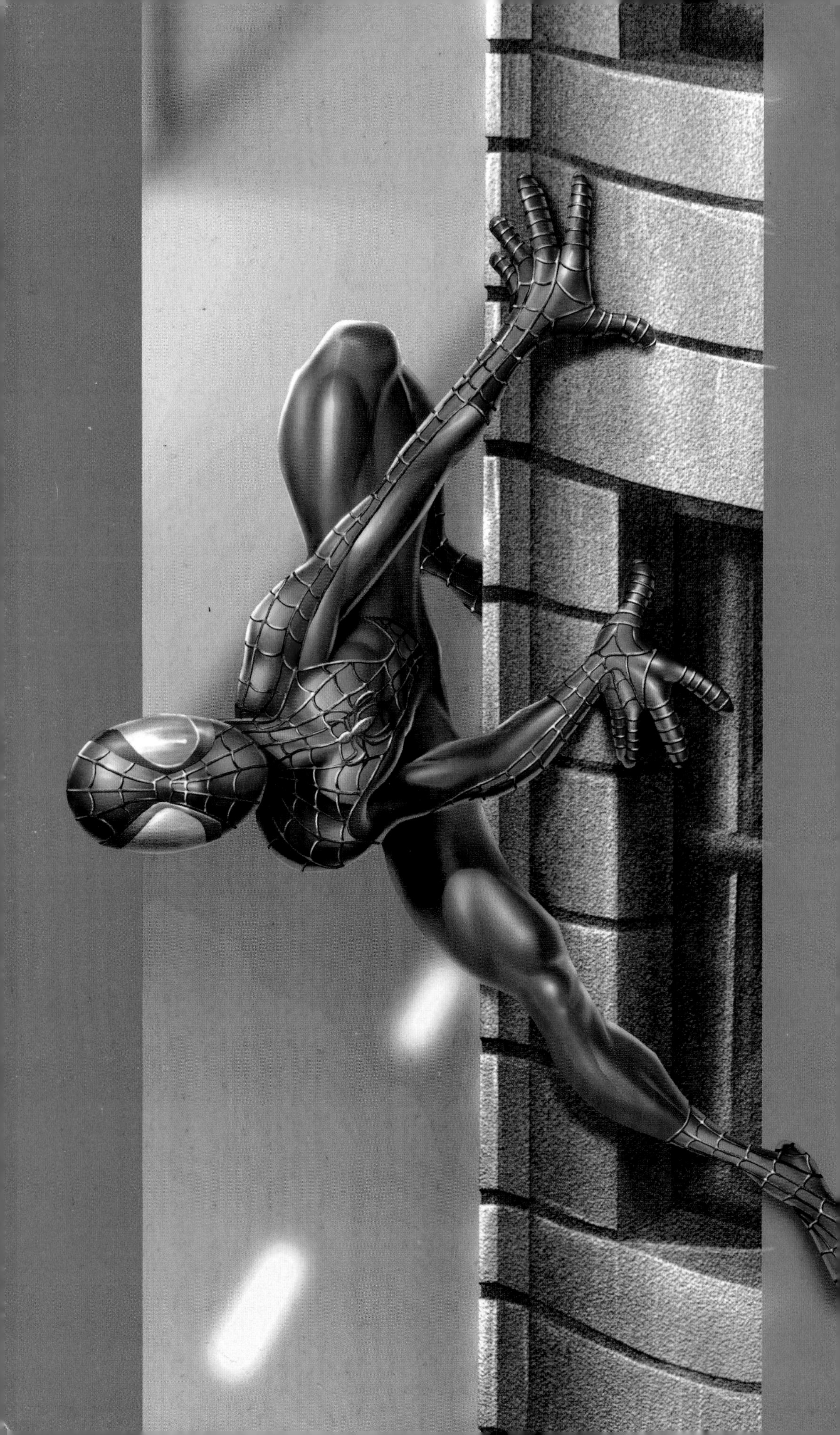

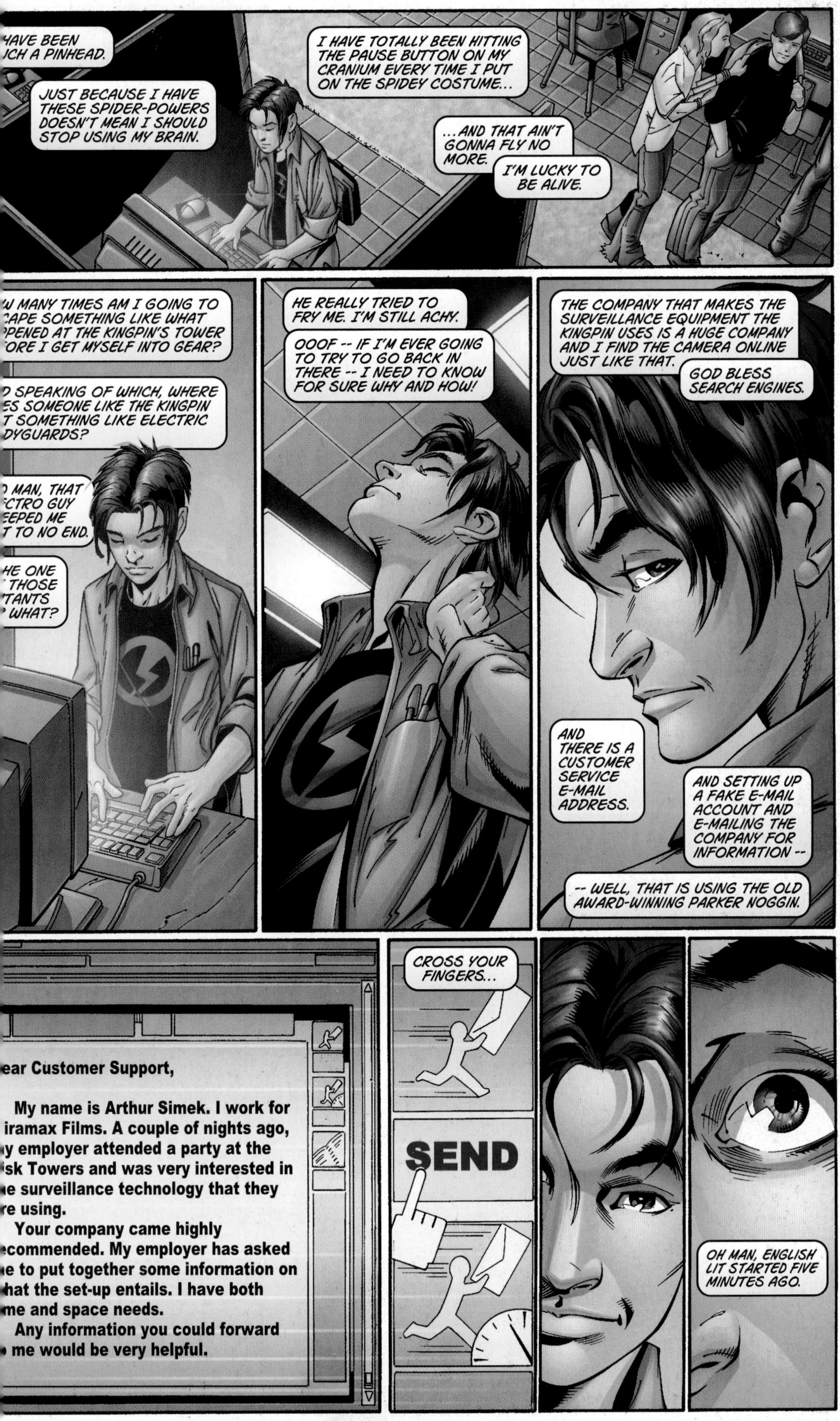
HAVE BEEN
ICH A PINHEAD.
JUST BECAUSE I HAVE THESE SPIDER-POWERS DOESN'T MEAN I SHOULD STOP USING MY BRAIN.
I HAVE TOTALLY BEEN HITTING THE PAUSE BUTTON ON MY CRANIUM EVERY TIME I PUT ON THE SPIDEY COSTUME...
...AND THAT AIN'T GONNA FLY NO MORE.
I'M LUCKY TO BE ALIVE.
W MANY TIMES AM I GOING TO
CAPE SOMETHING LIKE WHAT
PPENED AT THE KINGPIN'S TOWER
FORE I GET MYSELF INTO GEAR?
D SPEAKING OF WHICH, WHERE
ES SOMEONE LIKE THE KINGPIN
T SOMETHING LIKE ELECTRIC
DYGUARDS?
D MAN, THAT
ECTRO GUY
EEPED ME
T TO NO END.
HE ONE
THOSE
TANTS
WHAT?
HE REALLY TRIED TO FRY ME. I'M STILL ACHY.
OOOF -- IF I'M EVER GOING TO TRY TO GO BACK IN THERE -- I NEED TO KNOW FOR SURE WHY AND HOW!
THE COMPANY THAT MAKES THE SURVEILLANCE EQUIPMENT THE KINGPIN USES IS A HUGE COMPANY AND I FIND THE CAMERA ONLINE JUST LIKE THAT.
GOD BLESS SEARCH ENGINES.
AND THERE IS A CUSTOMER SERVICE E-MAIL ADDRESS.
AND SETTING UP A FAKE E-MAIL ACCOUNT AND E-MAILING THE COMPANY FOR INFORMATION --
-- WELL, THAT IS USING THE OLD AWARD-WINNING PARKER NOGGIN.
ear Customer Support,
My name is Arthur Simek. I work for
iramax Films. A couple of nights ago,
y employer attended a party at the
isk Towers and was very interested in
e surveillance technology that they
re using.
Your company came highly
ecommended. My employer has asked
e to put together some information on
hat the set-up entails. I have both
me and space needs.
Any information you could forward
me would be very helpful.
CROSS YOUR FINGERS...
SEND
OH MAN, ENGLISH LIT STARTED FIVE MINUTES AGO.

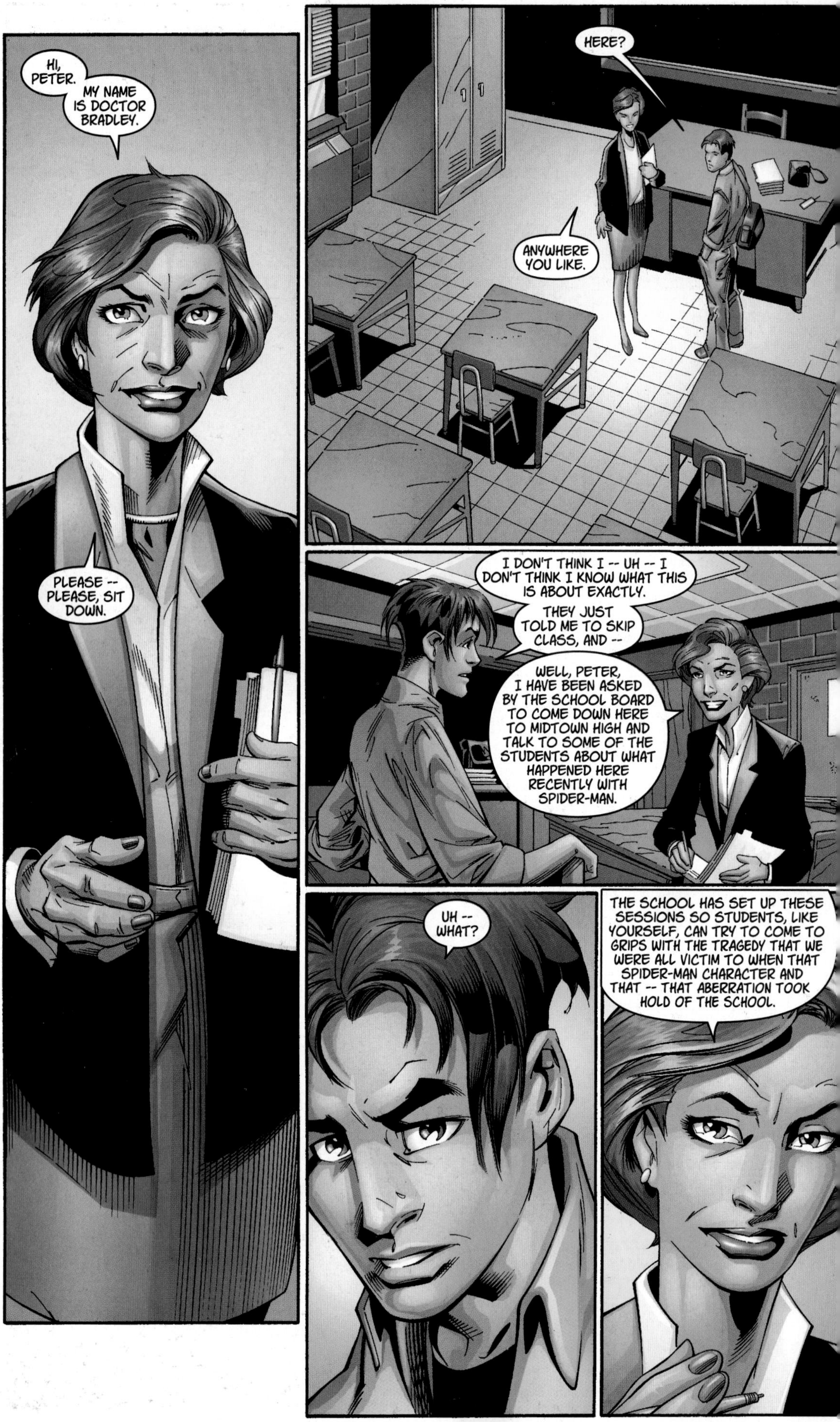
HI, PETER.
MY NAME IS DOCTOR BRADLEY.
PLEASE -- PLEASE, SIT DOWN.
HERE?
ANYWHERE YOU LIKE.
I DON'T THINK I -- UH -- I DON'T THINK I KNOW WHAT THIS IS ABOUT EXACTLY.
THEY JUST TOLD ME TO SKIP CLASS, AND --
WELL, PETER, I HAVE BEEN ASKED BY THE SCHOOL BOARD TO COME DOWN HERE TO MIDTOWN HIGH AND TALK TO SOME OF THE STUDENTS ABOUT WHAT HAPPENED HERE RECENTLY WITH SPIDER-MAN.
UH -- WHAT?
THE SCHOOL HAS SET UP THESE SESSIONS SO STUDENTS, LIKE YOURSELF, CAN TRY TO COME TO GRIPS WITH THE TRAGEDY THAT WE WERE ALL VICTIM TO WHEN THAT SPIDER-MAN CHARACTER AND THAT -- THAT ABERRATION TOOK HOLD OF THE SCHOOL.

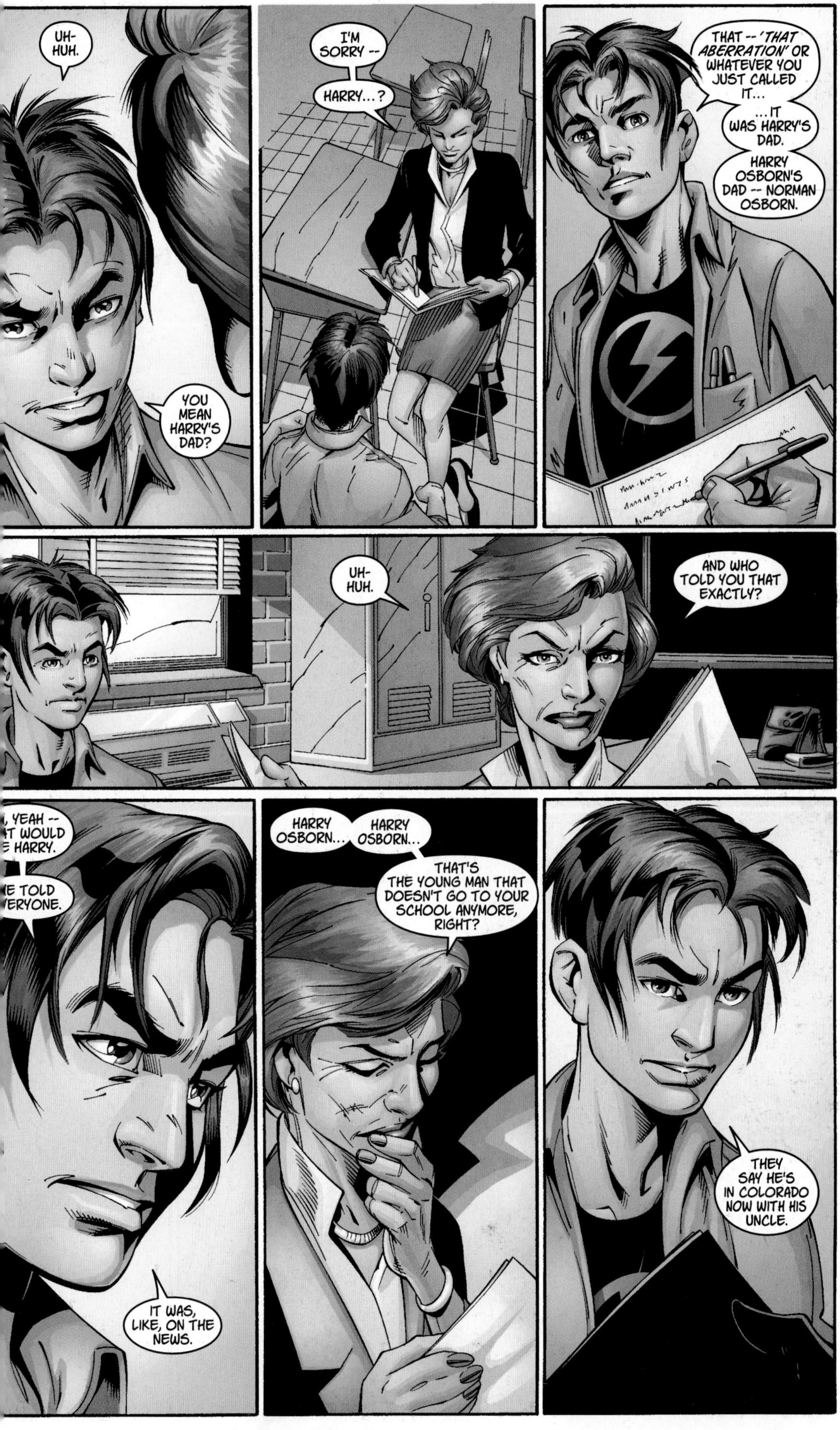
UH-HUH.
YOU MEAN HARRY'S DAD?
I'M SORRY --
HARRY...?
THAT -- 'THAT ABERRATION' OR WHATEVER YOU JUST CALLED IT...
...IT WAS HARRY'S DAD.
HARRY OSBORN'S DAD -- NORMAN OSBORN.
UH-HUH.
AND WHO TOLD YOU THAT EXACTLY?
, YEAH -- AT WOULD E HARRY.
E TOLD VERYONE.
IT WAS, LIKE, ON THE NEWS.
HARRY OSBORN...
HARRY OSBORN...
THAT'S THE YOUNG MAN THAT DOESN'T GO TO YOUR SCHOOL ANYMORE, RIGHT?
THEY SAY HE'S IN COLORADO NOW WITH HIS UNCLE.

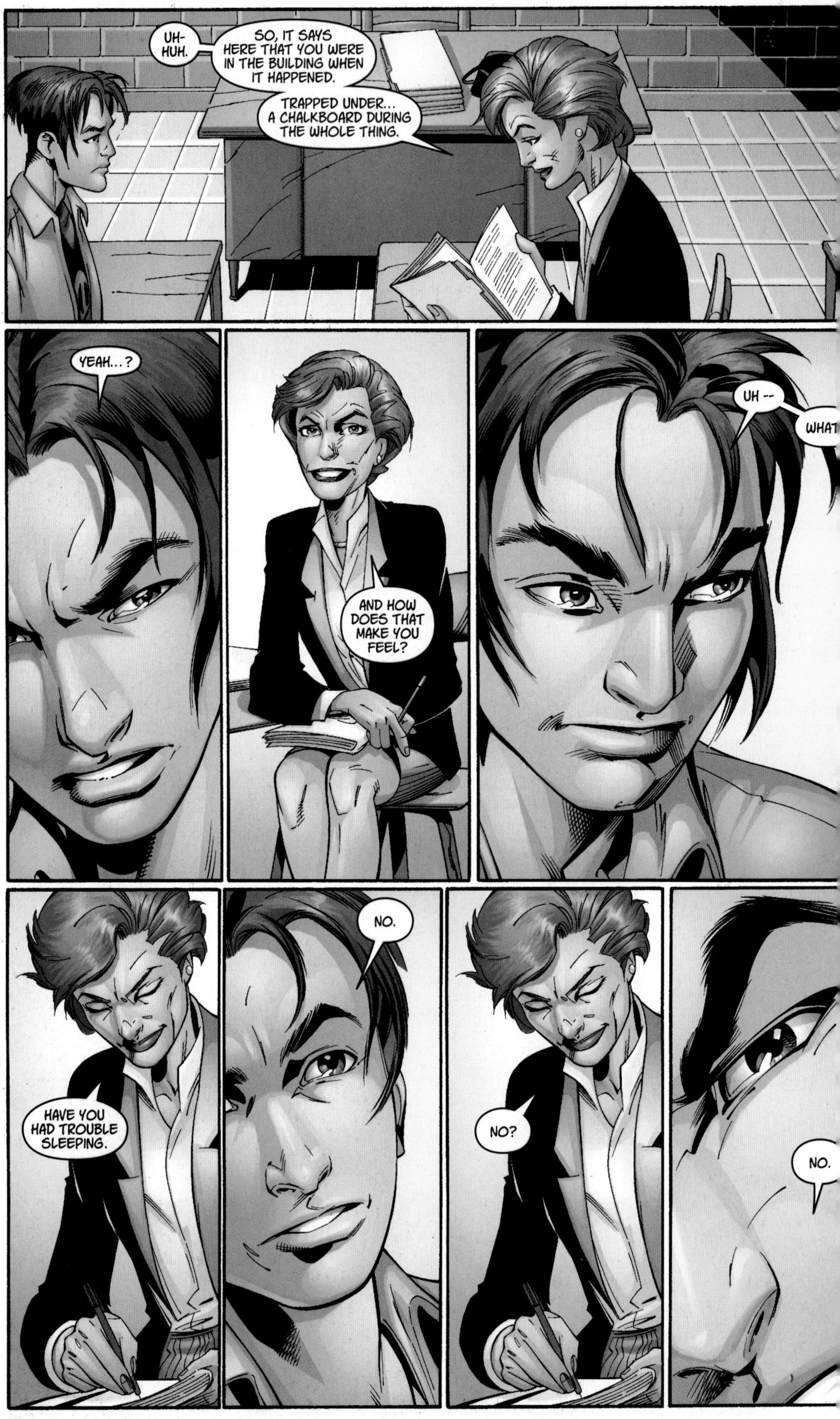
UH-HUH.
SO, IT SAYS HERE THAT YOU WERE IN THE BUILDING WHEN IT HAPPENED.
TRAPPED UNDER... A CHALKBOARD DURING THE WHOLE THING.
YEAH...?
AND HOW DOES THAT MAKE YOU FEEL?
UH --
WHAT
HAVE YOU HAD TROUBLE SLEEPING.
NO.
NO?
NO.

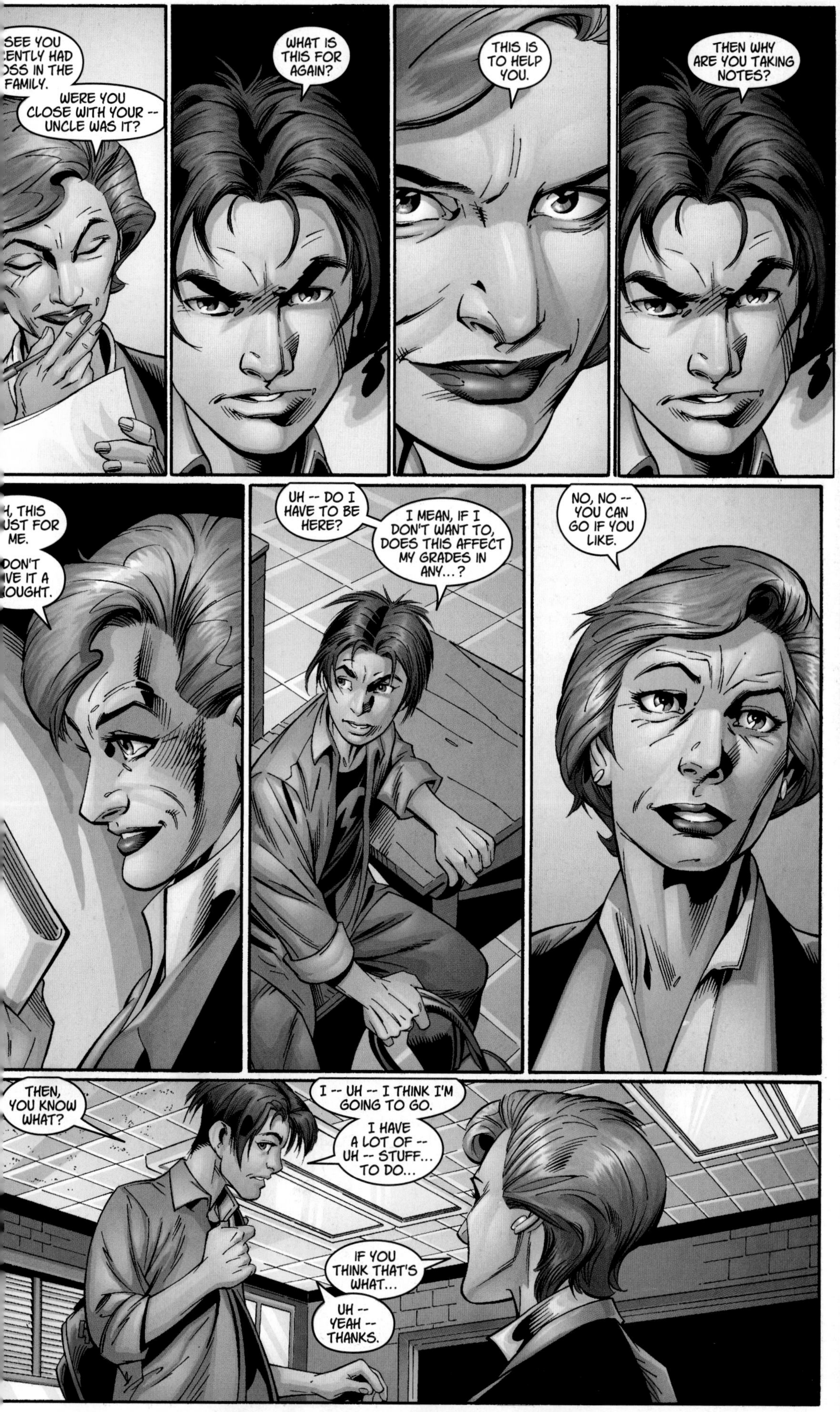

SEE YOU CENTLY HAD OSS IN THE FAMILY.
WERE YOU CLOSE WITH YOUR -- UNCLE WAS IT?
WHAT IS THIS FOR AGAIN?
THIS IS TO HELP YOU.
THEN WHY ARE YOU TAKING NOTES?
H, THIS UST FOR ME.
DON'T VE IT A OUGHT.
UH -- DO I HAVE TO BE HERE?
I MEAN, IF I DON'T WANT TO, DOES THIS AFFECT MY GRADES IN ANY...?
NO, NO -- YOU CAN GO IF YOU LIKE.
THEN, YOU KNOW WHAT?
I -- UH -- I THINK I'M GOING TO GO.
I HAVE A LOT OF -- UH -- STUFF... TO DO...
IF YOU THINK THAT'S WHAT...
UH -- YEAH -- THANKS.

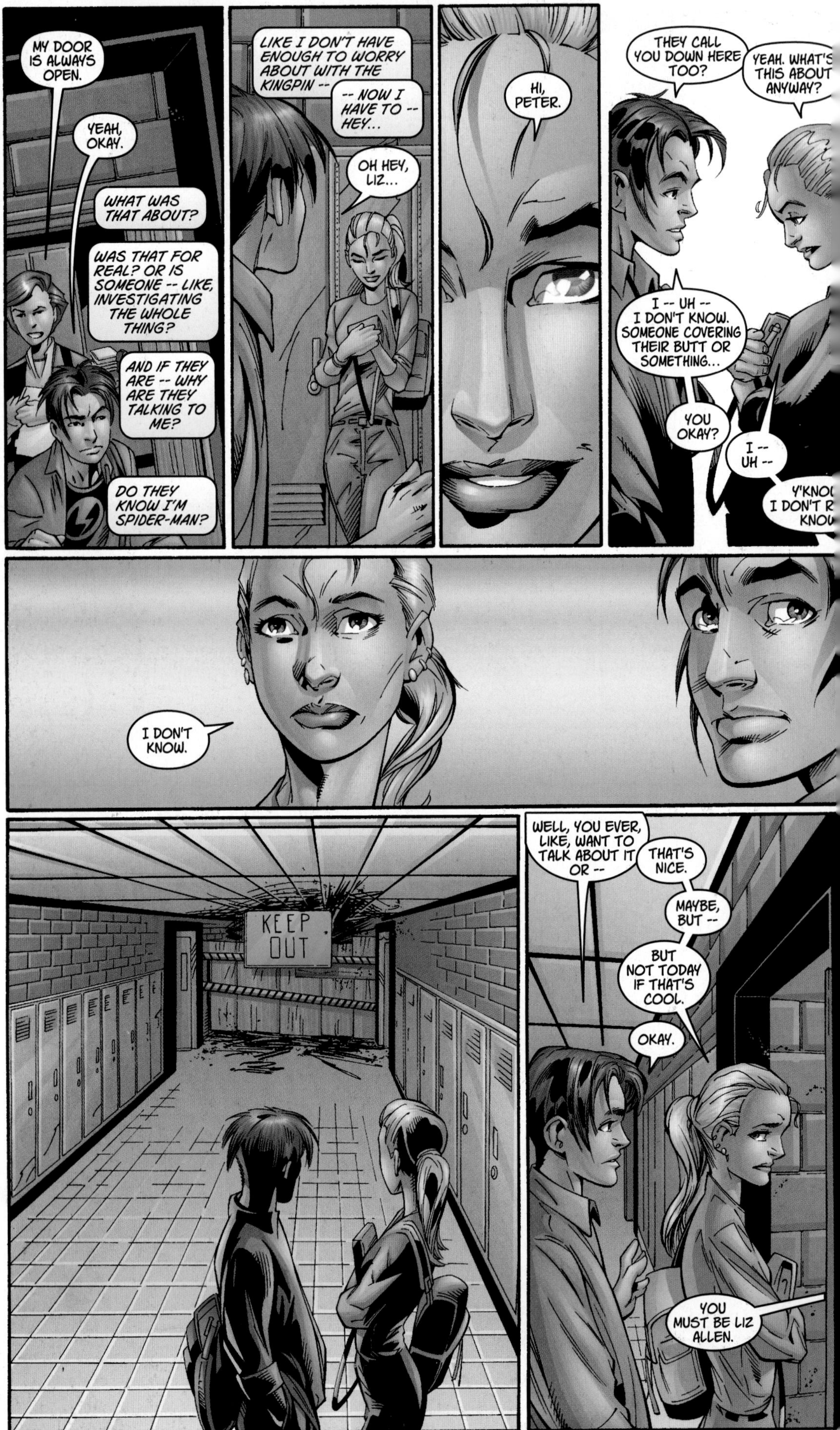
MY DOOR IS ALWAYS OPEN.
YEAH, OKAY.
WHAT WAS THAT ABOUT?
WAS THAT FOR REAL? OR IS SOMEONE -- LIKE, INVESTIGATING THE WHOLE THING?
AND IF THEY ARE -- WHY ARE THEY TALKING TO ME?
DO THEY KNOW I'M SPIDER-MAN?
LIKE I DON'T HAVE ENOUGH TO WORRY ABOUT WITH THE KINGPIN --
-- NOW I HAVE TO -- HEY...
OH HEY, LIZ...
HI, PETER.
THEY CALL YOU DOWN HERE TOO?
YEAH. WHAT'S THIS ABOUT ANYWAY?
I -- UH -- I DON'T KNOW. SOMEONE COVERING THEIR BUTT OR SOMETHING...
YOU OKAY?
I -- UH --
Y'KNO I DON'T R KNOW
I DON'T KNOW.
KEEP OUT
WELL, YOU EVER, LIKE, WANT TO TALK ABOUT IT OR --
THAT'S NICE.
MAYBE, BUT --
BUT NOT TODAY IF THAT'S COOL.
OKAY.
YOU MUST BE LIZ ALLEN.

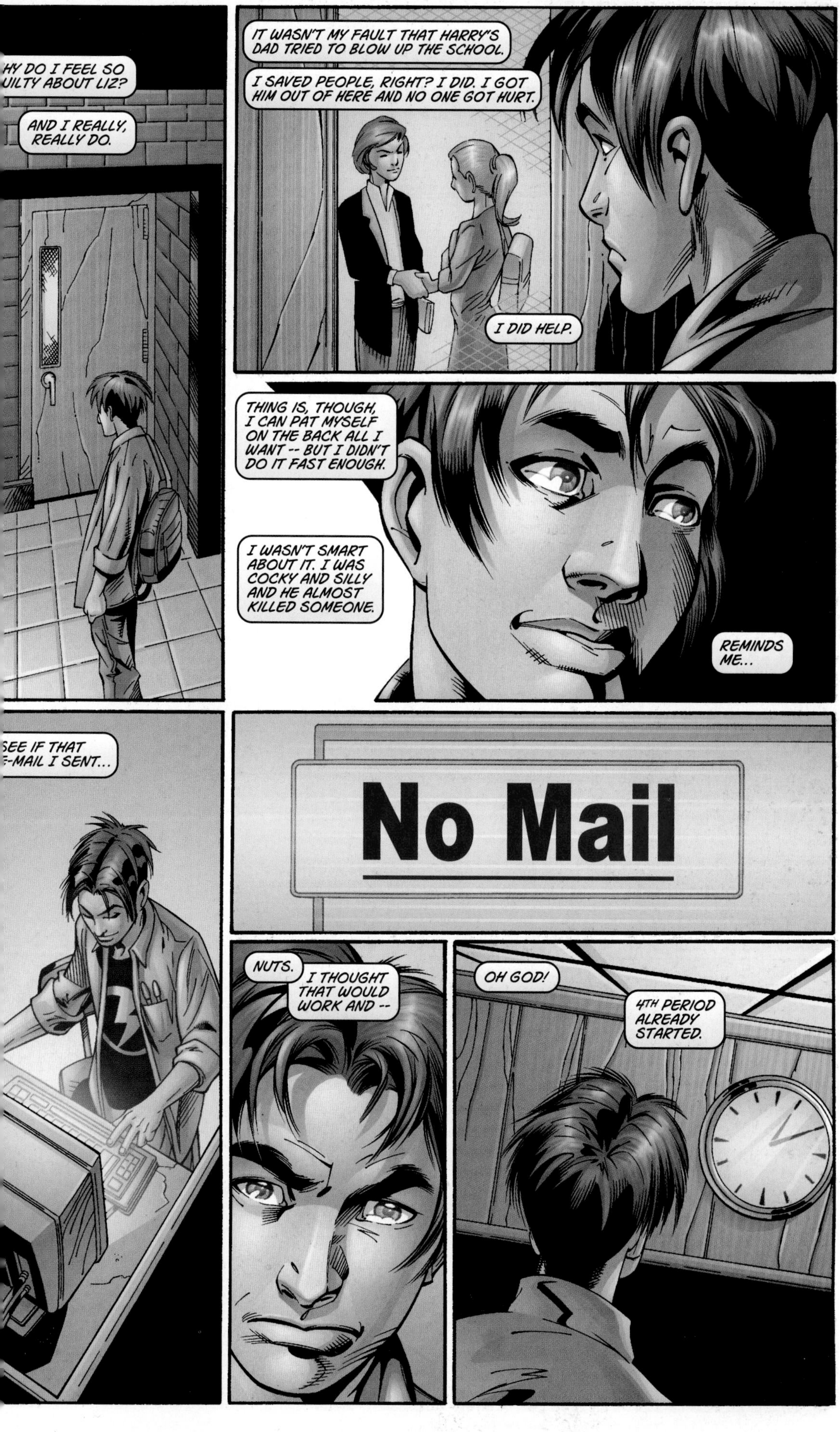
HY DO I FEEL SO
UILTY ABOUT LIZ?
AND I REALLY, REALLY DO.
IT WASN'T MY FAULT THAT HARRY'S DAD TRIED TO BLOW UP THE SCHOOL.
I SAVED PEOPLE, RIGHT? I DID. I GOT HIM OUT OF HERE AND NO ONE GOT HURT.
I DID HELP.
THING IS, THOUGH, I CAN PAT MYSELF ON THE BACK ALL I WANT -- BUT I DIDN'T DO IT FAST ENOUGH.
I WASN'T SMART ABOUT IT. I WAS COCKY AND SILLY AND HE ALMOST KILLED SOMEONE.
REMINDS ME...
SEE IF THAT
-MAIL I SENT...
No Mail
NUTS.
I THOUGHT THAT WOULD WORK AND --
OH GOD!
4TH PERIOD ALREADY STARTED.

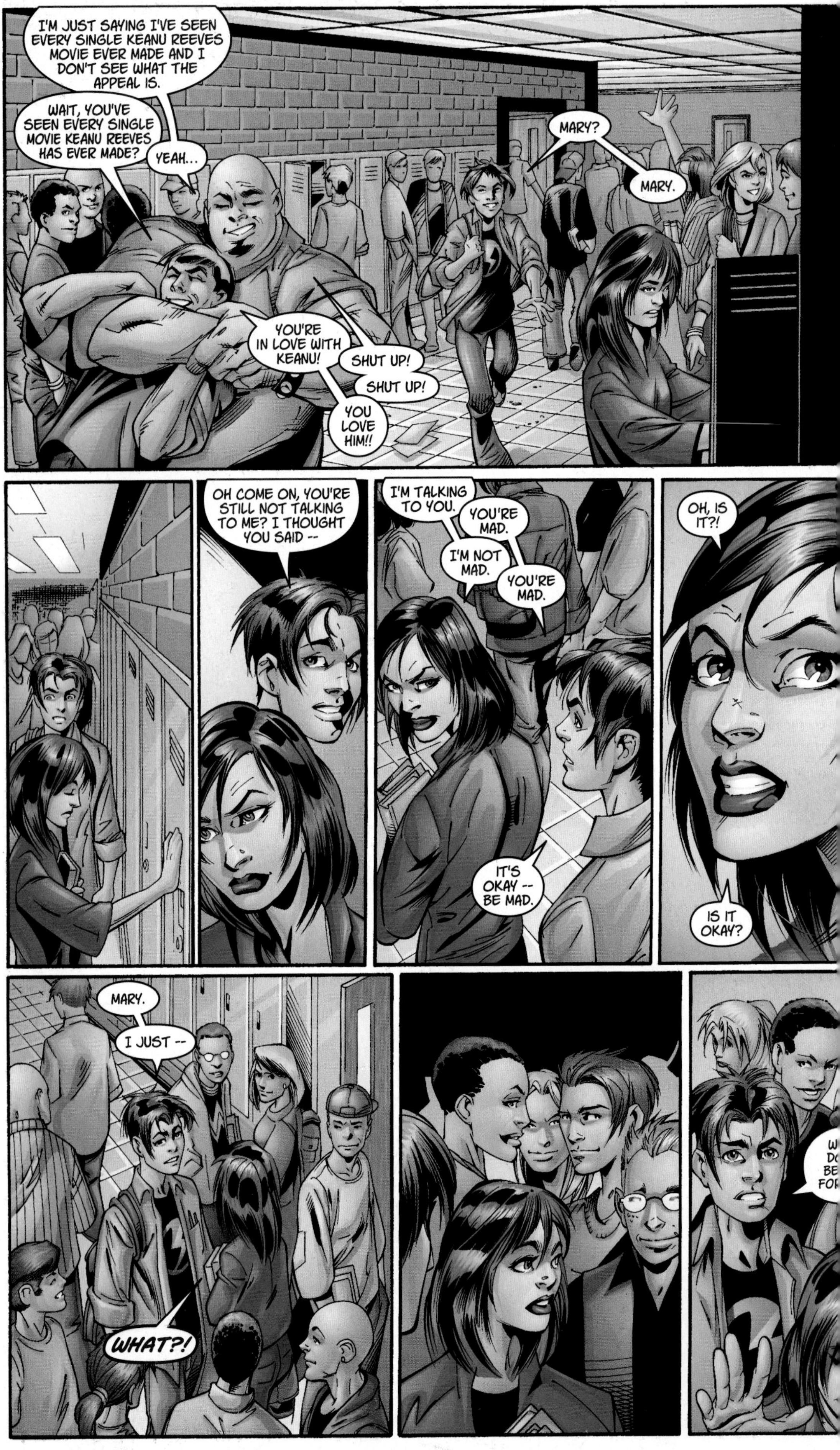
I'M JUST SAYING I'VE SEEN EVERY SINGLE KEANU REEVES MOVIE EVER MADE AND I DON'T SEE WHAT THE APPEAL IS.
WAIT, YOU'VE SEEN EVERY SINGLE MOVIE KEANU REEVES HAS EVER MADE?
YEAH...
YOU'RE IN LOVE WITH KEANU!
SHUT UP!
SHUT UP!
YOU LOVE HIM!!
MARY?
MARY.
OH COME ON, YOU'RE STILL NOT TALKING TO ME? I THOUGHT YOU SAID --
I'M TALKING TO YOU.
YOU'RE MAD.
I'M NOT MAD.
YOU'RE MAD.
IT'S OKAY -- BE MAD.
OH, IS IT?!
IS IT OKAY?
MARY.
I JUST --
WHAT?!

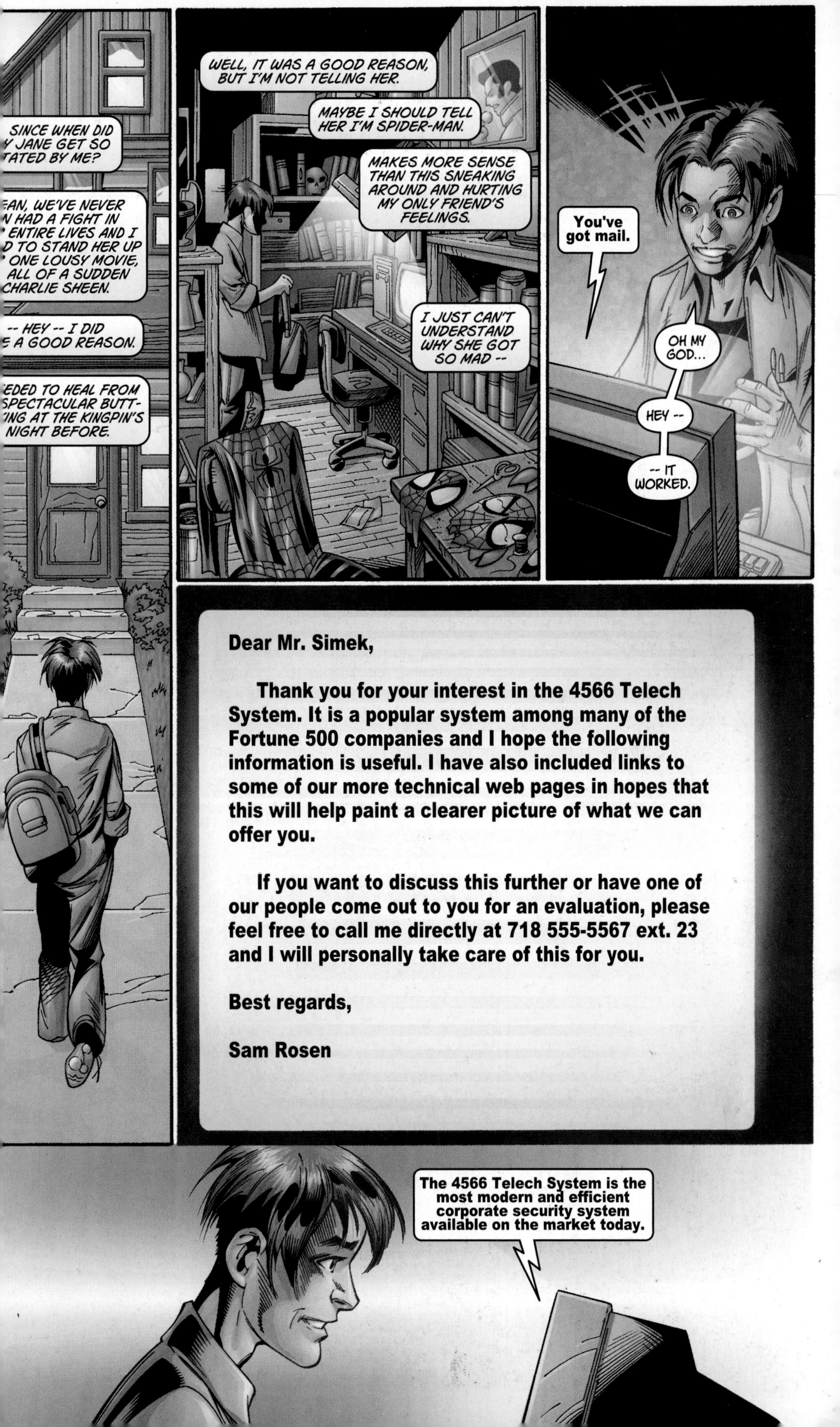
SINCE WHEN DID Y JANE GET SO TATED BY ME?
EAN, WE'VE NEVER N HAD A FIGHT IN ENTIRE LIVES AND I D TO STAND HER UP ONE LOUSY MOVIE, ALL OF A SUDDEN CHARLIE SHEEN.
-- HEY -- I DID E A GOOD REASON.
EDED TO HEAL FROM SPECTACULAR BUTT- ING AT THE KINGPIN'S NIGHT BEFORE.
WELL, IT WAS A GOOD REASON, BUT I'M NOT TELLING HER.
MAYBE I SHOULD TELL HER I'M SPIDER-MAN.
MAKES MORE SENSE THAN THIS SNEAKING AROUND AND HURTING MY ONLY FRIEND'S FEELINGS.
I JUST CAN'T UNDERSTAND WHY SHE GOT SO MAD --
You've got mail.
OH MY GOD...
HEY --
-- IT WORKED.
Dear Mr. Simek,
Thank you for your interest in the 4566 Telech System. It is a popular system among many of the Fortune 500 companies and I hope the following information is useful. I have also included links to some of our more technical web pages in hopes that this will help paint a clearer picture of what we can offer you.
If you want to discuss this further or have one of our people come out to you for an evaluation, please feel free to call me directly at 718 555-5567 ext. 23 and I will personally take care of this for you.
Best regards,
Sam Rosen
The 4566 Telech System is the most modern and efficient corporate security system available on the market today.

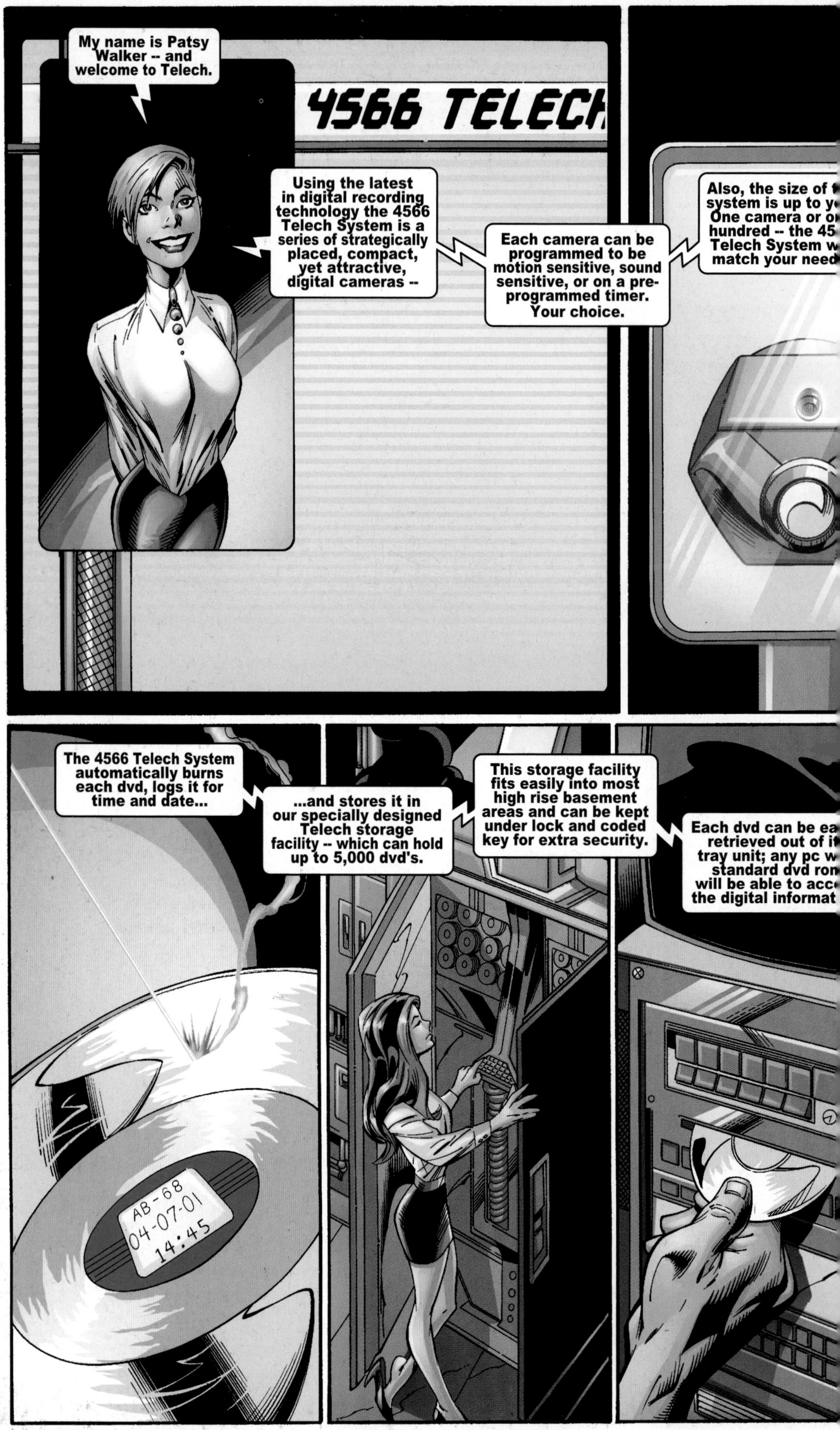
My name is Patsy Walker -- and welcome to Telech.
4566 TELECH
Using the latest in digital recording technology the 4566 Telech System is a series of strategically placed, compact, yet attractive, digital cameras --
Each camera can be programmed to be motion sensitive, sound sensitive, or on a pre-programmed timer. Your choice.
Also, the size of system is up to y One camera or o hundred -- the 45 Telech System w match your need
The 4566 Telech System automatically burns each dvd, logs it for time and date...
AB-68 04-07-01 14:45
...and stores it in our specially designed Telech storage facility -- which can hold up to 5,000 dvd's.
This storage facility fits easily into most high rise basement areas and can be kept under lock and coded key for extra security.
Each dvd can be ea retrieved out of i tray unit; any pc w standard dvd ro will be able to acc the digital informat

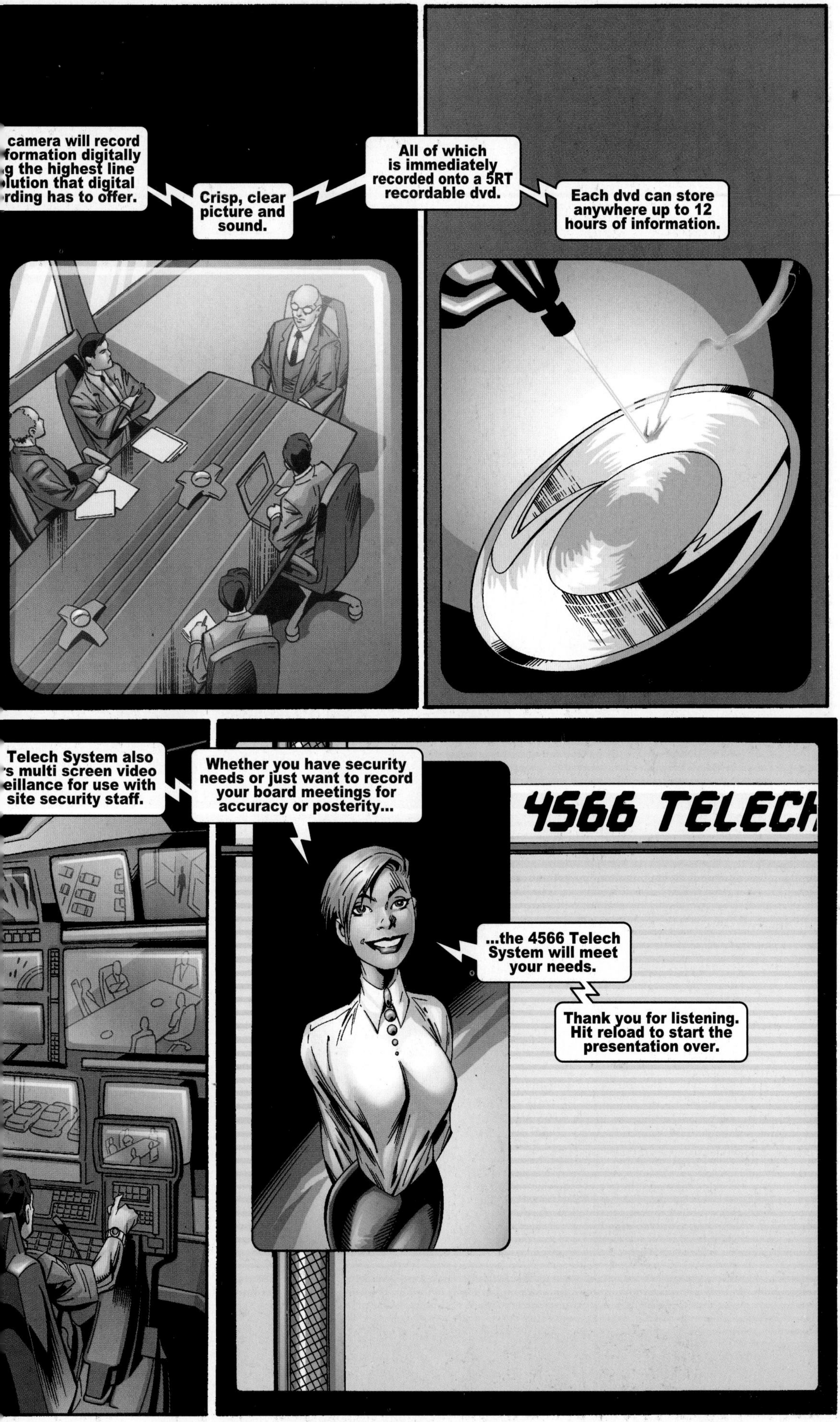
camera will record
formation digitally
g the highest line
lution that digital
rding has to offer.
Crisp, clear picture and sound.
All of which is immediately recorded onto a 5RT recordable dvd.
Each dvd can store anywhere up to 12 hours of information.
Telech System also
's multi screen video
eillance for use with
site security staff.
Whether you have security needs or just want to record your board meetings for accuracy or posterity...
4566 TELECH
...the 4566 Telech System will meet your needs.
Thank you for listening. Hit reload to start the presentation over.

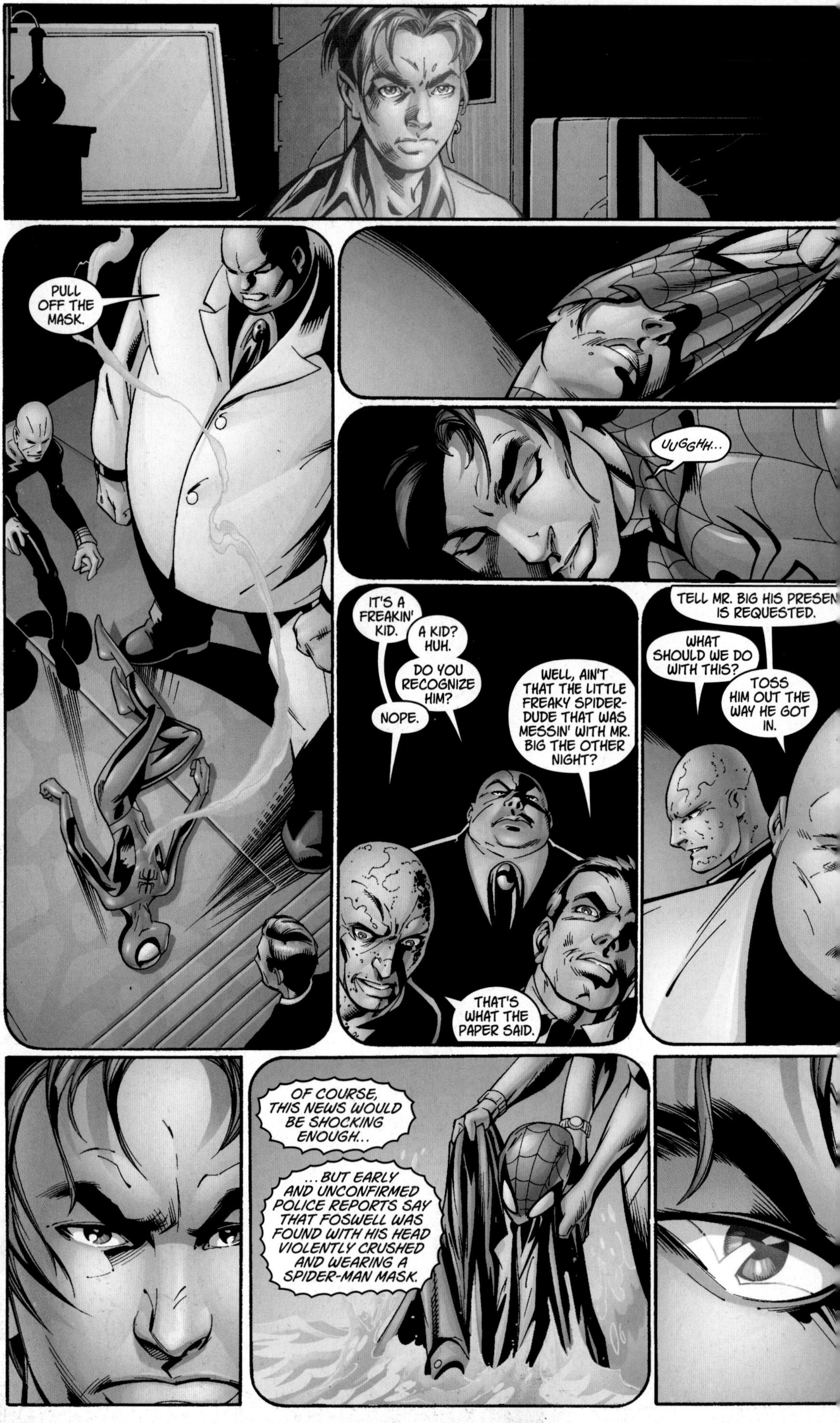
PULL OFF THE MASK.
UUGGHH...
IT'S A FREAKIN' KID.
A KID? HUH.
DO YOU RECOGNIZE HIM?
NOPE.
WELL, AIN'T THAT THE LITTLE FREAKY SPIDER-DUDE THAT WAS MESSIN' WITH MR. BIG THE OTHER NIGHT?
THAT'S WHAT THE PAPER SAID.
TELL MR. BIG HIS PRESEN
IS REQUESTED.
WHAT SHOULD WE DO WITH THIS?
TOSS HIM OUT THE WAY HE GOT IN.
OF COURSE, THIS NEWS WOULD BE SHOCKING ENOUGH...
...BUT EARLY AND UNCONFIRMED POLICE REPORTS SAY THAT FOSWELL WAS FOUND WITH HIS HEAD VIOLENTLY CRUSHED AND WEARING A SPIDER-MAN MASK.

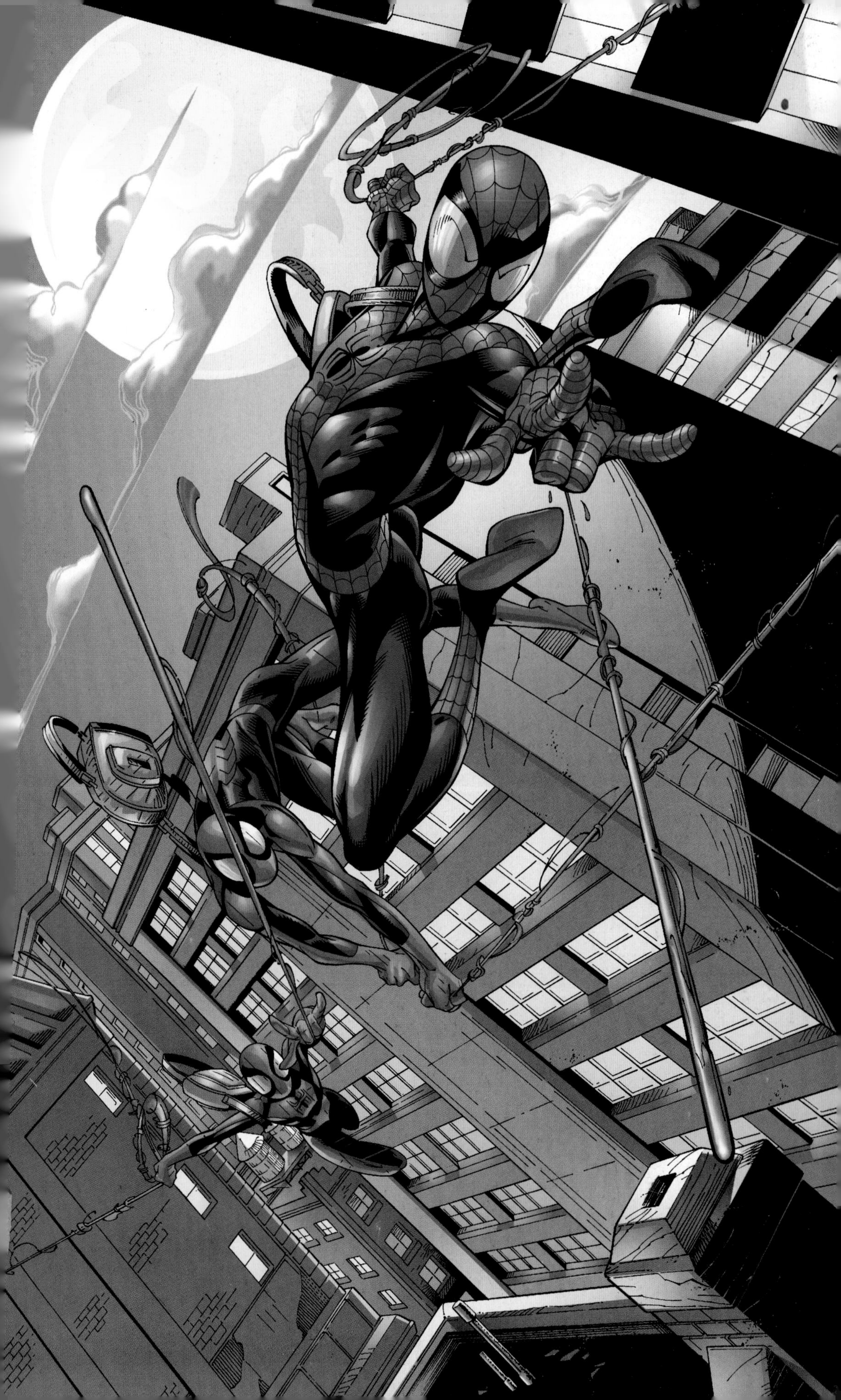

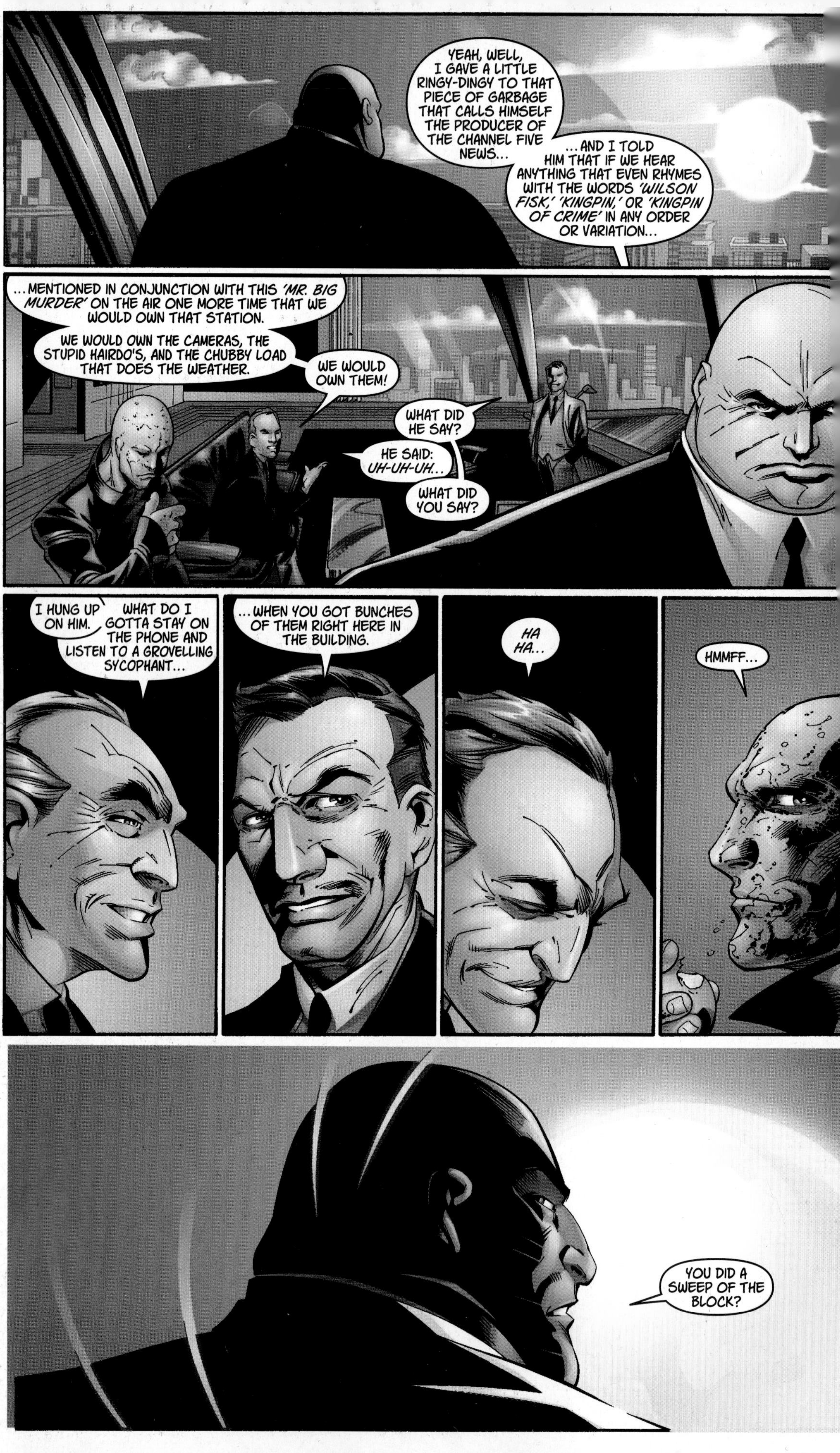
YEAH, WELL, I GAVE A LITTLE RINGY-DINGY TO THAT PIECE OF GARBAGE THAT CALLS HIMSELF THE PRODUCER OF THE CHANNEL FIVE NEWS...
...AND I TOLD HIM THAT IF WE HEAR ANYTHING THAT EVEN RHYMES WITH THE WORDS 'WILSON FISK,' 'KINGPIN,' OR 'KINGPIN OF CRIME' IN ANY ORDER OR VARIATION...
...MENTIONED IN CONJUNCTION WITH THIS 'MR. BIG MURDER' ON THE AIR ONE MORE TIME THAT WE WOULD OWN THAT STATION.
WE WOULD OWN THE CAMERAS, THE STUPID HAIRDO'S, AND THE CHUBBY LOAD THAT DOES THE WEATHER.
WE WOULD OWN THEM!
WHAT DID HE SAY?
HE SAID: UH-UH-UH...
WHAT DID YOU SAY?
I HUNG UP ON HIM.
WHAT DO I GOTTA STAY ON THE PHONE AND LISTEN TO A GROVELLING SYCOPHANT...
...WHEN YOU GOT BUNCHES OF THEM RIGHT HERE IN THE BUILDING.
HA HA...
HMMFF...
YOU DID A SWEEP OF THE BLOCK?

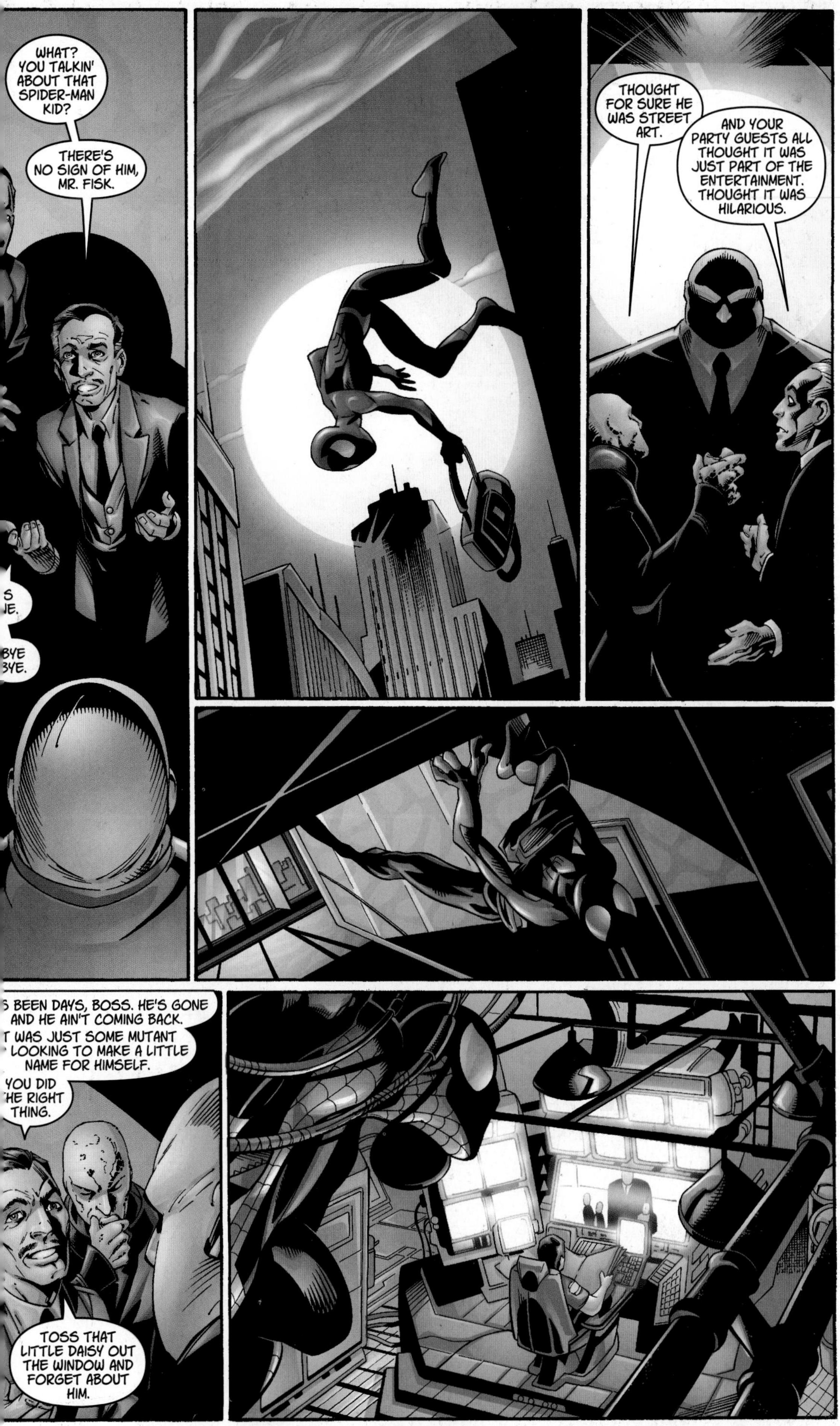
WHAT? YOU TALKIN' ABOUT THAT SPIDER-MAN KID?
THERE'S NO SIGN OF HIM, MR. FISK.
S
NE.
BYE
BYE.
THOUGHT FOR SURE HE WAS STREET ART.
AND YOUR PARTY GUESTS ALL THOUGHT IT WAS JUST PART OF THE ENTERTAINMENT. THOUGHT IT WAS HILARIOUS.
S BEEN DAYS, BOSS. HE'S GONE AND HE AIN'T COMING BACK.
T WAS JUST SOME MUTANT LOOKING TO MAKE A LITTLE NAME FOR HIMSELF.
YOU DID HE RIGHT THING.
TOSS THAT LITTLE DAISY OUT THE WINDOW AND FORGET ABOUT HIM.

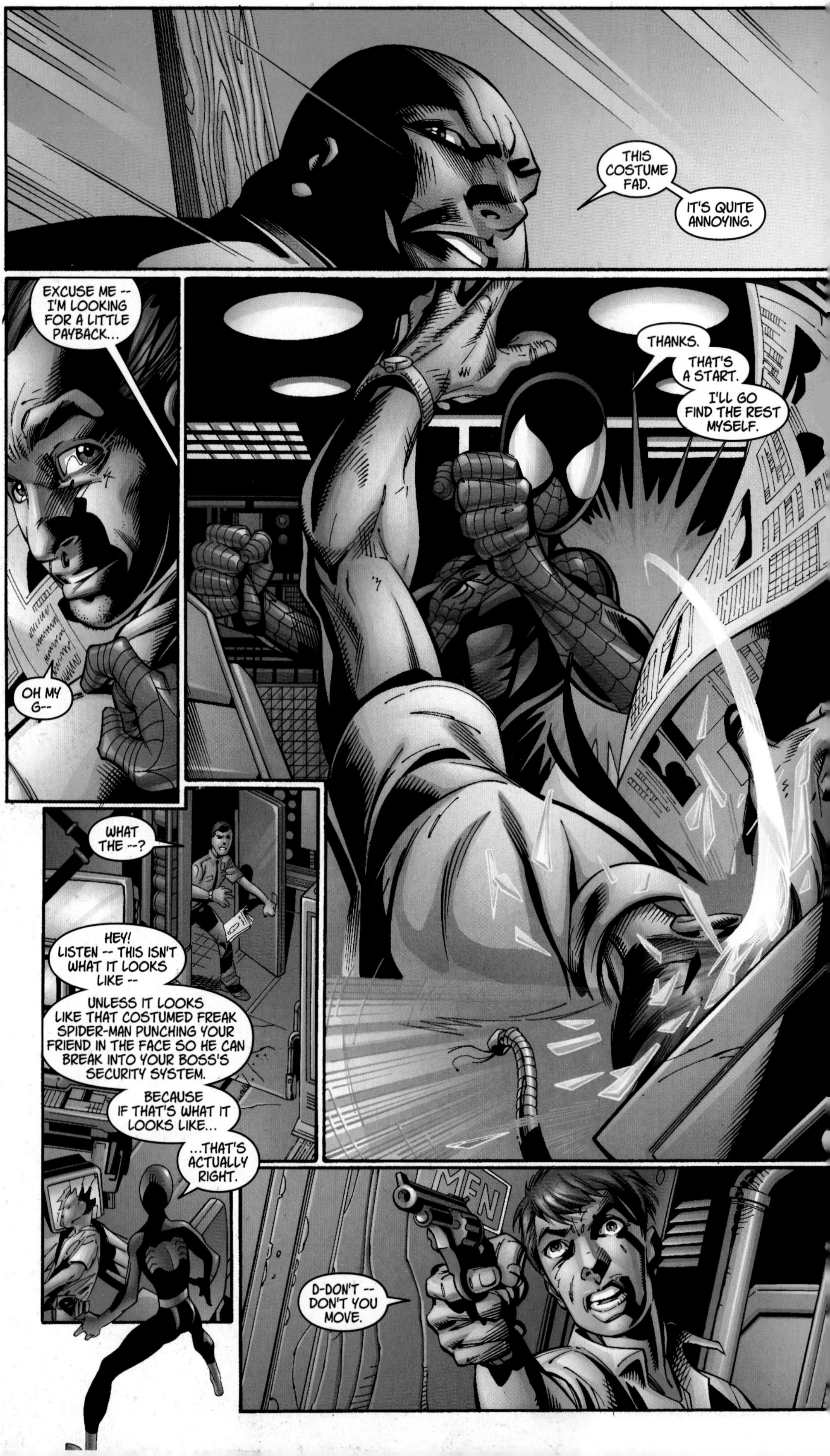
THIS COSTUME FAD.
IT'S QUITE ANNOYING.
EXCUSE ME -- I'M LOOKING FOR A LITTLE PAYBACK...
OH MY G--
THANKS.
THAT'S A START.
I'LL GO FIND THE REST MYSELF.
WHAT THE --?
HEY! LISTEN -- THIS ISN'T WHAT IT LOOKS LIKE --
UNLESS IT LOOKS LIKE THAT COSTUMED FREAK SPIDER-MAN PUNCHING YOUR FRIEND IN THE FACE SO HE CAN BREAK INTO YOUR BOSS'S SECURITY SYSTEM.
BECAUSE IF THAT'S WHAT IT LOOKS LIKE...
...THAT'S ACTUALLY RIGHT.
MEN
D-DON'T -- DON'T YOU MOVE.

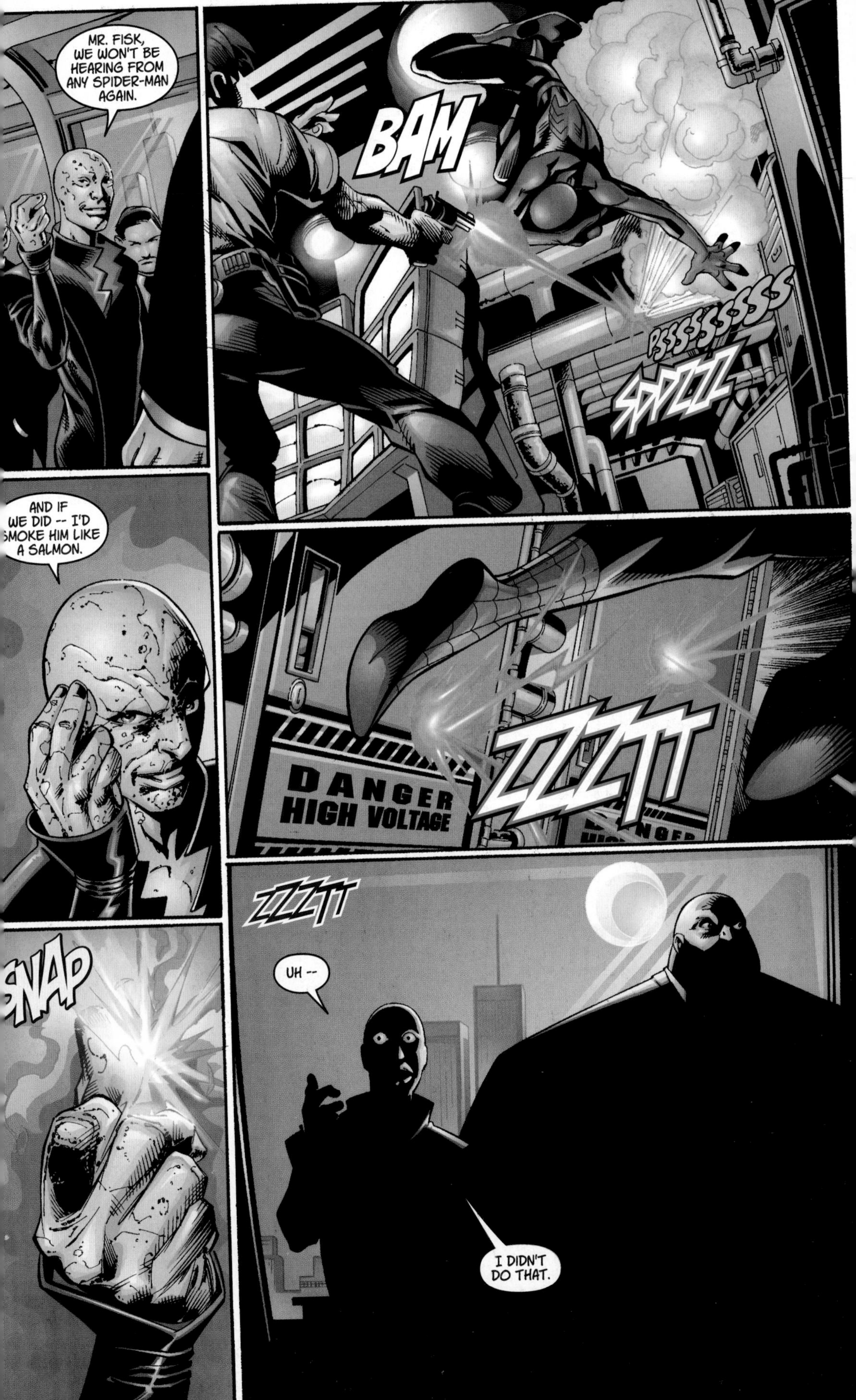
MR. FISK, WE WON'T BE HEARING FROM ANY SPIDER-MAN AGAIN.
BAM
PSSS-SSSSSSS
SPPZZZ
AND IF WE DID -- I'D SMOKE HIM LIKE A SALMON.
DANGER
HIGH VOLTAGE
ZZZTT
SNAP
ZZZTT
UH --
I DIDN'T DO THAT.

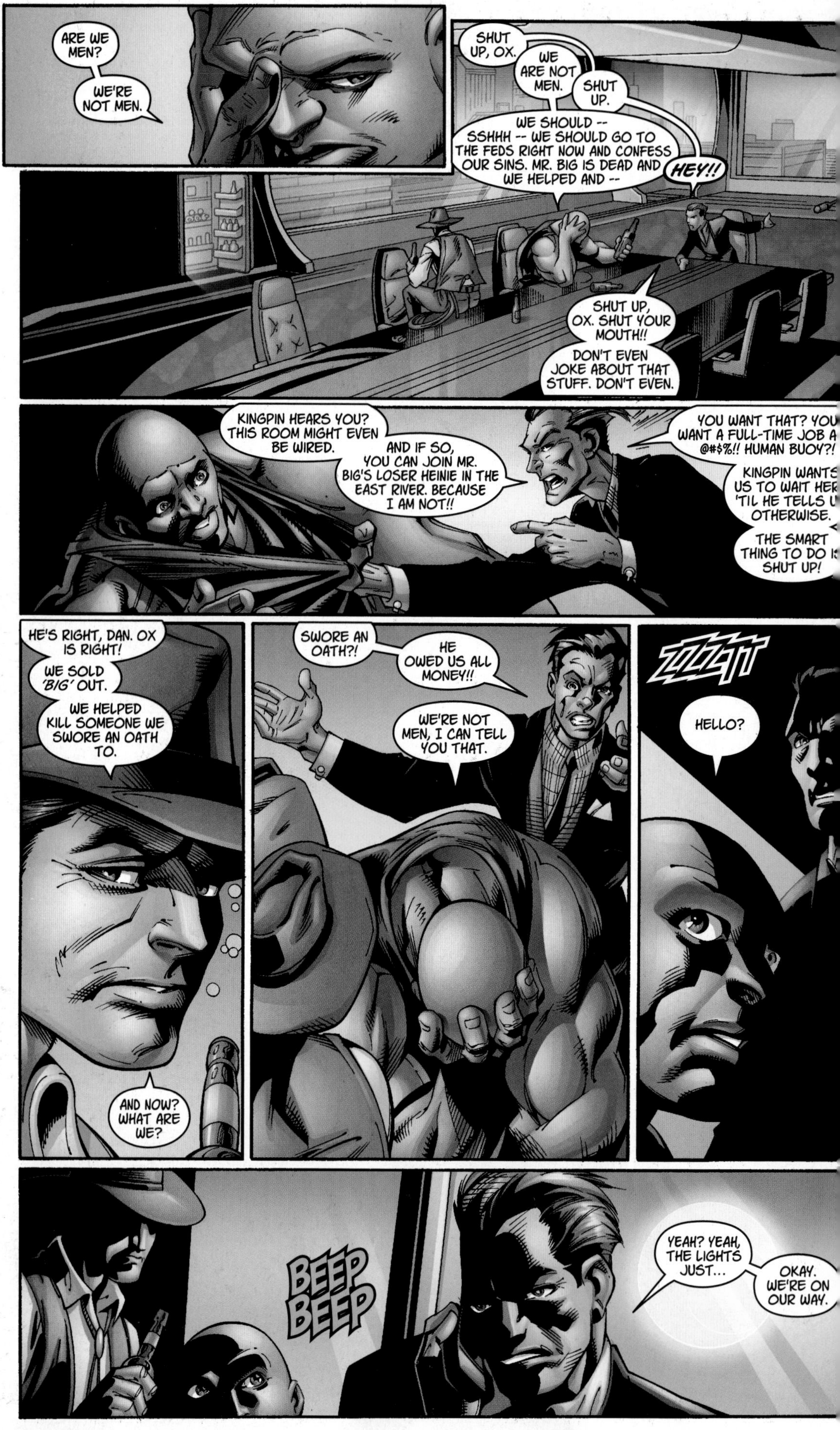
ARE WE MEN?
WE'RE NOT MEN.
SHUT UP, OX.
WE ARE NOT MEN.
SHUT UP.
WE SHOULD -- SSHHH -- WE SHOULD GO TO THE FEDS RIGHT NOW AND CONFESS OUR SINS. MR. BIG IS DEAD AND WE HELPED AND --
HEY!!
SHUT UP, OX. SHUT YOUR MOUTH!!
DON'T EVEN JOKE ABOUT THAT STUFF. DON'T EVEN.
KINGPIN HEARS YOU? THIS ROOM MIGHT EVEN BE WIRED.
AND IF SO, YOU CAN JOIN MR. BIG'S LOSER HEINIE IN THE EAST RIVER. BECAUSE I AM NOT!!
YOU WANT THAT? YOU WANT A FULL-TIME JOB A @#$%!! HUMAN BUOY?!
KINGPIN WANTS US TO WAIT HER 'TIL HE TELLS U OTHERWISE.
THE SMART THING TO DO IS SHUT UP!
HE'S RIGHT, DAN. OX IS RIGHT!
WE SOLD 'BIG' OUT.
WE HELPED KILL SOMEONE WE SWORE AN OATH TO.
AND NOW? WHAT ARE WE?
SWORE AN OATH?!
HE OWED US ALL MONEY!!
WE'RE NOT MEN, I CAN TELL YOU THAT.
HELLO?
BEEP BEEP
YEAH? YEAH, THE LIGHTS JUST...
OKAY. WE'RE ON OUR WAY.

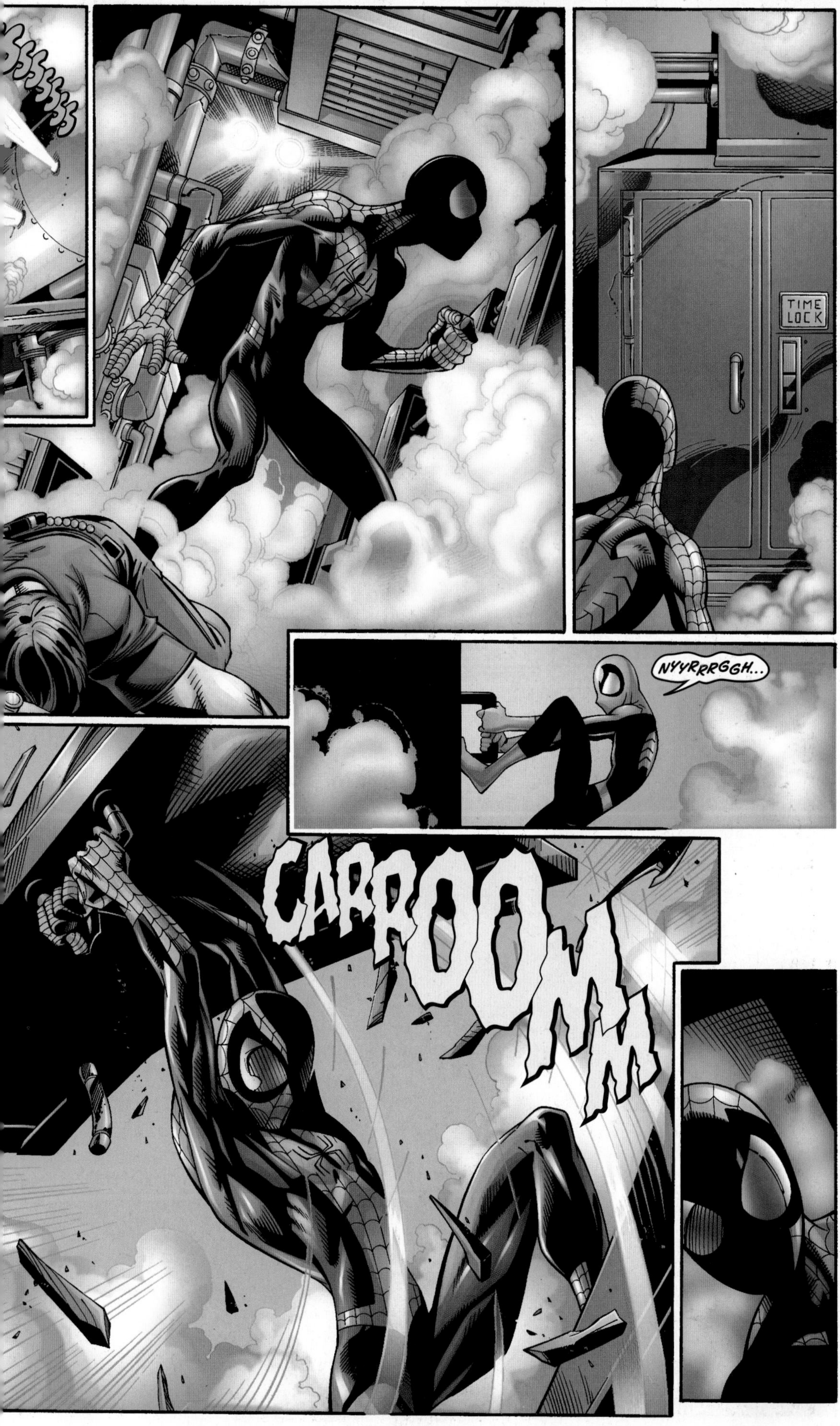
SSSSSSS
TIME LOCK
NYYRRRGGH...
CARROOM

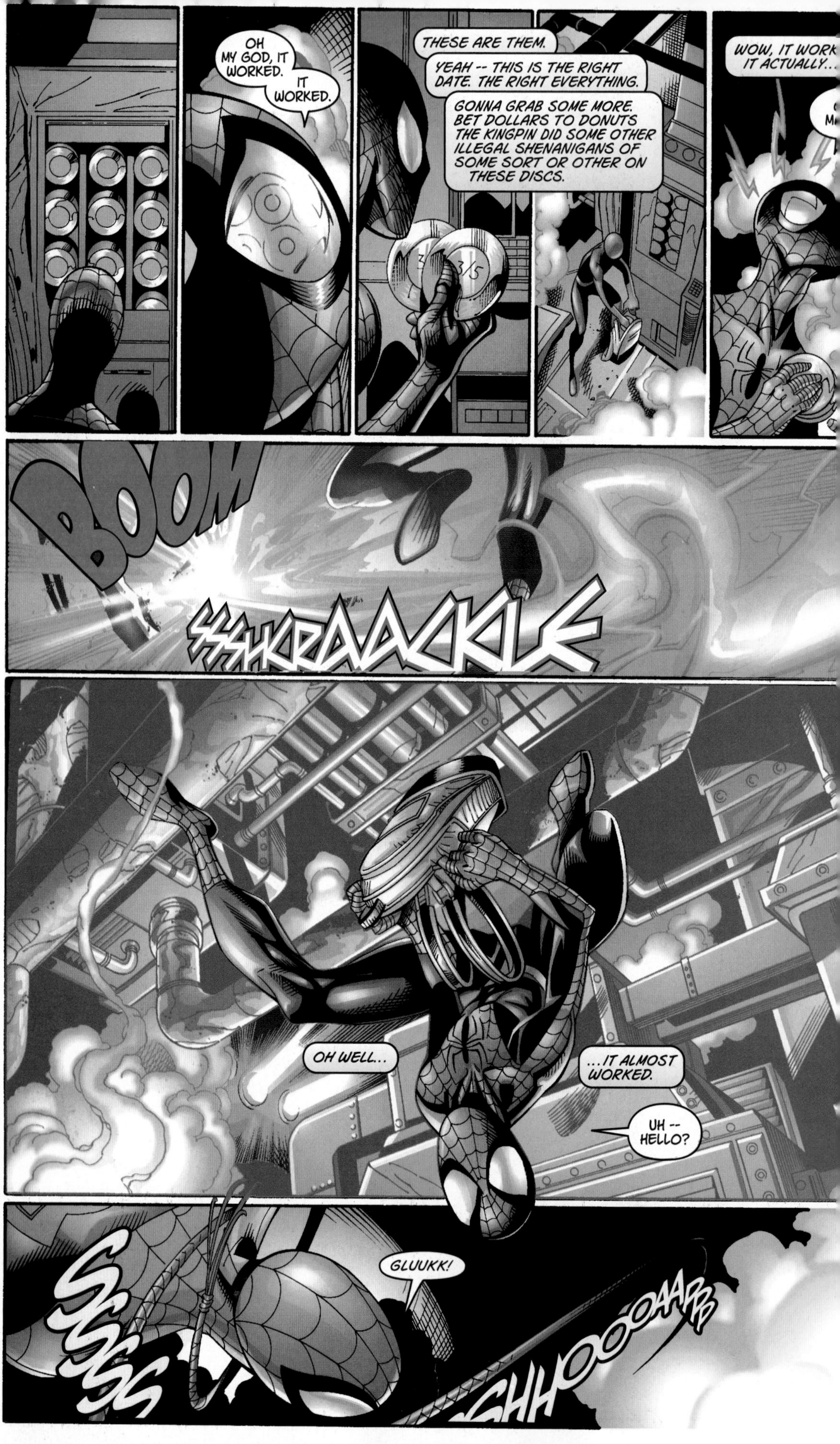
OH MY GOD, IT WORKED.
IT WORKED.
THESE ARE THEM.
YEAH -- THIS IS THE RIGHT DATE. THE RIGHT EVERYTHING.
GONNA GRAB SOME MORE. BET DOLLARS TO DONUTS THE KINGPIN DID SOME OTHER ILLEGAL SHENANIGANS OF SOME SORT OR OTHER ON THESE DISCS.
WOW, IT WORK
IT ACTUALLY...
BOOM
OH WELL...
...IT ALMOST WORKED.
UH -- HELLO?
GLUUKK!

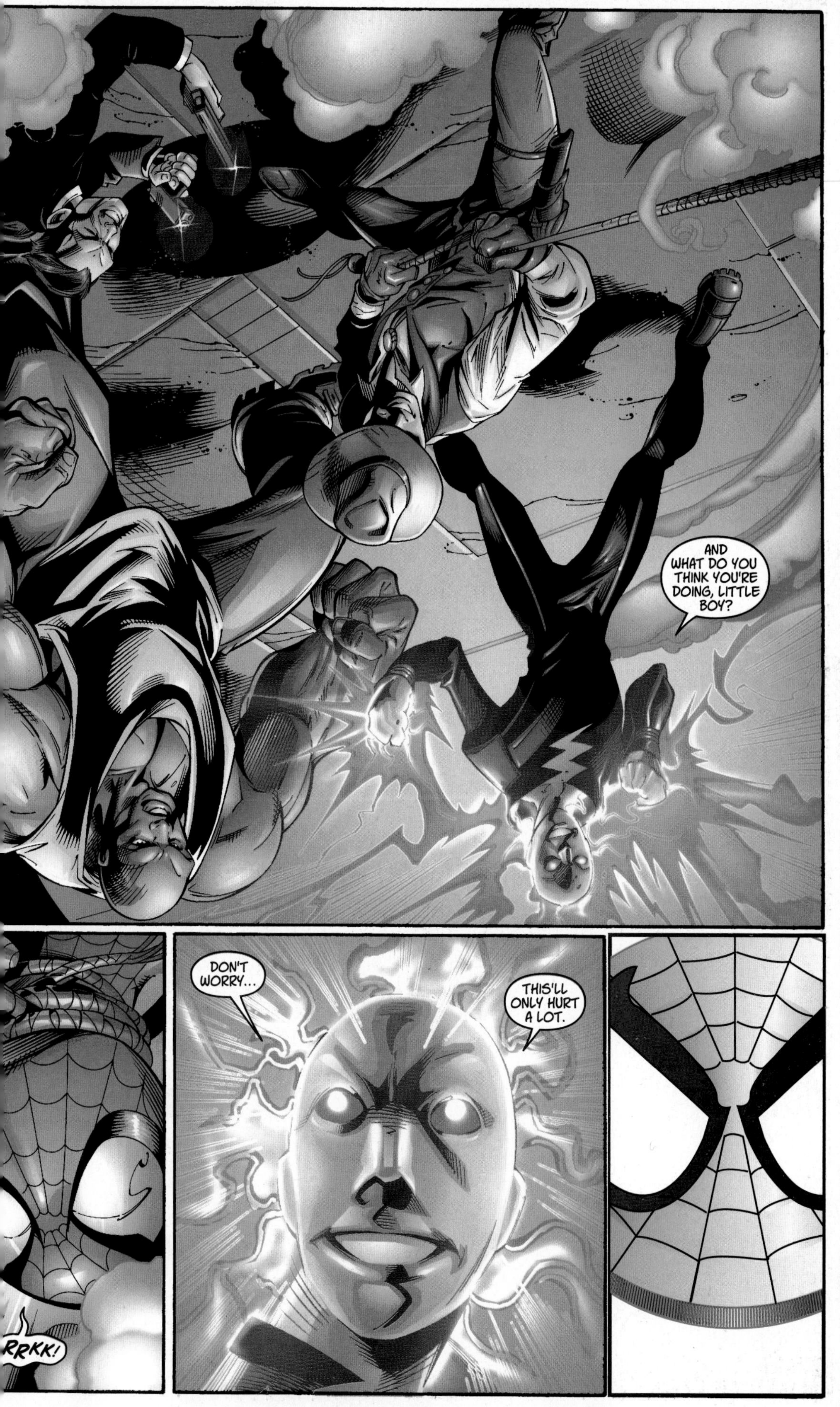
AND WHAT DO YOU THINK YOU'RE DOING, LITTLE BOY?
RRKK!
DON'T WORRY...
THIS'LL ONLY HURT A LOT.

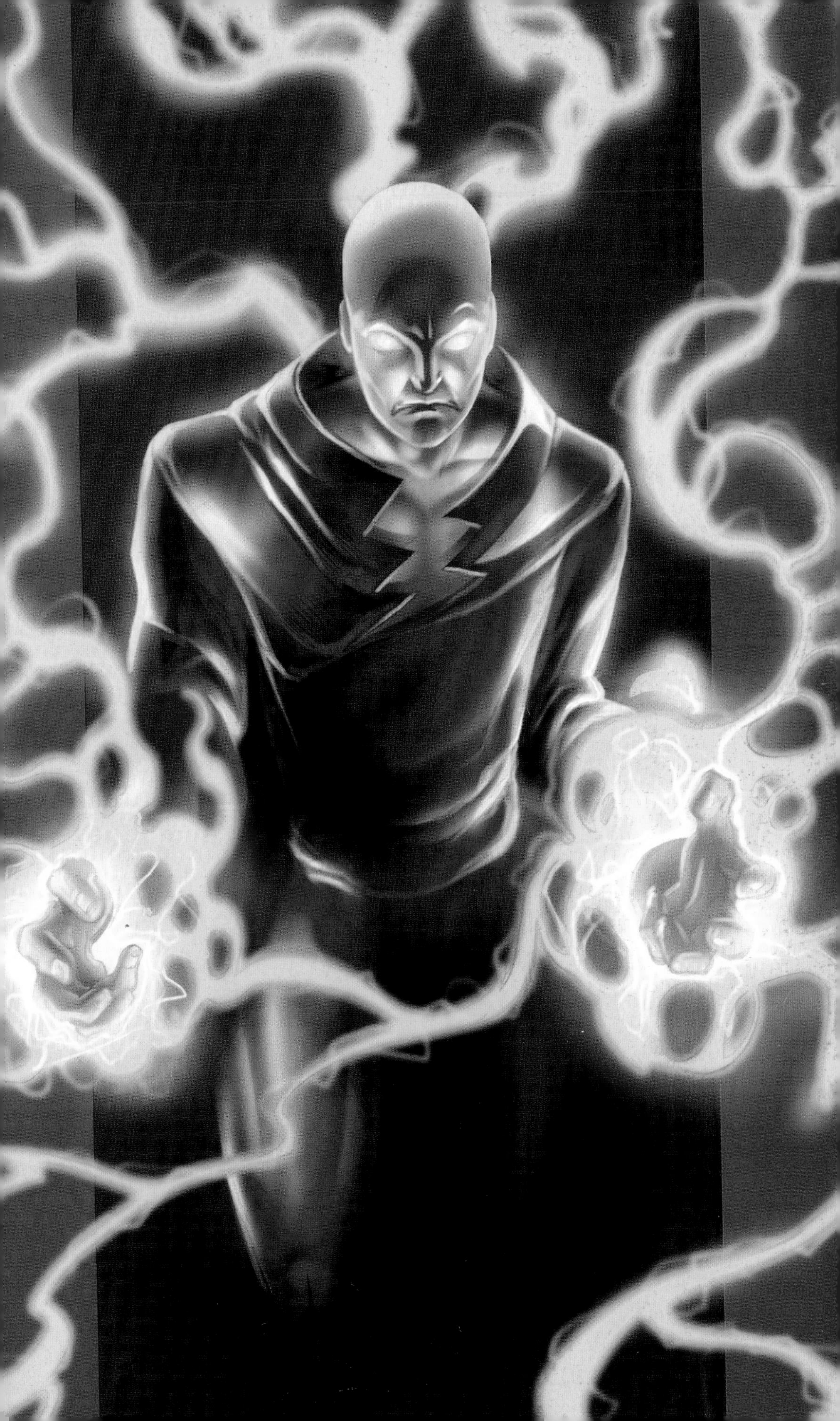

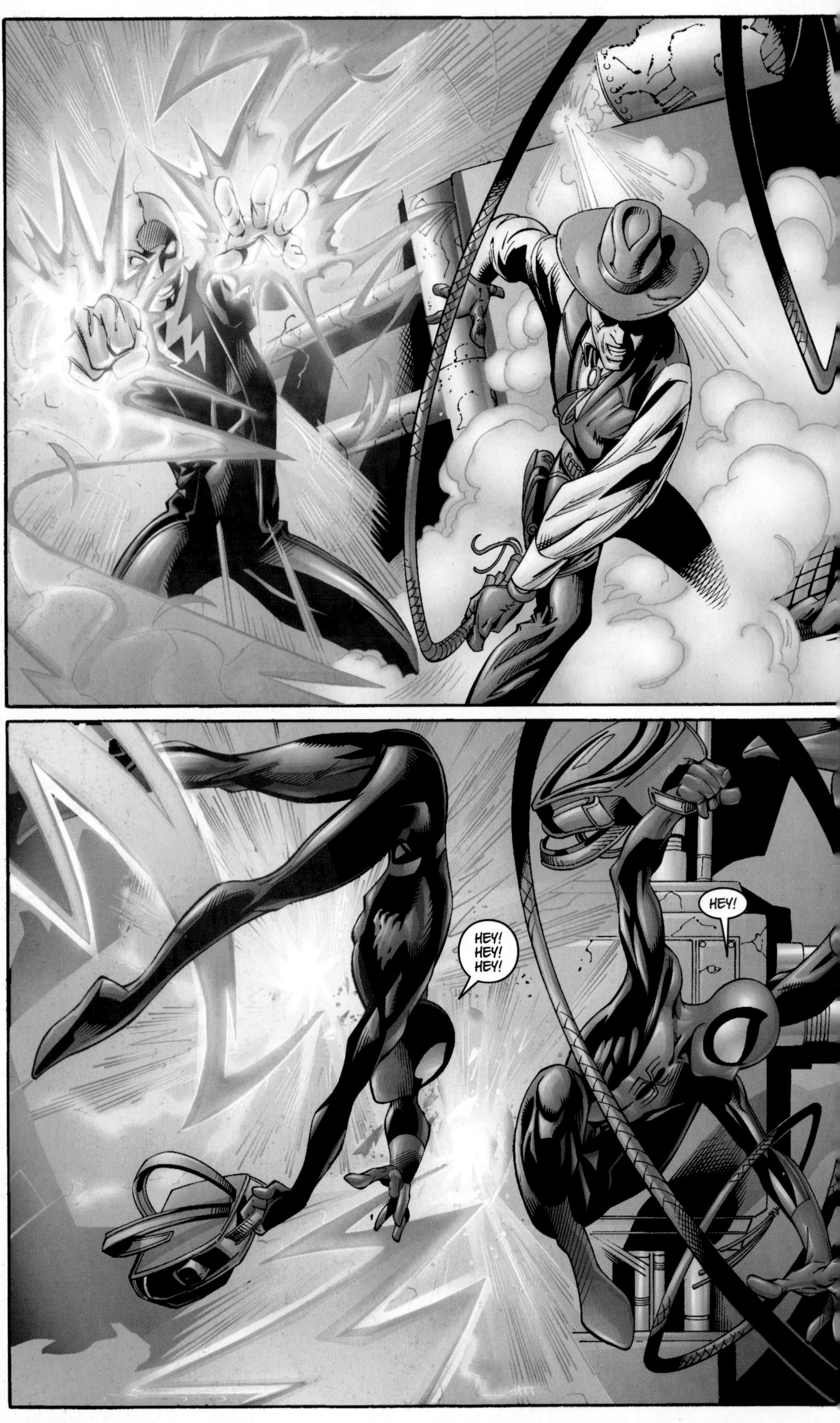
HEY! HEY! HEY!
HEY!

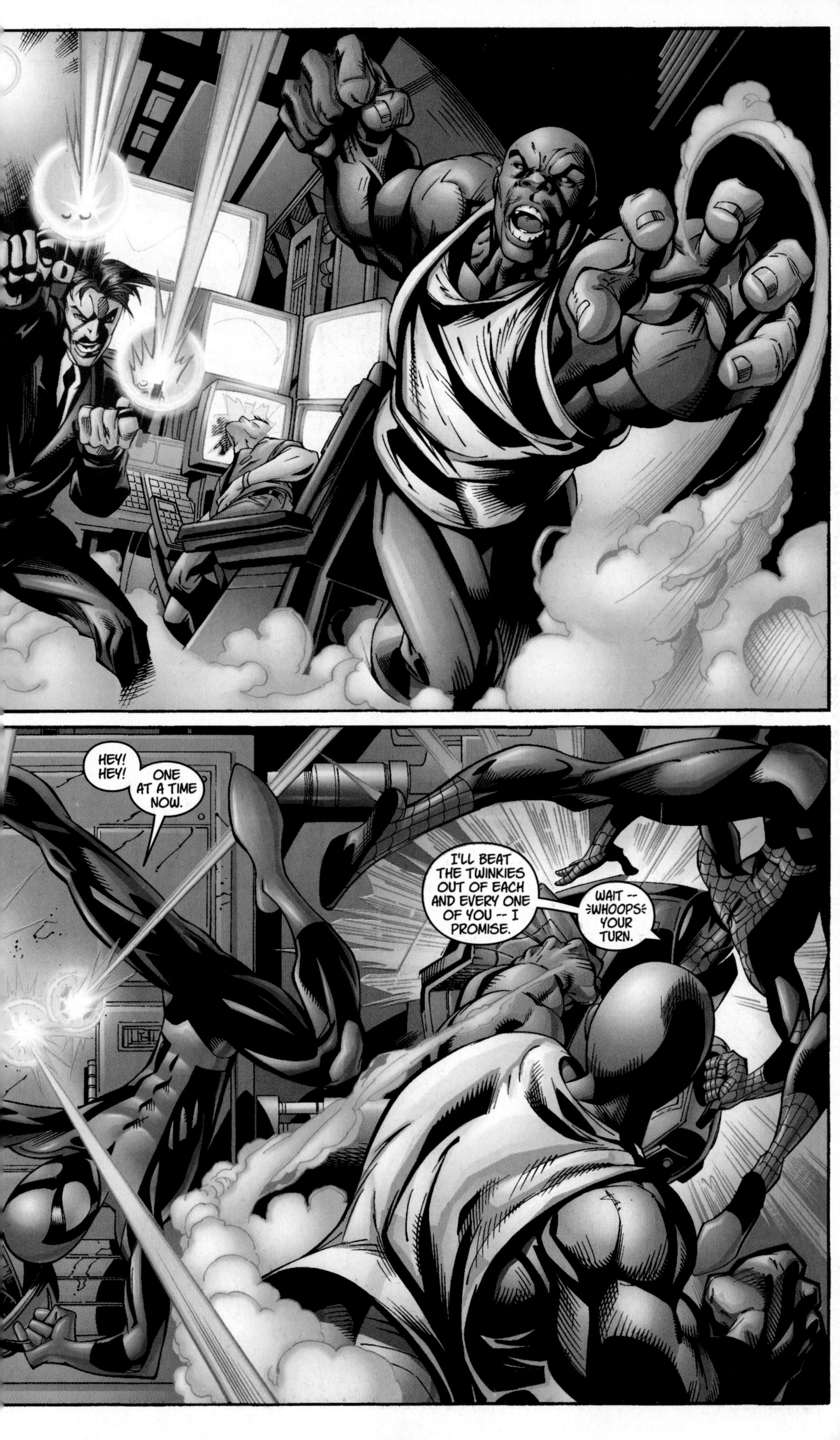
HEY! HEY!
ONE AT A TIME NOW.
I'LL BEAT THE TWINKIES OUT OF EACH AND EVERY ONE OF YOU -- I PROMISE.
WAIT -- WHOOPS YOUR TURN.

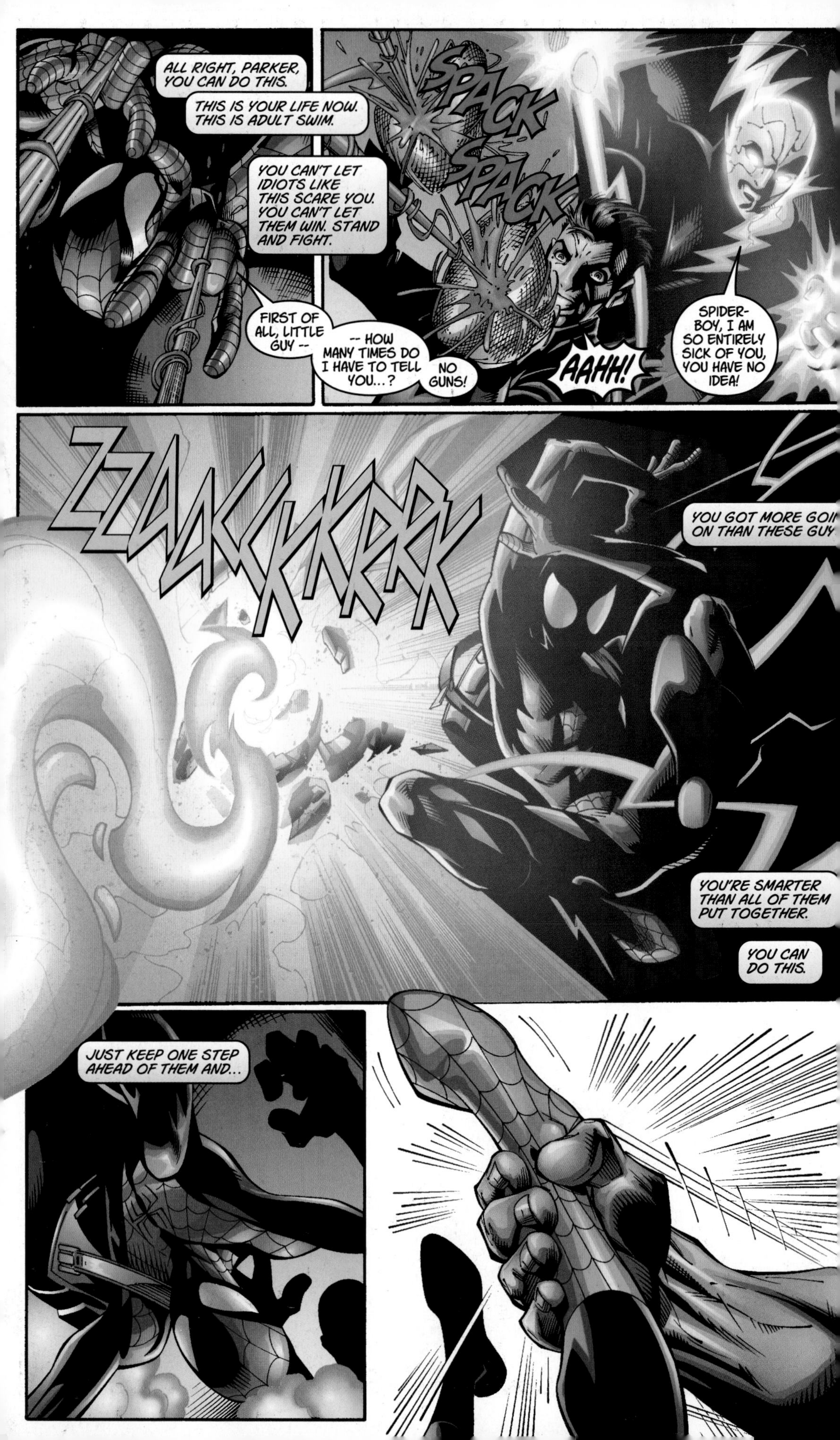
ALL RIGHT, PARKER, YOU CAN DO THIS.
THIS IS YOUR LIFE NOW. THIS IS ADULT SWIM.
YOU CAN'T LET IDIOTS LIKE THIS SCARE YOU. YOU CAN'T LET THEM WIN. STAND AND FIGHT.
FIRST OF ALL, LITTLE GUY --
-- HOW MANY TIMES DO I HAVE TO TELL YOU...?
NO GUNS!
SPACK
SPACK
AAHH!
SPIDER-BOY, I AM SO ENTIRELY SICK OF YOU, YOU HAVE NO IDEA!
ZZAACKKRRK
YOU GOT MORE GOI ON THAN THESE GUY
YOU'RE SMARTER THAN ALL OF THEM PUT TOGETHER.
YOU CAN DO THIS.
JUST KEEP ONE STEP AHEAD OF THEM AND...

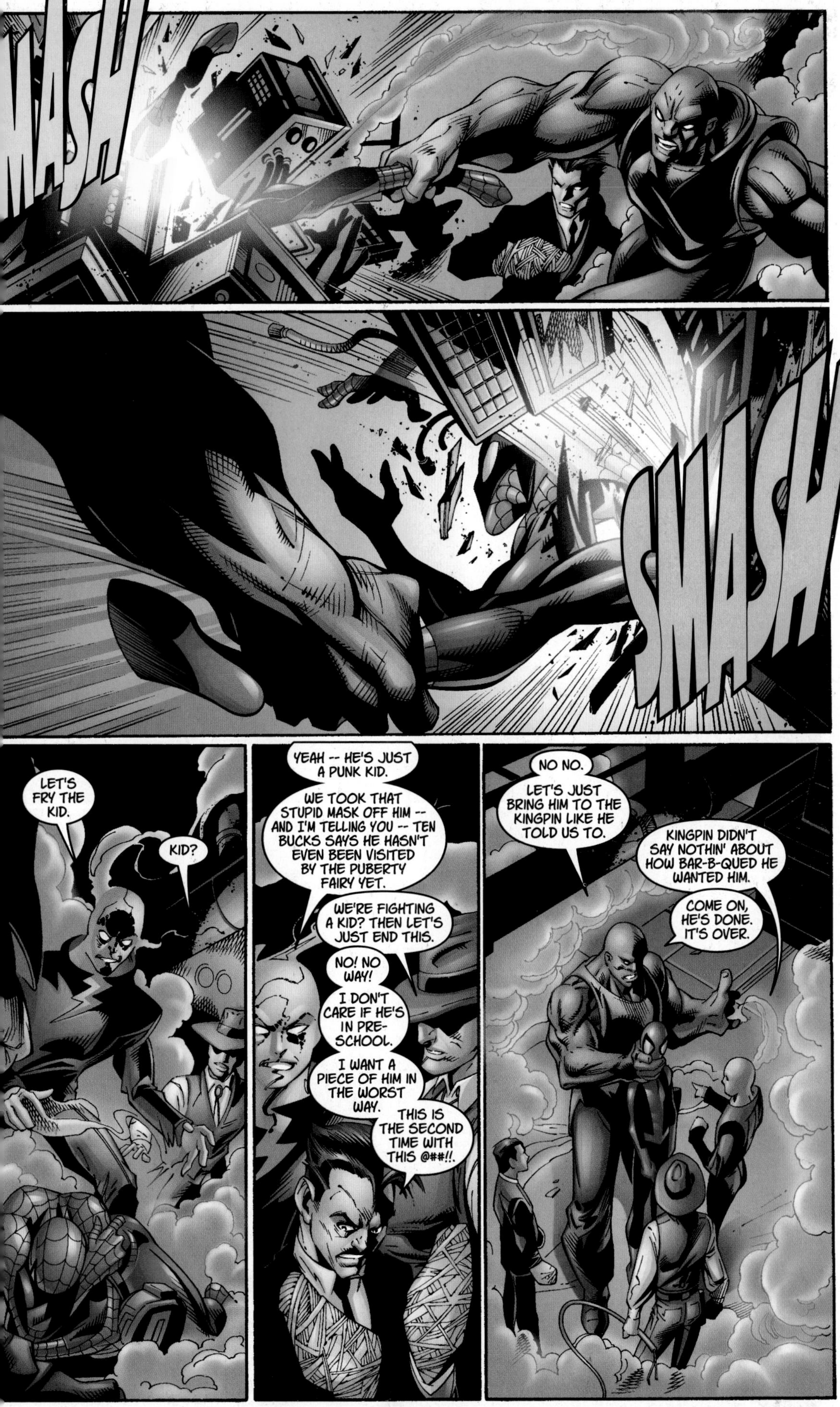
SMASH
SMASH
LET'S FRY THE KID.
KID?
YEAH -- HE'S JUST A PUNK KID.
WE TOOK THAT STUPID MASK OFF HIM -- AND I'M TELLING YOU -- TEN BUCKS SAYS HE HASN'T EVEN BEEN VISITED BY THE PUBERTY FAIRY YET.
WE'RE FIGHTING A KID? THEN LET'S JUST END THIS.
NO! NO WAY!
I DON'T CARE IF HE'S IN PRE-SCHOOL.
I WANT A PIECE OF HIM IN THE WORST WAY.
THIS IS THE SECOND TIME WITH THIS @##!!.
NO NO.
LET'S JUST BRING HIM TO THE KINGPIN LIKE HE TOLD US TO.
KINGPIN DIDN'T SAY NOTHIN' ABOUT HOW BAR-B-QUED HE WANTED HIM.
COME ON, HE'S DONE. IT'S OVER.

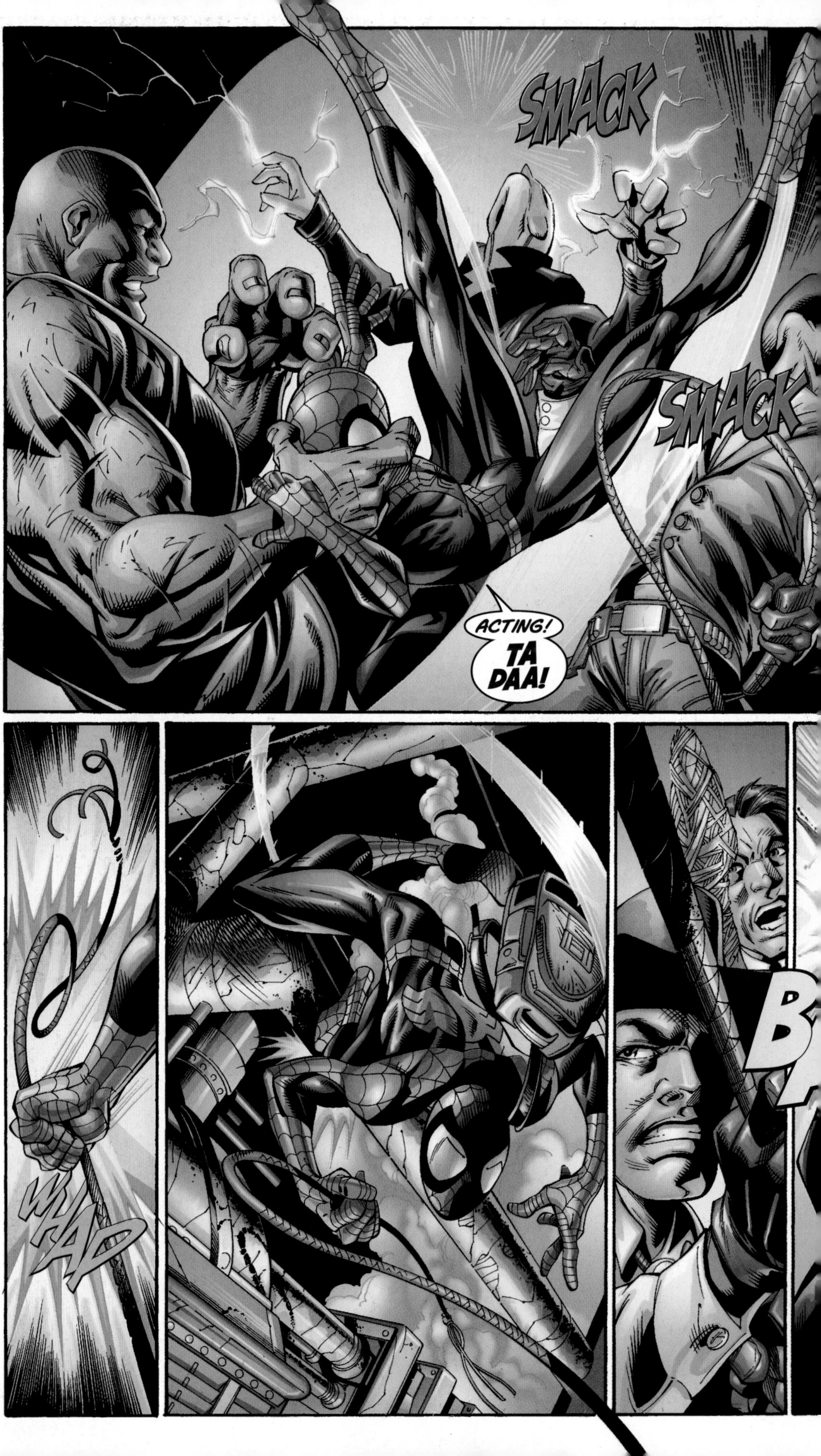
SMACK
SMACK
ACTING! TA DAA!
WHAP

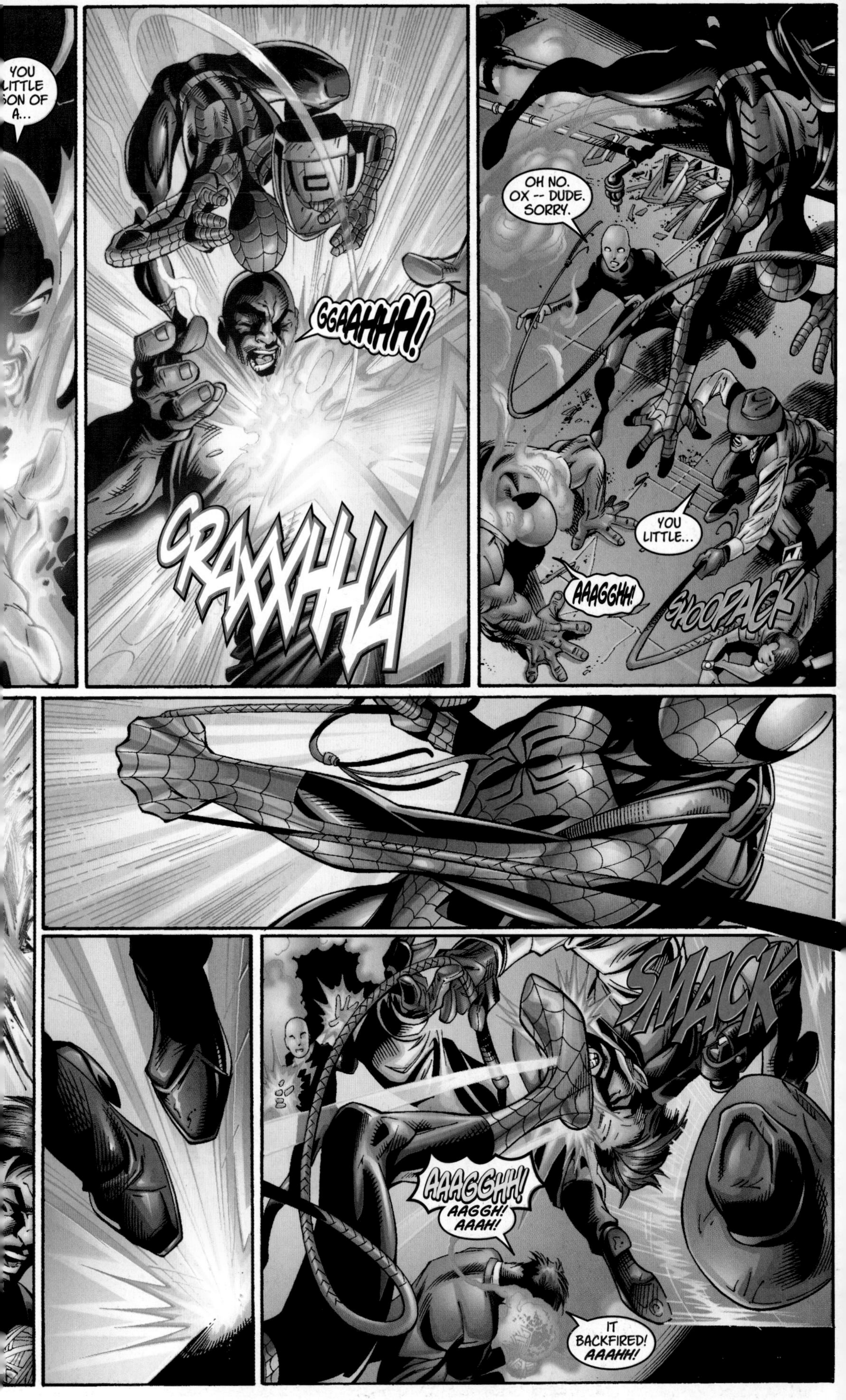

YOU LITTLE SON OF A...
GGAAHHH!
CRAXXHHA
OH NO. OX -- DUDE. SORRY.
YOU LITTLE...
AAAGGHH!
SHOOPACK
SMACK
AAAGGHH! AAGGH! AAAH!
IT BACKFIRED! AAAHH!

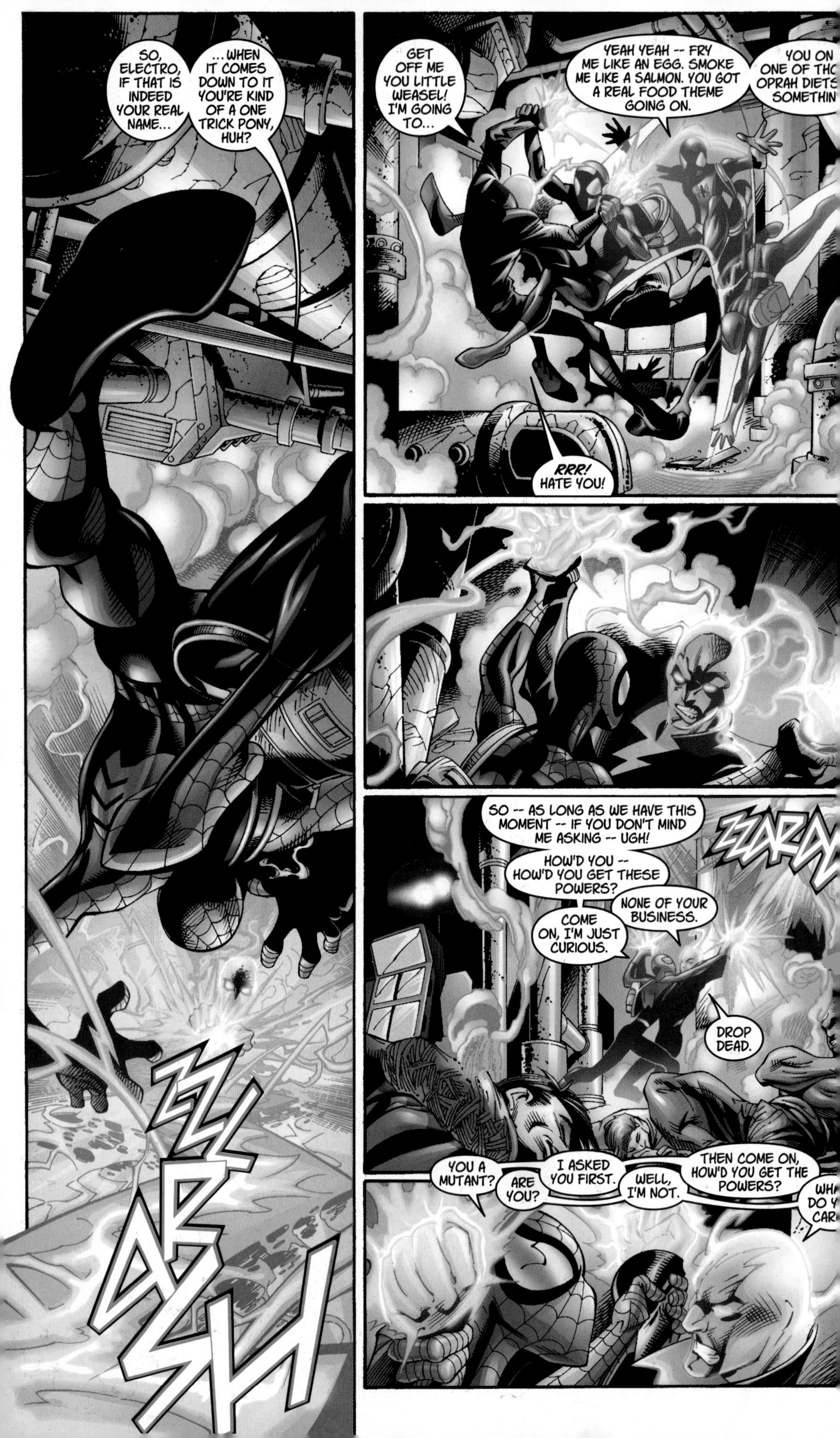
SO, ELECTRO, IF THAT IS INDEED YOUR REAL NAME...
...WHEN IT COMES DOWN TO IT YOU'RE KIND OF A ONE TRICK PONY, HUH?
ZZZARAKK
GET OFF ME YOU LITTLE WEASEL! I'M GOING TO...
YEAH YEAH -- FRY ME LIKE AN EGG. SMOKE ME LIKE A SALMON. YOU GOT A REAL FOOD THEME GOING ON.
RRR! HATE YOU!
SO -- AS LONG AS WE HAVE THIS MOMENT -- IF YOU DON'T MIND ME ASKING -- UGH!
HOW'D YOU -- HOW'D YOU GET THESE POWERS?
NONE OF YOUR BUSINESS.
COME ON, I'M JUST CURIOUS.
DROP DEAD.
YOU A MUTANT?
ARE YOU?
I ASKED YOU FIRST.
WELL, I'M NOT.
THEN COME ON, HOW'D YOU GET THE POWERS?

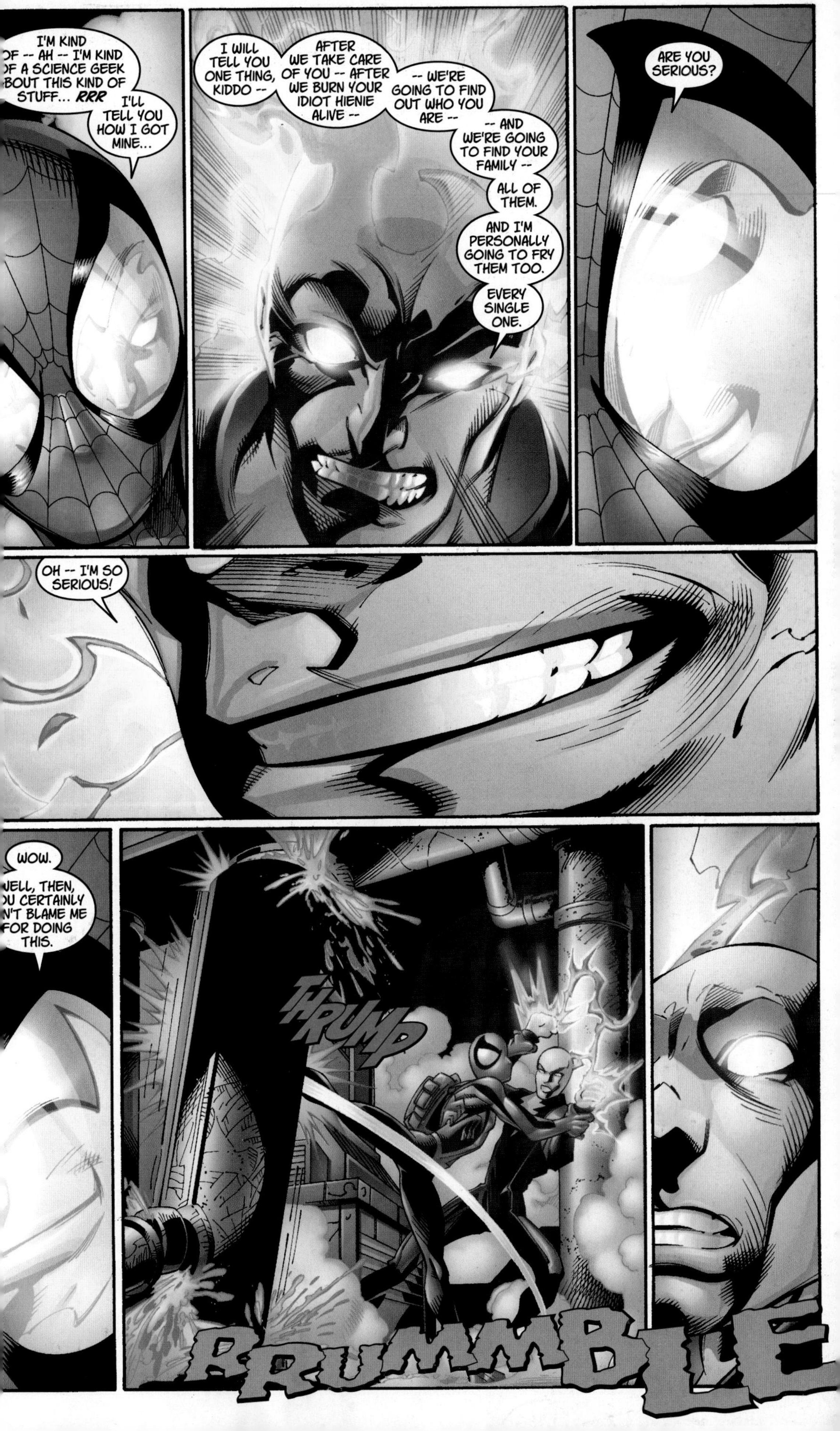
I'M KIND OF -- AH -- I'M KIND OF A SCIENCE GEEK BOUT THIS KIND OF STUFF... RRR
I'LL TELL YOU HOW I GOT MINE...
I WILL TELL YOU ONE THING, KIDDO --
AFTER WE TAKE CARE OF YOU -- AFTER WE BURN YOUR IDIOT HIENIE ALIVE --
-- WE'RE GOING TO FIND OUT WHO YOU ARE --
-- AND WE'RE GOING TO FIND YOUR FAMILY --
ALL OF THEM.
AND I'M PERSONALLY GOING TO FRY THEM TOO.
EVERY SINGLE ONE.
ARE YOU SERIOUS?
OH -- I'M SO SERIOUS!
WOW.
WELL, THEN, OU CERTAINLY N'T BLAME ME FOR DOING THIS.
THRUMP
RRUMMBLE

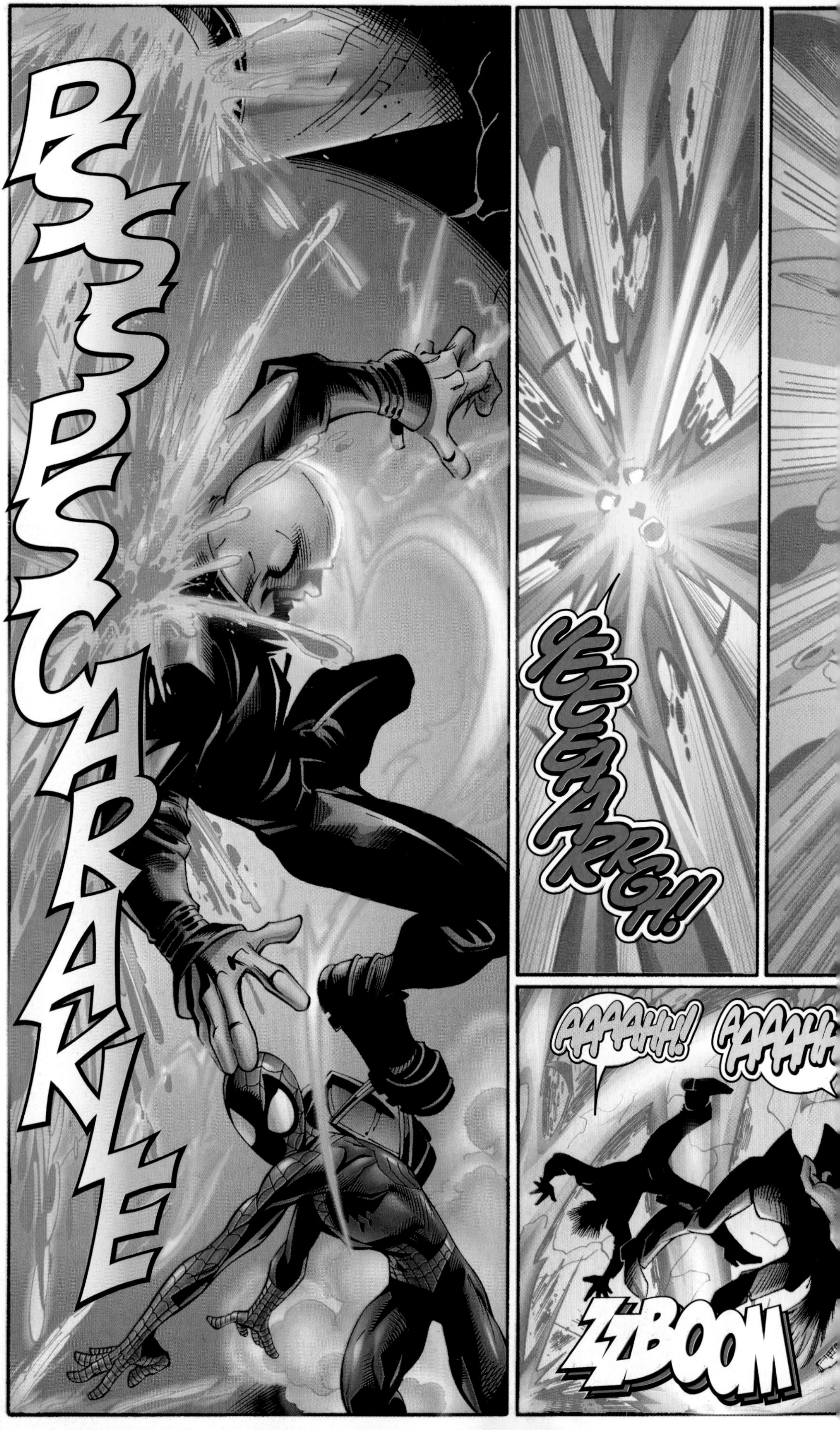
PSSPSCARAKLE
YEEEAARRGH!
AAAAHH! AAAAH
ZZBOOM

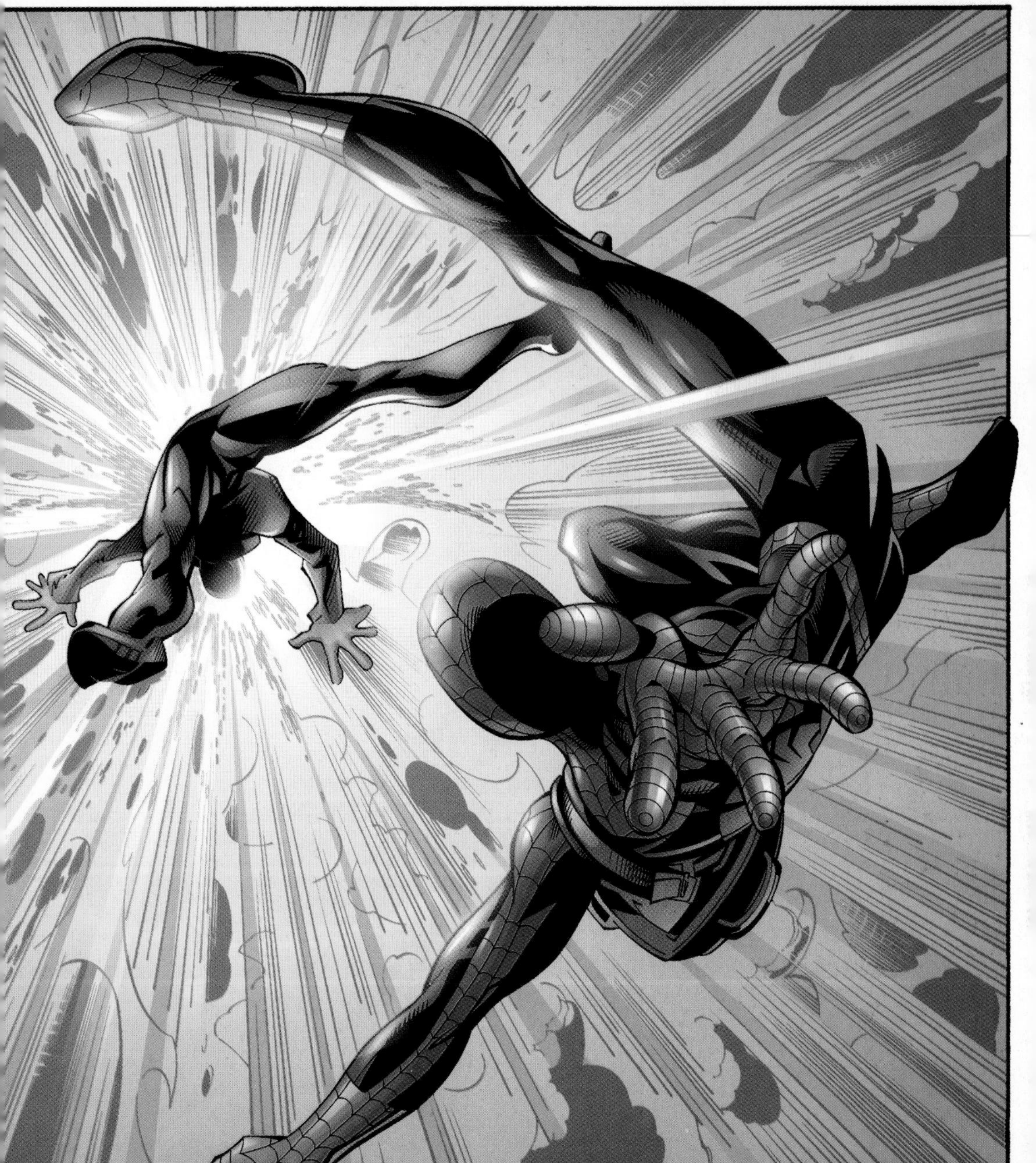

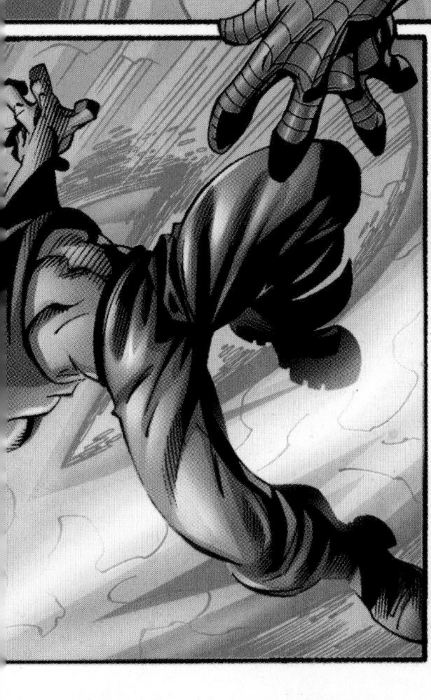

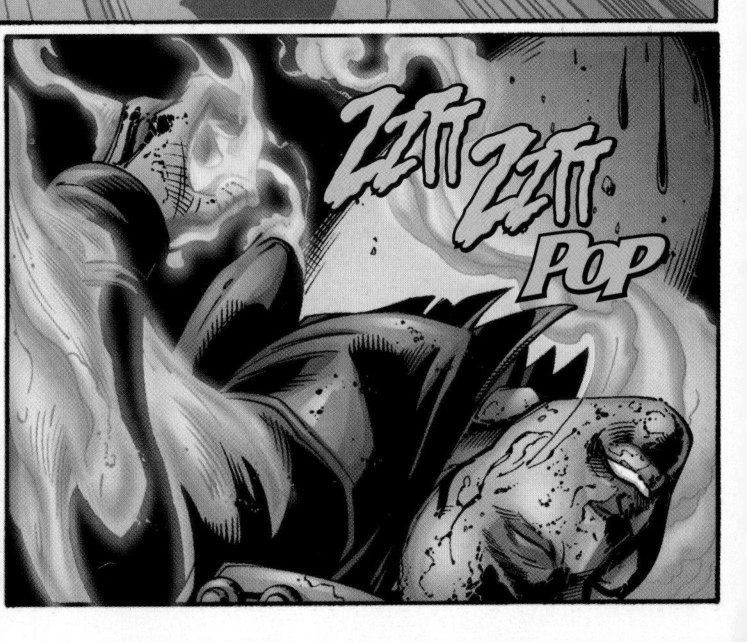
ZZFT ZZFT
POP

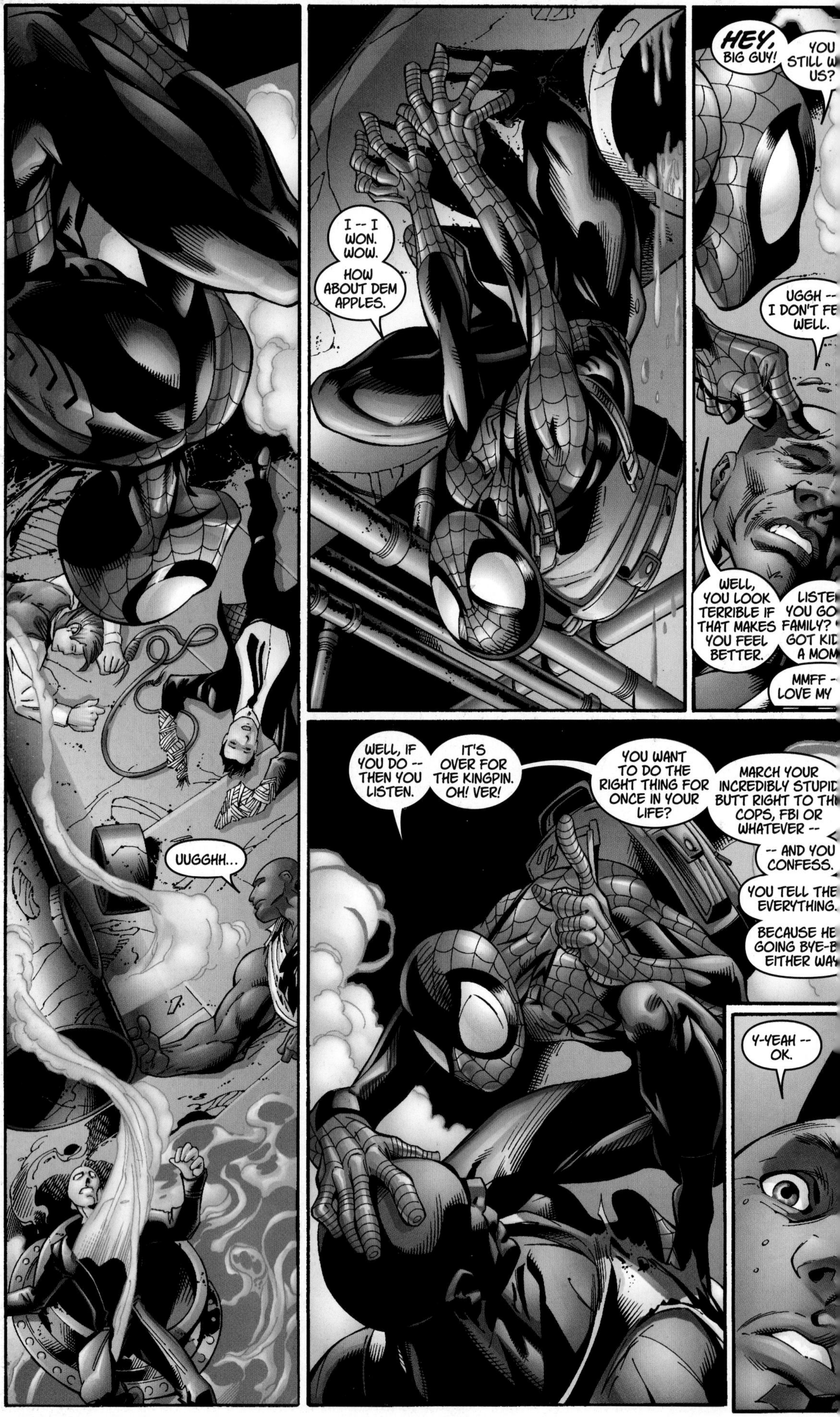
UUGGHH...
I -- I WON. WOW.
HOW ABOUT DEM APPLES.
HEY, BIG GUY!
YOU STILL W
US?
UGGH -- I DON'T FE
WELL.
WELL, YOU LOOK TERRIBLE IF THAT MAKES YOU FEEL BETTER.
LISTE
YOU GO
FAMILY?
GOT KID
A MOM
MMFF -
LOVE MY
WELL, IF YOU DO -- THEN YOU LISTEN.
IT'S OVER FOR THE KINGPIN. OH! VER!
YOU WANT TO DO THE RIGHT THING FOR ONCE IN YOUR LIFE?
MARCH YOUR INCREDIBLY STUPID BUTT RIGHT TO TH COPS, FBI OR WHATEVER --
-- AND YOU CONFESS.
YOU TELL THE EVERYTHING.
BECAUSE HE GOING BYE-B EITHER WAY
Y-YEAH -- OK.

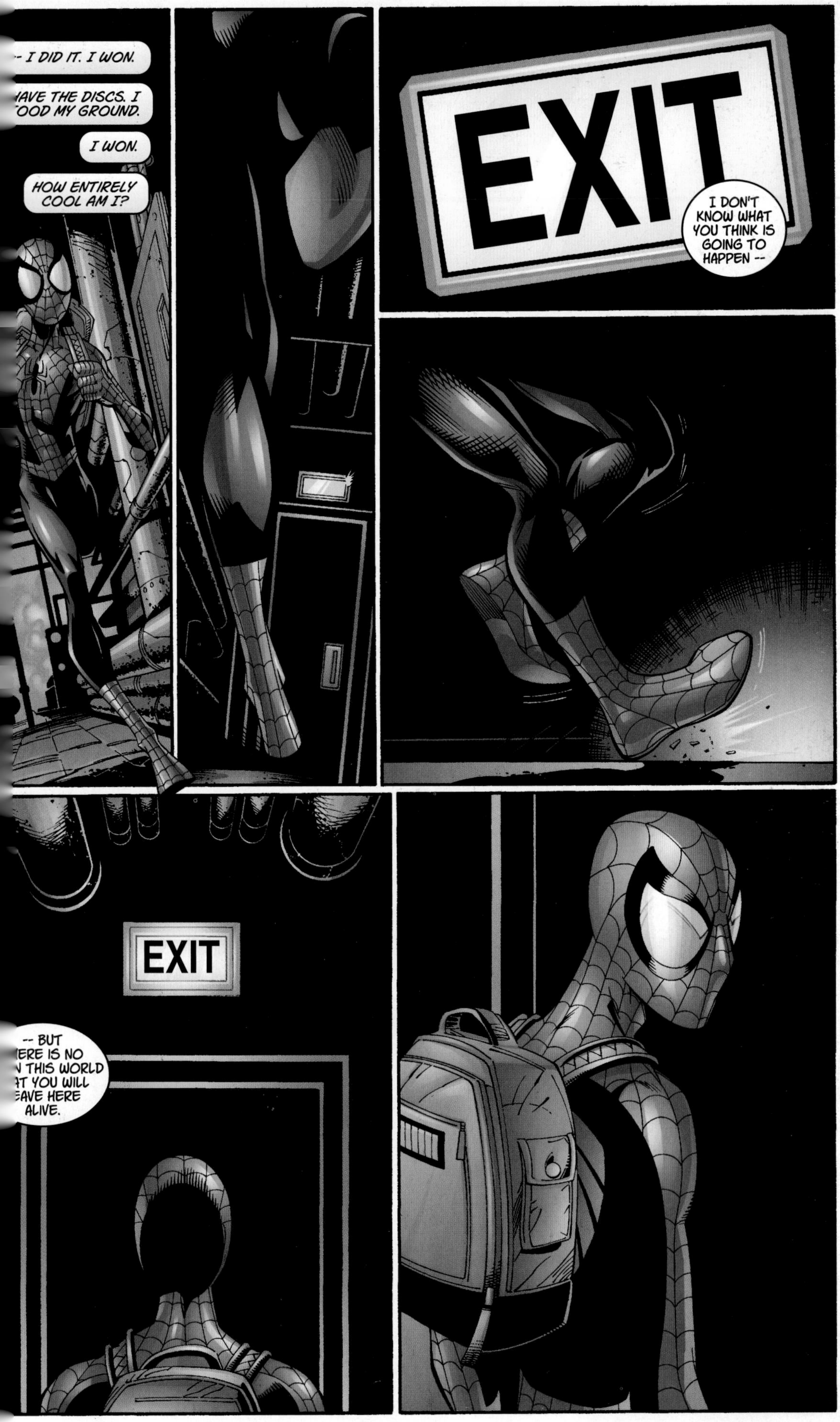
-- I DID IT. I WON.
HAVE THE DISCS. I
TOOD MY GROUND.
I WON.
HOW ENTIRELY
COOL AM I?
EXIT
I DON'T
KNOW WHAT
YOU THINK IS
GOING TO
HAPPEN --
EXIT
-- BUT
ERE IS NO
N THIS WORLD
AT YOU WILL
EAVE HERE
ALIVE.

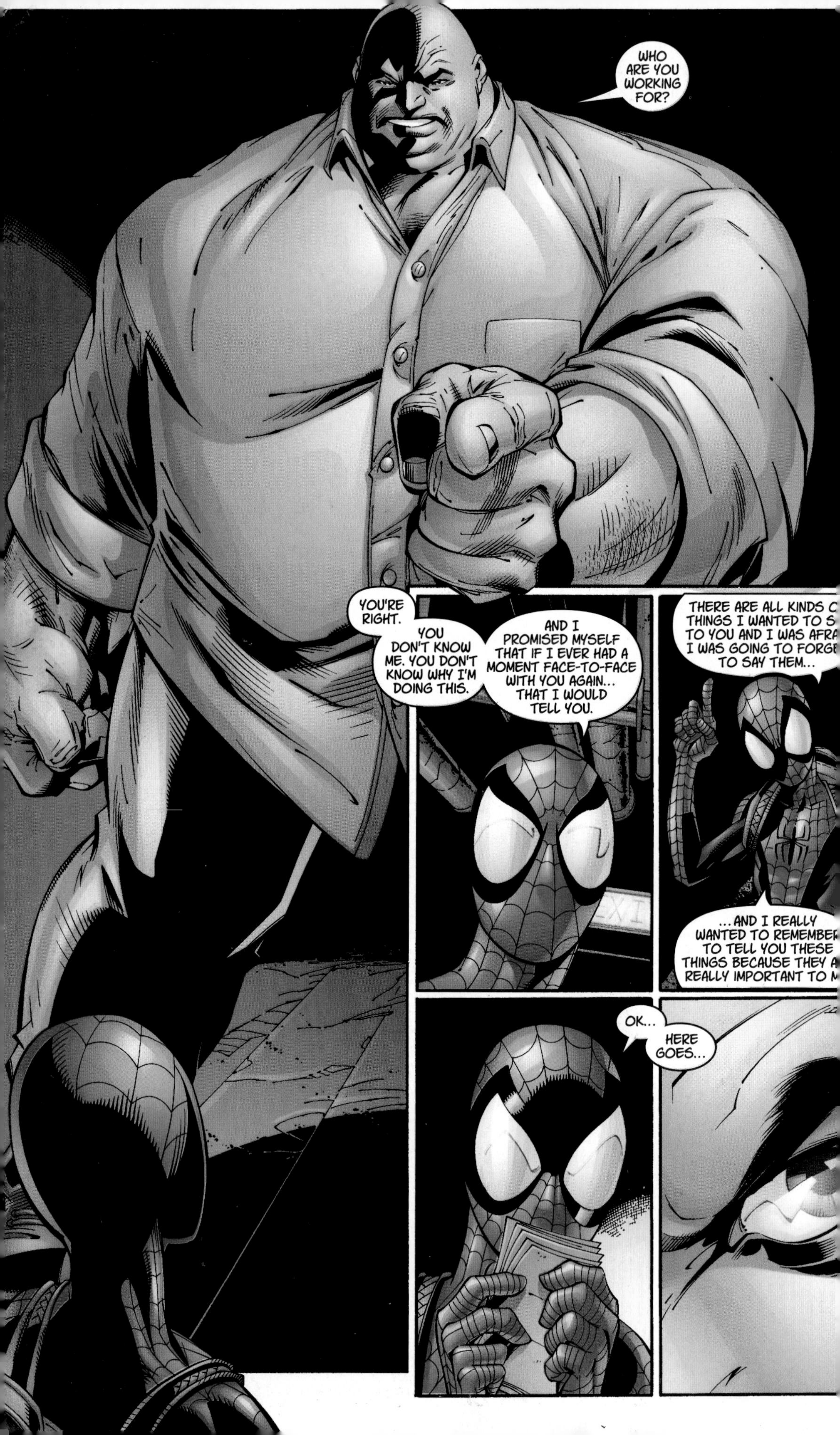
WHO ARE YOU WORKING FOR?
YOU'RE RIGHT.
YOU DON'T KNOW ME. YOU DON'T KNOW WHY I'M DOING THIS.
AND I PROMISED MYSELF THAT IF I EVER HAD A MOMENT FACE-TO-FACE WITH YOU AGAIN... THAT I WOULD TELL YOU.
THERE ARE ALL KINDS C THINGS I WANTED TO S TO YOU AND I WAS AFRA I WAS GOING TO FORGE TO SAY THEM...
...AND I REALLY WANTED TO REMEMBER TO TELL YOU THESE THINGS BECAUSE THEY A REALLY IMPORTANT TO M
OK...
HERE GOES...

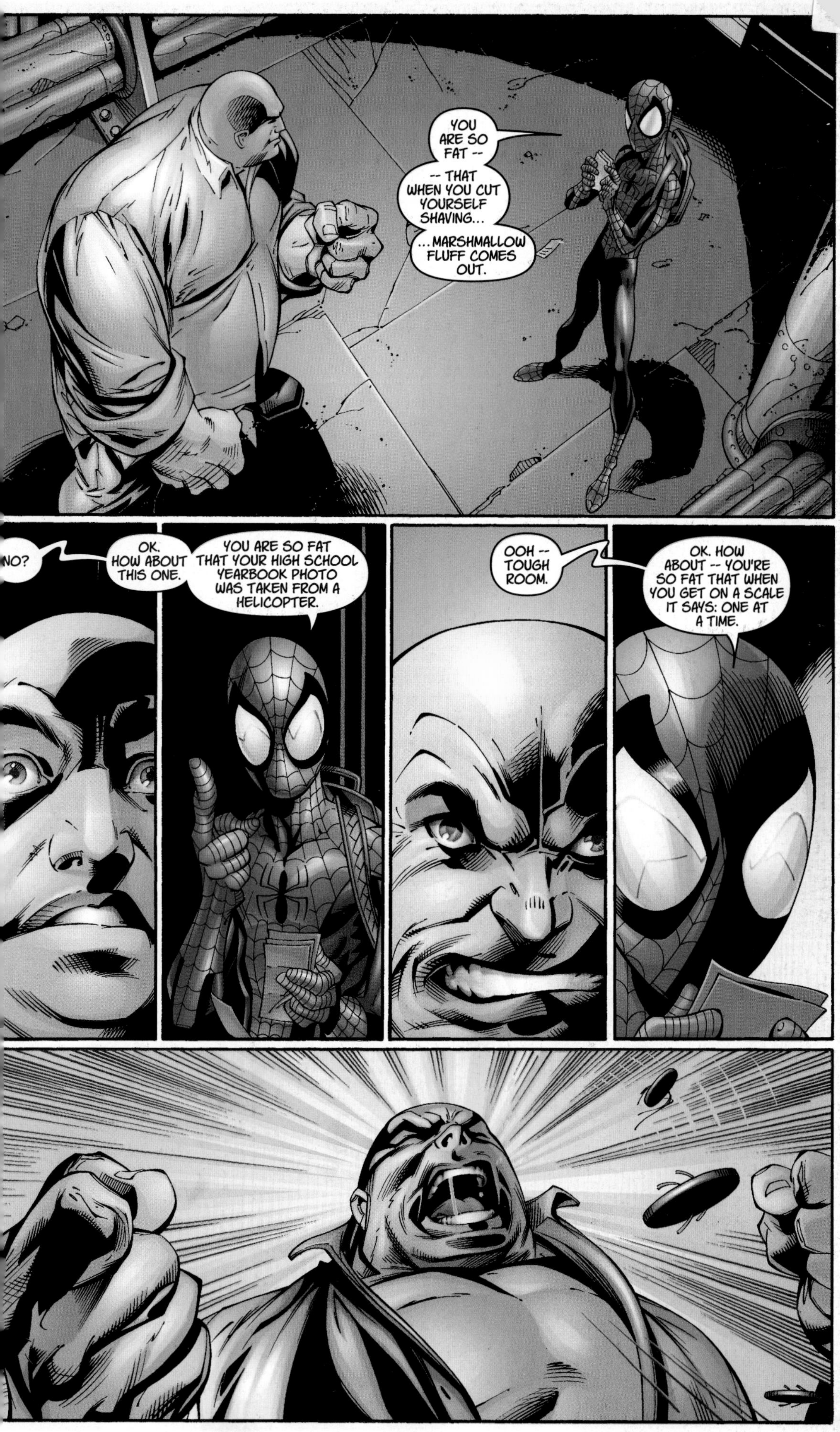
YOU ARE SO FAT --
-- THAT WHEN YOU CUT YOURSELF SHAVING...
...MARSHMALLOW FLUFF COMES OUT.
NO?
OK. HOW ABOUT THIS ONE.
YOU ARE SO FAT THAT YOUR HIGH SCHOOL YEARBOOK PHOTO WAS TAKEN FROM A HELICOPTER.
OOH -- TOUGH ROOM.
OK. HOW ABOUT -- YOU'RE SO FAT THAT WHEN YOU GET ON A SCALE IT SAYS: ONE AT A TIME.

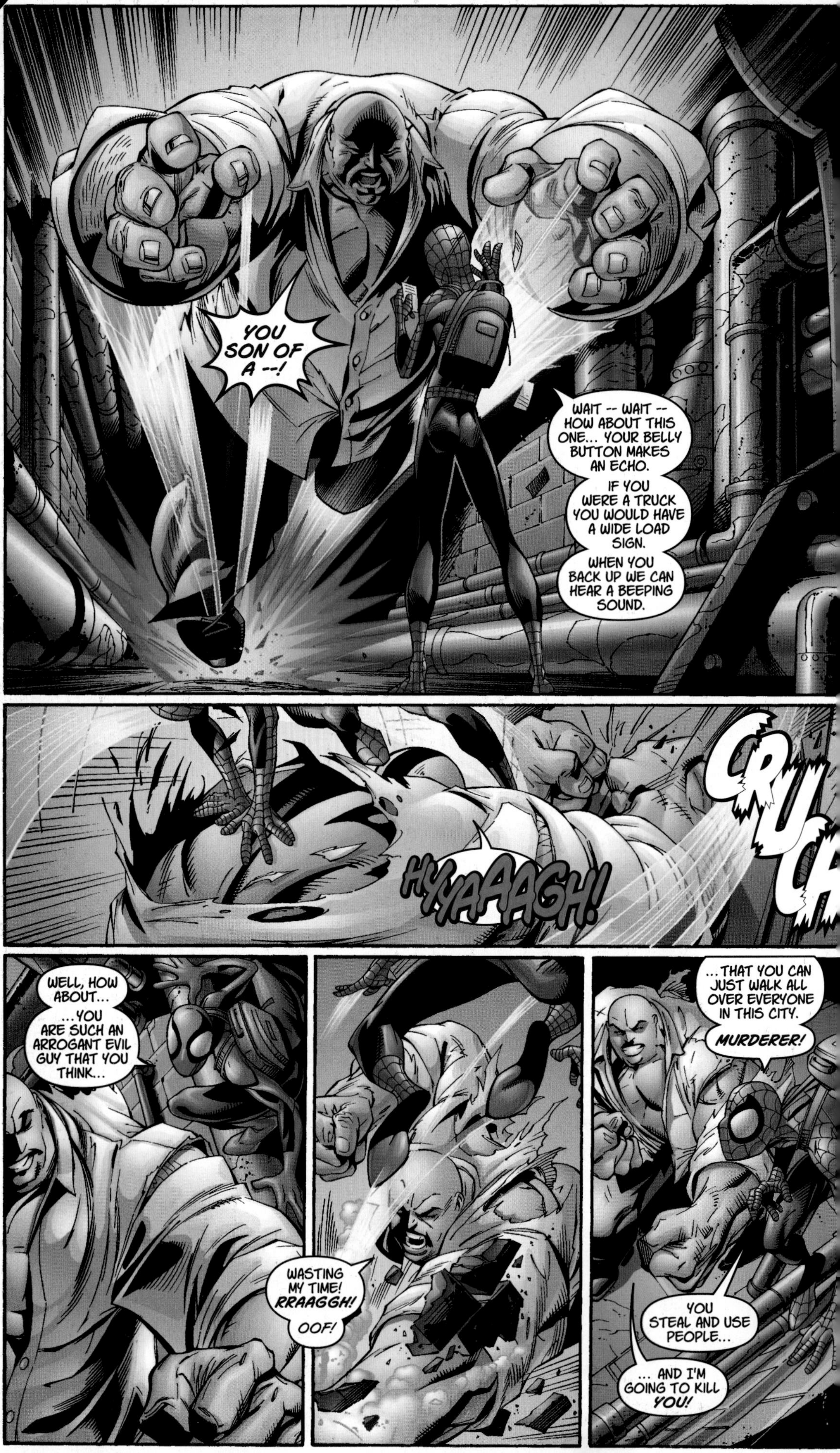
YOU SON OF A --!
WAIT -- WAIT -- HOW ABOUT THIS ONE... YOUR BELLY BUTTON MAKES AN ECHO.
IF YOU WERE A TRUCK YOU WOULD HAVE A WIDE LOAD SIGN.
WHEN YOU BACK UP WE CAN HEAR A BEEPING SOUND.
HYYAAAAGH!
CRUCH
WELL, HOW ABOUT...
...YOU ARE SUCH AN ARROGANT EVIL GUY THAT YOU THINK...
WASTING MY TIME! RRAAGGH!
OOF!
...THAT YOU CAN JUST WALK ALL OVER EVERYONE IN THIS CITY.
MURDERER!
YOU STEAL AND USE PEOPLE...
... AND I'M GOING TO KILL YOU!

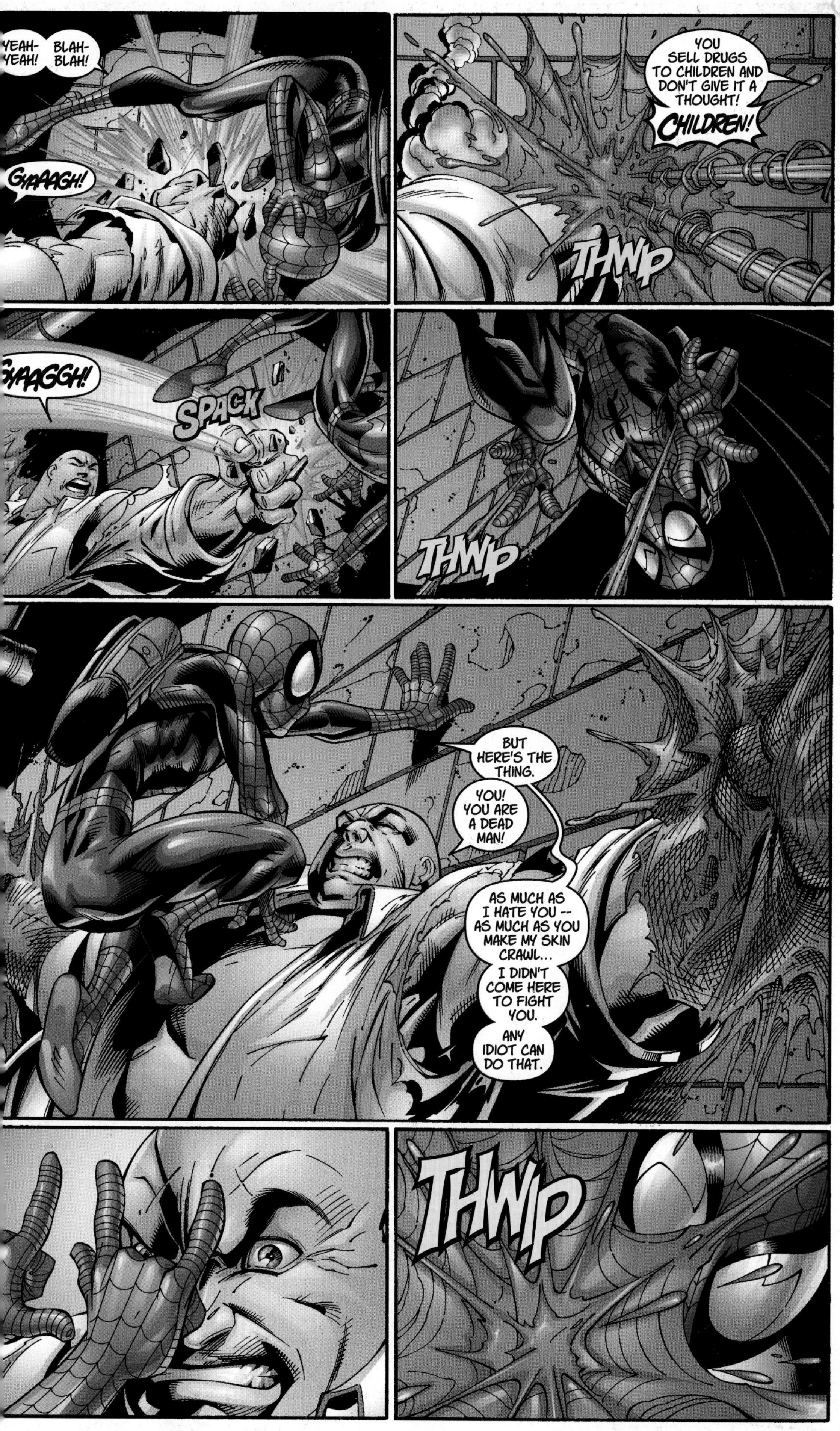
YEAH-YEAH!
BLAH-BLAH!
GYAAAGH!
YOU SELL DRUGS TO CHILDREN AND DON'T GIVE IT A THOUGHT! CHILDREN!
THWIP
GYAAAGH!
SPACK
THWIP
BUT HERE'S THE THING.
YOU! YOU ARE A DEAD MAN!
AS MUCH AS -- I HATE YOU -- AS MUCH AS YOU MAKE MY SKIN CRAWL...
I DIDN'T COME HERE TO FIGHT YOU.
ANY IDIOT CAN DO THAT.
THWIP

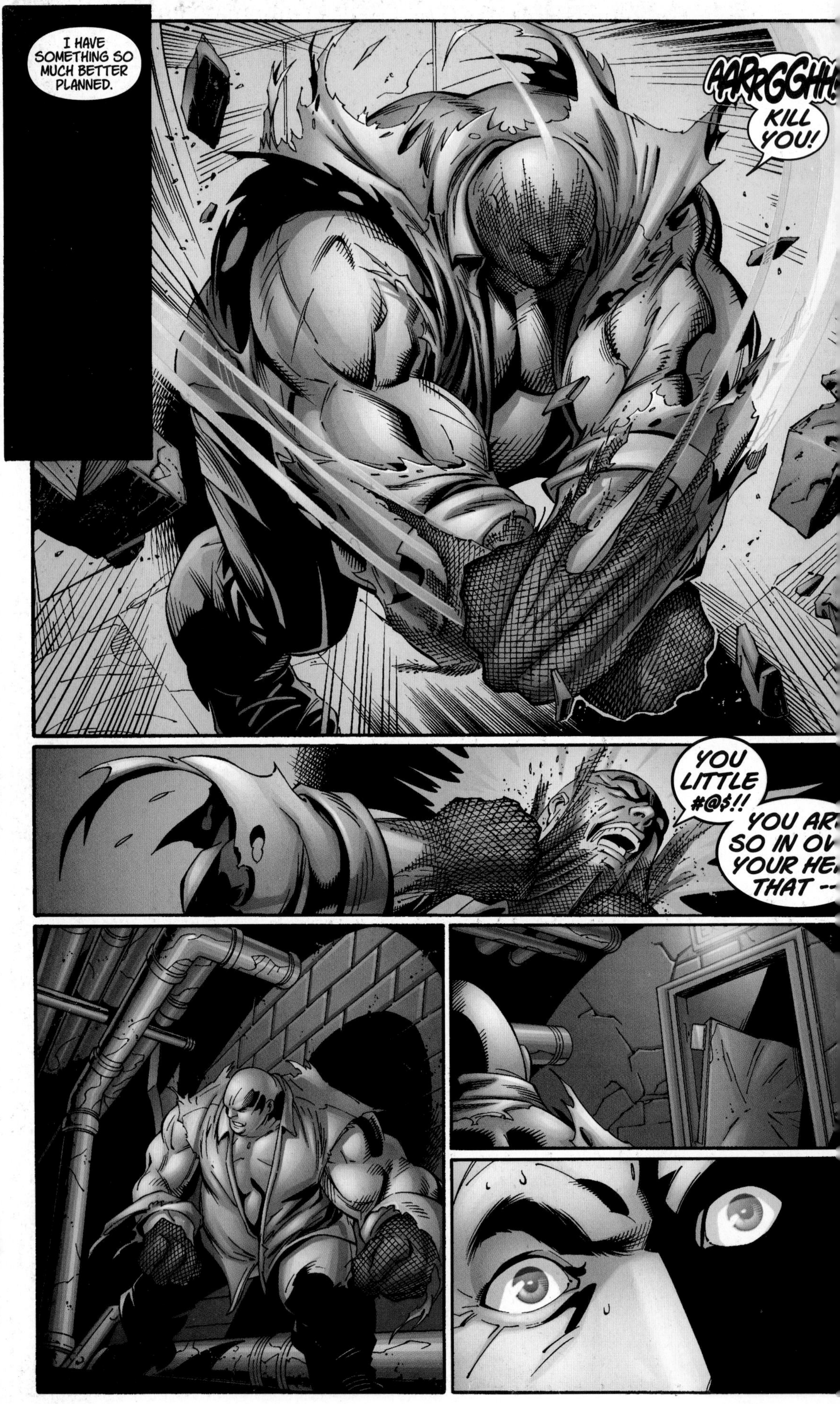
I HAVE SOMETHING SO MUCH BETTER PLANNED.
AARRGGHH
KILL YOU!
YOU LITTLE #@$!!
YOU AR SO IN OV YOUR HE THAT --

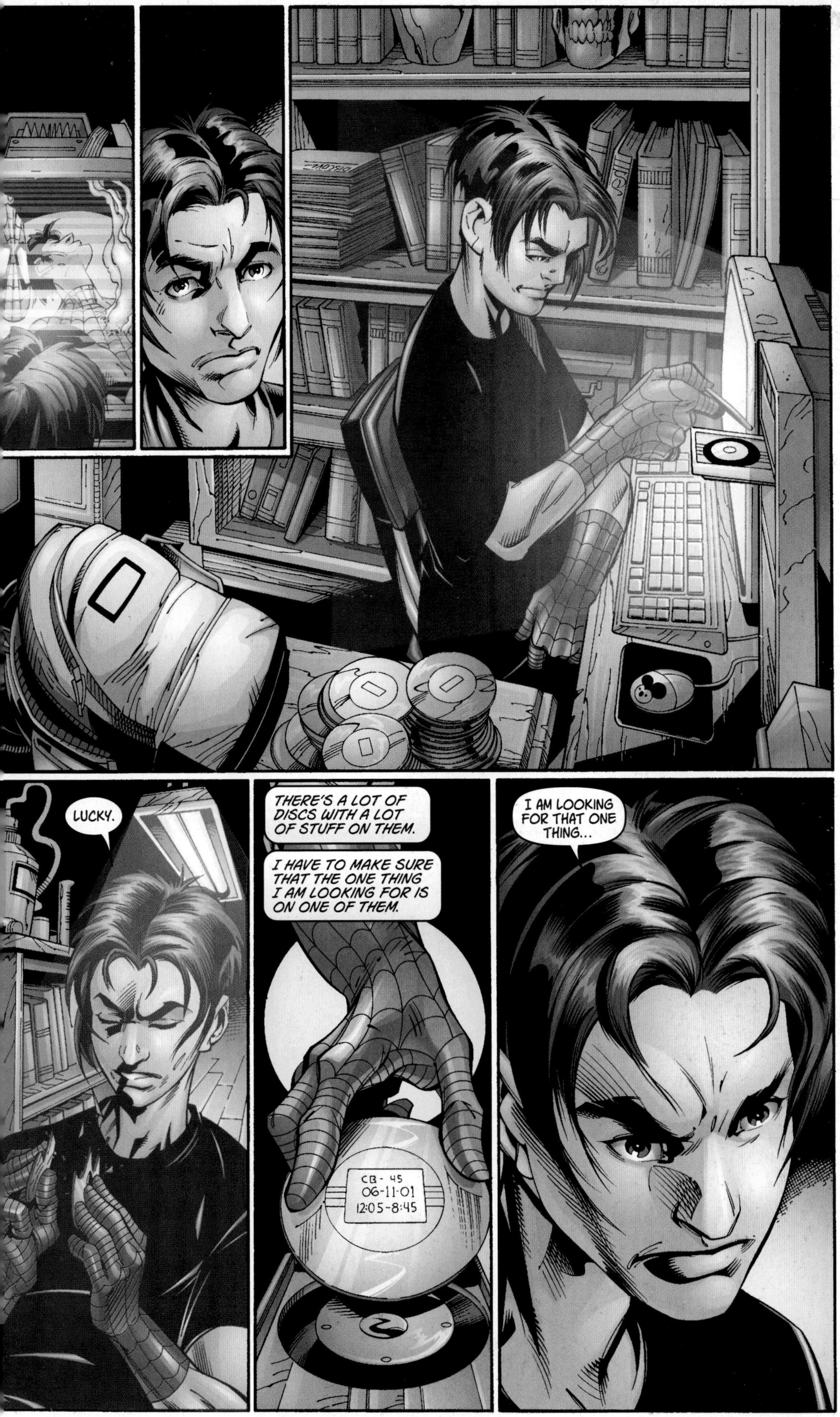
LUCKY.
THERE'S A LOT OF DISCS WITH A LOT OF STUFF ON THEM.
I HAVE TO MAKE SURE THAT THE ONE THING I AM LOOKING FOR IS ON ONE OF THEM.
CB - 45
06-11-01
12:05-8:45
I AM LOOKING FOR THAT ONE THING...

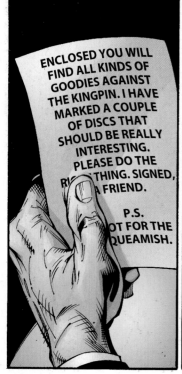

ENCLOSED YOU WILL FIND ALL KINDS OF GOODIES AGAINST THE KINGPIN. I HAVE MARKED A COUPLE OF DISCS THAT SHOULD BE REALLY INTERESTING. PLEASE DO THE RIGHT THING. SIGNED, A FRIEND.

P.S. NOT FOR THE SQUEAMISH.

OH MAN -- BETTY?

OY! WHAT NOW, URICH?

WOW UH -- UM -- DID YOU SEE ANYONE PUT THIS PACKAGE ON MY DESK?

NO.

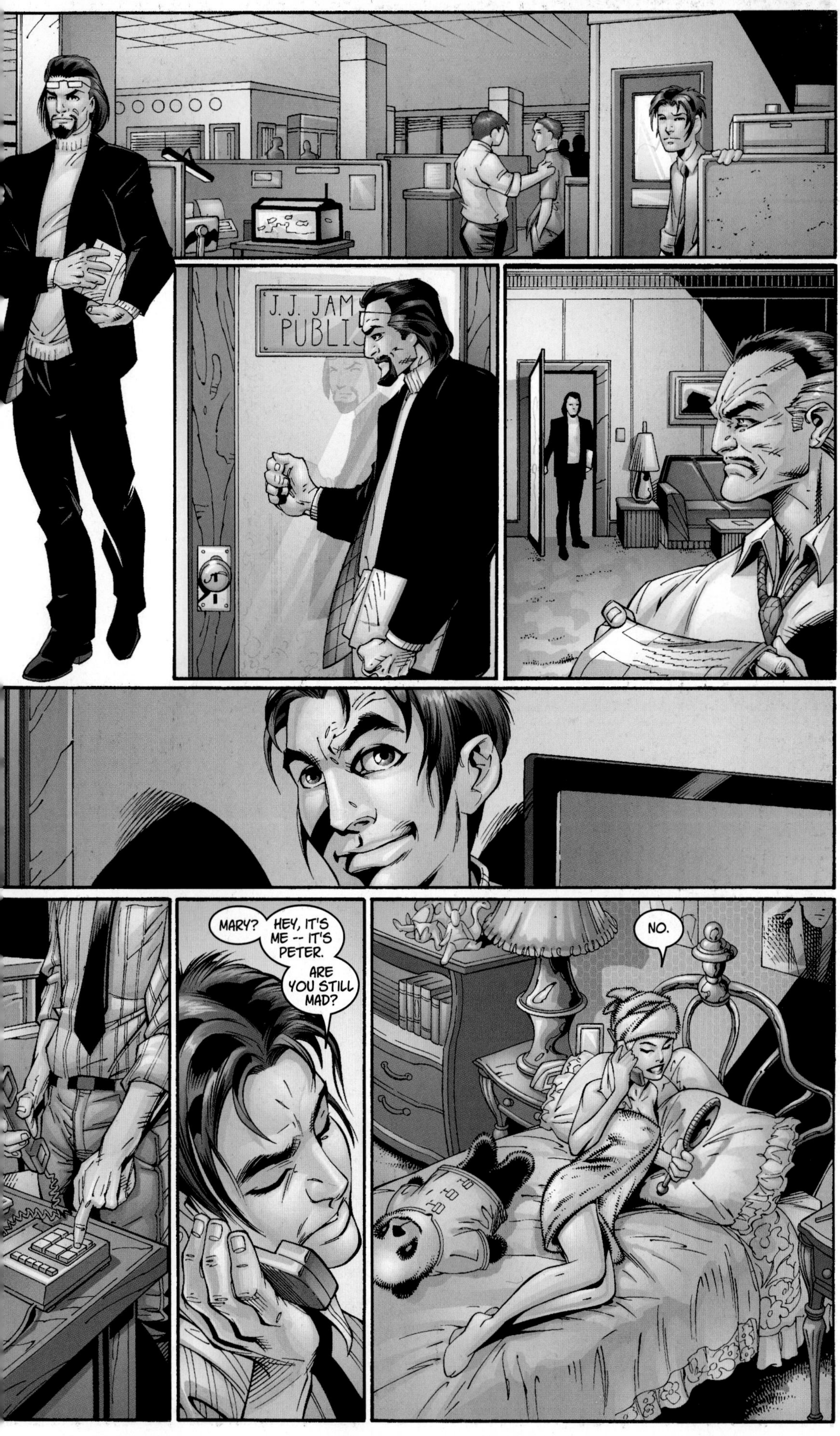
J. J. JAM
PUBLI
MARY?
HEY, IT'S ME -- IT'S PETER.
ARE YOU STILL MAD?
NO.

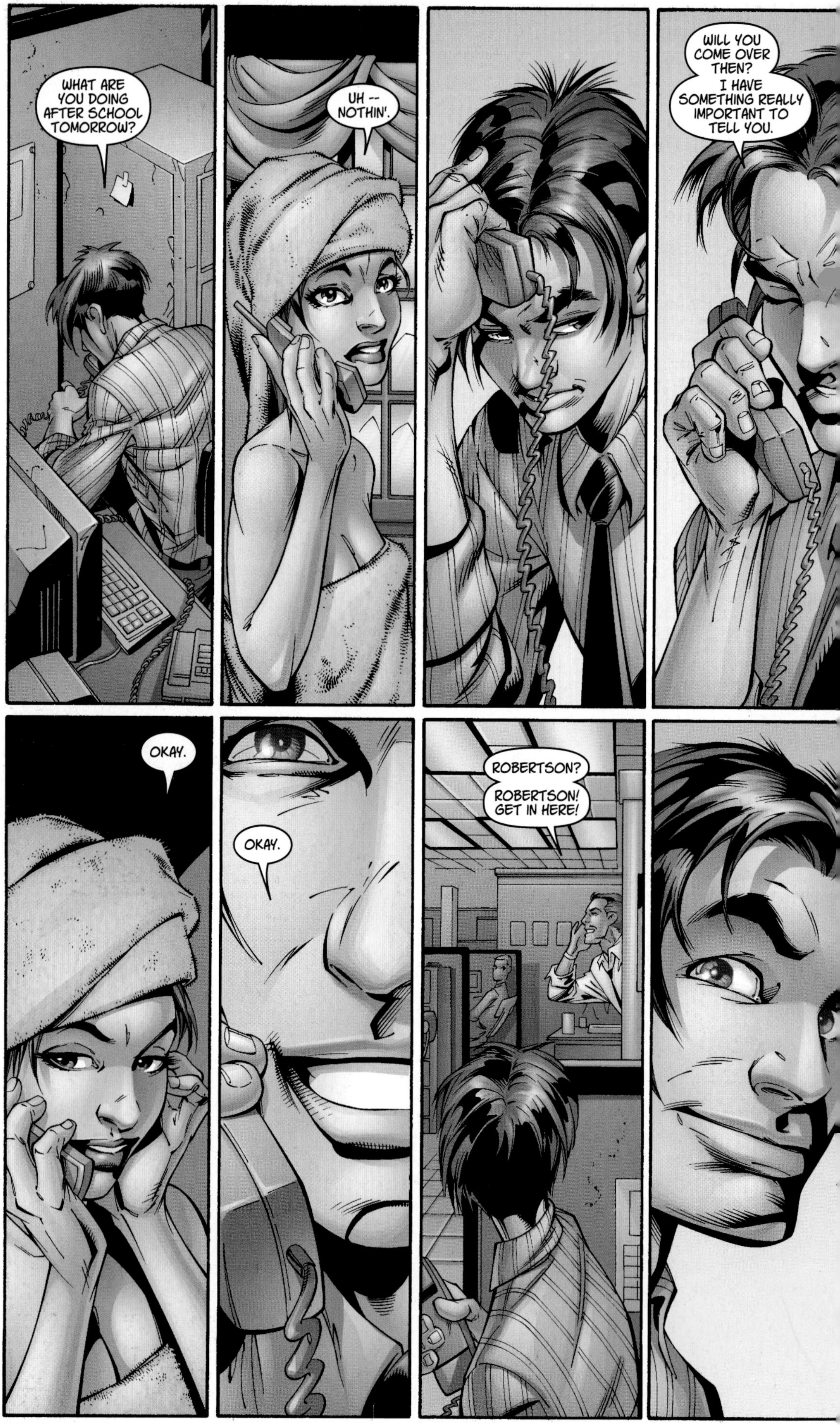
WHAT ARE YOU DOING AFTER SCHOOL TOMORROW?
UH -- NOTHIN'.
WILL YOU COME OVER THEN?
I HAVE SOMETHING REALLY IMPORTANT TO TELL YOU.
OKAY.
OKAY.
ROBERTSON?
ROBERTSON! GET IN HERE!

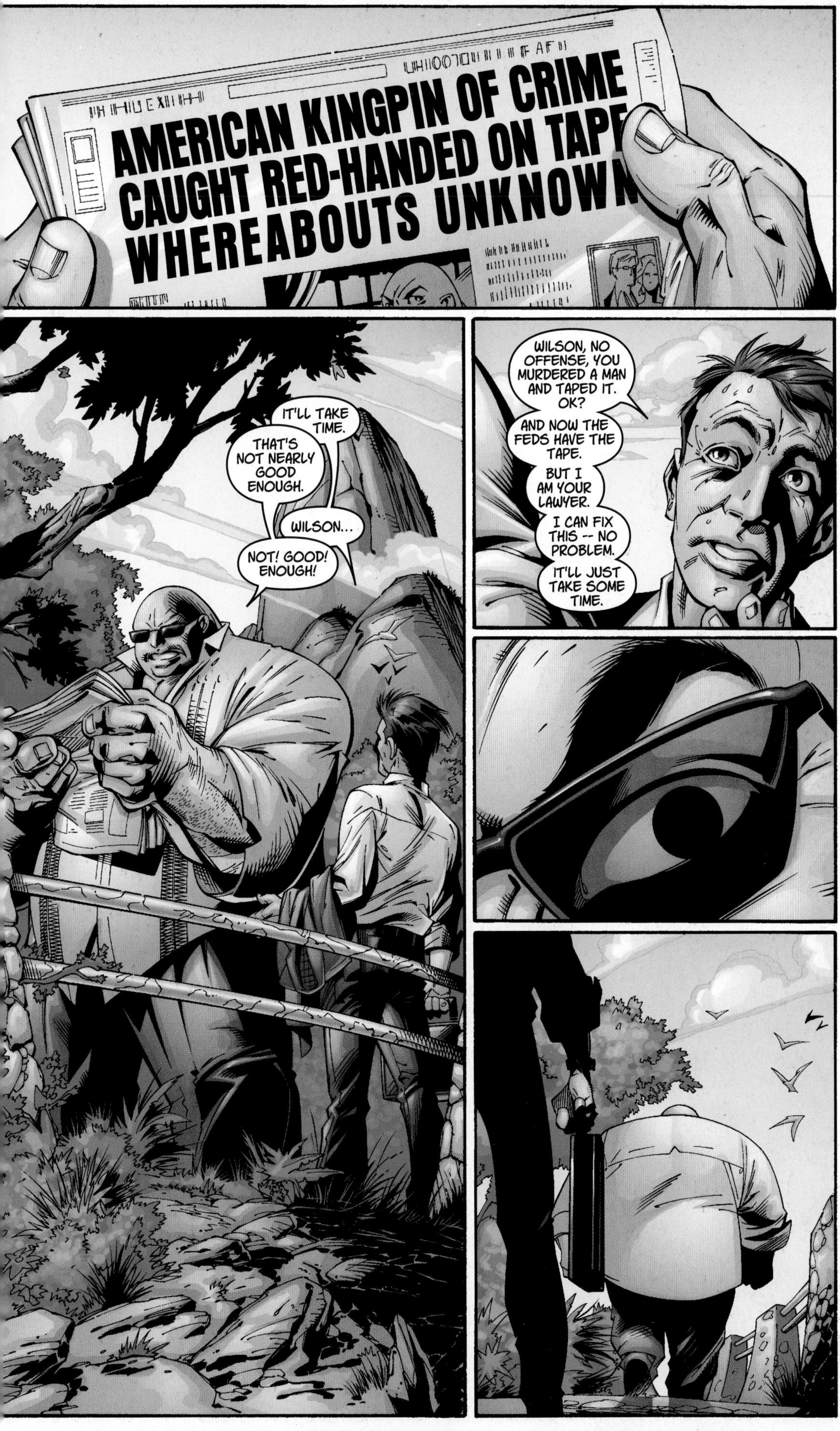
AMERICAN KINGPIN OF CRIME CAUGHT RED-HANDED ON TAPE WHEREABOUTS UNKNOWN
IT'LL TAKE TIME.
THAT'S NOT NEARLY GOOD ENOUGH.
WILSON...
NOT! GOOD! ENOUGH!
WILSON, NO OFFENSE, YOU MURDERED A MAN AND TAPED IT. OK?
AND NOW THE FEDS HAVE THE TAPE.
BUT I AM YOUR LAWYER.
I CAN FIX THIS -- NO PROBLEM.
IT'LL JUST TAKE SOME TIME.

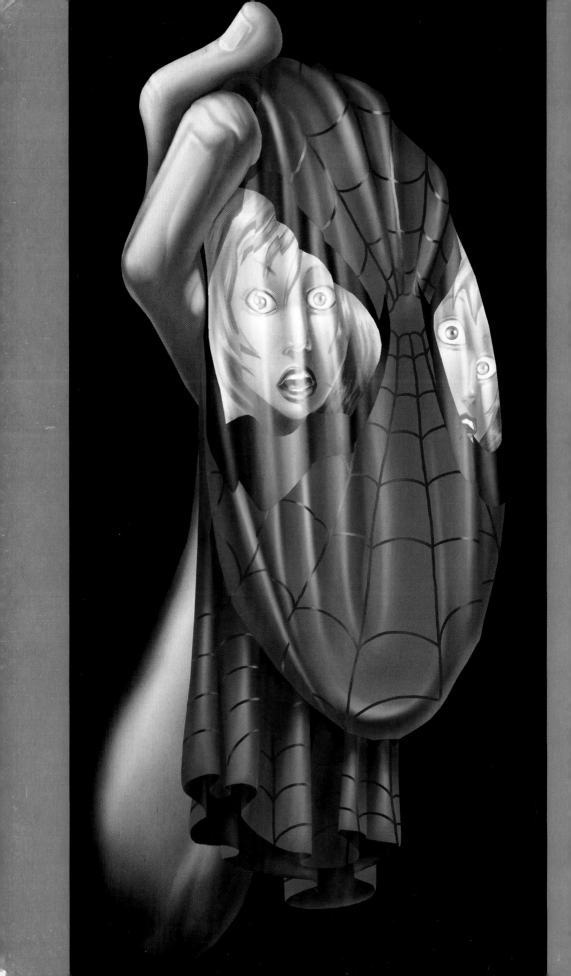

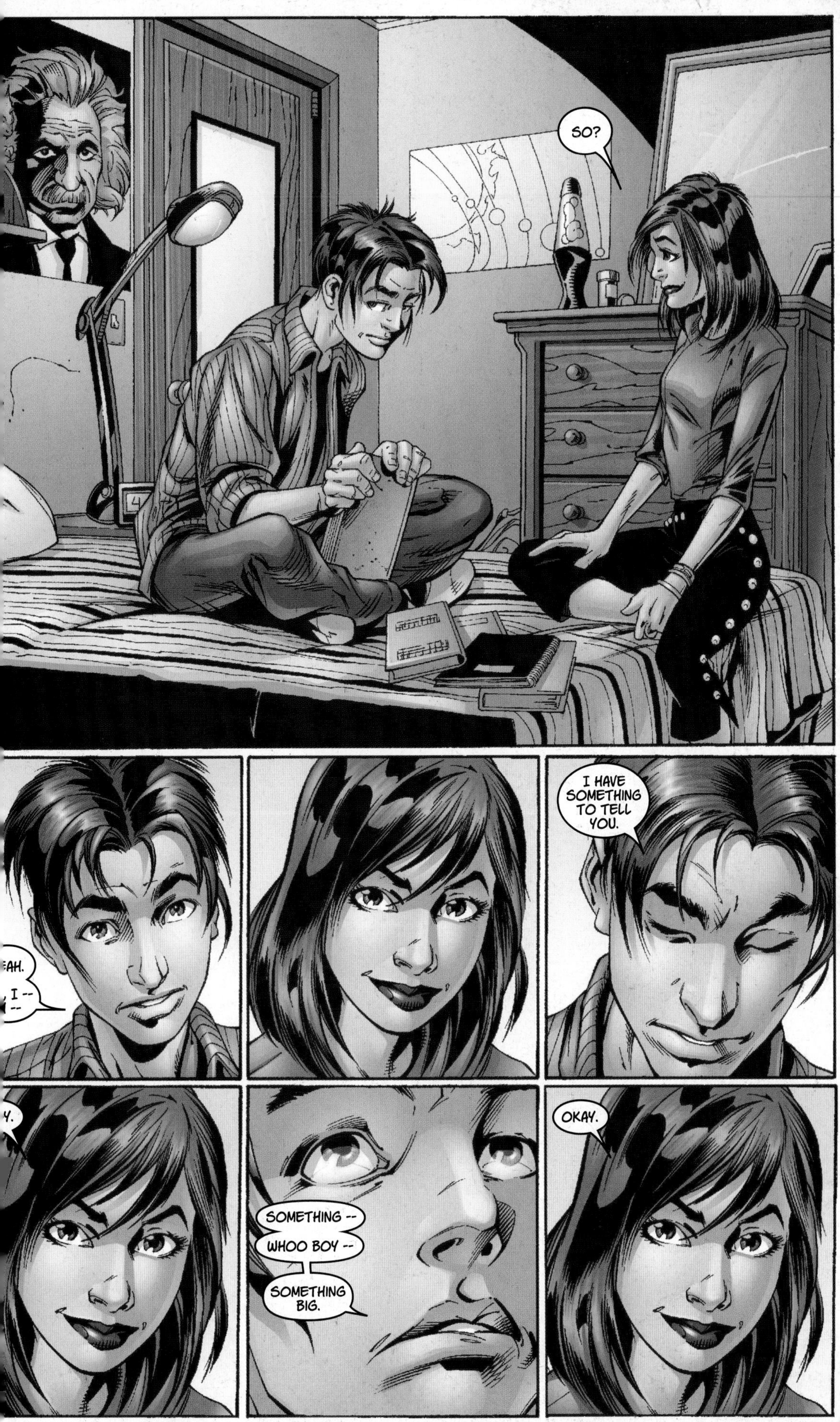
SO?
I HAVE SOMETHING TO TELL YOU.
SOMETHING --
WHOO BOY --
SOMETHING BIG.
OKAY.

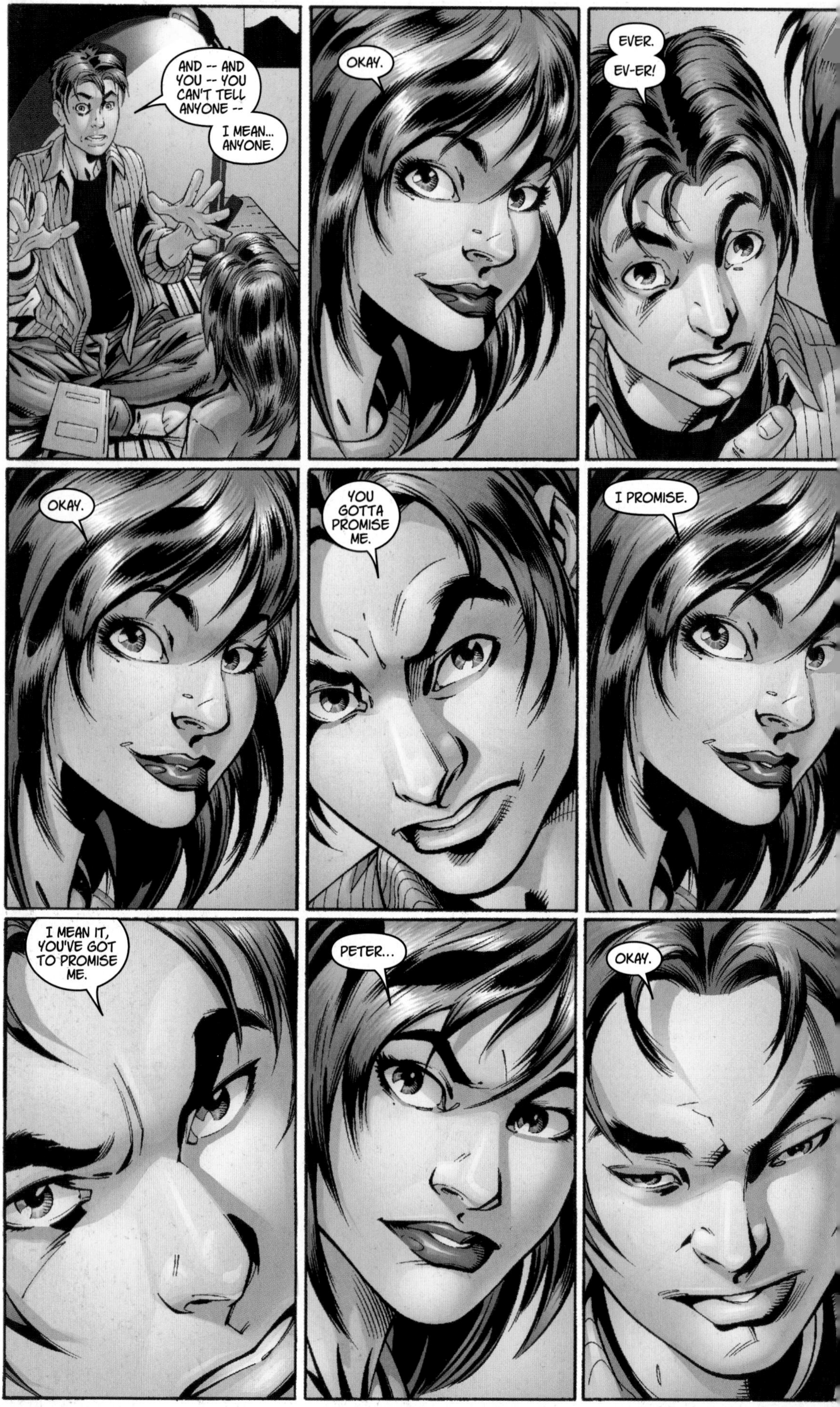
AND -- AND YOU -- YOU CAN'T TELL ANYONE --
I MEAN... ANYONE.
OKAY.
EVER.
EV-ER!
OKAY.
YOU GOTTA PROMISE ME.
I PROMISE.
I MEAN IT, YOU'VE GOT TO PROMISE ME.
PETER...
OKAY.

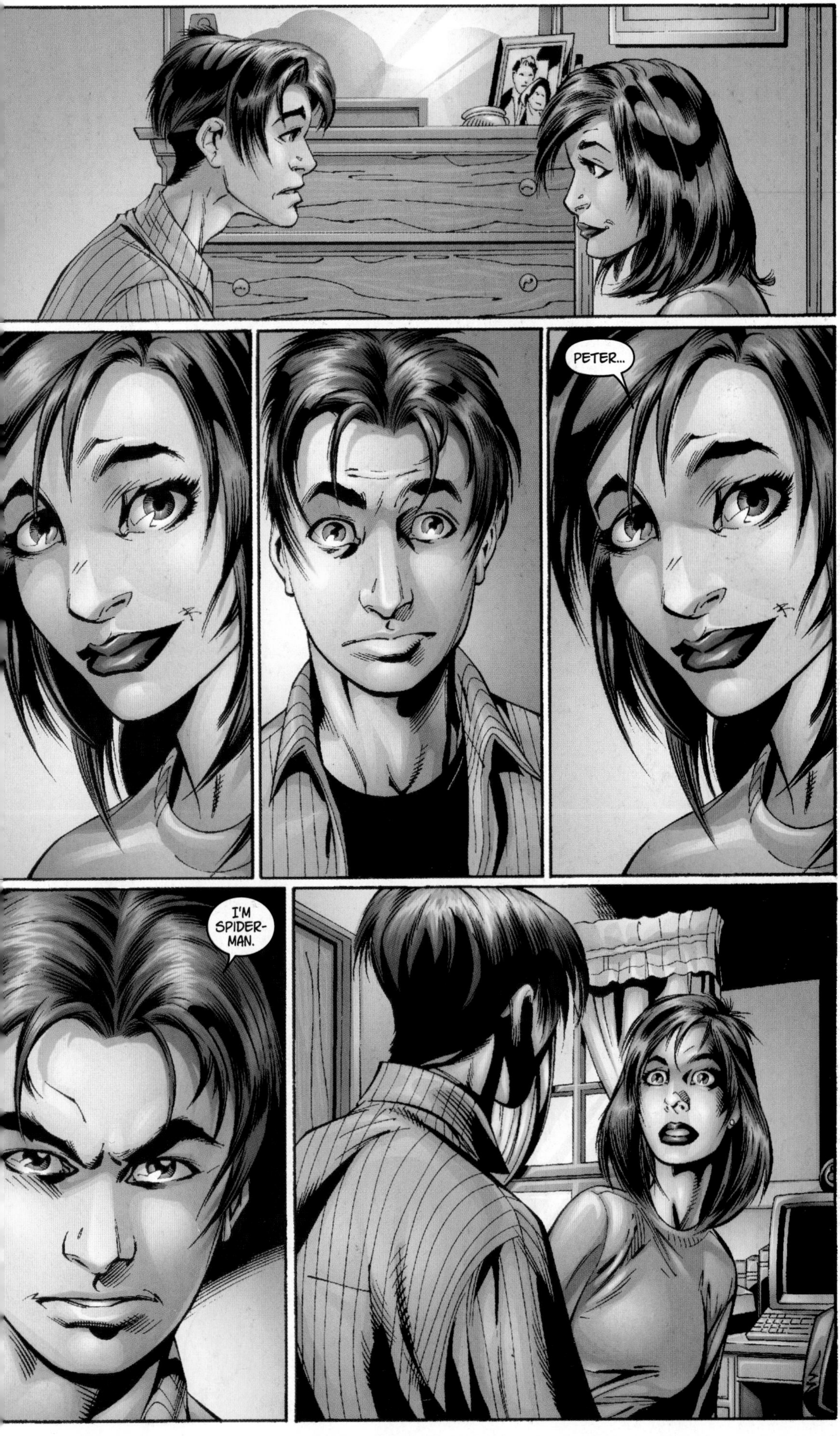
PETER...
I'M SPIDER-MAN.

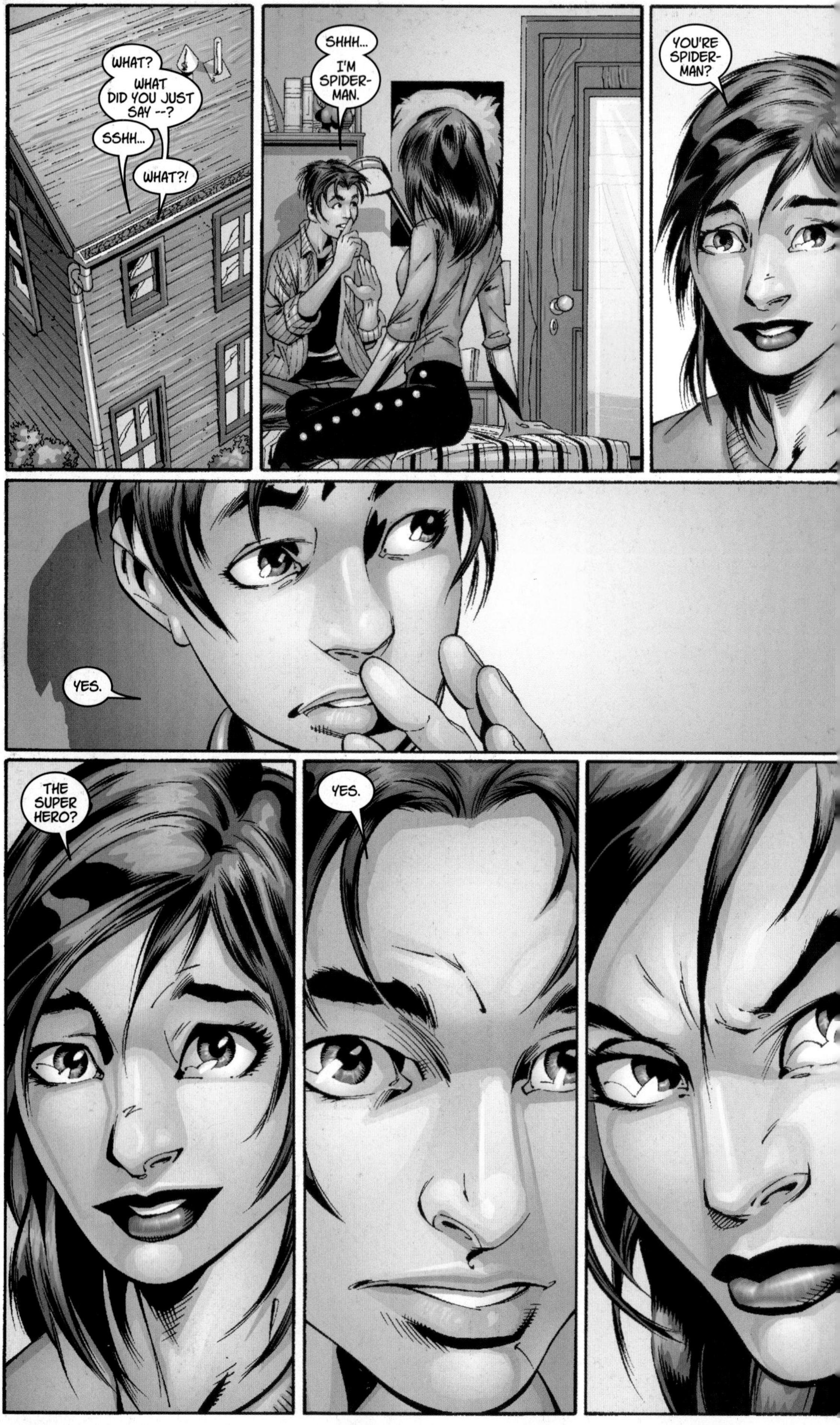
WHAT?
WHAT DID YOU JUST SAY --?
SSHH...
WHAT?!
SHHH... I'M SPIDER-MAN.
YOU'RE SPIDER-MAN?
YES.
THE SUPER HERO?
YES.

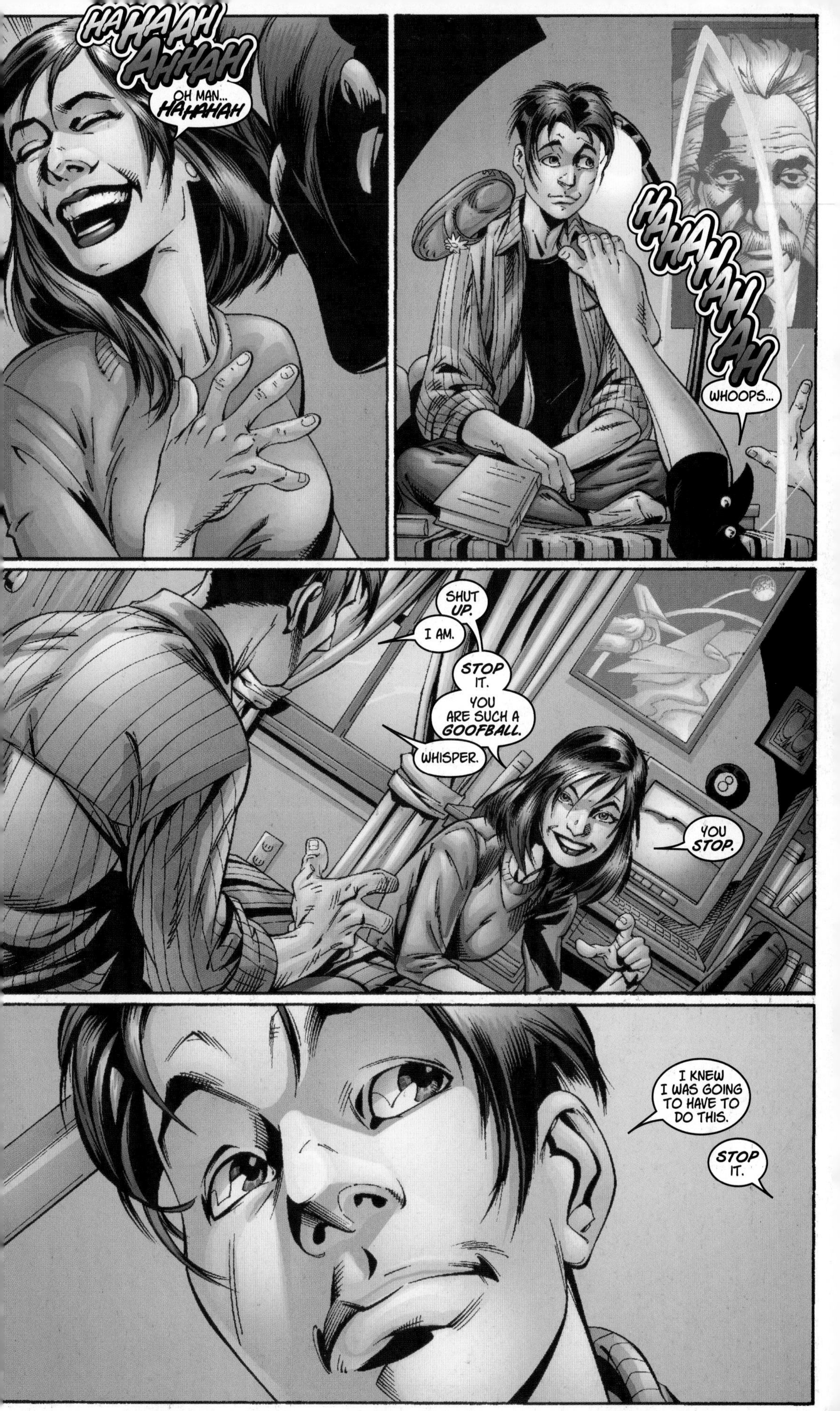
HAHAAH AHHAH
OH MAN... HAHAHAH
HAHAHAHAHAH
WHOOPS...
SHUT UP.
I AM.
STOP IT.
YOU ARE SUCH A GOOFBALL.
WHISPER.
YOU STOP.
I KNEW I WAS GOING TO HAVE TO DO THIS.
STOP IT.

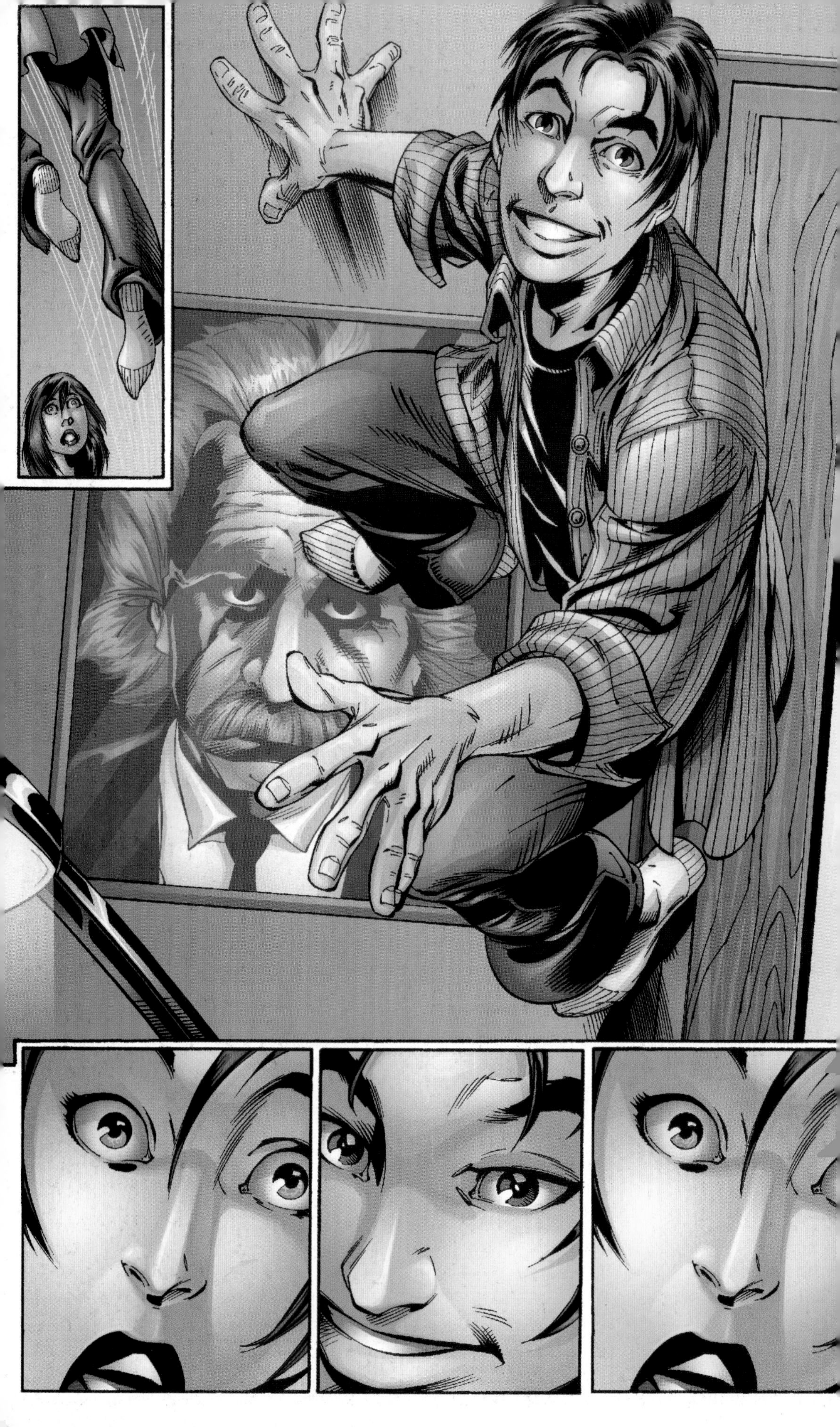

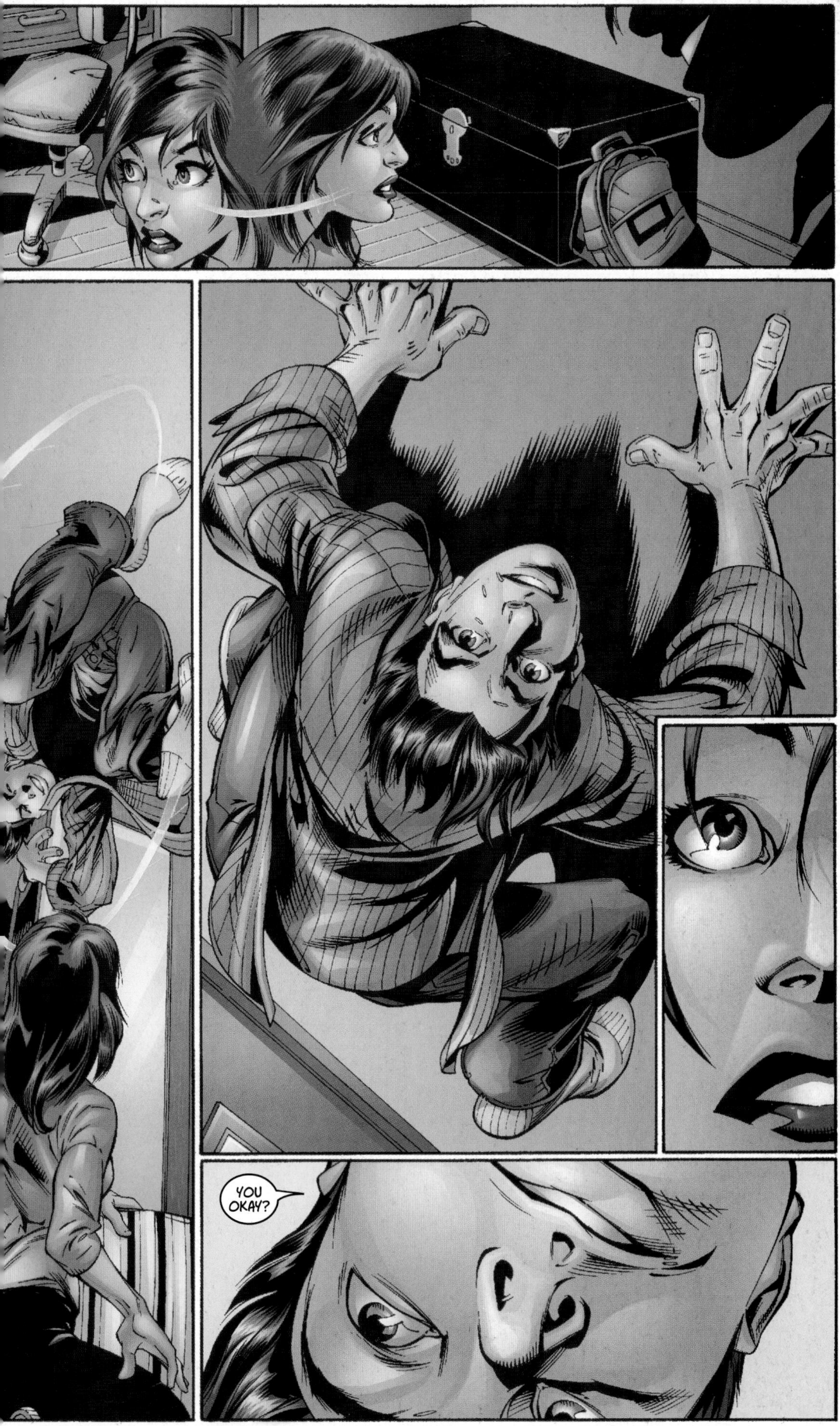
YOU OKAY?

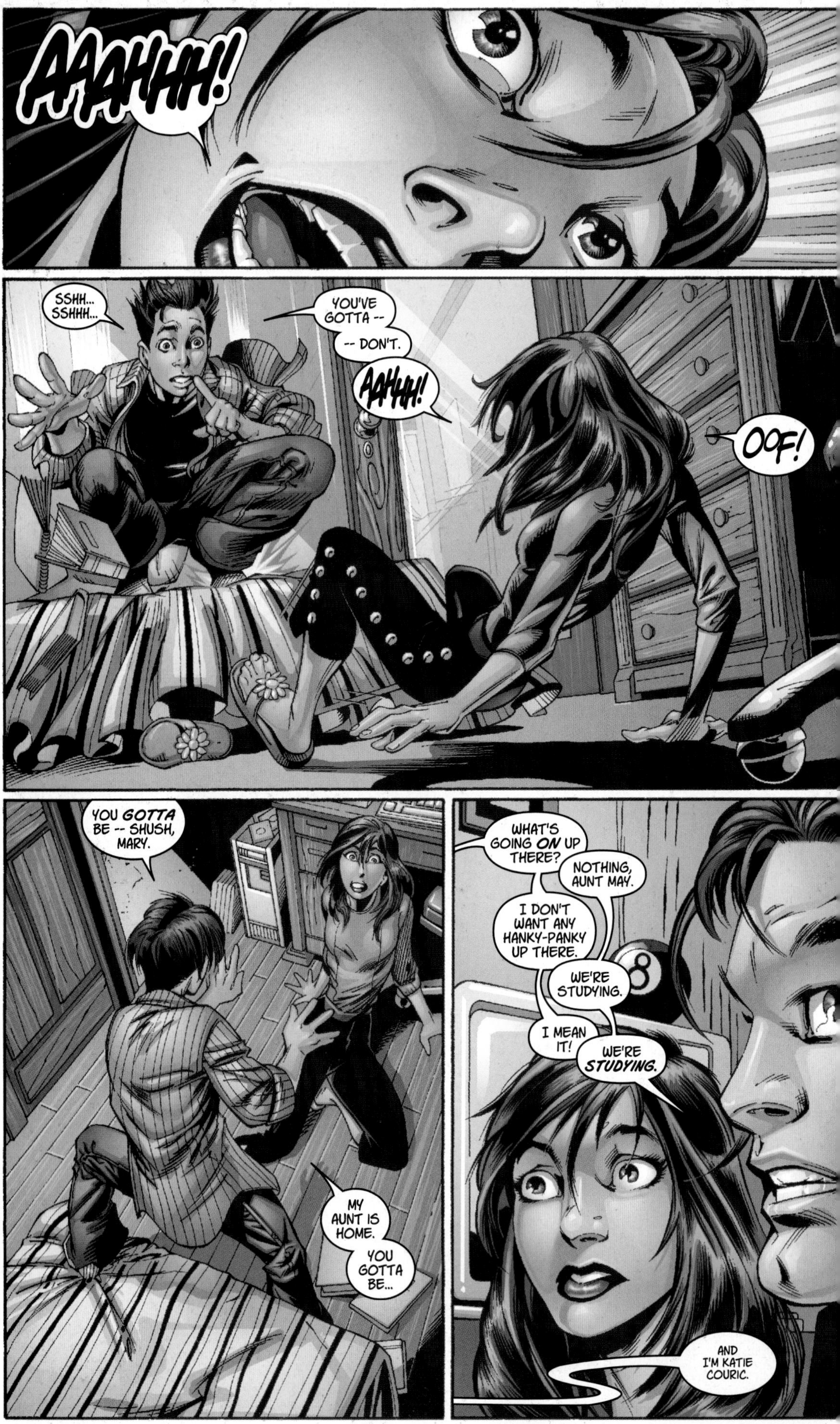
AAAHHH!
SSHH... SSHHH...
YOU'VE GOTTA --
-- DON'T.
AAHHH!
OOF!
YOU GOTTA BE -- SHUSH, MARY.
MY AUNT IS HOME.
YOU GOTTA BE...
WHAT'S GOING ON UP THERE?
NOTHING, AUNT MAY.
I DON'T WANT ANY HANKY-PANKY UP THERE.
WE'RE STUDYING.
I MEAN IT!
WE'RE STUDYING.
AND I'M KATIE COURIC.

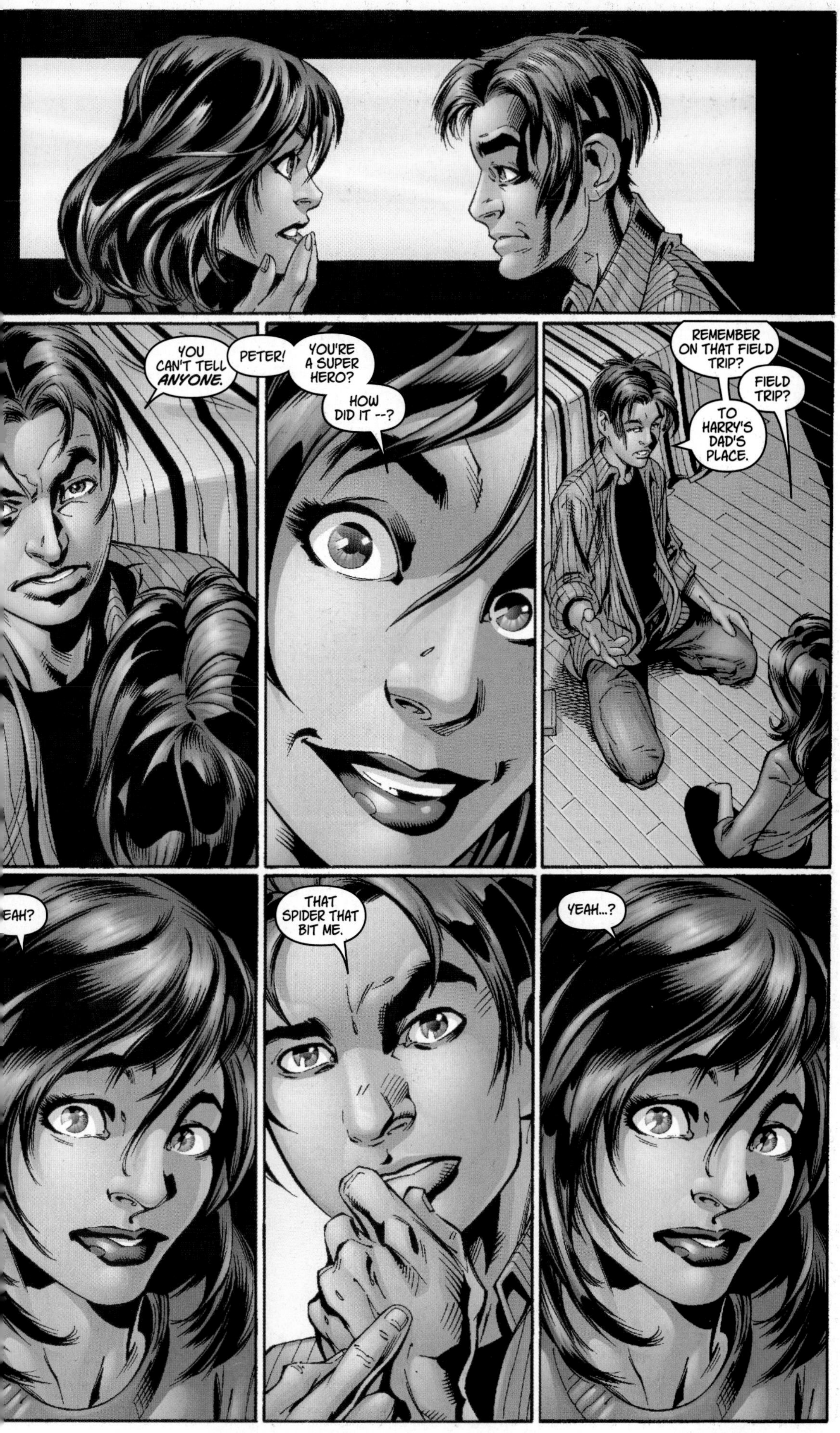
YOU CAN'T TELL *ANYONE*.
PETER!
YOU'RE A SUPER HERO?
HOW DID IT --?
REMEMBER ON THAT FIELD TRIP?
FIELD TRIP?
TO HARRY'S DAD'S PLACE.
EAH?
THAT SPIDER THAT BIT ME.
YEAH...?

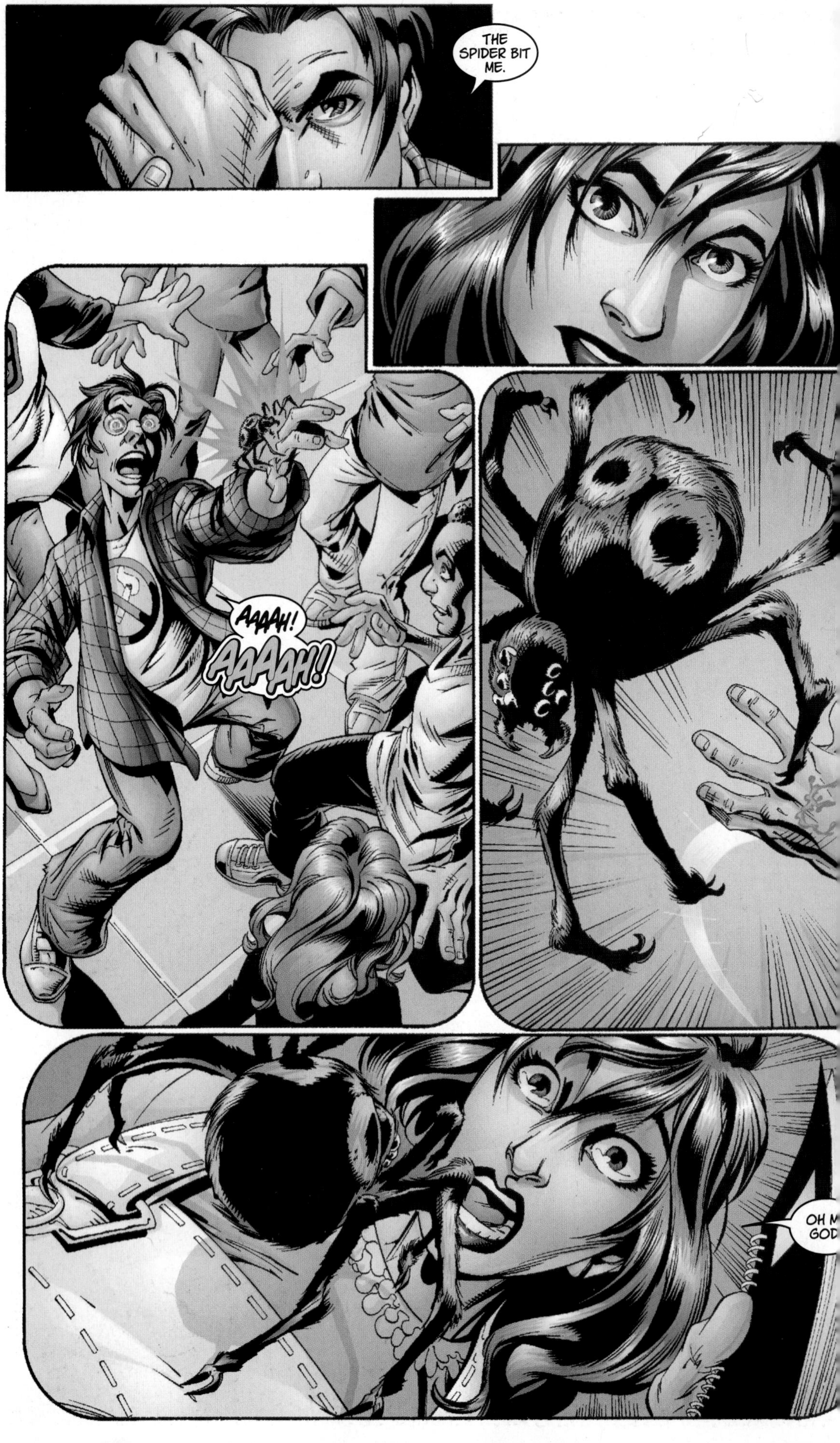
THE SPIDER BIT ME.
AAAAH!
AAAAH!
OH M
GOD

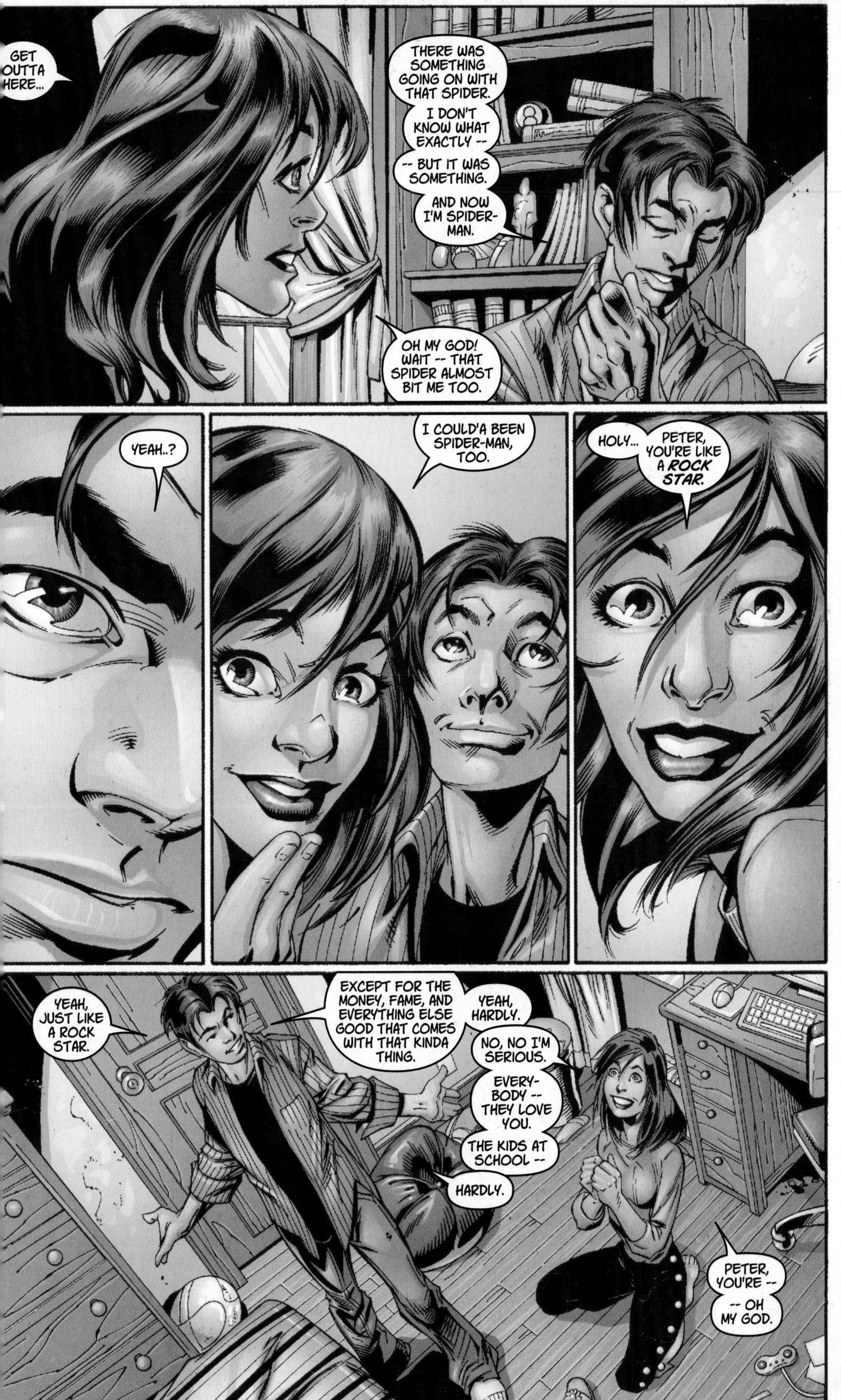

GET OUTTA HERE...
THERE WAS SOMETHING GOING ON WITH THAT SPIDER.
I DON'T KNOW WHAT EXACTLY --
-- BUT IT WAS SOMETHING.
AND NOW I'M SPIDER-MAN.
OH MY GOD! WAIT -- THAT SPIDER ALMOST BIT ME TOO.
YEAH..?
I COULD'A BEEN SPIDER-MAN, TOO.
HOLY...
PETER, YOU'RE LIKE A *ROCK STAR*.
YEAH, JUST LIKE A ROCK STAR.
EXCEPT FOR THE MONEY, FAME, AND EVERYTHING ELSE GOOD THAT COMES WITH THAT KINDA THING.
YEAH, HARDLY.
NO, NO I'M SERIOUS.
EVERY-BODY -- THEY LOVE YOU.
THE KIDS AT SCHOOL --
HARDLY.
PETER, YOU'RE --
-- OH MY GOD.

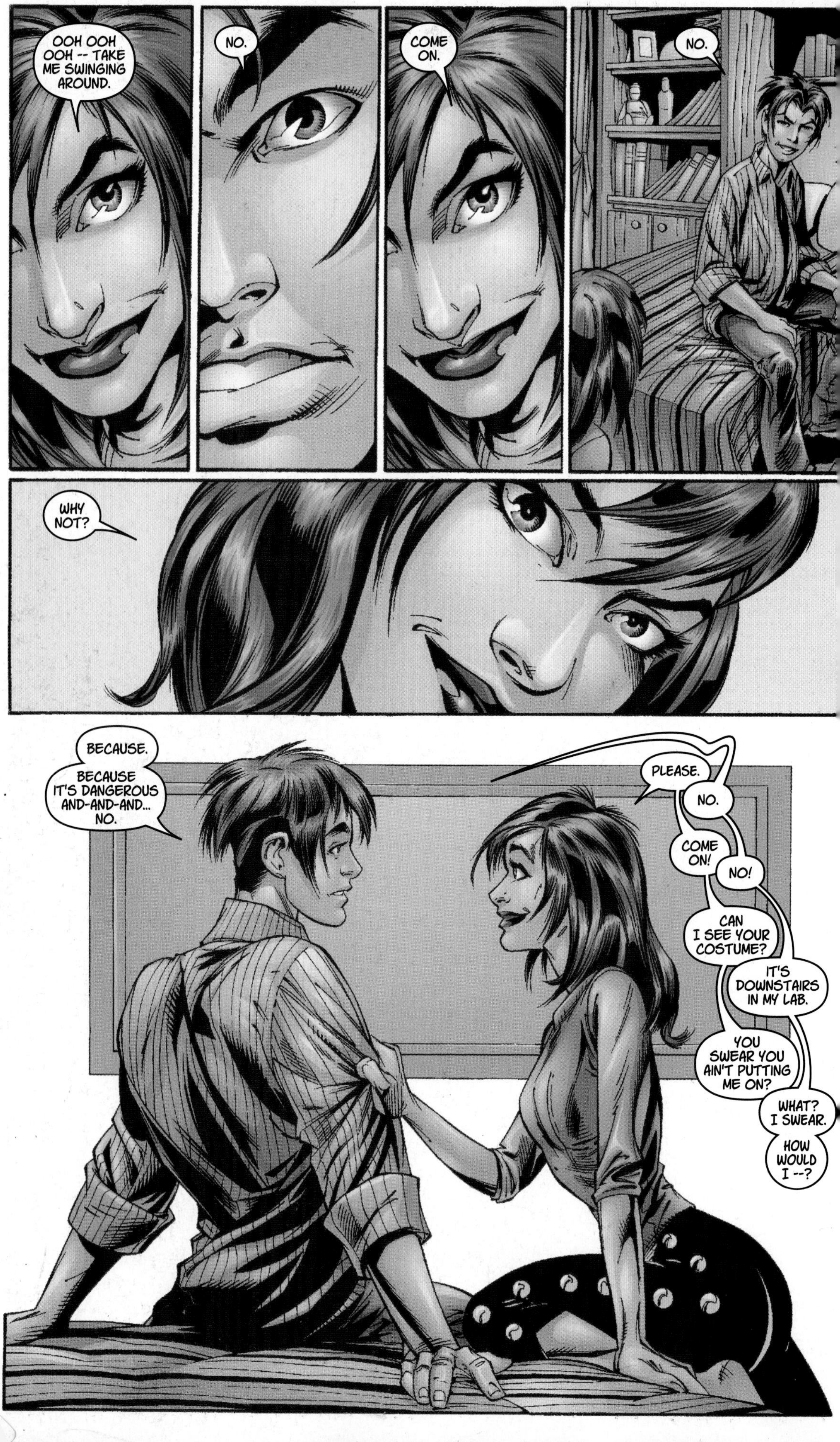
OOH OOH OOH -- TAKE ME SWINGING AROUND.
NO.
COME ON.
NO.
WHY NOT?
BECAUSE.
BECAUSE IT'S DANGEROUS AND-AND-AND... NO.
PLEASE.
NO.
COME ON!
NO!
CAN I SEE YOUR COSTUME?
IT'S DOWNSTAIRS IN MY LAB.
YOU SWEAR YOU AIN'T PUTTING ME ON?
WHAT? I SWEAR.
HOW WOULD I --?

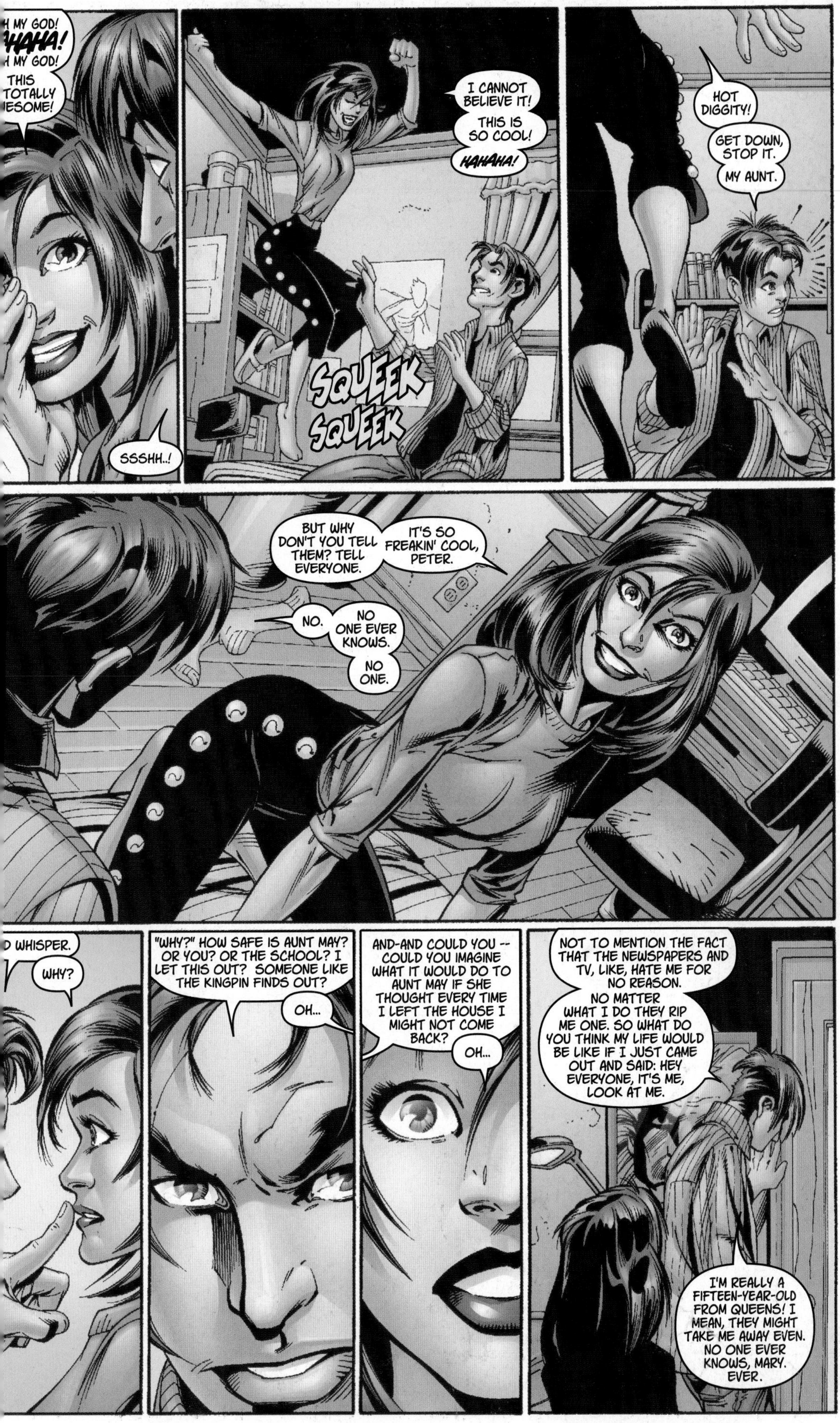
H MY GOD!
HAHA!
H MY GOD!
THIS
TOTALLY
ESOME!
SSSHH..!
I CANNOT BELIEVE IT!
THIS IS SO COOL!
HAHAHA!
SQUEEK
SQUEEK
HOT DIGGITY!
GET DOWN, STOP IT.
MY AUNT.
BUT WHY DON'T YOU TELL THEM? TELL EVERYONE.
IT'S SO FREAKIN' COOL, PETER.
NO.
NO ONE EVER KNOWS.
NO ONE.
D WHISPER.
WHY?
"WHY?" HOW SAFE IS AUNT MAY? OR YOU? OR THE SCHOOL? I LET THIS OUT? SOMEONE LIKE THE KINGPIN FINDS OUT?
OH...
AND-AND COULD YOU -- COULD YOU IMAGINE WHAT IT WOULD DO TO AUNT MAY IF SHE THOUGHT EVERY TIME I LEFT THE HOUSE I MIGHT NOT COME BACK?
OH...
NOT TO MENTION THE FACT THAT THE NEWSPAPERS AND TV, LIKE, HATE ME FOR NO REASON.
NO MATTER WHAT I DO THEY RIP ME ONE. SO WHAT DO YOU THINK MY LIFE WOULD BE LIKE IF I JUST CAME OUT AND SAID: HEY EVERYONE, IT'S ME, LOOK AT ME.
I'M REALLY A FIFTEEN-YEAR-OLD FROM QUEENS! I MEAN, THEY MIGHT TAKE ME AWAY EVEN. NO ONE EVER KNOWS, MARY. EVER.

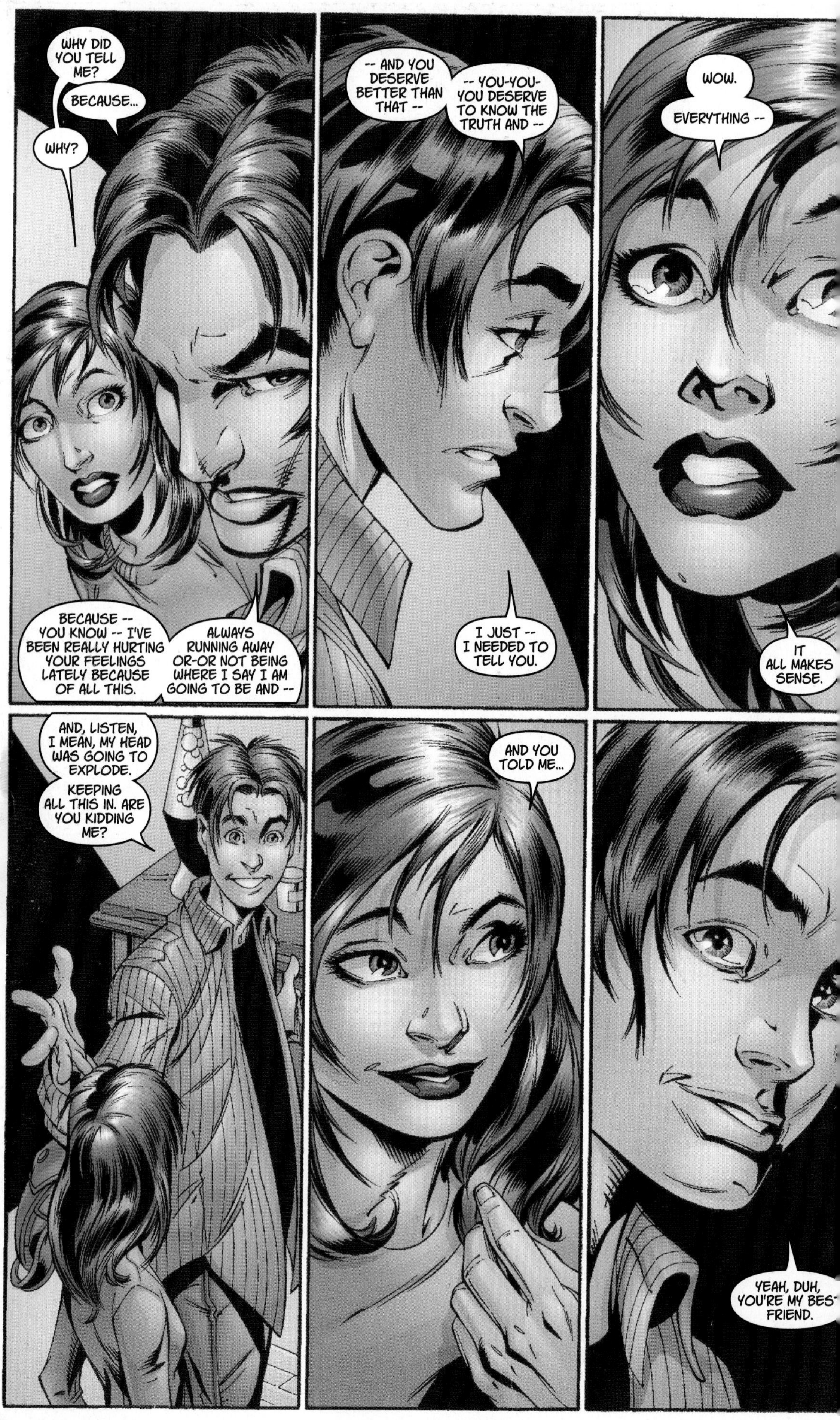
WHY DID YOU TELL ME?
BECAUSE...
WHY?
BECAUSE -- YOU KNOW -- I'VE BEEN REALLY HURTING YOUR FEELINGS LATELY BECAUSE OF ALL THIS.
ALWAYS RUNNING AWAY OR-OR NOT BEING WHERE I SAY I AM GOING TO BE AND --
-- AND YOU DESERVE BETTER THAN THAT --
-- YOU-YOU- YOU DESERVE TO KNOW THE TRUTH AND --
I JUST -- I NEEDED TO TELL YOU.
WOW.
EVERYTHING --
IT ALL MAKES SENSE.
AND, LISTEN, I MEAN, MY HEAD WAS GOING TO EXPLODE.
KEEPING ALL THIS IN. ARE YOU KIDDING ME?
AND YOU TOLD ME...
YEAH, DUH, YOU'RE MY BES- FRIEND.

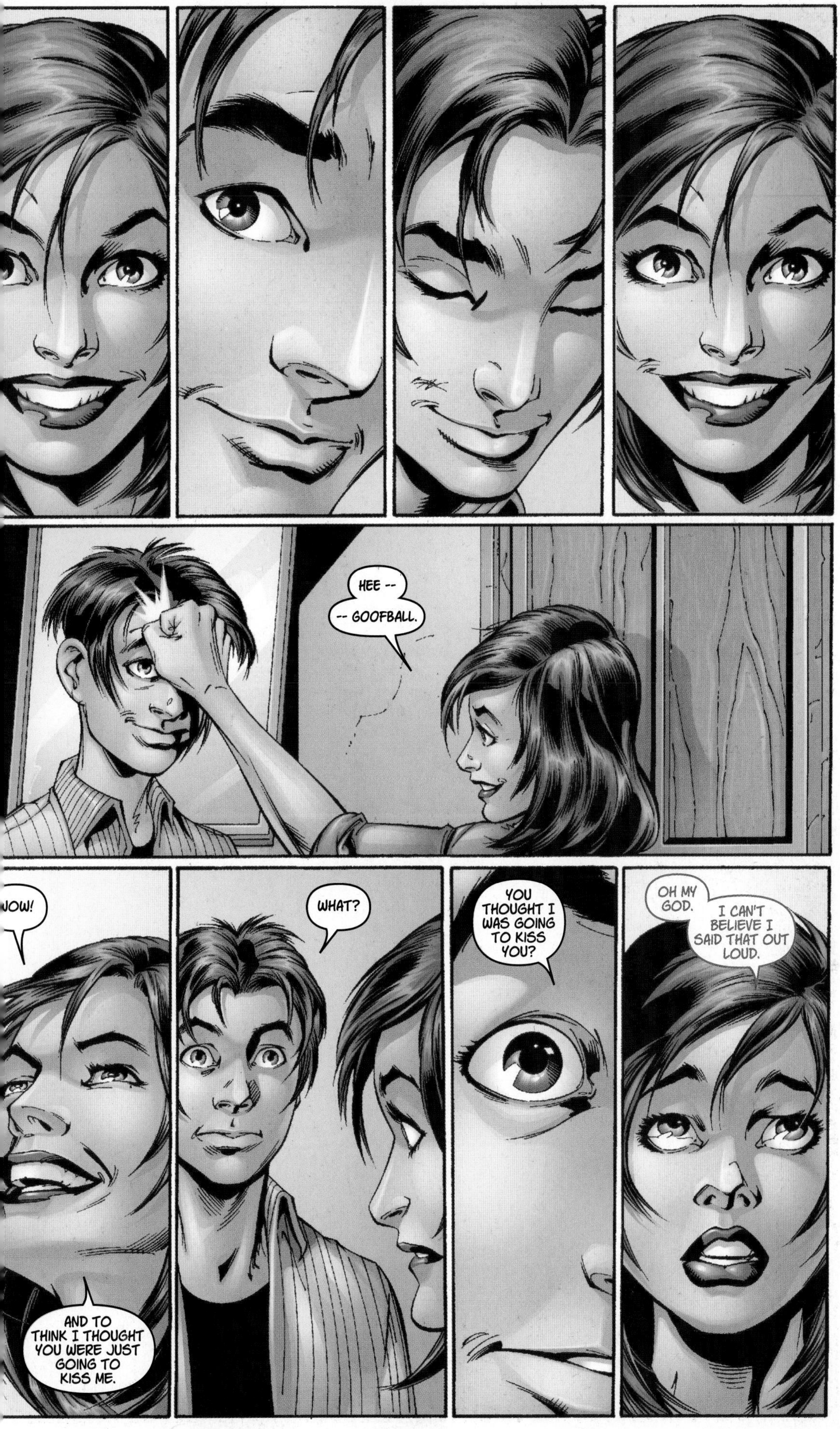
HEE --
-- GOOFBALL.
WOW!
AND TO THINK I THOUGHT YOU WERE JUST GOING TO KISS ME.
WHAT?
YOU THOUGHT I WAS GOING TO KISS YOU?
OH MY GOD.
I CAN'T BELIEVE I SAID THAT OUT LOUD.

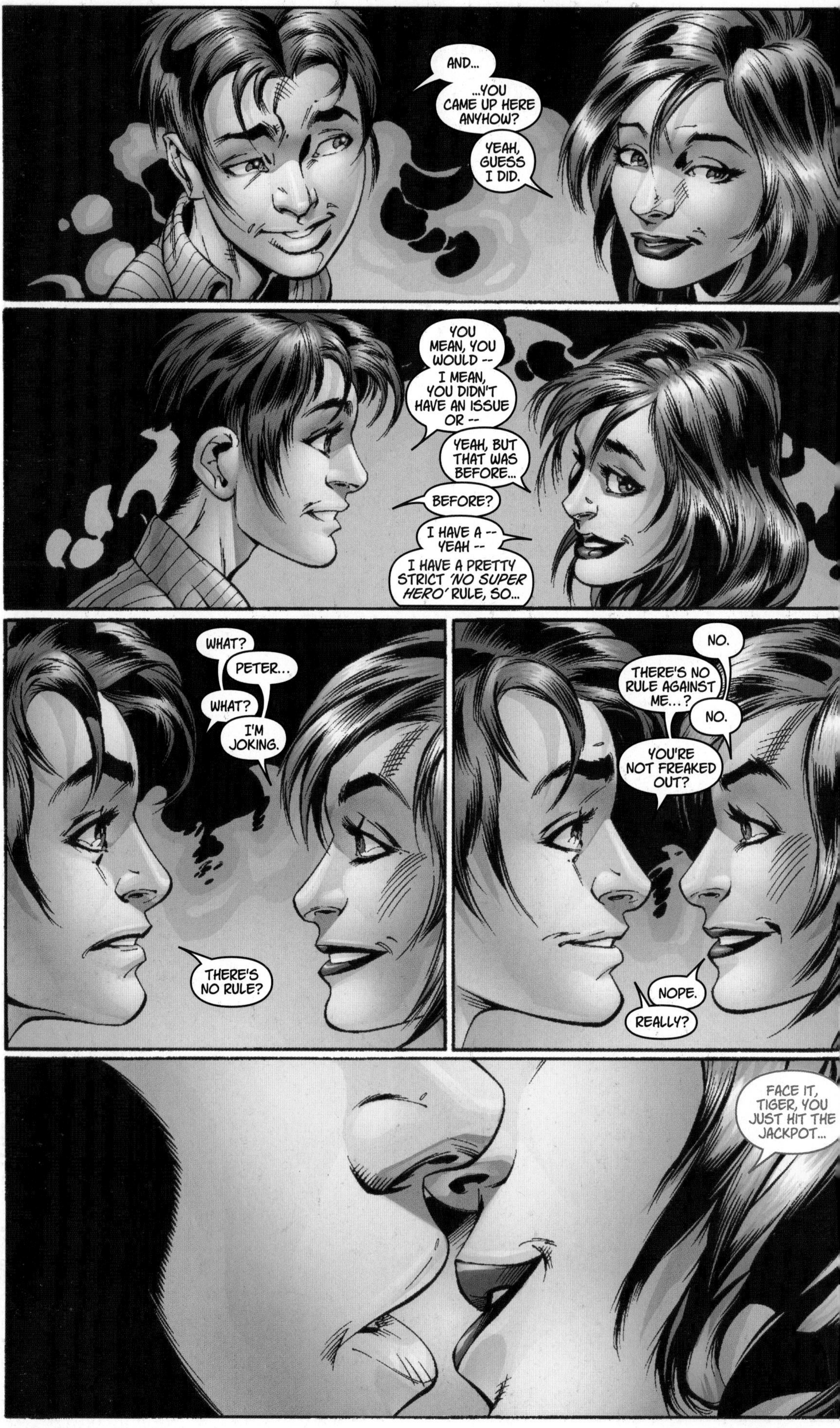
AND...
...YOU CAME UP HERE ANYHOW?
YEAH, GUESS I DID.
YOU MEAN, YOU WOULD -- I MEAN, YOU DIDN'T HAVE AN ISSUE OR --
YEAH, BUT THAT WAS BEFORE...
BEFORE?
I HAVE A -- YEAH -- I HAVE A PRETTY STRICT *'NO SUPER HERO'* RULE, SO...
WHAT?
PETER...
WHAT?
I'M JOKING.
THERE'S NO RULE?
NO.
THERE'S NO RULE AGAINST ME...?
NO.
YOU'RE NOT FREAKED OUT?
NOPE.
REALLY?
FACE IT, TIGER, YOU JUST HIT THE JACKPOT...

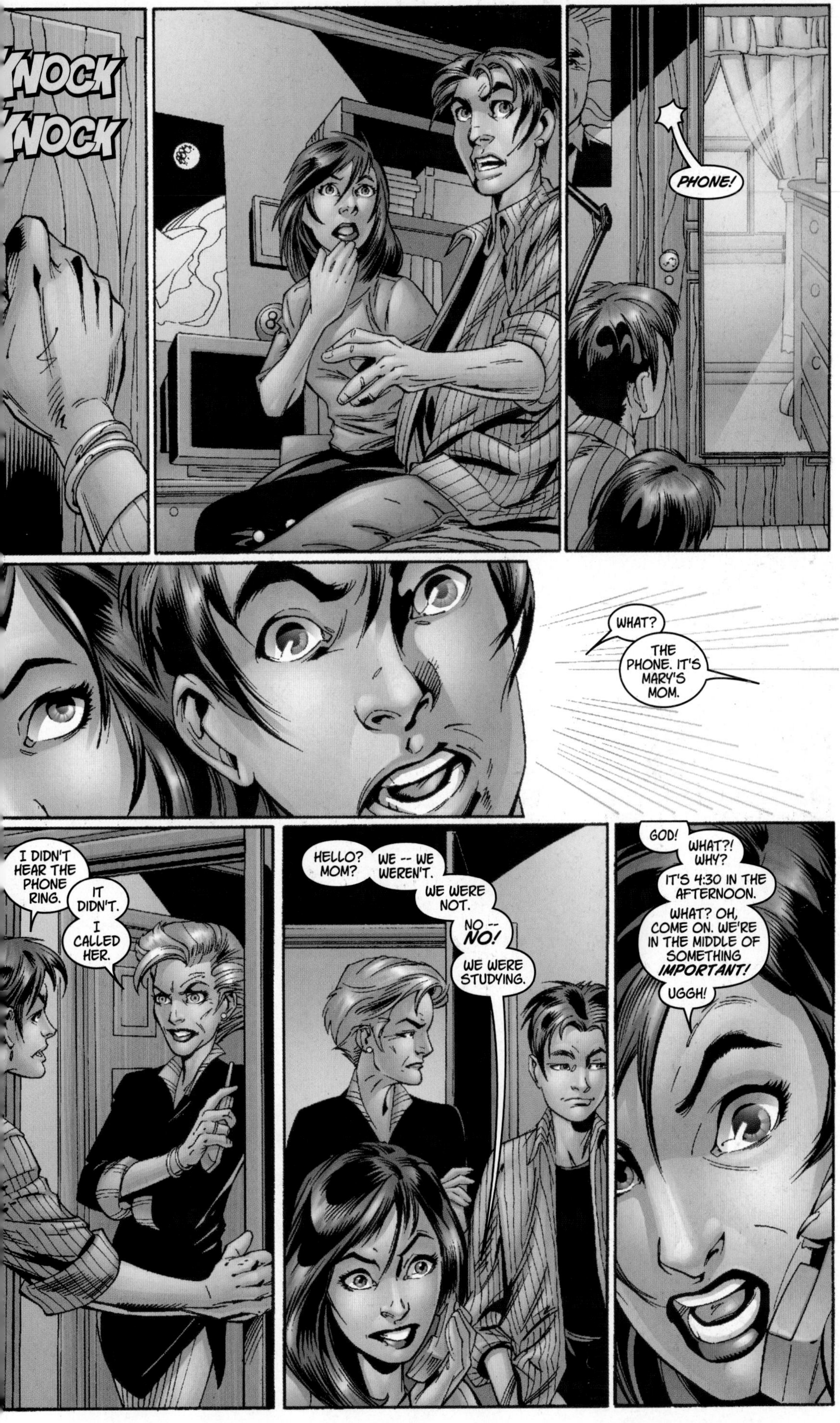
KNOCK
KNOCK
PHONE!
WHAT?
THE PHONE. IT'S MARY'S MOM.
I DIDN'T HEAR THE PHONE RING.
IT DIDN'T.
I CALLED HER.
HELLO? MOM?
WE -- WE WEREN'T.
WE WERE NOT.
NO -- NO!
WE WERE STUDYING.
GOD!
WHAT?! WHY?
IT'S 4:30 IN THE AFTERNOON.
WHAT? OH, COME ON. WE'RE IN THE MIDDLE OF SOMETHING IMPORTANT!
UGGH!

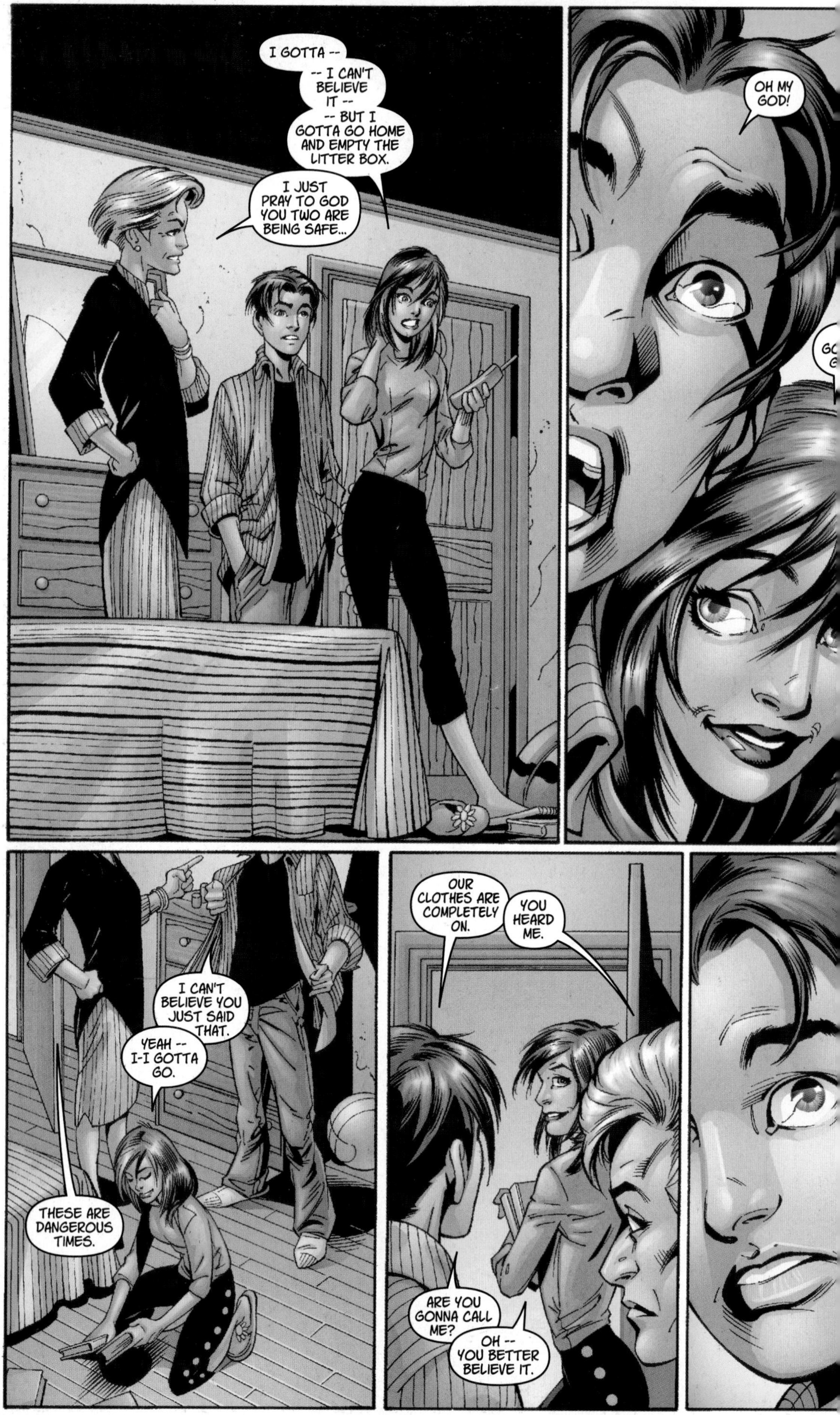
I GOTTA --
-- I CAN'T BELIEVE IT --
-- BUT I GOTTA GO HOME AND EMPTY THE LITTER BOX.
I JUST PRAY TO GOD YOU TWO ARE BEING SAFE...
OH MY GOD!
I CAN'T BELIEVE YOU JUST SAID THAT.
YEAH -- I-I GOTTA GO.
THESE ARE DANGEROUS TIMES.
OUR CLOTHES ARE COMPLETELY ON.
YOU HEARD ME.
ARE YOU GONNA CALL ME?
OH -- YOU BETTER BELIEVE IT.

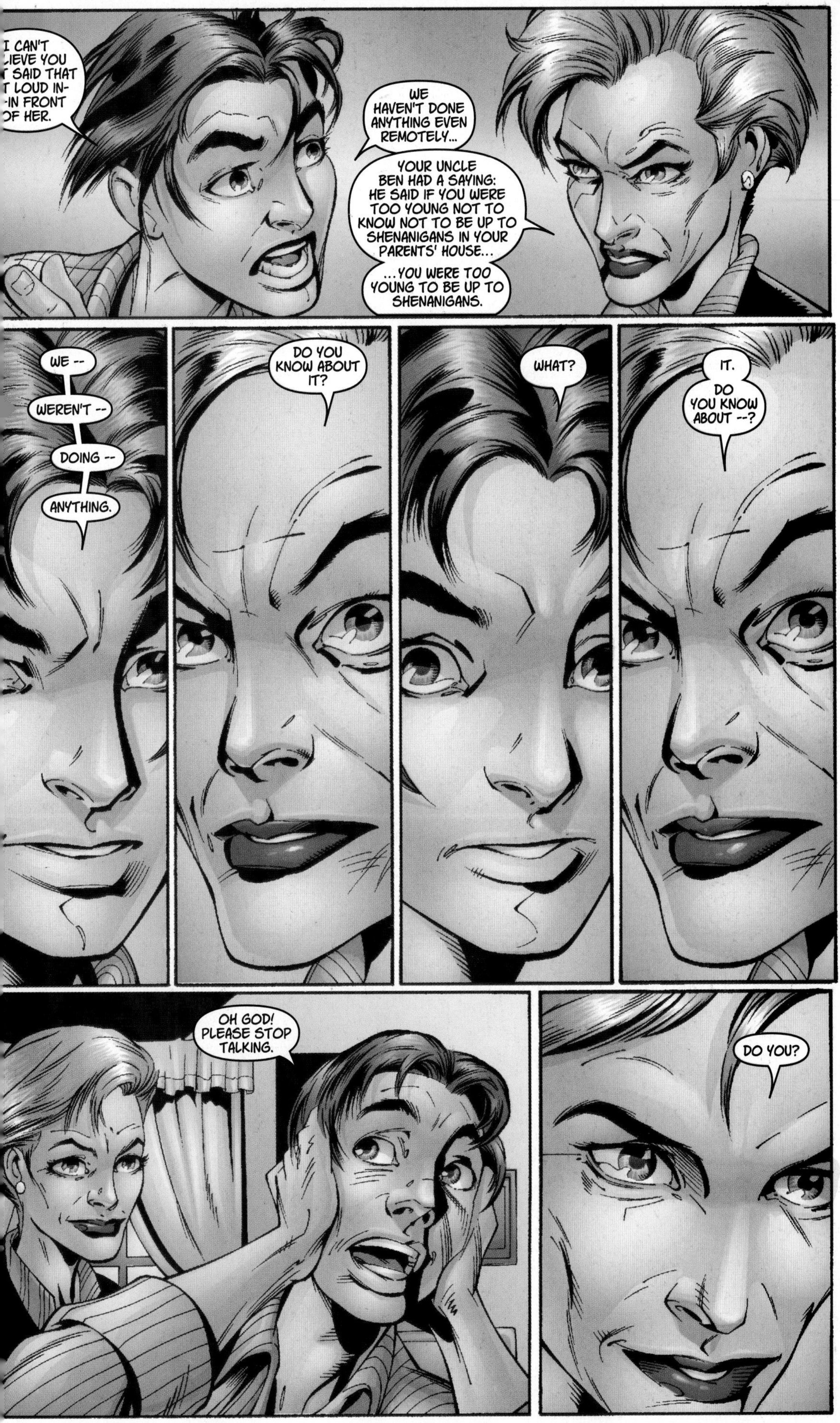
I CAN'T
-LIEVE YOU
-T SAID THAT
-T LOUD IN-
--IN FRONT
OF HER.
WE HAVEN'T DONE ANYTHING EVEN REMOTELY...
YOUR UNCLE BEN HAD A SAYING: HE SAID IF YOU WERE TOO YOUNG NOT TO KNOW NOT TO BE UP TO SHENANIGANS IN YOUR PARENTS' HOUSE...
...YOU WERE TOO YOUNG TO BE UP TO SHENANIGANS.
WE --
WEREN'T --
DOING --
ANYTHING.
DO YOU KNOW ABOUT IT?
WHAT?
IT.
DO YOU KNOW ABOUT --?
OH GOD! PLEASE STOP TALKING.
DO YOU?

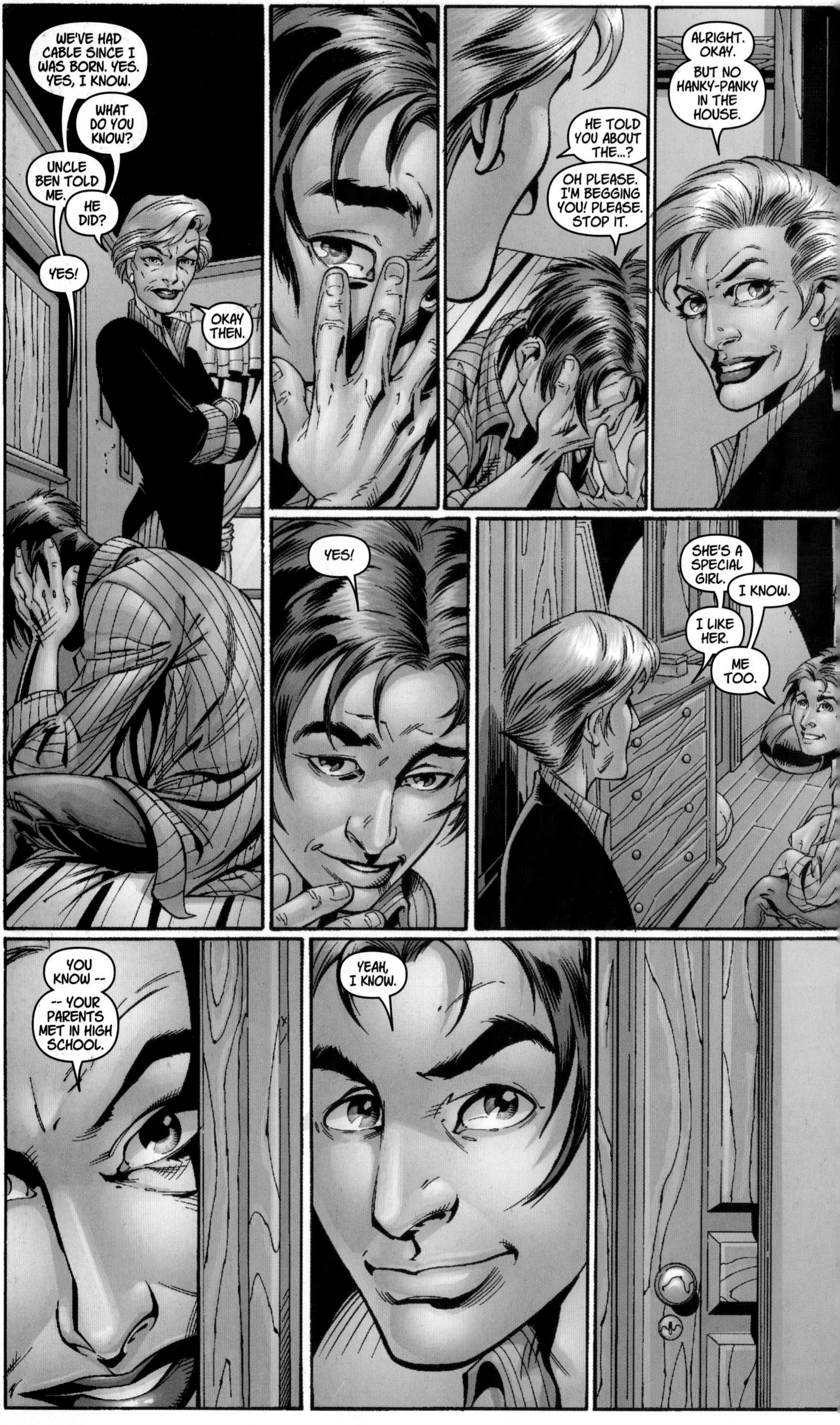
WE'VE HAD CABLE SINCE I WAS BORN. YES. YES, I KNOW.
WHAT DO YOU KNOW?
UNCLE BEN TOLD ME.
HE DID?
YES!
OKAY THEN.
HE TOLD YOU ABOUT THE...?
OH PLEASE. I'M BEGGING YOU! PLEASE. STOP IT.
ALRIGHT. OKAY.
BUT NO HANKY-PANKY IN THE HOUSE.
YES!
SHE'S A SPECIAL GIRL.
I KNOW.
I LIKE HER.
ME TOO.
YOU KNOW --
-- YOUR PARENTS MET IN HIGH SCHOOL.
YEAH, I KNOW.

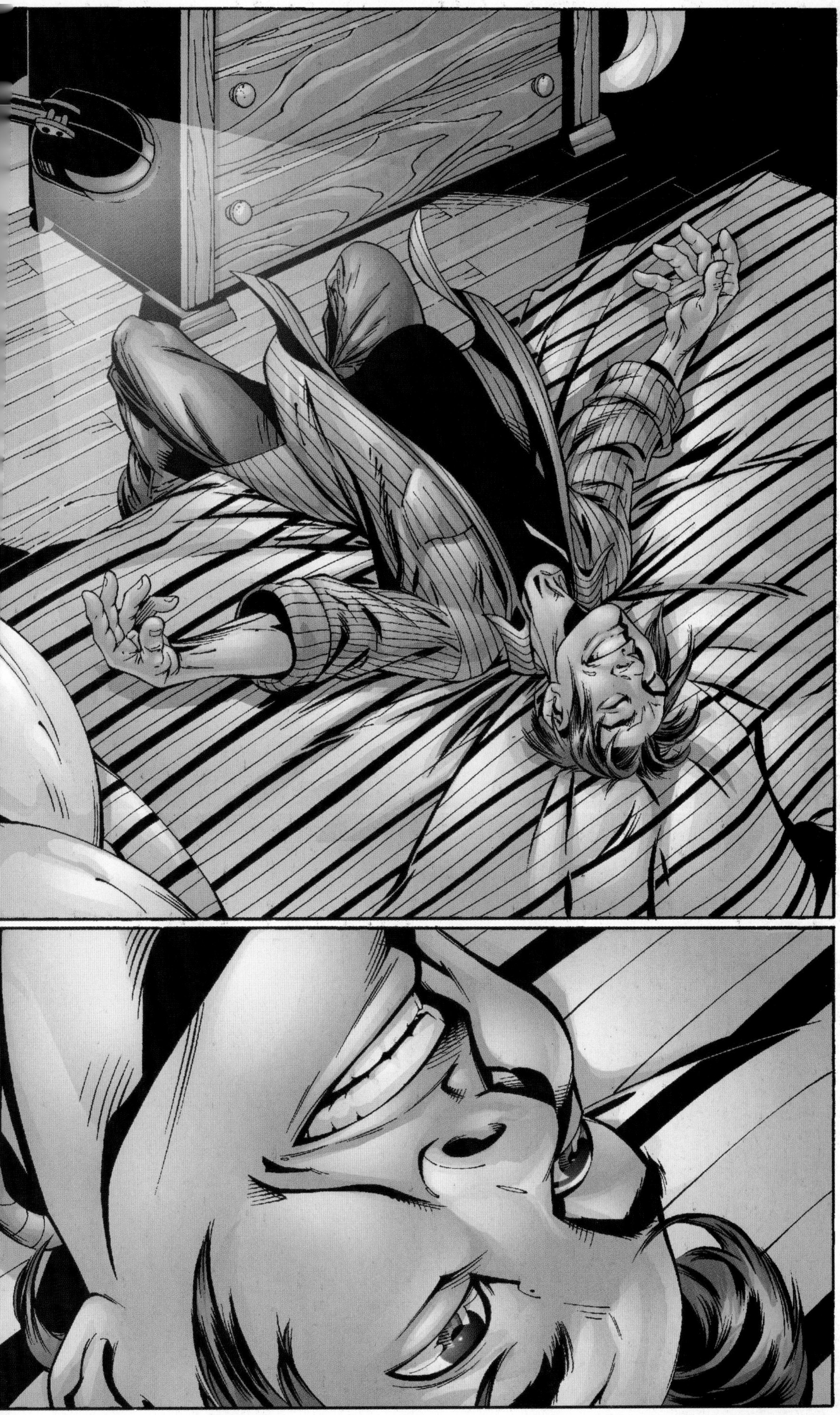

SPIDER-MAN

LARGE EYES

SPDEY- 5'9
ABOUT 135 lbs

SPIDER MAN
GROUND ZERO
3 VIEW

HE'S A TEEN AGE
SPIDEY. HIS HANDS
& FEET ARE LARGE,
AS IF HASN'T FULLY
GROWN INTO THEM.

VERY LEAN. HASN'T
BUILT UP MUSCLE MASS
FROM YEARS-O-WEB

MARY JANE